STUART SEATON

Inheritance

GW00691780

FONTANA/Collins

First published in Great Britain by
William Collins Sons & Co. Ltd 1985
First issued in Fontana Paperbacks 1986

Copyright © Stuart Seaton 1986

Made and printed in Great Britain by
William Collins Sons & Co. Ltd, Glasgow

MARK

from Lat. Marcus,
probably from Mars, God of War

I

The sky was mid-winter black, but a half moon hung low and the frost-sharpened speckle and gleam of stars silhouetted the tall chimneys and wide roof of the house. Lights slanted and flickered from big windows and were caught in yellow streaks by the thin covering of snow over the carriage drive and broad lawns. The old year was dying cold, but beyond the pillared door and solid stone and redbrick the house was warm and welcomed the people who gathered to celebrate the century's mid-point, for within three hours it would be 1850.

Roxton Grange took its name from the nearby village. It had stood for 200 years with its three storeys and sixteen rooms; the heart of the Roxton estate on the south-facing slopes a few miles from Exeter. Close by and sheltered by poplars and elms lay the low cluster of buildings around which the home farm fields spread and rolled away across shallow valleys and woodland; beyond again stretched the eight other farms of the estate – in all 2200 acres of pasture and cornland and timber which kept Rupert Haldane in prosperity. The 500-acre home farm was managed by Stanley Conway, the short-spoken and rugged steward who had served Rupert and his father before him for more than twenty years. The rest of the estate was tenanted; but Rupert knew every acre of it and ruled it all with studious devotion and obsessive concern for the health of the soil and the stock and the well-being of the seventy or more men and their families who, in various ways, derived their livings from it.

He had been born when the century was four hours old. Tomorrow was his fiftieth birthday and he had arranged a meal for the estate workers and tenant farmers to celebrate it – so far out of tune was he with the socially harsh times in which he lived.

But tonight was a more elegant and sophisticated affair. Tonight was his wife's night as hostess, and those who were invited considered themselves privileged and were envied by those who were not; for Caroline Haldane was still the toast of the West Country, ten years after her marriage to Rupert.

She was 32 years old, the daughter of a wealthy London shipper and banker who had not totally approved of the marriage because Rupert did not have the title he had wished for his eldest daughter's husband. But he had been persuaded by the Haldane family's land-holdings; besides, he had confided to his wife, an older man would be good for Caroline – slow her down a little, give her maturity and an awareness that there was more to life than London bright society and riding horses. And because of his age Rupert would, her father reasoned, want children quickly, which would slow her down still further and keep at greater distance some of the dashing male admirers with whom she had surrounded herself. So he had given his blessing even if, privately, he had not fully understood why Caroline had preferred the pleasant, educated but rather dull Rupert to other and younger and more exciting suitors.

But ten years later there were no children. Both Rupert and Caroline had apparently become resigned to that, although cynical friends whispered that Rupert would have a better chance of fatherhood if he devoted some of the time he lavished on his new-fangled breeding of pedigree cattle to a more enthusiastic physical relationship with his beautiful wife. The women secretly wondered if Caroline was frigid; the men, unprepared to accept such a suggestion about an eminently desirable lady, held that Rupert must have a problem of his own. Either way, it was obvious to their closest acquaintances that they had now ceased to enjoy their marital bed as fully as healthy folk should.

The first guests had already arrived, led by Morton Griffiths who owned the farm half a mile along the road and his massive, talkative wife Mary who had borne him eleven children of whom seven survived. With him was William Wright, tenant of the next farm in the opposite direction, for

8

unlike many of his contemporaries Rupert Haldane did not ask a man whether he owned or rented his farm before deciding if he was socially acceptable. There, too, was Wright's wife Jane, half-crippled with arthritis at the age of 42, heaving herself around defiantly on two sticks; and warming his back against the blazing logs in the stone fireplace which dominated one side of the great oak-panelled hall was George Callan, squire in the next village, smoothing the grey waistcoat over his ample stomach and fulminating loudly as he often did upon the whispered threats of workers banding together to demand more pay.

There were other early arrivals besides – twenty or more middle class country folk of varying qualifications in the social scale; and every few minutes a carriage or a ridden horse clattered over the frost-hard drive and Stanley Conway, less easy guiding guests than he was driving cattle or managing a farm labour force, directed drivers and riders and conducted new arrivals to Rupert and Caroline in the warmth of the big hall.

The wives swished and smoothed their hooped skirts as they complained about the cost of the village school which was now three pence a week for each child and, it was said, would soon be four pence. Their husbands talked guns and grouse and the price of livestock. Someone was concerned that his hay might not last the winter through, another asked who had seen the big bay gelding just bought by the Roxton blacksmith. There was need for a new carpenter and wheelwright in Roxton; and a new teacher, for old Fitzsimmons was past it – he could scarcely lift a cane these days and was not earning the money paid to him by the trust through which local landowners had founded the little school ten years before. There was a lot of fever in Exeter: was Dr Miller coming so that he could advise them if it was serious and if the water supply was to blame? Rupert nodded across several heads. Dr Miller would come.

Caroline moved about the hall and in and out of the long drawing room, chatting gaily first with one group, then another. She was tall and slender in grey satin, her flowing tiered skirt trimmed with red and black, the bodice close-fitting, high-necked and laced, and her long fair hair was coiled above her head. She saw Rupert in close conversation with Wright and Griffiths, and wished he would circulate more freely. She knew he would be talking about the home farm and the cattle, for he spoke of little else, and she felt a quick surge of impatience that on this night he could not find new topics for the enjoyment of his guests.

She checked the two serving maids as they offered drinks and canapes from silver trays; and relaxed when she saw they were already under the keen eyes of Nora Penryn who had been cook-housekeeper at the Grange for nearly as long as she had been mistress of the house.

Then, across the hall the inner door latch clicked and she turned to welcome the next arrival; and, fractionally, hesitated when she saw him. She was aware, too, of the momentary check in some of the talk around her as others also looked at the opening door and saw Conway first, and then Mark Helford.

He was mid-thirties; tall, rangy and dark-coated. He shook off his grey cloak and adjusted his cravat; and eyes that were as black as his hair swept over the room and the people, confident above a wide, assertive mouth. The tempo of conversation resumed; but the secret glances remained, and Caroline was glad to see her husband moving ahead of her towards the new arrival.

Helford owned ships, coasters mostly, running a brisk trade in anything down to Plymouth and Penzance, round to the Welsh ports and up the Channel to Southampton and London as well as across to Le Havre and Cherbourg. It was a successful business, not least because he dealt ruthlessly with debtors, was hard with agents, and by repute was worth any three men in a dispute on the tough south coast docksides or in the inns which surrounded them.

But the ladies in the room glanced cautiously and secretly at him for other reasons; for Helford, it was said, had a way with women. No one there had experienced that way; indeed no one there actually knew anyone who had. But behind the fans and the kerchiefs and in the boudoirs, when the men were at their port or working, they exchanged gossip which grew in detail with the telling – about the girls someone had seen calling at Helford's rambling house at night; about the society beauties who were said to await his visits to London; about the rumour that he had been caught in a titled lady's bedroom by his lordship's early return and the single blow with which he was said to have inflicted serious injury upon the unfortunate man; and, more secretly and only between intimate friends, about the skills and stamina which the stories said he possessed in bed.

Some of this was undoubtedly due to his appearance, which carried a hint of Latin influence only a generation or two back; and some, too, to the directness of his almost piercing gaze into the eyes of anyone to whom he spoke. Men found it unnerving until they became used to it; to women it was fascinating and dangerous – an invitation, a challenge, an intimacy almost as physical as a hand across their breasts or along their thighs.

Caroline Haldane was aware of it now. It was her second meeting with him. The first, two months before, had been brief but well-remembered. In the stone-built estate office alongside the house, Helford had been negotiating a deal with her husband for part of the season's wheat crop, and his near-black eyes had startled her to the point of a second's secret panic as she had accepted the courtesies of his greeting, exchanged formal pleasantries, and then – somewhat thankfully – had left the men to their business.

This time it was easier. She offered her hand and he raised it close to his lips but with no contact as he bowed his head and acknowledged Rupert's 'Of course, you've met Mark Helford, my dear, as I recall.'

'Indeed we have met. You are most gracious to invite me, ma'am.'

Caroline was cool and precise.

'The pleasure is ours, Mr Helford. We are delighted to welcome you among our friends on this happy night. So permit me to introduce you.'

As she presented him to the nearest group she saw the men nod briefly and cautiously; and the women studiously distant and wary, with heightened colour under his strange eyes. He was a head taller than most of the men around him as he greeted them quietly, correctly – and, thought Caroline as she turned back towards the door and another guest, slightly mockingly. She wondered if he knew anything of his reputation, and if he found it amusing.

'My dear doctor,' Rupert was saying as John Miller came through the door. 'So glad you came. Just getting anxious about you.'

Miller's lined face was tired. He handed his tall silk hat to the black-skirted, aproned maid beside the door, then his big coat with the long vent at the back which made it easier for the wearer to sit a saddle. He smoothed his creased tail coat and adjusted his high collar.

'Sorry I'm late, Haldane. Had a rather difficult call.'

Rupert raised his eyebrows.

'Nothing serious, I hope. We don't want that sort of thing during the festive season.'

Miller pushed long fingers through thinning grey hair.

'Less serious than I thought, I'm glad to say. Mrs Garton down the lane – her baby. But her husband works for Griffiths, so you probably didn't know. A difficult birth. But she'll be all right, I think. Handsome baby boy. Mrs Haldane, how charming you look. You are more beautiful every time I see you. Do you know of whom I speak? Yes, I can see you do. Biggest problem is that terrible cottage. And they're hungry, too.' He lowered his voice. 'You farmers don't pay these people enough, you know. Some of them can't feed themselves. Sorry, Haldane, I know you share my views. Your workers may be all right. But some of the others aren't.'

Rupert Haldane shrugged.

'I can't cure the whole county's social ills, doctor. Trouble is, after the bad times of the twenties and thirties, agriculture hasn't allowed its labourers to keep pace with the new prosperity. Memories are sometimes long, you know.'

'M-m.' Dr Miller looked sideways at his host. He knew his

12

man. 'Of course. Anyway, think I'll have a look at mother and baby again tomorrow. Probably call on you for a glass just before I do. Perhaps you'll have something left over from tonight I can take – help her to recover.'

He drifted away into the general conversations, accepting a glass of punch as he went.

Rupert watched him go. He knew only too well the problem Dr Miller faced. He could attend a difficult birth, either because he was paid to do so or – as in this case, undoubtedly – out of the goodness of his heart and his professional devotion; but he could not make good the ravages of undernourishment and squalid living conditions among some of his patients. Rupert paid his labourers ten shillings a week, with more for his senior men, and he was generous with his potatoes and vegetables, his cheese and home-made beer, and his logs. The ten cottages he owned were in a good state of repair. Often he paid doctors' bills for a hard-pressed employee, and when one of the sows on the home farm farrowed well he would reward a good labourer with a piglet to rear in his patch of garden. But he knew his generosity brought muttered criticism from some of his neighbours. Morton Griffiths was one. He paid two or even three shillings a week less than Haldane, was miserly with his gifts to labourers, and demanded the maximum working hours in all weathers. He owned several cottages, all in poor condition, and Garton and his wife lived in one of them. If the labourer wanted another job with a better master he would have to find one which carried a cottage with it, for he had no hope of saving money to buy one himself. And opportunities like that came rarely and were usually snatched up by a man already working for the owner.

'How's the new bull, Rupert?' The quiet voice was William Wright's. He was a small, wiry man with a thin face and bright, quick eyes over his high collar and white bowed tie. He shared Haldane's passion for improving the Shorthorn breed and had a small herd which was grading up steadily.

'Haven't actually got him yet, William. Next week he should be here and you can have a look at him. Only a youngster, of course. Have to make sure we don't use him too

13

heavily until we know what we've got. But he's well-bred and his dam and two of his sisters looked all right to me. All three have plenty of milk about 'em.'

'I'll be glad to see'm,' said Wright. 'Maybe I'll try him on one or two of my heifers.'

Haldane chuckled.

'Wait a while. I won't know what to charge you till I know what he can do. And by the way, I'm going to the January sale in Dorchester. There might be a heifer or two there worth picking up. Take three days altogether. Interested?'

Wright's eyes sparkled.

'I'll see if the good lady can cope. If she can, I'll join you.'

Haldane nodded. He would be glad of his friend's company.

'I'll talk to Stanley. He can lend her a hand if it's needed, and keep an eye on things. And Nora will be able to help her too.' He swept another glass of punch off a passing tray. 'How long's this happy upturn in our affairs going to last, d'you think?'

'Till the next war, if there ever is one. I reckon it'll see you and me into a comfortable old age, Rupert. All the corn trade forecasts were just scare talk. It's good, and it'll get better.'

Across the room Griffiths and Callan had come together before the wide fireplace, the stout squire and the big-shouldered red-faced farmer stabbing now at the grey waistcoat in front of him with a wide, blunt finger.

'With respect, sir, it's wishful thinking to keep talking about transportation. There'll be no more of that after the fuss over those Tolpuddle men all that time ago. We've got to handle 'em ourselves. And' – he lowered his rough-edged voice conspiratorially – 'our host is among those who don't help the situation, if I may say so beneath his roof. Give 'em an inch and they'll take everything we've got. Haldane gives far too much. It unsettles the whole labour force. You agree, hey?'

'Damn' right I agree,' the squire rumbled. 'There's too little respect and discipline. They're thieves and they're lazy. Heard any more of that damn' union talk lately?'

14

'No, not on my farm, I can tell you. They wouldn't dare let me hear a word of it. If I did, I'd take me crop an' drive the lot of 'em off the place. And they know it. Plenty more around who'd be glad of their jobs.'

While they talked, Rupert Haldane watched his wife. He felt momentary pride. She was by far the most attractive woman in the room. Half listening to Wright's forecasts of corn and cattle prices, he idly wondered what she really thought of him. He had no doubt that she was fond of him and respected him as a wife should. But he suspected that her affection did not go much further than that. Some of the time, he knew, she was bored. She was younger than most of his friends, and now rarely had the opportunity to see those who had made up her own social circle before their marriage. She took a genuine interest in the farm and the management of the estate and did not seem to resent his preoccupation with it. But sometimes he noticed that the gaiety and sparkling conversation for which she had been so much admired in her girlhood and in the early years of their marriage, and which was clearly captivating their guests now, was less spontaneous, less obvious. She read a great deal, rode often by herself if there was no one available to accompany her, and sometimes would stand in the wide window of the drawing room, looking across the walled garden and the fields beyond – yet, he felt certain, not seeing them; as if her mind were taking refuge in a private world which she could not, or would not, communicate to him.

Pity there were no children, he thought. But one could not order these things. And nowadays, with so much on his mind, there didn't seem to be much hope of a Haldane heir. That concerned him, for the estate had no future unless there was a Haldane to take it from him. But there was still time. She shared his bed still; although except for about once a month – or was it now two months? – they slept deep in their own halves of the feather mattress and scarcely touched each other. If he approached her she would respond, he knew: she always did; but less eagerly now. Years ago she had startled him sometimes with her passion; indeed, secretly he had not entirely approved of it, although it had been provocative enough. But now . . .

She was beside him, her dress rustling.

'I've asked Nora to make sure the food is ready for ten o'clock,' she murmured. She glanced quickly around the crowded room. 'It's all quite successful, I think, my dear. Rather like old times, all this noise of talk and the drinks going round and people laughing so much. I'm enjoying it greatly. Are you?'

He smiled, pleased by her pleasure.

'Of course. And I'm so glad you are.' He touched the lace at her sleeve momentarily and she flashed a smile at him. Yes, he thought, she's still fond of me, if nothing more. Perhaps tonight, being New Year and his birthday on the morrow, if the wine did not go to his head and send him to sleep the moment he got into bed – perhaps . . .

She edged away between the chattering people, intending a final inspection of the kitchen. From the doorway she glimpsed her husband as he turned to speak to Helford; saw the taller man's easy, courteous smile, and wondered if he was enjoying the occasion or if he found some of his companions frustrating. He was the stranger in their midst; the man from the city who was known and yet unknown, the man who lived privately in the public world of business, whose flamboyant reputation was mostly reflected in second-hand telling. And he was handsome in a way which set him apart from the others. Where did that black hair come from, she wondered; and those extraordinary eyes?

She knew little about him, except that he was a widower, that his father had died riding to hounds when his horse had refused a hedge to which it should never have been put, and that Helford had used the resultant small legacy to buy out a bankrupt merchant in Plymouth. From that small start, Rupert had told her, his business had expanded rapidly. He had bought schooners, then had rented warehouses on the Exeter quayside hard by the newly opened canal basin, exploiting the widened canal which enabled ships to be brought right to the ancient walls of the city or hiring lighters

16

to take cargo to and from bigger vessels which exceeded the canal's ten-foot draught limit. The city's importance as a port had increased via the canal, and Mark Helford's business had expanded with it. Now Caroline was aware of a stirring interest, for her own father's wealth had been earned from shipping.

Rupert was talking steadily. Caroline hoped he was not wearying their guest; then rebuked herself for the disloyal thought. But she knew Rupert could be wearying to anyone who did not share his obsessions. He's putting on too much weight, she thought as the crowd between them parted momentarily. She would have to speak to him about it. But he would take no notice of her. That was his way now. Fifty years old tomorrow. Sometimes she felt he was much older than that. She was painfully aware, these days, that their intimacy of thought was slipping away and she could not recall it. Communication was now too often a calculated thing; companionship had to be sought.

She pushed through the kitchen door, conscious of gathering depression, trying quickly, urgently, to dismiss it, telling herself that other women beyond that door shared her secret loneliness; her sense of isolation, even of failure. Dear God, she thought, why should it be like this? Yet why should she be anxious lest Rupert should bore his companions when many of them were incredibly boring themselves? Many; but not Mark Helford, she thought. He would be interesting.

The door opened and Nora bustled in, jolting her back to her responsibilities. She was hostess and this was a night of celebration. There was work to do. She fixed her smile and went back to the big hall and the chatter and was suddenly pleased by laughter and friendly faces, and her concerns receded until they were forgotten.

They ate well, those fifty or so guests of Rupert Haldane, landowner and farmer, cattle breeder, distinguished and satisfied citizen of rural Devonshire, and his young and beautiful and frustrated wife; for Caroline supervised her kitchen expertly, and Nora was a good and imaginative cook. They drank well, too, for the cellar at Roxton Grange was well stocked and there were new and interesting wines which Mark Helford had recommended as a result of his recent travels to France. And when the old year's final minutes slipped away and the toast was 1850 and the prosperity of all under the lofty roof of the old house and God's gift of health to the young queen and her family, the glasses were raised with high enthusiasm and the voices were loud and the cigar smoke curled around the yellow lamplight. Then someone remembered that it was now their host's birthday and the congratulations were long and noisy as the logs crackled beneath the wide chimney, and Dr Miller looked into the cold night beyond the shining windows and thought about the baby boy in the damp candle-lit two-roomed cottage along the lane and the thin pale woman who had produced him from her inadequate body and the harassed, defeated eyes of her weary husband.

Miller was the first to leave the party. He rode slowly past the cottage where the child had been born in the last hours of the old year, and reined in to listen. But there was no sound on the crisp air except the distant screech of an owl, and no light in the window. He rode on, feeling more at ease, his long coat with its big collar close about him and his tall hat silhouetted against the stars.

Much later, when the last of the guests had gone, Rupert and Caroline climbed into their wide bed and he fell asleep without touching her, for the wine had indeed got the better of him. And she lay staring into the darkness for a long time.

II

The Rising Sun was well named, for it stood at the southern end of the narrow street around which Roxton centred and faced east across the rolling fields towards distant Dorset. Half-timbered and thatched, with an entrance wide enough for coaches – although few stopped there, for this was no main thoroughfare – it enjoyed a pleasant reputation for food and drink and good fellowship under the watchful eye of landlord Frederick Walton.

Its traditions included the annual New Year's Day meet of the district's hunt. And on New Year's Day in 1850 the occasion drew more people than usual, for the weather was fine with a clear pale blue sky, and while the wind was thin it was no more so than one might expect with a dusting of snow on the surrounding fields and the temperature scarcely above freezing point for the last three days.

They stood in groups, scattered across the green in front of the inn and up the narrowing cobbled street between the windows and doors of little houses and shops below their smoking chimneys. The village women, mostly in drab, heavy woollens – wide, thick skirts concealing black boots, coats pulled tight, scarves at their necks and close-fitting bonnets concealing their hair and shielding their ears from the wind – stood with their cord-trousered, heavy-booted men, some of whom wore long top-coats with tall collars, others fustian jackets with scarves wrapped around them, and tight-brimmed bowlers or flat-topped silk hats. Many of the farmers who had ridden in for the occasion were still mounted; others had tethered their horses and stood, heads together in talk of ditching and hedge-laying and winter threshing of last season's corn. They wore wide cord breeches and leggings above stout boots, and thick jackets buttoned over woollen shirts. Nearly all had black or brown bowlers on their heads. Between the groups the children ran, mostly in tattered hand-me-downs in wool or corduroy, tousle-haired and jumping up and down to keep the cold out of their inadequately-clad bodies.

In the crowd was Peter Parker, cowman on William Wright's farm. He and his master had milked the fifty Shorthorn cows that morning and washed down the byre. Then he had left a fellow labourer to drive the cart which took the milk churns down to the Exeter dairy. Now he turned to Billy Tregoney who worked for Morton Griffiths, and muttered: 'Your gaffer must've bin to a party last night – 'e looks like a sick dog.'

Tregoney hitched his breeches and spat. He was big-shouldered, with dark curly hair which extended down his cheeks to a fringe of greying beard below his heavy mouth.

'Mebbe 'e'll die like one – if we're lucky,' he growled. He looked at his companion. 'You 'eard about the party, then?'

Parker shook his head.

'No. I was just talking. Was there one?'

Tregoney turned, scanning the crowd nearby. He caught sight of a boy wearing patched corduroy breeches and a tattered woollen shirt under a long coat that would have fitted a grown man better than his thin twelve-year-old frame, and beckoned.

The boy dodged between people to reach him.

Tregoney said: 'Come 'ere, young Bob. Tell Mister Parker what we saw last night.'

The boy looked up at the two men. He had his father's dark hair and the same mouth.

'You mean all them folk going to the Grange, papa?' Tregoney nodded and the boy grinned. 'Carriages,' he said. 'Lots of 'em. An' horses. All going to the big house. We watched 'em for an hour, didn't we, papa?'

'We did that, lad. Stood in the window, counting 'em, till we got tired of it. Going past us, one after another. Must've bin fifty or sixty people. Think o' the money that lot cost to feed, an' all that drinking. Makes you sick, it does. Don' you forget it, lad. That's all rich folk 'ave to do – drink an' eat. They eat as much in a night as we do in a week. Idle bastards. Don' you forget it. That's the world you're growing up in – rich folk showing off while the rest on us slaves for a few bob a week to make 'em richer. You remember what the Haldanes are like, son – throwing their money around eating and drinking.'

The boy looked up at him. He remembered the previous evening with exceptional clarity, for it had startled him and what he had heard had kept him awake well into the night; for as the carriages had clattered past the cottage his father had shaken a fist towards the house and had said: 'Be you cursed, Rupert Haldane. You an' all in your house. May there be no more of you. May you be forever childless an' your money an' your land scattered as if you'd never been.'

The boy was still shaken by the vehemence in his father's voice – but impressed by the message. Why should some men have so much money, and others so little? Why should they give it all to their sons and none to other people who worked much harder? He thought his father was right. The squire of Roxton should not have sons. Then his money and his land would come to the men who had made him rich. The boy did not know how that might happen, but he was sure his father understood it all.

Beside them Peter Parker said nothing. He did not want to encourage Tregoney, for he knew the big man's hatred of the squire of Roxton. Once Tregoney had worked as a labourer on the estate – until, two years before, he had punched the farm steward to the ground. Rupert Haldane rarely dismissed a worker, but he had no stomach for violence and had sent Tregoney packing. After nearly a year without regular work the labourer had stood at the hirings and Griffiths had taken him on. Since then he had loudly blamed that misfortune upon Rupert Haldane. Parker had seen him several times, standing at the door of his cottage within a hundred yards of the gates of the Grange, staring at the big house sullenly, bitterly. Parker guessed he often stood there, watching. He knew Tregoney's hot temper and his brawls in the village

21

when he had had too much ale, and did not want an argument now. So he turned to watch the mounted men and the yelping hounds and the restless villagers standing aimlessly, stamping feet and rubbing hands in the cold air, waiting for something, anything, to happen. When the hunt moved off they would move too – the men into the Rising Sun or the smaller Dog and Partridge for ale and more talk before going slowly home where, in the little farm houses and cottages, the women would be preparing a meal. Except for the afternoon milking there would be little work that day; even farming's tempo slowed on the first day of the year. Meanwhile they watched, looking for old friends and old enemies, marking who talked to whom and which huntsmen put heads together, saddle-to-saddle, and wondering what they were planning and how it might affect the land which was their living. There was one consolation to be derived from the cold weather – wherever the hunt went today, and no matter how furious the chase, the horses were unlikely to do much damage, for the land was hard and there was little growing that would take much harm.

Sir Henry Wallingford, deputy lieutenant of the county and squire of the great hall and all that could be seen from its thirty-six windows – which did not include Roxton, for the village was four miles and three hills from his family seat – surveyed his mounted fellows with satisfaction on his round, whiskered face. They were as fine a body of English country gentry as he could wish to see, with their pink coats and glossy horses and shining harness under the bright morning sun. And the pack was turned out well under young Wardley, too – fourteen couple of the best hounds in the county. It was no wonder the folk turned up in such numbers to see and admire them, and follow them on foot or horse if they could. If Reynard obliged, it would be a good day.

He checked the shifting, stamping gathering of horses and riders as Master Walton moved among them with his hot stirrup cup. Thursgood – Martindale – Callan – Griffiths; he turned in his saddle, counting more. Where was that Shorthorn breeder fella who had all the land on the south side of the village? – ah, there – 'Morning Haldane, and the kindest wishes for the New Year to ye.' – and his delightful lady – not hunting today; pity – marvellous horsewoman – always good to watch. Good God she's a beauty – never will know how Haldane managed it. Still, he's a wealthy man – a lot of land – good catch for any young woman. 'Morning Lawton – how's business? Hope the year's a prosperous and healthy one for ye.' – 'This is an excellent sample, Walton – right up to your usual standard.' Who the hell is that? – dear God, that Exeter ship fella Helford come to have a look. Like a damn' half caste – must say he can sit a horse, though – but we won't have him as a member until he has land, that's sure, no matter what they say about his money. Not the only thing some people say about him, either. Looks a rake through and through – obviously not British . . .

A nearby horse wheeled, whinnying, and Sir Henry lost sight of the knot of spectators which included Helford and turned his attention to the hounds which were milling back and forth between the horses and the groups of villagers and farmers.

Helford edged his black gelding along the fringe of the crowd where it spilled from the street and over the green in front of the inn, nodding a greeting here and there, his strange eyes flicking from face to face. He wore a quiet check jacket and high-collared shirt atop his riding breeches, and heavy leather gloves, but was hatless – almost the only mounted man present without headgear of some sort. Across the chattering, shifting groups of people and horses and hounds he had seen Caroline Haldane, and was moving unobtrusively towards her.

She wore black, with a satin-faced jacket fitting close about her trim figure, buttoned high up around her neck and showing a frill of white lace at her throat. Leather gloves with long gauntlets protected her hands and wrists, and a narrow-brimmed grey hat was held in place by a pinned veil. She was a striking personality among the spectators, sitting side-saddle with the elegance and confidence of a thoroughly experienced rider. But then those who had ridden to hounds with the lady of Roxton Grange knew that there was no better horsewoman

23

in Devonshire – and probably not for many a mile elsewhere, most reckoned.

Today, as Sir Henry Wallingford had noted, she would not hunt but had come to watch her husband set out with the others, before cantering back to the Grange, escorted by the faithful and attentive Conway. But Conway was on the other side of the village street at that moment, and the horse that sidled alongside hers was Helford's.

'You look charming this morning, Mrs Haldane. I must thank you again for a most delightful evening.' His voice was just loud enough for her to hear, and for no one else's ears.

She turned, surprised, off guard, and felt his eyes.

'My word, Mr Helford, I didn't expect to see you here. Are you going to tell me that you rode all the way home after our party, and then returned for the meet? You must have had no sleep at all.'

He laughed. It was an easy, controlled sound, deep in his throat.

'No, ma'am. I don't have so much energy. I spent the night here, with our good landlord. And a pleasant and comfortable place he has. So I'm as fresh and rested as any other of your guests who've made the effort to be here.'

She looked at him curiously.

'You stayed at the Rising Sun? Was that because of the meet – or the party?'

He shrugged slightly, checking his horse as it stamped and swung its quarters.

'A little of both, perhaps. I have business hereabouts. But I suppose it could have waited. I could certainly have returned home after your excellent party, but it would have been a long ride so late at night. So – the party – the meet – the business: it made good sense to stay. And now –' again the dark straight gaze and the half smile and the hint of inexplicable mockery '– now the bonus of meeting you again. My New Year has started well.'

She inclined her head graciously, but her eyes did not leave his.

'You have a charming turn of phrase, Mr Helford.' Now

24

she was mocking, gently. 'I was tired this morning, and nearly did not come. On another occasion I would have joined my husband and followed the pack. But certainly not today.' She laughed quickly. 'I think I shall spend a very lazy day, apart from the meal we have arranged for the workers and tenants. Did my husband tell you about that?'

'No.' His eyebrows slanted. 'Are you hostess on two successive days?'

'Oh no.' She shook her head, swaying slightly as her mare tossed its mane. 'Nora and other ladies are in charge, I'm glad to say. But we are providing the food and the drink. It's by way of celebrating my husband's birthday – he is exactly as old as the century, you see.'

A child ran close beneath Helford's mount's nose, and he reined firmly. The horse backed two or three paces, snorting, breath rising in the cold air. Caroline turned the mare towards him, stirrup to stirrup.

'How remarkable.' For a moment Caroline wondered if there was sarcasm there, then decided it was simply his naturally slightly sardonic manner of speech. 'Does he take a close interest in his workers?'

'Of course.' Caroline's voice was cool, slightly defensive. 'And should he not do so?'

'My dear Mrs Haldane, please do not misunderstand me. I would not suggest that for a moment.' Helford was apologizing for the mistake, yet somehow making clear that it was hers, not his. 'But you must admit not many men in his position are much interested in their labourers – certainly not sufficiently to provide them with food as part of a birthday celebration.'

'That's true.' She was still wary, but less so. His eyes held her gaze, and she was conscious of his smile. 'And he doesn't do such a thing every year, by any means. But he felt this year was rather special. And some of the men have been with him and with his family for a long time.'

'Is he a good employer?' The question could have been impertinent, but there was no accusation in the quiet voice, and the half smile was easy and friendly.

25

'Oh yes,' she said swiftly. 'He pays as well as he is able – better than most others. And he is much concerned for their welfare. If they are ill he takes them food and pays Dr Miller to attend them. And he repairs their houses, even without being asked. They think a great deal of him.'

He looked at her thoughtfully.

'And you are proud of him for it.' A statement; an observation.

'Naturally.' She was cool again. 'For that and many things. Perhaps you do not know him well, Mr Helford.'

He laughed at her, but it was an inviting sound.

'I confess I do not. But I am getting to know him better by the minute – through you. I admired him already as a shrewd businessman and a gentleman. Now I realize there is much else to be admired in him. But I am afraid I do not know too much about the land, Mrs Haldane. I'm more at home with ships and cargoes and buying and selling.'

'So I hear. 'Tis said you are a hard businessman, Mr Helford.' She was testing his sense of humour.

'Business is hard, Mrs Haldane. A man must be equally so, to be successful.' He did not sound particularly interested. 'And the more –'

'Morning, Helford.' Suddenly Rupert Haldane was beside them. Neither had heard his approach in the moving throng of horses and people. 'We really must try to get you elected – you should be riding with us today.'

Helford looked sideways at him.

'You're kind, sir. I shall have to apply. It's a remarkable day. You should enjoy the chase.'

'Hope so – sure we will.' Haldane steadied his restless horse, a rangy bay gelding that looked too big for his slightly overweight figure, then spurred the mount forward as the frosty air was split by the silver-sharp notes of the horn summoning the hunt on its way. The riders formed into groups of two and three behind Sir Henry and, with hounds in attendance, they moved up the village.

Helford said, 'Shall we follow?' and they swung their mounts and rode side by side among the crowd behind the hunt. As they did so the stocky figure of Conway, riding a big bay mare, fell in behind them.

'I see we are accompanied.' Helford's voice was just loud enough for her to hear above the hubbub of voices and hooves and snorting horses.

She looked at him sharply.

'Mr Conway is to escort me home,' she said. Her eyes held his in quick challenge.

His smile was disarming.

'But of course. I should have realized. A pity, though – I was hoping you might have permitted me the pleasure.'

She laughed, relaxing again.

'There is no limit to numbers. Why don't you ride with us part of the way?'

A little later, the hunt gone away at a canter and the sightseers dispersing, they turned off the end of the village street into the lane leading towards the Grange, the estate's lady and Helford side-by-side, Conway just behind. He had acknowledged Helford with no more than a curt 'Morning, sir' and now his hard eyes were fixed on the long straight back and black hair, his face expressionless as he rode.

They talked little. Caroline enjoyed the bright morning and heady air, and watched the rooks and starlings in the fields beyond the hedgerows. But occasionally she glanced covertly at her companion. He seemed to pay her little attention apart from an occasional comment on the scene, and she wondered if he resented Conway's presence and silent disapproval.

'Do you enjoy riding – for its own sake?' she tried.

He looked round, almost as if he had forgotten her.

'I suppose so. Never thought about it. I do enjoy a good gallop, particularly with a companion. That seems to make it much more interesting – more competitive, perhaps. A sharing of pleasure is important, don't you think?'

Suddenly she felt sorry for him. She had forgotten he was a widower. Perhaps his hard, confident exterior was a shield for loneliness.

'I'm sure of it.' She hesitated, choosing her words – and then in the same instant wondering why she found it necessary

27

to do so. 'Perhaps you would care to join me – Rupert and myself – for a canter sometime. There are some good rides here, both on our own land and away from it.'

His eyes looked into hers. She wondered if he had noticed her hesitant inclusion of her husband, and whether he knew that these days Rupert hardly ever rode with her for pleasure. Why had she said it? This was foolish – the man was dangerous – everybody said so.

'You're very kind.' There was no way that Conway, behind them, could have heard him. 'I would enjoy that – and especially the pleasure of your company.'

She straightened her back and wrenched her eyes away from the intensity of his gaze. It was almost a physical severance. She was suddenly very aware of Conway's presence, as if the farm steward might in some way be able to read her confusion. Mark Helford's words had been a harmless courtesy; yet subtly, indescribably, he had conveyed in them a significance that tightened the muscles across her chest.

She said hastily: 'The land looks good for the time of year, I think.' She pointed her riding crop towards the rolling red earth rising beyond a wooden field gate.

'I am not an authority,' his easy voice said. 'What makes it look good to you, Mrs Haldane?'

She raised her crop again, deliberately concentrating her gaze on the fields and the low hills.

'Do you see the cattle? They're next season's breeding heifers. The men are feeding them little but hay, I'm told, although they're carrying calves. But see how fit they look. Now notice the land, Mr Helford. It's clean – little sign of puddling, even around the gates. It was a dry autumn – remember? – and there's been relatively little rain since. And until the frost of the past week, not too much cold weather, either. The cattle like that. They're wintering well, Conway tells me. We're getting through the season nicely.'

She could feel his eyes on her and sensed his curiosity.

'Do you understand the business of farming? I must say you appear most knowledgeable.'

She flicked a glance at him. He was not mocking her, she was certain.

'It is my husband's business, sir. I am most interested, of course.'

Ahead, along the lane, a rabbit ran down a hedge bank, paused, hesitating; then darted away, white tail towards them. Helford watched it go before he said: 'Your husband is not a farmer, ma'am. He owns land – but your man Conway does the farming for him, and his tenants do the rest. With respect, I would have expected that your station would have distanced you from the practicalities.'

'Good gracious, Mr Helford.' She turned to face him now as they rode stirrup-to-stirrup. 'Indeed you do not know my husband well. Conway may be our steward, and the daily conduct of the home farm may be in his hands. But Rupert loves this estate, and is proud of it. He knows every yard of our land, every beast in our herds and most of the sheep flock, too. He would be quite capable of undertaking much of the practical work if it were ever necessary, I assure you. There is little that occurs on our land that he does not understand at least as well as the steward or the tenants.'

'And he discusses such things with you, ma'am?' He was watching her with quiet interest, his eyes no longer challenging.

Her shoulders moved in a slight shrug.

'I am not sure that discussion would be a totally accurate description. He certainly tells me a great deal. I do not have his total understanding, for I come of different stock. But I have learned much from him through the years, I do assure you.'

He nodded gravely.

'That is evident enough, ma'am. I envy you your knowledge – and the opportunity to experience a world of which I am relatively uninformed.'

She looked away quickly, unsure of him again, and watched a buzzard circle slowly on wide dark wings above the edge of a copse beyond the nearest field. He followed the direction of her gaze.

'He's hunting,' he said softly. 'That's what the countryside is all about, isn't it – death to provide life – down to the insects in the hedgerows. And man is part of the pattern; except that we have the supreme advantage that there is no one to hunt us. Our society may be harsh, but it is constructed less brutally than that of the buzzard and the rabbit, or the fox and his prey. Yet still harshly enough, don't you think?'

She hesitated, surprised.

'I am not sure that I understand you clearly, Mr Helford.'

He said, very quietly: 'There's a man in the wood, to the right of the hawk. I trust he is not poaching on your land. But if he is, it may not be entirely for greed. It could even be a matter of survival for him, and his family. What do you do with poachers, Mrs Haldane?'

She searched the distant trees; saw no movement. Then she looked at him sharply.

'I? I do nothing with poachers. Conway deals with them if they're caught.'

'I'm sure he does.' Helford turned to catch a glimpse of the mounted figure a dozen yards behind them. 'And most competently, I am certain.'

She stared at him, head up now, quick anger in her gaze.

'What are you meaning to say to me, Mr Helford?'

But his smile was easy again, and she was surprised to see a hint of humour in his deep dark eyes.

'Nothing I have not already said. My impression of Conway is one of total competence. And poaching cannot be allowed to run out of hand, no matter what our social problems. Please do not take offence, for none was intended.'

She inclined her head, meeting the challenge, accepting the hint of apology, wondering if he had tried to provoke her and had succeeded. She struggled to distance herself, and failed as his wide mouth curved again, and could think of nothing else to say.

A minute later they reached a row of farm cottages – crumbling brick and chipped plaster, tattered thatch above; two small windows each, one above the other, and a door set in a shallow porch. As they came abreast of the first she reined in abruptly.

'Mr Helford, there is something I have to do. There is a woman here with a newly born baby. I must enquire after her health, and that of her child. I – I may be some time.'

His eyes hinted amusement, as if he thought she was making an excuse to be rid of him and he found the idea vaguely entertaining.

'I understand. I'll leave you here. Thank you for allowing me to ride with you. I'll take up your invitation one day, if I may. I hope you find the lady in good health.' He turned his horse as he spoke, and there was interest, even curiosity, in his gaze as he glanced quickly across the grimy wall of the little cottage. 'My regards to your husband.' He spurred his mount. 'Good day to you, Conway.'

'Morning, sir.' Conway made his second contribution to the day's conversation.

Helford kneed his horse into a canter. He did not look back.

Caroline said quietly, 'Hold my horse, please,' and Conway jumped to the ground and took her mare's head. She slid from the saddle easily, expertly, without waiting for his assistance, and smoothed her skirt.

'I'm going to see Mrs Garton. I think I should.'

Conway concealed his surprise, but could not resist a question.

'D'you know her, Mrs Haldane?'

He sounded as if he did not expect an affirmative answer, but Caroline nodded.

'Slightly. Her husband passes our gate regularly, I have spoken with her in the village on occasion. She is a courteous woman, if very poor. It would be a neighbourly thing to ask after her health – and her baby's.'

Conway nodded. He was a man who rarely wasted words. But if Caroline noticed his puzzlement she did not show it. She walked down the two rough steps to the little door and knocked. The door was opened almost immediately by a man wearing a ragged shirt and rough faded trousers secured at the waist with cord. He was mid-thirties, big and strongly made. But his hair was tousled, his shoulders stooped and his pale thin face lined with exhaustion. His eyes blinked in the bright light, and then widened in astonished recognition.

'Good morning, Mr Garton.' Caroline's voice was gentle. 'I trust this is as happy a New Year's day for you as I am led to believe.'

Albert Garton gulped.

'I – oh yes – Mrs Haldane – I didn't expect –'

She shook her head.

'Of course. I was passing. How is your wife – and your son?'

He edged back into the dimness of the cottage, embarrassed, but his pleasure showing slowly.

'She's – she's all right, I think. She's asleep. And the baby – he – he's fine. A lovely boy. Ma'am – you're very kind to ask.'

'Not at all. I was anxious to know.' She paused as he stared at her awkwardly, not knowing what to say next. 'Well – aren't you going to invite me to step inside?'

He nodded; then shook his head, confused.

'Oh, ma'am, this place isn't – I mean, it's not fit to receive 'ee. 'Tis honoured we are – an' you're most welcome – but –'

'If I'm welcome then I'll come in,' Caroline said firmly.

He retreated before her, backing into the half-dark of the tiny room. It was both living room and kitchen, with a blackened chimney and a poor fire, a dented kettle and a cooking pot in front of the low flickering flames, two wooden chairs, a small rough-hewn box and a battered dresser beside the little window. The floor was rough stone and the walls stained and unpainted plaster. The smell of dampness met her like a physical barrier.

She said: 'Your wife is asleep? Please do not disturb her.' Her eyes became more accustomed to the gloom and she realized that the box beside the fireplace was a crude cradle. She crossed to it and stood, looking down at Albert and Grace Garton's day-old son. The child was quiet, but not asleep. She said, almost to herself: 'I came to see your baby as well as your wife.' Gently she pulled aside the sacking that covered the cot and lifted the bundle of tattered blankets. The baby stared up

32

at her with the uncomprehending eyes of the newly born. Albert Garton stood behind her, wondering, proud, confused. She held the baby across her arm for a moment, swaying slightly to console it.

'What name will you give to him?'

'Name, ma'am? Frank, ma'am. My father's name. If 'e lives. We've lost two children.'

She nodded. It was commonplace.

The child gurgled, then was quiet again as she cooed in response. She walked to the light of the window, turning so that she could see the tiny face. Pale sunlight brought life to her fair hair beneath her grey hat and veil. Garton watched, wordless.

She said: 'You need a better fire. Do you have much fuel?'

'No – no. Not much,' he stammered. 'I 'ave to make it last. The nights are cold –'

'I'll send some wood. You must keep him warm – warmer than this. And well fed. Did the doctor say anything about that?'

'The doctor – 'e said Grace would feed 'im – that she could –'

'Then she must have good food.' She remembered what Miller had said the night before. 'I think Dr Miller will call again, probably today. Take notice of what he tells you.'

'Oh, Mrs Haldane – you're very kind.' The words tumbled out. 'The midwife, she sent for the doctor to come. Said it was going to be a difficult birth. I told 'er we couldn't pay anything but she wouldn't listen. 'E mustn't come agin – I –'

'Nonsense. He will be the judge of that. And he will not charge you if you cannot pay. That is Dr Miller's way. He is a good man. You must trust him.'

The child stirred a feeble arm. She stroked the tiny hand, feeling the fingers trying to close around her own. She turned her back towards Garton, looking at the baby's round pink face in the thin light from the grimy window, feeling quick life in the helpless limbs. A sudden slight shiver passed across her shoulders.

Silently, the lady of Roxton Grange was crying.

III

***

By the evening of the third day of the year the villages around Exeter and the little ports along the nearby coast were abuzz with rumour and excitement. The events which had startled the little town of Teignmouth the previous day were being eagerly reported, first by the few witnesses then by second and third hand listeners, gaining detail and drama on the way.

They were dramatic enough, in truth; though no more so, the wise men said, than one might have expected in view of the principal participant.

In the sheltered waters behind Teignmouth's sand bar, where the fast flowing channel below the steep red cliff and the tiny fishing village of Shaldon widened into more peaceful shallows on either side of the winding river, the 220-ton schooner *Western Belle* lay at the wooden quayside. She had come in at high tide several days before Christmas with mast and rigging damage after a storm off the Lizard and had lain alongside over the holiday. The forward mast had now been replaced, but much of the rigging remained to be refitted.

Only two men were visibly working on her when Mark Helford arrived. Still in the saddle, he looked along the length of the ship with hard eyes and tight jawline; then he swung from his horse, tethered it, and with his customary grey cloak hanging loose from his shoulders, walked with long strides to the gangplank and ran up to the deck.

A thickset man in his thirties, with a craggy face and a mop of fair hair, looked up from the block on which he was working.

'I'm Helford. I own this ship. How many men are working here?' Sharp-edged words.

The man wiped thick-fingered hands down his stained

leather waistcoat and nodded to another figure forward on the ship.

'Two.' He glanced again at the visitor's height and wide-legged stance and added '– sir.'

'Where's the foreman?'

The man clambered to his feet, went to the rail, pointed to a wooden hut thirty yards away and in front of the line of single-storeyed buildings backing the quay.

'That's where he likely is, this time o'day.'

Helford said: 'What's his name?'

The man looked wary, and curious.

'Willis. John Willis.' He added again '– sir.'

Helford leaned over the rail, cupped his hands, and bellowed the name. His deep voice echoed back from the buildings.

The door of the hut opened and a man peered out.

'Who's that?' he shouted, his eyes searching the waterfront.

'Willis – I want you here – on the *Western Belle*.' Again the buildings threw back the bark of the voice.

The man focused on the schooner and the figure at the rail. He came out of the hut – above six feet, balding, a tangled mass of hair at the back of his head and extending down his cheeks to the angle of his strong jaw. He had wide shoulders and long arms. A bottle was clutched in one fist.

'Who are you?' His voice was as aggressive as his appearance.

'Helford. Owner of this ship. Come over here.'

Along the quay men raised their heads, straightened their backs, sensing conflict. Another man stood at the rail of a barque tied up further along the quay, and watched.

The foreman glanced back into the hut, said something, hitched his leather-and-cord breeches, began to walk slowly along the quay. Two more men clad in woollen shirts, heavy leather waistcoats, thick trousers and leggings, came out of the hut behind him and shuffled in his wake. Helford hooked thumbs into his trouser pockets, watching them come. At the foot of the gangplank they stopped, eyeing him. Willis raised his bottle, looked at it, put the neck in his mouth and drank. He dragged the back of his hand across his lips and passed the bottle to one of the men flanking him.

'Where's your manager – Mr Trevelyan?' Now that the men were closer Helford's voice had dropped. But it had lost none of its razor edge.

The foreman stared back insolently. Then he turned to his companions, exaggerating the move.

'Now where'd he go, lads? Exeter, wur it? Or Land's End?' The group grinned at each other, and Helford heard one of the men on the deck cackle. 'No – I remember – Plymouth. Ye'll have to wait around a coupla days if ye want to see him, mister. Get yur fancy clothes wet – it's gonna rain afore long.'

Helford said steadily: 'This ship is due away on the evening tide tomorrow. The master will be here this evening. The crew will be here tomorrow morning. The contract was for four men to work on her. If four men start work immediately, and you join them, Willis, you might just have her ready. Start now.'

The foreman's eyes narrowed. For seconds he stared up at Helford. Then he muttered to his companions. One moved towards the bow, the other went aft, taking another swig from the bottle as he walked. They went quickly, reaching the two mooring bollards at the same time – and with rapid, deft movements, cast off the rope hawsers which held the ship close against the quay. As they did so Willis roared, 'Rob – Tom – get off there – fast!' and the two men who had watched the exchanges from the deck behind Helford darted for the rail, vaulted over, and dropped to the quayside eight feet below. As they landed Willis heaved at the gangplank, trying to pull it away from the ship.

The schooner shifted. The fast ebb tide caught her stern and she started to swing. Helford stepped back, grabbed the deck end of the gangplank and pulled, bracing himself with one foot against the rail. The planking dragged on the quay and slid back as the ship moved away. Willis suddenly added his weight at the other end and roared with laughter as

Helford staggered across the deck, the plank slamming into him as he wrestled to control it and prevent it damaging the deck fittings.

By the time he had secured it roughly with two turns of a loose rope, the *Western Belle*'s stern was a dozen yards into the river and her bow was six feet clear of the quay. As Helford ran for the wheel he heard the jeering laughter of the men, and then ducked as the bottle they had been sharing was flung at him, hit a mast and splintered against the base of the compass housing. Along the quay men were gathering, staring open-mouthed, motionless.

The tide carried the drifting schooner broadside as Helford unlashed the wheel and spun it frantically, his grey cloak flying out from his shoulders in the chill wind, the half-rigged masts stark against the threatening clouds. The ship cleared a barge moored in the river, rolling as she turned in momentary answer to the helm. Then the tide caught her again and the stern swung until she was drifting across the tideway.

For minutes Helford fought at the wheel as she neared the faster waters at the narrow point of the sand bar. Then a freak channel and tide brought her round and she drifted to the limit of the stream, turning slowly into the calmer waters, and drove her bow hard into the shingle that bounded the Salty from the quay out to the end of the sand bar.

Men were running from huts and cottages along the shore line. One swung a rope, hurled it. Helford ran forward, grabbed the end and secured it. Ashore two men heaved on the other end, found a post, lashed it. Another rope streaked aboard. Within minutes the *Western Belle* was secured, hard aground, against the receding tide.

Helford picked up a rag, wiping his hands as he walked forward. He swung his long legs over the rail, balanced for a moment, then jumped. The shingle was wet enough to cushion his fall. The men ran to him, extending hands; then stood, not touching him, when they saw his face.

He said: 'Thank you. Stay here and I'll see that you're rewarded for your assistance.' Then he brushed between them and stalked across the shingle onto firmer ground, turning upstream towards the end of the quay a hundred or more yards away.

The men watched him go, silent. Then one jerked his head at the other.

'Better send word for a constable to come,' he said, and he moved to follow Helford. His companion nodded and ran up the shingle towards the low line of wooden shacks and the fishermen's cottages.

Helford walked with long, fast strides. He had lost his cloak somewhere on the ship, and his riding boots, grey trousers and long black coat were stained with grease and mud. He moved with surprising speed, his face rock-carved, ignoring the men and women who peered from windows and came from the houses above the shingle to watch him. A sudden flurry of cold rain spattered across the water. He appeared not to notice it. At the end of the quay he climbed a rusting steel ladder three rungs at a stride. At the top he checked momentarily, his near-black eyes glinting in the dull light from the scudding grey clouds. Three men who had watched the schooner cast adrift stood twenty yards away. They saw his face and eyes and, even at that distance, instinctively backed away. Beyond them was the hut from which the foreman and his men had emerged earlier. In the distance were more men, watching. There was no sign of Willis or his companions.

He resumed his fast walk towards the hut. Halfway there he veered suddenly and picked up a short wooden stave propped against a capstan. Nearer the hut he heard voices raised, and harsh laughter heavy with drink.

Then he was at the door, measured his distance, and lashed out with his foot. The door cracked wide, and the violent sound echoed into the sudden silence within.

The man to whom Helford had first spoken on the deck of the schooner stumbled into the daylight. He opened his mouth to shout, and the sound was choked to a sobbing gurgle as Helford's stave slammed across his throat. He staggered back, clawing at his face and mouth, colliding with another man who half-fell in his headlong rush outside. Helford let him come, raised his stave and as the man swerved and lifted

38

an arm to ward off the blow, kicked him savagely in the crotch. The man screamed, doubling up, falling forwards as the stave slammed down across the back of his neck. The only sound as he hit the ground was the scrabbling of his boots before he was still.

Then the other three were out in the open – Willis last, with a bottle in his great hand. Helford swerved left, and the man on his right came in fast and low, his arms outstretched for Helford's legs. Helford's stave, now in his left hand, lashed out, momentarily keeping the other two at bay, and the blade of his right hand smashed into the neck of the man whose head was now level with his waist and whose hands clawed at his thighs. The clutching fingers froze and Helford kneed the man clear as he rolled over, face down against the wooden boards of the quay. He made no sound.

The other two hesitated, unbelieving. The reduction in the odds had been so sudden, so violent. Willis took a half-step back to get a clearer sight of his target; his companion glanced round, thinking the foreman was retreating, panic on his face. His head swivelled and he saw deep-dark eyes that seemed to shine cold lights into him in their hatred. The three motionless bodies stretched out from the door of the hut, the stave now shifting from one waiting hand to the other, the tall black-haired man's wide thin mouth and hunched shoulders, were suddenly more than his nerves could take. Words bubbled: 'God – dear God – he's bloody mad – he'll kill us all – bloody mad –' and he stumbled sideways, away, half falling, recovering, ignoring Willis's snarling 'Grab him – get the bastard' – breaking into a shuffling crab-like scrabble of boots to get away. His breath whistled in terror and he fell, scrambled to his feet in final panic – and ran.

Helford took a long, deep breath.

'Now – just you and me, Willis.' The words were scarcely above a whisper.

Men stood at a distance, frozen, fascinated, horrified. One said, 'Oh Christ,' as Helford suddenly whirled his stave – and threw it in a long, high arc away towards the water.

'I don't need that to deal with you.' His voice was louder,

39

cutting against the wind, reaching the astonished watchers. Then Willis darted sideways. His bottle smashed against the ground and came up jagged glass, spilling the remains of the liquor. He held it in front of him, low, like a knife, weaving it from side to side. Helford jumped back, turning as if to move left, and lashed out with his right foot. The toe of his riding boot thudded into the foreman's wrist and the remains of the bottle spun away. Willis swore, scrambled after it before Helford could move again, caught it as it rolled. Behind him two policemen ran between buildings forty yards away, truncheons drawn. Willis straightened, the razor edges of the glass in his right hand flashing up. But Helford was on him, fingers locked around the wrist, his rush carrying the man back in violent collision as Willis jabbed with his fist, gashing the side of Helford's face, hammering his head forward at the taller man's mouth.

Helford jerked sideways, and the fingers of his right hand, steel-straight, divided into a vee, stabbed out; and Willis shrieked, reared, his free left hand across his eyes, and then his thin cry exploded in a strangled cough as Helford's right arm pistoned back, fingers curled now, locked, and slammed forward, bone-jarring below the heart. Willis swung, almost suspended by the wrist Helford still held aloft, his head back and his mouth open, retching, blinded, as the two running policemen reached him, one on either side, clubbing him across the shoulders.

Helford jumped back, blood streaming from the gash along his cheekbone. The broken bottle dropped from the foreman's helpless fingers and he crumpled, one of the policemen falling on top of him, pinning him.

The other swayed in front of Helford, panting. 'I saw the bottle, sir – thought you were a goner. You got a nasty cut –'

Then there were men running, crowding, but silent in the wind, now standing and looking at the figures on the ground – and keeping an arm's length from Helford.

The policeman looked around, puzzled.

'Who else was in this? Who done those?' He waved his truncheon at the prostrate, sprawled men.

Helford straightened. The savage light was still in his eyes, but fading now. He felt for a kerchief, held it to his face.

'No one else, officer. I'll give you the details in due course.' His voice was low and quite steady, his breathing long and deep.

Willis moaned as his captor shifted his weight and stood up. A spectator jabbered: 'Bloody hell – never seen anything like that.' And to Helford – 'They were terrors, sir. None of us dared go near 'em when they were drinking –'

'You did all this?' The policeman stared at Helford incredulously, then looked around. 'All this? This lot?' He shook his head as he saw the nodding crowd, mystified.

Helford turned. The men parted in awe. He walked between them towards his tethered, forgotten horse which stamped and snorted at the sight of him.

IV

Moses Dodman swung the sledgehammer back, balanced, then heaved it round, over his shoulder and down with a satisfying thud on the four-inch square top of the fencing post. Robert Clement, who had been steadying the post, straightened, rubbing his aching back, and said: 'Reckon it'll do, Mose.'

It was the last of a dozen posts they had placed to cover gaps in a thorn hedge through which sheep had begun to stray several weeks before. The hedge would have to be laid and interplanted; meanwhile it had to be made stock-proof, and wooden fencing from the estate's workshop was the only quick answer. Ten of the posts had already been linked with three horizontal slats nailed into place. Now only the last two posts remained. The two men worked, sweating in the cold winter air, hammering in the final nails. Their breath steamed around their heads and their boots crunched the frosted soil.

When they had finished they stood back, regarding the work with satisfaction, and began to gather their tools. Dodman said: 'I'm hungry. Time t'go back.'

Clement grunted his agreement. They dragged their equipment across to the flat cart on which they had brought the fencing posts and slats from the farm buildings three hundred yards away, Dodman heaved himself onto it and picked up the reins and Clement turned the patient carthorse. Then he jumped up beside his companion and the cart lurched away from the hedge.

'Hear about the fight in Teignmouth, two-three days back?' asked Dodman, stuffing tobacco into a clay pipe.

'Heard something. Not much, though. On the quay, weren' it?'

'Oh yes. They say 'twere that feller Helford – took on

half-a-dozen men 'n beat hell outa all of 'em. They'd cast his ship adrift, or something. You ever see'm around the farm 'ere?'

'Once.' Clement took the reins while Dodman fiddled with matches. 'Wouldn' like to tackle'm meself. It's not just as 'e's big – it's the way 'e looks. You ever see'm, Mose?'

Dodman puffed smoke from the pipe and nodded.

'Twice I seen'm. Tough as they come, 'e is. Where'd you reckon 'e's from, then? Looks like a furriner.'

Clement flicked the reins, shouted 'Giddup – giddup', then said: 'France or Spain or somewhere, wouldn' be surprised. Not 'im, mebbe – 'is father, I suppose. 'Tis said 'e was hurt.'

'Oh yes, I 'eard that too. Gashed with a bottle, 'tis said. But folk say 'e nearly killed two o' those fellers. All by isself, too.'

'Don' believe that – not one agin six. No man could, 'cept with pistols, or somethin'.'

'Let's ask Mr Conway, then.'

They saw Stanley Conway as the cart rattled over cobbles around the corner of the stables, turned the horse towards him and slid to the ground.

'Hey boss – you 'ear about that fight in Teignmouth? Few days back, 'twere. On the quay – Mr Helford –'

'I heard,' Conway interrupted. 'What about it?'

''Tis said Mr Helford beat six men, all by isself. Is that right?'

Conway shook his head.

'I don't know about six. I only heard about it this morning. Suppose I'd better see if Mr Haldane knows – him being a friend of Mr Helford's.'

'Better tell'n Mr Helford's hurt, then,' said Dodman.

'Is he?' Conway eyed him suspiciously. 'How d'you know that?'

Dodman puffed energetically at his pipe, the smoke hanging around his head.

'All over the village, boss. All over. Gashed with a bottle, 'e was. Must've bin a good fight. Like t've seen that – eh, Rob?'

Clement grinned, watching Conway turn away.

'M-m. Fair sport, by the sound.'

'Get along to work,' growled Conway over his shoulder, and the two men winked at each other and led the horse across the cobbled yard. Within minutes they had backed the cart into the long shed, released the horse from the shafts and stabled it, their morning's work done.

In the estate office alongside the house Rupert Haldane and his steward compared notes on the Teignmouth fracas. Rupert had not heard about the injury to Mark Helford and was alarmed.

He went into the house, found Caroline reading.

'My dear – after lunch I shall go to see Mark Helford. He has apparently been involved in a fight at the Teignmouth dockside. One of his ships was set adrift by a gang of drunken labourers. He appears to have inflicted considerable damage among them – a remarkable story indeed – but he has been hurt also.'

His wife was on her feet, wide-eyed.

'Oh, Rupert – he's hurt? How badly? Tell me –'

She checked, aware that her voice was rising, that her book had fallen to the floor.

Rupert put a reassuring hand on her arm.

'Don't excite yourself. I do not hear that he is in any danger. But I was told he fought a man who had a bottle – a broken bottle – and has been slashed. It's nearly an hour's drive, but I think it would be a courtesy to call on him.'

'Yes. Of course. And I would like to come with you. We must see if he needs help.' She was in control now.

He frowned, shaking his head.

'There is no need to trouble yourself, my dear. Indeed I did not expect you to be so anxious. I am sure we shall find that there is no need for alarm. I will go, and I will tell you about it when I return.'

She gathered her skirts about her.

'No. I will come with you.' She was firm. 'You know nothing of bandaging.'

'It was two days ago,' he said sharply. 'And I am sure he will have summoned a doctor if there is need.'

'I'll still accompany you. I'll ask Nora to hurry our lunch.'

She swept her long fair hair back across her shoulders and hurried from the room, her face masking the turmoil in her mind. She knew that her confusion lay not only in the sudden news of Helford's injury but in her own reaction to it. She saw the danger signals clearly, and the perils they heralded. Yet she was unable to turn away from them. Her mind said, 'Don't go – there is no need', and she rejected the thought. Then again, 'Keep away – there must be some ground for his reputation', and she ignored that, allowing it to be swamped by the memory of his voice and his eyes and the glimpse they gave her of unimaginably exciting worlds. And the ultimate argument, 'You fool – what are you doing – you're married –' left her cold and angry with herself, for she knew there was no answer to it and, because of that, she did not want to hear it.

Meanwhile Rupert looked after her as she went, still frowning, puzzled. Then he shrugged to himself and walked slowly from the room.

An hour later one of the farm men put two quiet mares between the shafts of a Victoria carriage as Rupert told Conway: 'You'd better come with us, Stanley. It may be dark when we return. And it's a lonely road.'

The steward nodded, wordless. Haldane's precaution was wise and needed no comment. There were always a few thieves about – often men from ships in the Exe, the Teign and the Dart. And a woman as strikingly beautiful as Caroline needed especial protection. He came out of the office, pulling on his heavy cord coat and cramming a cap onto his head as he felt the chill wind.

Their journey was uneventful. Once they bumped past a small coach carrying half-a-dozen passengers in the opposite direction; then two riders approached and Rupert leaned from the window and raised a hand in greeting as they cantered by – one was the Reverend James Lethbridge, vicar of St Thomas's church which served Roxton and the neighbourhood. Otherwise they saw no one until, with cold rain pattering on the roof of the carriage, they reached the outskirts of Exeter city and the big town house which Mark Helford had bought two years previously.

Conway turned into the short drive and Rupert Haldane alighted.

'Wait in the carriage, my dear,' he called back as he walked up the three wide steps to the door.

Caroline watched as he hammered on the oak panelling. She sat on the edge of the seat, one hand to her throat, the tension suddenly aching in her body. Throughout the journey she had responded briefly to Rupert's desultory conversation while her mind had raced back and forth over the sketchy details she had of the Teignmouth incident, trying to reassure herself that Helford would not be badly hurt, then wondering at her anxiety, telling herself that she was being foolish, behaving like an impressionable girl instead of the wife of a mature and respected landowner. As Rupert waited now at the door she made a physical effort to relax; then held her breath as the door opened.

A middle-aged woman, grey-haired, round-faced, dark-clothed, was speaking to the caller. Then Rupert went inside. The door remained open, and Caroline could see the woman beyond it, in the hallway. Within a minute Rupert came out, down the steps, and opened the carriage door.

'Mr Helford is delighted to see us,' he said. Caroline thought the words were pompous, then stifled the reaction and allowed her husband to hand her from the carriage. Her apprehensive eyes searched Rupert's face, but she would not allow herself to ask the question that dominated her mind.

In the doorway the woman half curtsied.

'Good afternoon, ma'am. I'm Mrs Tovey. Mr Helford's housekeeper. He's waiting for you.'

'Thank you.' Caroline hardly heard her own words. She looked past the woman into a long dim hall, with wide stairs ascending on the left and doors on either side. In the doorway of the room at the far end stood Mark Helford.

In the half-light she could see little of his face. His black hair and dark complexion seemed to merge with the oak panelling. He wore dark trousers, a grey waistcoat, but no coat over it. She hesitated, calming herself, waiting for him to move.

'I am honoured, Mrs Haldane. This is an unexpected pleasure.' His voice seemed to float along the hall. Then he came forward, into the light from the still-open door behind her, and she gasped audibly as she saw the angry wound along his cheek and the bruising; then, under control, extended her hand, smiled her greeting, exchanged the necessary courtesies. They followed Helford into the drawing room – high and wide, with darkly upholstered chairs, small occasional tables, rich brocade curtains framing a small neat garden outside.

Rupert was demanding: 'My dear Helford, tell us what happened. Are you badly hurt? We have heard the strangest rumours.'

He said quietly, almost humorously: 'I had a disagreement with some unpleasant fellows. I'm pleased to say they regretted the encounter. Mrs Haldane, do sit down. Mrs Tovey will bring tea for you.'

He gestured to a chair, and his eyes met hers and held them as she walked past him. She dragged her gaze away, down to the slowly healing gash on his cheek, and stood quite close to him, inspecting it.

'You have been hurt,' she said. 'Have you allowed a doctor to treat that?'

Half his mouth smiled, the other half taut under the bruising.

'I have. There is nothing much amiss. It is more spectacular than serious.'

They sat on comfortable chairs. Mrs Tovey brought tea for Caroline; Helford poured whisky for Haldane and himself. Then, under Rupert's questioning, he related the outline of the violence at Teignmouth; quiet-voiced, factual, clinical.

'My God, man – you tackled five? On your own? You're lucky to be alive.' Rupert was incredulous.

'They had done my property considerable damage. I was not able to let the matter rest.' He was almost indifferent. But again his eyes held Caroline's for a second as he reached for his glass.

They talked for half an hour or more about the incident, about the police, about the four injured men – all pronounced seriously hurt with various broken bones, one initially paralysed from the savagery of Helford's blow to his neck, the foreman blinded in one eye and injured in the other; about the police assurance that Helford was considered only to have defended himself after their initial attack on his ship and their throwing of the bottle at him as he tried to free the wheel. Helford confided that he regarded himself fortunate that the police had seen the foreman thrusting at him with the broken bottle. That had convinced them that he had been the victim of a vicious assault and they had not enquired too closely into the start of the fight. Caroline listened, breathless, captivated, tense and enthralled by his clipped, harsh story and offhand dismissal of talk of danger.

Finally they rose to leave. Conway came through from the kitchen where he had spent the time in Mrs Tovey's company. They stood in the hall, exchanging final pleasantries. And as Helford raised Caroline's fingers in the gesture of tribute she felt a quiver of response within herself; felt his strange eyes touch hers as bright lights in a private darkness; and then the almost imperceptible pressure of his hand, so slight that for an instant she wondered if it were a product of her imagination, and in another knew it was not – and that her recognition had been communicated by some secret means she could not identify.

With the others looking on, and totally unaware, he had sent his message and she had responded.

She was no simple country wife, but a sophisticated and experienced woman whose consciousness of her body and her needs was beyond Rupert's stereotyped imagination. Now, unbidden but encouraged within herself by her boredom and scarcely-interpreted frustration, she found herself facing a new release; recognizing it, accepting the inevitability of it. And Mark Helford, whose intrusion had initially been merely instinctive experiment spurred by her beauty, watched her

48

departure and found awareness of his conquest abruptly disturbing as he realized there was more to Caroline Haldane than his basic male hunting instincts had contemplated.

On the Thursday of the following week, the day after Rupert Haldane and William Wright had left for the Dorchester Shorthorn sale, Caroline called on the Gartons again. It was a spur of the moment decision, a product of loneliness and depression. For a week she had thought of little else than Mark Helford and her own confusion. Sometimes fear gripped her, for she was fully aware of what was happening and of the possible consequences. Helford's attraction was physical; the fascination of his flamboyance, his handsome face and lithe body, the magnetism of his eyes, were a combination that had touched instincts and passions which she had schooled and disciplined until they had been all but forgotten. Now she was not only aware of them again, but they were tempting her. That morning she had sat in her bedroom, away from Nora and the servant girl Mary, staring out of the window at bare trees and thin hedges and the grey winter sky, struggling with her problem, arguing with herself that she had misread Helford's eyes and fingers and subtleties and knowing she had not; then, briefly until she wrenched herself away from the disturbing fantasy, trying to imagine what sort of a lover he would be.

In the afternoon, despair turned her thoughts to the baby in the cottage along the lane, and she recognized the stab of envy, even jealousy, which surged suddenly within her. She took a long coat, her warmest bonnet and a scarf, told Nora where she was going, and set out to walk the short distance to the cottage.

Albert Garton was away working at Morton Griffiths's farm half a mile away. His wife admitted her visitor cautiously, reluctantly, her face pale in the winter dimness of the cottage.

' 'Tis very kind of you to call, ma'am,' she said defensively. She lit two candles standing in cheap brass holders on the scrubbed table with the cracked top. Caroline saw the baby in the wooden box beside the low fire and asked after him.

'Doing well, 'e is,' Grace Garton said. She stood awkwardly beside one of the chairs. Caroline sat down on the other chair without waiting for an invitation she felt would not come.

'And are you now feeling stronger?'

'Oh yes'm.' The pale woman perched on the edge of the hard chair, the candlelight throwing gaunt shadows over her thin face and deep-set eyes. Hair that might have been fair or grey straggled from beneath her muslin cap. 'I'm all right. Better'n I've been after my other babies.'

'I sent some wood. Do you now have enough to keep a good fire, to keep the child warm?'

A nod; the flicker of a smile on the guarded face.

'T'were kind of you, ma'am. Aye – we can keep a fire all day now as well as in the evening. 'Tis better for the baby – for me, too.'

Caroline looked at the box with its sacking cover. She said very quietly: 'May I see him, Mrs Garton? May I hold him for a moment?'

The mother shuffled her feet. Fingers plucked nervously at the coarse cotton apron over the heavy woollen brown frock.

'He's asleep, ma'am. He's been a long time going off. If you don't mind –'

Caroline nodded, smiling stiffly.

'Of course. I understand.' She stood up, peering at the tiny head just visible in the box. She smelled stale urine and damp wool. She said: 'I have a blanket you could cut up for him, to provide fresh bedding. I'll send it. Change his bedding as often as you can. I'll send some more wood for the fire to help you make sure the bedding is dry after you've washed it. I know it's very difficult at this time of the year, to have a new baby.'

The woman's fingers plucked away at the apron. She swallowed, hesitating.

'I don't want to be disrespectful, ma'am – but why are you

50

helping me?' Her voice was low, defensive; not hostile, but wary.

'Because we are neighbours,' Caroline said firmly. 'Because we must all do what we can to help each other.' She returned to her chair. 'I always try to help the wives of the estate workers if I can. I'm sure you know that.'

The woman said stubbornly: 'But Albert don't work for you. 'E works for Mr Griffiths. This is Mr Griffiths's cottage.'

Caroline nodded. 'Of course. It makes no difference. We are neighbours. That is reason enough. For your baby's sake I do urge you to accept any help I can give.' She hesitated, just for a moment; then added: 'I do not have children, Mrs Garton. It gives me pleasure to help others who are more fortunate.'

The woman blinked at her, tears suddenly in the eyes that were now resentful. She muttered: 'One day I might be willing to change my child for your money, ma'am. Having children's all right if you can bring 'em up healthy. We don't have enough money for ourselves. When the baby's weaned, I don't know what I'll feed him on, so's he'll grow strong.'

'Then I'll have to help you,' Caroline said. 'Don't turn it away, Mrs Garton. You need a little help, and I'm able to give it.'

Then, tactfully, she turned the conversation to the cottage's food supplies and to how often the woman was able to breastfeed her baby and how the child responded, and the problem of keeping him dry and warm and clean, until half an hour had passed. Then she left, and was conscious of the wary eyes which watched her as she climbed the two steps up to the flint-and-mud road, and she walked back through the grey afternoon, aching in her heart and mind.

Tethered to the rail near the door of the house was a black gelding. She knew immediately it was Mark Helford's.

He was in the hall. Nora, busy and motherly as ever, was telling him anxiously that Mr Haldane was away and Mrs Haldane had gone visiting.

Caroline checked, holding herself back for a moment, calming her face until he turned and saw her.

51

His cheek was no longer swollen, although the bruising still discoloured the skin slightly, and the scar of the gash was a wide, dark line.

She said: 'Mr Helford – how pleasant to see you. This is unexpected.'

He nodded, and she thought his eyes were humorous.

'I'm sorry about that, Mrs Haldane. But I had some business to discuss with your husband. Your good lady tells me he is away. That's a disappointment. But the matter will wait. When do you expect his return?'

She said to Nora: 'May we have afternoon tea, please?' She turned back to Helford. Her gaze was level and cool and composed. 'You will take tea with me, Mr Helford? I am aware of much of my husband's business. Perhaps we can discuss what you have in mind.'

Nora bustled away and she led him into the drawing room, closing the door quietly. They stood still, facing each other. Then Caroline took off her coat and her bonnet, shook her hair loose, held out her hand for Helford's cloak and placed the garments together over a chair. She stood with her back to the door, facing him.

'You knew Rupert was away,' she said. It was neither accusation nor complaint; a statement.

For whole seconds their eyes locked. Then he turned, walked to the wide, heavily curtained window. Without looking round he said: 'Your garden is charming. Do you plan it yourself?'

She watched his dark outline.

'Yes – and enjoy working in it – at least in the spring and summer. Do you really have business to discuss with Rupert?'

He watched a flight of starlings circle the nearby elms, black whirling shapes against the grey clouds as they sought roosting for the night.

'I bought corn from him recently. I'm sure you remember. I want to talk about next season.'

'But you knew he was away,' she persisted.

He turned slowly.

'If you say so.' Very quietly, easily.

52

She was a statue; only her breathing stirred her shoulders.

'Very well. Since you can't talk to him – talk to me. Not about corn – about yourself. Tell me where you came from – why you are the sort of man you are.'

She moved then, sat on the edge of a couch and gestured to a chair. He said, 'Thank you,' and crossed from the window.

'I don't know what would interest you.' He sat down, leaned back comfortably. The scar on his face looked suddenly more angry as he turned.

She said quickly: 'No – first tell me how you are – how well you are recovering.' She realized that she was no longer using his name, and that he was no longer calling her 'Mrs Haldane' or using his slightly mocking 'Ma'am'.

'I am recovered,' he said. He touched his cheek. 'This is healing. It will simply take time to disappear.'

It will not disappear, she thought. He's marked for life. Then he was talking again.

'Tell you about myself? What a strange request. There's little to tell. I own ships. They carry cargo for others, and my own cargoes. It is a limited but profitable business. That you know. Originally my father sent me to work in Plymouth – a shipping office – that was where I learned the trade. I was married once. Sadly my wife died. But that was a long time ago. What else may I tell you?'

She said quietly, evenly: 'Where did your family come from?'

Then he laughed at her; a quick, pleasant sound.

'You're asking me if I'm totally English, aren't you?' His candour took her by surprise. She felt herself flush, and hoped he would not see it. Before she could think of a reply he went on: 'I'm not. My father was a Devon man, from a line of Devon men. My mother was born in Plymouth, as the result of a visit there of a Portuguese ship's master whose vessel was wrecked along the coast. He stayed long enough to marry my grandmother – and sire my mother. He told my grandmother he was the son of a pirate who preyed on shipping along the North African coast. If that was true – and she certainly

53

believed it was – one can only guess to what country he owed his allegiance. Spain – Morocco – Algeria – who knows? It's an intriguing question. Tell me why you married your husband.'

She held her breath; then realized his question was only slightly more impertinent than the implication of her own. She thought she ought to be angry, but was not. And then, suddenly, she wanted to tell him things she had told no one else.

Almost as if she were a spectator to the conversation she heard her voice saying: 'Looking back – I'm not sure. At the time he was kind. I thought he was good-looking. He had – has a quick mind. He's interesting. He offered me security. He was older than my friends at the time – the young men who were my escorts. He was more mature –'

She turned, startled, at a knock. The door latch rattled. Nora came in, carrying a tray of tea, scones and cakes. Caroline said quickly, covering her sudden silence, 'Oh Nora – thank you – please put it here.' She pointed to a round inlaid mahogany table.

The housekeeper nodded with the comfortable familiarity of the established principal family servant. She put the tray down carefully, began to pour the tea. As she did so she glanced carefully at the silent Helford, then at the mistress of the house; hesitated, then said: 'What shall I do about Mrs Wright? You did promise that I would see if she needed help today.' She looked quickly, uneasily, at Helford, then back at Caroline. 'Shall I send Mary instead?'

Caroline took a long breath, concentrating on the housekeeper's steady, capable hands busying around the tray. Without lifting her eyes she said: 'No – no. I don't think that would be sufficient. I would prefer that you should go. It would be far more helpful to Mrs Wright. She cannot manage well on her own, and her husband will be away for several days. No – you must go. And –' she hesitated, then rushed on '– and take Mary with you. She will be useful for a hour or two, and company for you coming home. I – I don't want an early meal. There's no inconvenience.'

54

Nora finished pouring the tea. She looked doubtful. Then she nodded.

'As you say – Mrs Wright can't help herself much. Very well. I'll see her right for the next day or two. I won't stay longer than I must.'

She moved to the door. Caroline said: 'There is no hurry. Don't rush yourself.'

The housekeeper, with a last, still-worried glance at Helford, was gone. The room was suddenly silent, and the two people in it motionless; until Helford stirred.

'How far away does Mrs Wright live?'

'Not far. A quarter of a mile.'

Her voice was quiet in the still room. The afternoon light was fading early beyond the windows. She should have been lighting a lamp. But she did not move. She heard Nora's footsteps somewhere beyond the hall; her voice, distant, as she spoke to the servant girl.

Mark Helford watched her in the gathering dark.

'Was it really necessary to send them both?' His voice was so low that if there had been any other sound at all she would not have heard it clearly.

'Yes. Yes, of course. They will do more work. And come back in the dark. It's better that – that they go together.'

He appeared not to notice her tension. Presently he said: 'You haven't answered my question. You haven't told me why you married your husband. Many men are kind and good-looking and intelligent. You are kind – and beautiful – and intelligent. But you are much more.'

Footsteps in the hall. They both heard, and listened to them. The outer door swung, creaking closed, the sound echoing briefly. Footsteps then on the gravel outside the window; crunching, fading.

He eased out of the chair, crossed to the table, picked up a cup and saucer. She watched him, wishing she could see his face more clearly; so that she might know what he was thinking. Two steps. He was holding the cup and saucer towards her.

'Thank you. I should have done that, for you.' Her voice

was little more than a whisper. She reached forward, and felt his fingers. Instead of trying to take the saucer she kept her hand still, against his.

Gently, unhesitatingly, as if he had intended it all along, he took the cup and saucer in his free hand and put it back on the table. His fingers twined into hers, and then she was standing, looking up at him, searching his face in the dim, quiet room, feeling herself drawn close to him. His voice was a breath in her ears: 'This was bound to be. Nothing could have stopped this.'

It was a long kiss. She drew back momentarily to whisper his name. The second kiss was harder, searching, urging and demanding, her arms at his shoulders then sliding around his neck; his hands moving around her waist, along her back. And they were lost, and won, and the stillness of the room yielded to the tempo of their breathing, and their bodies met and merged and her secret excitement was secret no longer as he received it and returned it and took it back again.

Afterwards neither knew how long they were in that darkening room and what words they said; or what signal took them from it, across the hall and up the staircase into the room above with its wide bed and sheets that were cold to their bodies. She was glad it was almost night, for it was too soon for him to see her, and it was easier to surrender and then to demand. They lay side by side and face to face, her breasts against his chest and the nipples hard against his skin, her hips moving slightly, rhythmically, unashamedly; synchronized with his own as she wondered, marvelled, at his strength. Their hands held tight around each other, then explored, unhurried yet urged by their breathing. No words, until his murmured 'Please – please –' and hers, 'Oh yes – yes – Mark – yes', and they rolled, her breath hissing as she felt him hard and sure and heard his moan. They were locked then, and he was overwhelmed by her need and she by his skill and care and power, and they dissolved together, writhing and crying out, and there was no end to it until she sobbed against him and he whispered 'Caroline – Oh God – Caroline' and shuddered, down and down and breathless and still. The exhausted passion of their helpless bodies ran together, and her tears with it as they clung to the wonderment and the memory and the warmth.

V

―――――

The elder of the two boys was fair-haired, tall for his ten years, and solid, with a pleasantly rugged face that might have belonged to a child several years older. He stood, woollen shirt with a tear at the shoulder, ragged breeches calf-length, legs spread for balance on the trunk of a fallen tree, looking down at his companion, challenging him.

The other boy, a year or so younger, contrasted. Dark hair and eyes, high-cheeked, lightly built, tanned skin; he was quieter, more serious, almost withdrawn in his play. His knee-breeches were well-fitting, his shirt a cotton check and neat except for soil-smudges on the sleeves. He surveyed the fair boy's advantage on the tree, turned as if to retreat – then threw himself at the other's legs, locking arms about them, dragging him to the ground.

In an instant they were scrabbling, punching, wrestling in concentrated fury, the fair boy grunting, the dark one silent as they fought.

It lasted for minutes. Then they both heard a cart rumbling along the track nearby and, as one, tumbled apart and ran together to the hedgerow and dropped into a shallow ditch, panting.

The two-wheeled cart, piled with brushwood and drawn by a big gelding, passed; the driver oblivious of their youthful drama.

They raised their heads, looking after it, then at each other. Both had bleeding noses; the dark boy had a half-closed eye. Their hands were scratched.

The fair boy said: 'You're a good fighter.'

The dark boy rubbed his face carefully, looking at the blood on his fingers.

'So are you. But I'd have beaten you if that cart hadn't stopped us.'

Without animosity they sat on the grass, inspecting each other – ten-year-old Frank Garton, son of a farm labourer, and nine-year-old Randolph Haldane, heir to the Roxton estate.

It was the spring of 1860.

Albert and Grace Garton had produced one more child after their first surviving son – a frail girl. She had died of fever at two years of age. But Frank had thrived, strong from the beginning, to become the undisputed physical leader of the local village boys of his age.

Randolph was born on 15 October 1850, nine months and five days after Mark Helford and Caroline Haldane had joined in their desperate passion. Before Rupert Haldane had returned home three days later she had had time to think, to agonize, to decide. She had met her husband at the door, welcoming. And that night she had turned to him in bed, caressing and encouraging. Their intercourse was brief and reasonably satisfying, and she had thrust out of her mind comparison with the man who had lain with her in that same bed such a short time before. It was, for her, an essential precaution, and she wept secretly later, for she knew it had been no more than that.

When Dr Miller had confirmed her pregnancy she had spent weeks in private mental confusion, alternating between joy and despair. But Rupert had known nothing of that. He was delighted that, at last, there was to be a Haldane child; and the more so when it was born a boy with hair as fair as Caroline's and dark eyes that seemed to relate to neither of them but were of no significance because of that.

Mark had visited them occasionally in the early part of her pregnancy, but there had been no opportunity for them to talk privately until three months had gone. Then, in the few minutes they had together she had clung to him and told him her secret, and he had held her and asked the inevitable question: 'Could it be Rupert's?'

She had whispered against his chest, 'Yes. It could be. I – I made sure of that.'

His laugh was gentle in her ear.

'Then you're a clever girl. Do you think it's his?'

'No.' She hid her face against him. 'I don't. Why should it be, after all this time? It's yours, Mark – it has to be. God knows how I'm going to go through with it. But I have to. I want to – so much. Don't ever give us away – please. And – keep coming to see me. I couldn't bear it if you didn't.'

He said something then that he had never expected to say.

'I'll keep coming. I'll never let you down. I'll be there, whenever you need me. Always. And – I love you.'

He meant it.

In the following months she had come to terms with the future, and gradually was happier, more contented, than she had been for years. When the child was born it was easy, although she was frightened until she saw the baby in case it was too obviously Mark's. Rupert, for his part, was happy too, and for a while even spent more time in the house than usual, away from his cattle and his herd books.

But babies change as they grow. By the time Randolph was four years old his fair hair had become black, and his complexion was just a little darker than the summer sun justified, and his dark eyes were compelling. Dr Miller said he would be taller than Rupert; a lot taller, he expected. The boy's personality was different, too; he was cool and calculating in childish crises; loving to his mother, a little reserved towards Rupert. And there was a secret part of his quick mind that neither could understand, or even identify.

Caroline knew beyond all doubt that Mark was his father. Rupert seemed to notice nothing untoward.

The boy went to the local school – 'so that he will learn early that life can be hard' Rupert had said. But there was a place reserved for him at Marlborough as soon as he reached the age of twelve. In the meantime he played with the village children but made few friends, apart from Frank Garton.

Their friendship was founded on mutual respect. Frank was the unchallenged leader of the pack, simply because he was bigger and stronger and more aggressive than the others. But he learned quickly that the boy from the Grange, although smaller, had a ferocious streak if he was roused. They fought regularly – at first because they were seeking mastery; then, when they realized there was little to be found, simply because they enjoyed it.

By 1860 they were fast friends. But it was a friendship which had had to survive opposition and mature in secret.

At the end of a summer's day when Randolph was seven years old the two children had played in the hay loft above the long stable. A quarrel resulted in punches and a discoloured eye for Randolph. Afterwards he and Frank, their difference forgotten, had sat in the dust by the gate which separated the big house's carriage drive from the farm buildings, and Randolph became aware that Rupert was watching them from the estate office window.

Later he went inside, and Caroline exclaimed in anxiety over his swollen eye, and sat him in the big kitchen alongside the long cooking range and the Welsh dresser while Nora bathed his face.

When Rupert came in he stood in the doorway and said: 'What happened to you, Randolph?'

The boy ducked away from the cold flannel.

'Nothing really, father. Frank did it. We had a fight. But we're friends again.'

Rupert walked into the kitchen, smoothing his tweed waistcoat and adjusting his jacket pretentiously. His side-whiskers were thick and grey and his mouth turned down at the corners.

'I think you should stop playing with that boy,' he pronounced. 'I have discussed it with your mother. He is not the sort of boy with whom you should associate. He is not – our type. I will be obliged if you cease to spend your time with him.'

Randolph slid off his high stool in alarm.

'But father, he's my best friend. He didn't mean to give me a black eye – and I don't mind. I gave him a bleeding nose last week –'

'It is not a question of your fighting, boy,' Rupert said severely. 'Although for my life I cannot understand how you can say he is your friend when all you seem to do is fight. No – you have to remember who you are, Randolph. You are my son – the heir to this estate. Frank Garton is a labourer's son. You belong to different worlds. It is as well you do not associate closely. You are picking up rough speech from him. Kindly do as I have said.'

The boy blinked back sudden tears.

'But father – he's my friend. He's –'

'Be silent,' Rupert snapped. 'Remember what I have said.' He turned and marched from the room.

Randolph stood, irresolute, staring after him. Then he turned, and Caroline saw that the tears had been replaced by anger deep in his dark eyes, and she said quickly: 'You'll have to take notice of your father, Randolph.' Her voice was quiet and reassuring. 'I know it's difficult for you to understand. But you'll have to take notice.' Her troubled glance met Nora's for a moment, and then she hurried from the kitchen in her husband's wake, her skirts swishing against the doorframe.

The next day, when Alice Romney, prim in her black ample-skirted dress and white bonnet, rang the handbell to signal the end of schooling, and the forty children scampered out across the school yard, Frank ran up to Randolph, grabbed his arm and cried, 'C'mon – let's go fishing in the pond.' Then he saw the expression on Randolph's face and checked. 'What's the matter, then?'

Randolph pulled his arm free and muttered: 'Can't tell you. Least – I shouldn't.'

Frank stared at him, sensing some unusual crisis.

'Go on – tell me. What is it?'

They fell into step, walking out through the school gate, ignoring the other running, shouting children.

Randolph mumbled: 'I've got to stop playing with you. We can't go fishing – or anything else.'

Frank stopped walking.

'Why not? We're still friends – aren't we?'

Randolph nodded, staring miserably at the ground.

'Yes. Only –' he hesitated, then rushed on '– only my father says I mustn't play with you.' He glanced up, flushing. 'I can't help it. That's what he said.'

Frank clutched the school book in which he had written the day's exercises, and walked on slowly. Randolph followed him half a step behind.

'Don't 'e like me?'

'I dunno.'

They walked a few more slow paces.

'I wasn't going to tell you. My mam says I shouldn't play with you.'

Now it was Randolph's turn to stop.

'Me? Why?'

' 'Cos you're posh, she said. I dunno what's the matter with her. My dad don't say it – 'e don't care. I think it's 'cos your family's rich an' we're poor.'

Randolph kicked at a stone, watched it roll away across the lane. The other children had gone now. A curlew cried beyond the hedge.

'Am I posh? D'you think I am?'

A shrug.

'Dunno. Suppose you are, really.'

Another kick at another stone.

'My father says I'm picking up rough words from you.'

Frank started walking again.

'What's rough words?'

'Don't know. Don't care, really. D'you care if I'm posh?'

'No.'

They walked on; silent, subdued.

'Why can't grown-ups mind their own business?' Randolph demanded.

'Dunno.' A few more paces. 'We're still friends, aren't we?'

'M-m. 'Course. I don't care what they say.'

Frank looked sideways at his companion.

'Then we won't tell 'em. Won't tell 'em we're playing. We'll have a pact – a secret pact. Like smugglers.'

Randolph scuffed his shoes.

' 'Tisn't easy. They might find out.'

'They won't. We'll keep it secret. You can say you're playing with Peter. I'll say I'm playing with Colin. They'll not know. They don't care who we play with, s'long as it's not you or me.'

Challenge lit Randolph's face.

'That's right. Only we can't play in our fields. But we can go to Mr Wright's field. He doesn't mind who plays there. He's got a wood. We can go there, too. Tell you what – we can think of a code, and leave messages on the wall by Mr Wright's farm. We'll invent a code so we can meet.'

Excited now, they fell to their invention. And afterwards strange chalk signs appeared on the end of William Wright's wall, and two small boys found a way of defying their parents, and their friendship grew in secrecy while Rupert Haldane and Grace Garton forgot their prejudices to such a degree that when Frank reached thirteen years of age Stanley Conway gave him a job at the estate's home farm, and neither parent objected – Rupert because he was not interested, Grace Garton because she was thankful for an extra four shillings a week with the promise of more as the boy grew, and did not care where it came from.

Later in the same year Randolph was to go to Marlborough. But before that moment arrived there occurred an incident which was to confirm their friendship dramatically.

Ever since six men from Tolpuddle in Dorset had been transported to Australia in 1834 for attempting to start an agricultural labourers' trade union, talk of organizing farm labour had been largely muted. But by 1860 harsh conditions in the cottages and on the farms were once more prompting the reformers.

The targets were more often farmers than big landowners, for many of the latter had become, to varying degrees, reformers themselves as they had gradually sought to better the lot of their employees. The majority of farmers had less money to spare, long memories of hard times past and a growing instinct that more were on the way; so wages stayed low, malnutrition remained a scourge, and long working hours under hard physical conditions were the norm.

When Peter Trimble came to the Exeter area in 1863 he had already stirred the smouldering embers of rebellion in the Midlands' shires. Meetings had been held, workers here and there had gone to their employers in a body to ask for higher wages. Some had gained an extra shilling or two apiece; a few had lost their jobs as startled farmers had hit back. Meanwhile Trimble's reputation had gone ahead of him so when the news went out that he was to address a meeting in an upstairs room at the Dog and Partridge inn, at the far end of Roxton's main street from the more salubrious Rising Sun, he was guaranteed a good audience.

But news of his coming reached many farmers, too. The day before, the ageing and increasingly irritable George Callan nailed a notice to a barn door threatening that if any of his employees even went to the meeting he would dismiss them. Morton Griffiths said nothing publicly but spent the day calling on neighbours and talking darkly with them. Rupert Haldane refused to discuss the issue with his more volatile associates, telling Caroline privately that since he paid more than most, a labourers' union was not likely to trouble him greatly.

On the day of the meeting Albert Garton stumped down the narrow stairs of his darkened cottage before five o'clock in the morning, fastening the wide belt around his thick corduroy trousers and tucking in his grey woollen collarless shirt. His heavy boots and woollen stockings were in front of the cold chimney and he pulled them on before going out of the back door to the tumbledown privy in the little garden. Then he brought wood and a little precious coal in to start a fresh fire.

Presently his wife joined him, patting into place the muslin cap which she wore from sunrise to bedtime. She lighted a candle on the table and checked that there was water in the iron kettle before placing it carefully on the hob over the small fire. When the water was hot she made kettle broth, the breakfast of the poorest labourers and their families – bread well salted and soaked in hot water. By this time Frank had come down the stairs from the tiny room which led off his parents' bedroom, and she handed him the earthenware dish containing his food.

The boy sat alongside his father and ate hungrily, glancing first at one parent then the other, sensing tension.

Presently Grace Garton said: 'Will you be going, then?'

Her husband nodded briefly in the dimness.

'Aye. Just to listen. Be as well to find out what's brewin'.'

Frank swallowed his last piece of bread.

'Where're you going, papa?'

Albert looked sideways at his son. He smoothed the fringe of beard around his chin.

'The Trimble meeting, o'course. They musta bin talking about it at your work?'

'Oh yes. All yesterday. Some will go – some won't. Mr Haldane pays well – like you said. So not many'll go.' The boy hesitated, looking uneasily at his mother. 'May I go with you, papa? Never bin to a meeting. I'd like to watch – see what it's like.'

Grace Garton snapped: 'Keep out of it. No good'll come of it – I've said so all along. Keep away.'

'The lad should go if he wants to,' Albert growled. 'Teach him things.' He glanced at Frank. 'It starts eight o'clock. 'Spect I'll go straight there. Won't have time to come home. You come if you want, boy.'

He stood up and reached for his fustian jacket. Hanging on a peg behind the door was his billycock, and he crammed it on his head. He patted the pockets of his coat, checking that he had with him the right forefoot of a hare which he always carried to ward off the rheumatism which was everyone's enemy. His wife handed him his canvas bag containing the daily bread and cheese, and sugar in a screw of paper for the tea Morton Griffiths would provide. He paused at the door, looking back.

'Don' worry, Grace. It'll just be words. As well to go, though.'

She shook her head, tut-tutting as he went out.

The day passed quietly enough on the district's farms. Yet on many there was a vague wariness, a caution between the men and their employers. All knew about the meeting; few wanted to confess that they would go, and few farmers felt it wise to imply their concern by asking. But all thought about little else despite pressures of spring ploughing, harrowing and seeding.

On the Roxton home farm Sam Veryan was light ploughing after winter vegetables. Seagulls wheeled across the fields – twenty or thirty curved-winged birds against the sky, swooping suddenly to the red earth, perching, pecking, cackling behind Veryan whose corded arms wrestled with the plough and the two big bay carthorses. Used to the task, the horses strained against the stiff compact soil, steady in the traces, hearing the ploughman's cautioning, encouraging voice, responding to the guiding rein instinctively. Just as instinctively Veryan was keeping the shallow furrow as straight across the field as if it had been drawn with a tape between two posts. His mind was back in the big stone coach house with the stables alongside, hearing Bob Tregoney muttering: 'I'm going. I don' care if old Haldane do pay more'n most. I'm going.'

Tregoney had grown to be like his father. Now, at 25 years old, he stood two inches under six feet and weighed well over thirteen stones. His dark hair curled down over his collarless shirt and his scratched and scarred arms were thick and strong. He had worked on the Roxton estate for the past five years or more and throughout had shown little regard for his employer or for the day-to-day business of ploughing and harvesting and heaving crops and manure. Sam Veryan knew, as most of the local labourers knew, that the young man had been brought up by his sullen father to resent the Haldane family's wealth and the prosperity of the estate and he was not surprised that he should be going to the Trimble meeting. But he would be going without Sam Veryan, who had worked for Rupert Haldane for eight years and lived in a home farm cottage with his wife and their four children. He was head ploughman and earned twelve shillings and sixpence a week. Only the head cowman and the shepherd earned more. At 37 years old he reckoned he knew a lot more about the world than did youngsters like Bob Tregoney – and had said so.

'If you stay here a few more years, young Bob, you'll find out when to keep outa trouble. Mr Haldane's a good 'un. It'd be an insult to go to that meeting.'

'I don't care about insulting him,' Tregoney snapped. 'Just looking after meself. An' I can't do that without joining up with everyone else. We can't stand up agin farmers unless we do. All right – the boss pays more'n most do. But he's no better'n the rest. Filthy rich – an' look at us. We've got to fight all of 'em –'

He checked at the sound of boots on the cobbles outside the heavy wooden doors of the coach house. Both men turned and saw Frank Garton who nodded to them warily.

'Come 'ere, young feller,' Tregoney said. He waved a hand. 'We're just talking about Trimble's meeting.' His lip curled. 'Don't expect to see you there – too busy playing around with the boss's lad most of the time.'

Frank stepped back to keep out of arm's reach.

'Don't know, Mr Tregoney,' he said. 'But I'll likely go. My dad –'

'Just be careful you don't go talking to young Haldane,' muttered Tregoney threateningly. 'If anything gets back to the boss about who's going upalong tonight I'll have the skin off your back, sure I will. Time you stopped mucking about with 'im. You're a working lad now –'

'Leave'm alone,' Veryan said. 'Let the lad do what he wants. Off y'go, lad – get on with your work – quick now.'

Frank went, thankfully, as Tregoney said to the older man: 'Don't trust that boy. Too pally with the Haldane lad. None of us know what 'e's telling.'

Sam Veryan stooped as he paced behind the plough, lining up a tree on the far side of the field with a nick he had cut in the short cross shaft attached to the harness. The shaft prevented the horses coming together. Most ploughmen had a similar device which they usually made themselves according to their individual preferences. Many sharpened the ends of the shaft but Veryan did not approve of extremes for he respected his horses. He thought young Frank was unlikely to tell Randolph Haldane much about the men working on the home farm or around the estate; and he had an instinctive feeling that Randolph would mind his own business even if he were told something that might not please his father. Veryan was puzzled by Randolph. He thought he was of a different stamp to Rupert Haldane, and had said as much to his wife. 'Don't know how the boss managed to breed a lad like that,' he had said. 'He's different – not just his looks but the way he behaves. Don't know what it is – almost as if he don't belong here – he could be someone else's kid.' His wife had rebuked him for the thought, and he smiled now to himself as he flicked the rein. He had not meant to be uncharitable. Yet he still thought Randolph was out of place.

A mile away Billy Tregoney halted his horse. There was a large stone caught in the chain harrow and he bent to free it. Ahead and to the right Tom Newton was harrowing with tines, making fast progress behind two of the biggest horses on the farm. Tregoney would have liked to stop and talk with him but he knew Morton Griffiths wanted the field sown down to barley that week and it would go hard with them both if the farmer caught them gossiping. Like Veryan, he was thinking about the Trimble meeting. There was no doubt in his mind about what he would do. He would be there, and he would ask questions, and if Mr Trimble wanted a local organizer he would volunteer; secretly, of course, because he did not have to be told that it would cost him his job if Griffiths found out. And he knew that virtually every one of the men currently working for the stout farmer would be at the meeting. He kicked at the stone and it fell free. He hated Griffiths. And he hated Haldane. He hated all farmers and landowners. He was a serf; a slave – like all his fellows. Lost men, for they would always be serfs and slaves. But not their sons. Times were changing. Young Bob would see to that. And others like him. Young Bob had ideas. He was only waiting for the right time. And he was young enough to wait. He would work behind closed doors, in the night, in his mind, in other men's minds. The farmers would never know until it was too late. And Bob was hard – harder than he, his father, was. Bob wouldn't stop at words. If men were hurt, so be it. That was the only way. There had been violence before, many years before. But it had achieved little. Next time it would be different. He felt satisfied. He had brought his son up the right way – told him the things he had to know. Bob would be a leader. But he, Billy Tregoney, would know who had struck the spark in his son. He was getting old now. But there was still fight left in him – enough to keep the spark glowing and the fires growing, enough to make sure his son didn't forget what he'd been taught.

He turned suddenly, picked up the heavy stone, and hurled it savagely up into the air, towards the nearest hedge.

At seven in the evening Morton Griffiths clattered up to the Grange on his horse. Randolph sat in a corner of the dining room studying the books on history and geography which his father provided to augment Miss Romney's simple schooling. He heard his father's welcome for the visitor and the murmur of voices in the hall, but took no notice until the voices began to rise and he detected impatience in both.

'Ye'll be one of the few missing, Rupert. There'll be at least ten of us, mebbe more.'

'I've told you – I'm not concerned. And I don't intend to suggest I am concerned by being seen in your party. I have good relations with my men and I'm going to retain them.'

'We've got to show we're all standing together. It's essential. If one or two show weakness, they'll blackmail the lot of us. And if you think paying an extra bob or two'll protect you, you're making a mistake. They'll twist your arm same as everybody else's if they get a chance.'

'You can't stop them meeting, Morton. In the end they'll get together if they want to. And you know it.'

'We can. If we all walk in on them tonight, and make a show of writing down their names, it'll scare 'em to death. And when some lose their jobs tomorrow, and maybe one or two their cottages as well, it'll frighten the rest still more. I can afford to get rid of a few. Soon replace 'em if I want. We've got to show we won't stand for it.'

'I'll have no part in that, either.' Rupert's voice was angry. 'It isn't right to dismiss a man just for going to a meeting. And I've warned you already – you're risking violence. If you and the others crash into that meeting, anything could happen.'

'Rubbish, Rupert – rubbish. There's only one door into that room. We'll just block it, and they can't get out. Then we write down their names. There'll be no violence. They'll be petrified. Now come with us.'

'Definitely not. And that's final. And if you take my advice you'll just call it off.'

'Too late for that. We're meeting there at half past eight – and that'll be that. If ye won't come, Rupert – goodnight to ye.'

Heavy boots stamped in the hall, the voices receded, and Randolph sat at his table, listening anxiously but now in vain. Then he heard Griffiths's horse outside, and the front door closed as Rupert re-entered the hall.

It was exciting, he thought. He had heard talk of the meeting all week, without taking much notice. But now, if the farmers were to invade it as Morton Griffiths suggested, the drama heightened. He did no more work then, sitting back and trying to imagine the scene at the inn later in the evening.

Half an hour went by before he thought of Frank, and remembered him saying that he thought his father would go to the Dog and Partridge. He stood up then, alarmed, recalling Morton Griffiths's words – 'when some of them lose their jobs – maybe one or two their cottages' – and suddenly he was scrambling his books together.

The hall was deserted and he guessed his parents were in the drawing room. He went quietly up the stairs to his room and stood there, hearing the farmer's words again, seeing Frank and his ragged parents in their cottage, picturing the meeting suddenly disrupted and Morton Griffiths writing down Albert Garton's name in his notebook. Then, still quietly and very calmly, he returned to the hall, put on a coat and cap, and walked softly out into the night.

71

As he went quickly down the lane he wondered if he was betraying his father's friends. But they were not such good friends, he thought; the sharp exchange with Griffiths had demonstrated that. If he were found out he knew he would be in trouble, and the thought quickened his pulse – not with fear but with excitement. He would have to be sure he was not found out. He began to run and was breathless when he hammered on the cottage door.

It opened cautiously, just a few inches, and Grace Garton peered at the dim, panting figure in the dark.

'Mrs Garton – please – may I see Frank?'

She opened the door wider.

'What are you doin' here at this time, boy? No – you may not see Frank.' Severe, defensive.

'But Mrs Garton – please – it's terribly important – just for a minute –'

' 'E's not here,' she snapped. 'That's why you can't see 'im. 'E's out with 'is father.'

Randolph stood on the step, staring. Of course. If Albert Garton was at the meeting, why not Frank as well? He would go with his father – he would be at the inn – would be there when the farmers marched through the door with their sticks and their angry faces and Morton Griffiths at their head.

Then he was running, leaving the woman wordless in the doorway, back along the lane, cramming his cap into his pocket, then tearing off his coat and stuffing it under a hedge and running on, faster. He knew the time must be past eight o'clock; how long past he did not know. The meeting would have started, the farmers would be gathering – somewhere . . .

Half a mile of running brought him to the green and the yellow windows of the Rising Sun. Panting, his legs and chest aching, he peered through a window at the crowd of men inside, looking at faces through the steamed glass. He could not see Griffiths, but he saw three farmers he knew were among Griffiths's close friends, and heard horses tethered in the stable yard. He went on, walking now, not wanting to attract attention in the village street, past the little shop windows in darkness, and the curtained lighted windows of the cottages and the bigger houses, past the church and the graveyard and more cottages.

When he reached the inn he hesitated. He had never been inside it – nor inside any other inn. But there was no fear in him, only wariness as he pushed open the door and found himself in a low-roofed room crowded with men and noise and tobacco smoke and the smell of ale. No one seemed to notice him and he sidled along a wall towards a grimy curtain. As he pushed it aside and saw stairs, two men looked at him and one started to say something and Randolph pulled the curtain quickly back behind him and ran up the narrow stairs lit by a paraffin lamp in a niche at the top. The voices behind him faded and ahead he heard new ones – a murmur, then one voice raised, then the murmur dying and the voice louder, and he reached a closed door and listened. Again he was not aware of fear, although he did not know what to expect in the room, or what he would do once he was inside. He stood, grasping the door latch, a twelve-year-old breathless, red-faced boy on the brink of a man's world – and for all he knew a hostile world.

He fixed his mind on Frank, raised the latch, and pushed the door open.

There were thirty or forty men in the room, all sat quietly on benches and chairs facing one man, young, black tousled hair, heavy moustache, bright eyes, arm raised, voice raised – 'not let it go on – all brothers – we will only find the strength we need in unity' – as faces turned and eyes stared at the boy in the doorway. A man lifted one finger to his lips and Randolph nodded at him, closing the door quietly. He felt agonizingly conspicuous, and edged away from the speaker towards the back of the room. Now he began to look for Frank but could not find him. Panic surged inside him; then he saw Albert Garton looking at him and beckoned. Garton stared, then turned his head away, and Randolph saw Frank sat next to his father, and Frank caught the slight stir of interest and looked round and saw the boy by the wall and instinct brought him from his seat, stumbling over heavy

73

boots and past cord and leather-clad knees to the intruder's side. Randolph jerked his head in instruction and Frank followed him to the door. The voice was louder – 'if every man joins together with us no one can be harmed and our strength will be irresistible' – and then they were in the corridor and Randolph hissed: 'Mr Griffiths and a lot of farmers are coming – going to take names of everyone here – I heard him say he'd dismiss some of his men if they were here – throw them out of their cottages – tell your father – get out – quick – my father says there'll be violence.'

Then, for the first time he was afraid of what he was doing and turned and ran along the corridor and down the stairs, head down and furtively through the crowded room and down the village street into the darkness as fast as he could make his aching legs move.

Fifteen minutes later Morton Griffiths led his followers into the inn, brushing past the alarmed landlord, through the curtain and up the narrow stairs, and burst into an empty room.

At about the same time Randolph stealthily let himself into the house, crossed the still-deserted hall and tip-toed up the stairs to his room. He stood inside controlling his breathing, calming his nerves, listening. Then he filled his basin with water from the big jug on the wash-stand and reached for soap and a towel.

Two days later Morton Griffiths called. He went to the estate office, planted himself legs astraddle in the doorway and said to Rupert: 'You know what happened at the Dog, at that meeting. Someone warned the bastards we were coming. I'm told a boy went in a few minutes before we arrived, then ran off. I'm also told he looked remarkably like your Randolph.'

Rupert regarded him coldly.

'Then you'd better tell whoever told you that he should have looked more closely. Are you suggesting I sent the boy there?'

'I'm not suggesting anything. I'm telling you what's being said.'

'Randolph was in the house all evening, working at his books,' Rupert said brusquely. 'I was here, so was my wife. He could not possibly have gone out without our knowledge. I certainly didn't send him – and he didn't know what you were planning. Forget it, Morton. You're just angry because you didn't get what you wanted. Now if you'll excuse me I have a lot to do.'

Griffiths grunted and left. Rupert watched him through the window, his eyes thoughtful. He sat still for several minutes, frowning at his desk.

Frank Garton had also watched Morton Griffiths's departure on the seventeen hands grey hunter he always rode. The boy stood at the corner of the hay barn, looking across the long yard to the white gate that separated the farm from the house and its sweeping carriage drive. He had seen Griffiths's scowling face and wondered what the big man had wanted at the Grange. He was afraid of Griffiths; afraid for his father, and for himself and his mother. He had not seen Randolph since the episode at the Dog and Partridge, and wondered if Griffiths had found out who had warned the men gathered at the inn that night. Bob Tregoney had been the only Roxton home farm labourer at the meeting and had been sitting at the front of the crowd; Frank thought he had not seen Randolph's surreptitious entry. But others had and gossip might well have got back to Randolph's father. He wanted to warn Randolph about the visitor, but knew he could not loiter around the buildings for another hour until his friend came home from school.

When Randolph sauntered up to the house later, Rupert came out of the estate office to intercept him.

'Was school interesting today, m'boy?' he enquired stiffly.

Randolph shrugged. He was used to the enquiry, for Rupert was permanently anxious about his progress.

'Not really, father,' he said politely. 'But I got some good marks for English and writing.'

'Excellent. You'll need to keep studying hard. Marlborough has high standards.' Rupert paused, his heavy eyebrows drawn together as he looked down at the twelve-year-old. 'I hear something happened at the Dog and Partridge – that dreadful little inn at the top of the village near the church – a couple of nights ago. I expect all the children are talking about it, eh?'

Randolph looked at him innocently.

'Do you mean the Trimble meeting, father? I heard something. Not much, though. Didn't a lot of farmers go there, wanting a fight? That's what everyone's saying. Why did they do that, father?'

Rupert eyed the boy suspiciously.

'I don't know exactly what happened,' he said. 'But I understand there was no fighting because the meeting had ended before the farmers arrived. Apparently someone went there to warn the labourers. Did the other children talk about that?'

Randolph stood his ground, meeting Rupert's gaze.

'They didn't tell me about it,' he said evenly. Then he added: 'Perhaps it was a good thing it happened. Otherwise there might have been a fight, and men might have been hurt. Do you think so?'

'I don't know,' Rupert said heavily. 'But I understand the warning might have been delivered by a boy.'

Randolph's dark eyes were steady.

'I thought boys weren't supposed to go into an inn like the Dog and Partridge,' he said. Then his mouth widened. 'But I know some boys at school who have. They say it's full of smoke and smells a lot of ale and all the men swear. Is that true?'

Rupert knew when he was beaten. He grunted and turned away.

'Most inns are like that,' he said over his shoulder. 'Now go into the kitchen and wash yourself.'

Randolph watched Rupert's broad back for seconds, his face expressionless. Then, abruptly, he ran after the receding figure, calling: 'Father – please may I go onto the farm first – just for a while?'

Without turning Rupert snapped: 'Yes. But only for half an hour. And don't dirty your clothes.'

76

Randolph made for the white gate, and then the stone buildings beyond. He walked into the barn, then on into the dairy and watched the cows being milked, listening to the soft drilling sound of the milk spurting into the pails and the grumbling and shuffling of the cows. He liked the smell of boiled oilcake, chopped roots and hay which had been mixed with chaff and steamed to provide a production ration for the cows. He liked the smell of the cattle, too; it hung, close and clinging beneath the tarred rafters and tangled cobwebs of the low roof, a warm smell of fur and skin and breath. He waited until the nearest of the four cowmen had pushed himself upright from his milking stool and said: 'Where's Frank, please?'

The man lifted the half-full pail in a big hand.

'In the sheep paddock, Master Randolph. Lambin'll start any day. 'E's putting up the foddering rail.'

Randolph wandered outside, then broke into a trot. The paddock used for lambing the Dorset ewes was only a hundred yards away. When he cleared the buildings he could see Frank working alongside one of the men, holding stakes which the man was driving into the ground. They would be used to construct a crude temporary fence and hay would be spread along the line to provide fodder for the ewes and also some shelter. Elsewhere in the field half-a-dozen rough pens had been created from the same materials to protect the ewes at the moment of lambing if the wind should rise.

By the time Randolph had reached the centre of the field the last of the stakes had been driven in and the man had turned away to the nearby cart and its load of wood. Randolph caught Frank's eye and the two walked out of range of the man's hearing.

Randolph whispered: 'My father's just been asking questions about the meeting. Said a boy warned the men that the farmers were coming.' He grinned. 'I wonder who that could have been.'

'Mr Griffiths was here,' Frank muttered. 'Not an hour ago. Reckon he must've told your father something.'

Randolph nodded. 'I expect so. But he couldn't have

known it was me – otherwise father would have said so.' He grinned again. 'I don't care, anyway. Even if he beats me.'

A voice shouted from the direction of the cart: 'C'mon, young Frank. Get some bloody work done – I ain't doing it all, I can tell 'e.'

'Coming,' Frank shouted back. 'Just talking to Randolph for a minute.'

The man looked across the cart. He did not like to complain about the squire's son, so he grumbled under his breath but said nothing more.

The two boys walked a few steps further away, staring down at the spring grass. Frank prodded the turf with an outsize boot that had been his father's.

'Why'd you do it, Randy?'

Randolph glanced sideways. His eyes were dark and cool and confident.

'Because I wanted to. I heard Mr Griffiths telling father what was going to happen. I wanted to stop it.'

Frank concentrated on the ground at his feet.

'Did you do it 'cos of me, an' papa?'

'Yes.' The answer was unhesitating. 'And because of the others.' He swung suddenly to face the other boy. 'Why shouldn't you go to a meeting if you want to? I know what old Griffiths says – that the men are trying to gang up on the farmers and force them to pay higher wages. Well, maybe the men wouldn't need to gang up if some of them paid more money.'

Frank looked at him awkwardly.

'You shouldn't talk like that,' he said. 'You ought to be on his side – Griffiths, an' all the farmers.'

'You mean because I live in a big house and my father owns the estate?'

'Yes.'

'That doesn't stop me thinking.'

Frank wiped grimy hands down the thighs of his rough breeches. He was clearly troubled.

'You shouldn't be on our side,' he muttered stubbornly.

78

'I *am* on your side. Same as you're on mine. Like we've always been.'

The other boy shook his head.

'I know that. But why're we like that? Shouldn't be. The men think I'm crawling to you. They say I'm trying to speak like you – they say I shouldn't 'cos you're the squire's son. They don't understand. They're so – so – prej –' He stopped, seeking the word.

'Prejudiced,' said Randolph. 'Like old Griffiths. Even my father is – though in a different way, really. He does try to help the men. I'm glad he does. Otherwise I'd hate him.'

They turned and began to walk slowly back towards the cart. The horse between the shafts watched them, tossing its head.

'D'y'think we'll always be friends, Randy?'

'Of course. Why not?'

'Even when we grow up an' you've bin to that posh school? We can't be friends then – you in that big house, an' me living in the cottage, an' being a labourer.'

Randolph stopped walking. He said, so quietly that Frank hardly heard him: 'Nobody will stop us being friends, if we want to be. Nobody will stop me doing anything, when I grow up, if I want to do it. You see.'

Frank stared at him; at the untidy black hair and the deep-set near-black eyes and the light in them, and the tight mouth. He did not speak, because he did not know what to say. He had seen Randolph like this before; had felt himself distanced, because he did not understand. At such moments his companion left him uneasy; doubtful not of their friendship but of the driving force within the other boy. Were all boys who were squires' sons and lived in big houses like that? No, he knew they were not. No one was like Randy; at least, no one he had ever met.

He said suddenly: 'I'd better get on – do some work – or he'll tell Mr Conway.' He jerked a thumb at the man who was struggling with wooden laths beside the cart.

Randolph nodded. 'All right. I suppose you'd better.' He wandered away, back towards the buildings. After a minute he turned and stood still, watching Frank from the distance. He heard the other boy's words. 'You shouldn't be on our side.' Whose side was he on? He knew the answer – no one's except his own. Sometimes he felt apart from everyone – except his mother. He was sorry for the men, except when he thought they were lazy or lying; then he despised them. But he despised Morton Griffiths and George Callan more, for they were bullies. He knew how to deal with bullies at school. But men were different. Some men were bullies not because they were bigger than other men but because they had more power. He knew even now that when he grew up he would not be able to beat bullies like that by fighting them. And it was bullies like Griffiths and Callan who threatened his friendship with Frank by making the differences between them deeper and wider and more noticeable. At least he thought so. But he was not always sure. That was why he had made up his mind a long time ago that when he grew up he would fight for all he was worth for the things he wanted, whatever they were, against the Griffiths's and Callans and the labourers and anyone else who tried to stop him. And he had no doubt that he would win, for he could conceive of nothing else. He and Frank together, probably; for they had always been together. But if he had to fight alone, he would still win.

VI

Rupert Haldane had chosen Marlborough College for Randolph's education because he vaguely believed it was a 'country school' and therefore appropriate. It was scarcely a dozen years old and unproven when he did so, although the clergy had given it their blessing by negotiating discounts for their sons' tuition there – a factor that had done nothing to avert its early reputation for excessive bullying and lack of discipline. Caroline had been disturbed by the choice, for in 1851 the school had been the scene of a week of anarchy among the pupils which the staff had been unable to contain. A change of headmaster had resulted in considerable improvement, but in many parents' eyes the stigma had remained and several of the Haldanes' friends had raised questioning eyebrows when they had learned of Rupert's decision.

But he was by no means unaware of the boy's considerable physical prowess and his capacity for taking punishment without complaint when he tackled someone bigger and stronger than himself.

'Don't you worry, my dear,' he had told Caroline. 'We have bred a boy who will acquit himself well. It will be a big strong lad who will get the better of him. Boys of his sort are never the subject of bullying, I assure you.'

To that extent he was perceptive. By the time Randolph arrived at the school the problem of violence among the pupils had been reduced considerably – although it certainly still existed – in step with the introduction of physical sports and the shrewd government of the headmaster Dr Bradley, who was a disciplinarian who could yet command the respect of the boys through the strength of his personality as well as his arm. And Randolph showed quickly enough that any boy who gave him trouble, unless considerably bigger and stronger, was unwise.

Scholastically he was an average pupil. But he excelled in sports both because of a natural skill and because he demonstrated disregard for personal discomfort. He was also adventurous, and the tribes of boys (as they were known) who were allowed to gallop through parts of the neighbouring Savernake Forest were soon to adopt him as one of their leaders.

By the time he was fifteen he was playing cricket against the local grammar school and other organizations, his performance on the embryonic rugby field was quietly cunning and physically deadly, and he proved himself incredibly accurate with the squaler, that distinctively Marlburian weapon that was nominally intended for hunting squirrels and other small game in the woods.

A squaler – a piece of lead shaped like a pear and attached to the end of eighteen inches of cane – was part of the equipment of every boy considered by his fellows to be worth his salt. Randolph could hurl it further, and with greater force, than any of his associates – and with an accuracy which other boys regarded not just with envy but with fear, for there was something in the gaze and manner of the dark-haired Devonian which hinted that he would use the weapon in any way that was necessary if he found himself in desperate straits.

One October evening he excelled himself, and gained a reputation that was to dominate the hero-worship to which the younger boys were already inclined when they pointed him out to newcomers.

He was already a captain of his room – a rank which brought the privilege of being allowed unsupervised into Marlborough High Street. On that Saturday evening he hired a pony from the hostelry in the middle of the little town and, with two other boys similarly mounted, set off into the forest.

Deer were commonplace, and often came quite close to the outlying buildings of the town. But they were protected by the tough guardians of the forest who were considered by the local poachers to be formidable opposition, and the Marlborough boys usually left them strictly alone. But on this occasion Randolph heard a young buck bellowing on the outskirts of a small herd of does, watching an old stag warily, for this was rutting time. He signalled the other boys to dismount, tethered his pony, then whispered: 'See that one? I reckon I could get him from here.'

The other two stared at him, suddenly scared.

'Randy – you'd better not. There might be a gamekeeper around,' one muttered. No boy had ever felled a deer, to their knowledge.

Randolph grinned in the gloom.

'You do what you like. I'm going to have him.'

He edged through the undergrowth, using all the skills he had learned and practised with Frank Garton in the woods of the Roxton estate, until he was within close range. The young buck was too preoccupied with the females to notice him, and the squaler flashed through the evening light and struck dead-centre into the stag's forehead, just above the eyes, with tremendous force.

The victim dropped, quivered and kicked, lay still. The rest of the herd turned, startled; the old stag roared his alarm, and they crashed away through the woods.

The two boys who had watched stood frozen, wide-eyed, disbelieving. They listened. But the gamekeepers were not around that night. Several minutes passed, then they crept forward to inspect the victim.

'Still alive,' said Randolph. He straddled the young buck, knelt on its shoulders, seized the muzzle and head, and heaved up and back, twisting and wrenching and grunting; until the deer's neck broke.

'He's dead now,' one boy whispered. He looked sad. 'What are you going to do with him?'

'Sell him, you fool – what d'you think?' Randolph retorted. 'Come on.'

Accepting his leadership, they helped him to drag the deer into a dense patch of undergrowth, then returned to their ponies and trotted along a ride for half a mile towards the town.

A small thatched cottage was Randolph's objective. He went to the door and knocked. The man who opened it was wiry, sharp-featured, roughly dressed.

'Hullo, young Haldane,' he growled. 'Coming in?' He held the door wide.

The boys filed into the little room, which smelled of wood smoke and dogs. Randolph said: 'Billy – I've got something for you. What'll you give me for a young stag – two years maybe – fit and clean?'

Billy Carver, renowned among the Marlborough boys and others besides as poacher *par excellence*, was suddenly wary.

'You mean you killed 'un?' His voice was low, hardly believing.

Randolph nodded. 'Yes. He's hidden. I'll tell you where, if you give me ten shillings.'

'It'll not be worth that.' The poacher's eyes were narrowed. 'And what about the keepers? How d'you know they ain't on to you?'

'They're nowhere around. I promise you. It's easy. I'll help you to bring him in if you like. But ten shillings first.'

'You help me bring 'un in, and I'll give y'five bob.'

'Ten. And that's it.'

Billy Carver grinned, showing blackened teeth.

'And what'll y'do with 'un if I won't give y'the money? Leave 'un to rot?'

Randolph shrugged, eyeing the man.

'I'll tell you what I'll do. I'll go back when I'm ready, cut up the carcase, and sell it in the town. I can do it – my father owns farms – I've cut up pigs and lambs before now. I don't reckon a deer is much different. And I've been around this town long enough to know where to sell venison. So please yourself, Billy. Ten bob to you – or nothing.'

Carver knew the price would leave him a handsome profit, and now he realized Randolph knew it too. He reached for his coat.

'All right, you young bastard. God, you're a hard'n. Wouldn' like t'do business with you when you grow up.' He went to a corner cupboard, rummaged inside, came out with money in his hand. 'There y'are. Ten bob. I'll keep it in m'pocket till we get back. Then it's yours.'

Randolph nodded. Everyone knew the poacher never double-crossed one of his kind.

'Come on,' he said. 'It's dark now. We'll soon get it back here.'

They did. Randolph gave his companions two shillings each for helping to drag the carcase. And because they talked as soon as they got back to the school his fame spread as rapidly as young tongues could wag. Nobody had ever tried to fell a deer with a squaler before, let alone done so. The accuracy and the force required were almost beyond belief. If there had been only one witness no one would have believed it. But there were two – and Billy Carver's cottage was no strange place to many of the boys. No one doubted the story for long.

A week later Horner, an assistant master who taught latin and history, stood in a first floor corridor, watching boys below in the quadrangle. He said: 'Foster. That boy there – the tall one with the dark hair – he's one of yours.' It sounded like an accusation. That was Horner's way.

Foster peered, stuck out his ample stomach, fingered his watch chain.

'Haldane. From the West Country. Yes – he's my house.'

'There's a story going round among the boys that he killed a deer in the forest – with a squaler. Have you heard it?'

Foster sighed and smoothed his thick grey side-whiskers.

'Yes. I've heard it. Preposterous. Totally impossible. But he's the sort of boy who attracts that kind of story. Take no notice.'

Horner shook his head. His baldness shone in the midday sunlight through the leaded lights in front of them.

'You don't know your boys as well as you should, Foster,' he rebuked. His black beard wagged as he spoke. 'I've seen that boy all by himself with a row of stones on the ground, hitting them one after another with that infernal weapon. Practising, practising. I've seen him hit a bottle at twenty yards – I'll swear to that. And he throws with incredible force. Have you asked him about the story?'

Foster looked wearily at his companion.

'I have not. Aside from whether I believe it or not, what would be the point? There is no proof.' He levelled a finger. 'Never accuse a boy unless you have proof. That's the only way to make them respect you.'

Horner's head reflected the light as he moved, pulling his gown about him.

'You'll get no respect out of that boy, proof or otherwise. He's trouble, Foster. Mark my words. There's something odd about him. That's why the other boys leave him alone. I've been here longer than you. I remember when he came here. Just a stripling. Boy of fifteen, big for his age, mocked him about something. Haldane ignored the boy – kept on ignoring him. Until the boy threw ink at him. Then he hit him so fast and so hard that the bigger boy never had a chance to defend himself. After that I watched Haldane. There's a funny look about his face – his eyes – when he's provoked. He never starts a fight. But when somebody starts one Haldane finishes it very quickly. He'll get himself into trouble one day. Be advised. Keep a close and wary eye on him.'

Despite the forecast Randolph avoided serious trouble. Every half year he returned to Roxton taller, wider at the shoulders, more confident – yet still reserved, almost introspective; as if life held patterns for him which he could not trace but which he sought constantly. Rupert Haldane, now 65, white-haired and stooping a little with rheumatism, told Caroline he was confident the boy would do well enough to go to Oxford – Marlborough's favourite university – and would then return to take over the estate's management. Caroline, still slender and, it seemed, scarcely touched by the passing years, assured him she agreed; yet secretly wondered, for reasons she could not identify.

She saw Mark Helford frequently, usually in Rupert's presence, occasionally alone when they could arrange it; and there had grown between them a deep, unspoken understanding which stolen embraces and kisses punctuated and strengthened. For fifteen years she had locked away her secret, playing her dull, stereotyped role as mistress of the big house

86

and wife to its ageing, narrow-visioned owner; but nourishing a dream, never forgetting Mark for long, always searching for her next chance to see him, always cherishing the memories of their rare private moments together. Randolph brought her closer to Mark, too, for in so many subtle, miniature quirks of behaviour he mirrored his father, and she saw them with secret delight. Outwardly she remained loyal to Rupert; but in her mind she was Mark's lady, and she learned to control and partition accurately and dispassionately the dual personality which resulted.

Meanwhile Helford derived consolation from his business, frequently travelling to France, building more ships, increasing his trade. When Randolph was at home he contrived to visit Roxton Grange frequently, until one day the young man returned suddenly more mature and Helford realized that he was looking at a youthful replica of himself. After that he tried to avoid meeting his son, for the risk of gossip – to say nothing of Rupert's curiosity – was obvious.

Randolph himself realized that one day the estate would be his for the taking, and found the prospect interesting if unexciting. He had been delighted when Conway had employed Frank Garton, for it enabled them to see more of each other. Half-hearted parental opposition to their friendship was now ignored and the two boys spent as much time as possible together in Marlborough's half-year holidays. Frank was by now no longer the bigger of the two although he was still thicker-set; but in any event the physical rivalry between them declined as they grew up. Instead they planned their futures – always distant, vague; but always with Randolph owning the estate and Frank managing the home farm for him. And gradually, instinctively, Frank modelled himself on Randolph in speech and manners, so that even Rupert became aware of a change in the young labourer, and Frank's mother was openly distressed by her son's behaviour, declaring it to be 'unnatural – like 'e don't belong 'ere'.

By the time he reached his sixteenth birthday Randolph was vice captain of the college's cricket team and had won the coveted silver replica of a bat as cricketer of the year in consequence of a ferocious attack on the bowling of the Savernake Club which gave him a century within an hour and took his season's tally to over five hundred.

But it was rugby he enjoyed most. The Big Games of up to sixty players were now out of favour; occasionally forty boys took part in a game, but the more usual team was twenty and Randolph's ruthless physical ability was seen more and more as the confusion of the Big Games gave way to the more open play possible with smaller teams.

Sergeant Adams, the Crimean War veteran who was still the college gym sergeant, watched him critically, confiding in Voss, who occupied the lodge: 'That boy could be the best rugby player in the country, either forward or back, if only he'd concentrate on it instead of spending time in the back rooms of the Red Lion.' And Goaty, who paraded along the Bath Road just outside the lodge, wearing his high hat, white smock and knee breeches and selling ginger beer and fruit from his barrow, leaned over the gate to watch the play and nodded approvingly when the dark-haired boy streaked clear of the pack with a flying ball, or crunched an attacking opponent to the ground.

It was rugby which brought Randolph his most famous victory – in a corner of the college known as Fleuss's Arch where tradition demanded that affairs of honour be settled.

The incident arose out of a house rugby match in which Randolph had been brought down by one of the biggest boys in the school, a twelve-stone sixth former named Webster. The two had always disliked each other, and as they rolled apart after the whistle Webster lunged a second time. They went down and Randolph jabbed backwards with his elbow into the bigger boy's face, snarling: 'Get your hand away from my balls or I'll break your bloody neck.'

Several boys checked, turning, listening – in time to hear Webster retort: 'Sorry. Thought you liked that sort of thing. You farm boys are supposed to – always messing about with the back ends of animals.'

Somebody in the pack sniggered. Randolph climbed slowly to his feet. His dark eyes riveted on the other boy. He said, loudly enough for half the team to hear: 'Fleuss's – after the game. I'll show you whether I like it or not.'

Webster was big enough to be confident in spite of Randolph's reputation. By the time the protagonists arrived, seventy or eighty boys had gathered, for the word had spread quickly that Randy was going to fight. Dr Bradley himself, attracted by the noise, watched from a window but did not interfere, for he knew better than most that the tradition of Fleuss's Arch provided a discipline and a distraction worth preserving.

A fight there had to be in accordance with certain unwritten rules – fists only, no kicking, no weapons. It was won and lost when one boy surrendered and apologized, or could not stand.

Bloody battles of fifteen and twenty minutes were on record, and the shouting, pressing mass of spectators relished the prospect of such a contest now.

They were disappointed. The two came together, handed their coats to watching boys, faced each other. The crowd hushed. Randolph snapped: 'You ready?' Webster grinned, lifted his fists, started to say, 'You won't catch me turning my back on –' when Randolph hit him – a feint to the head, an explosive smash just above the waistline and an uppercut that lifted the bigger boy's feet clear of the ground and sent him rearing up, pawing at the air, poised and placed for the hammer blow that went in under his heart. As he jerked forward, Randolph stepped sideways and hit him below the left ear. Then, without looking round and almost before the other boy had hit the ground, he took his coat from the frozen arm of the boy who held it and turned to leave. He did not even inspect his bruised knuckles.

Those nearest to him fell back, parting, forming a silent corridor, suddenly afraid. As he went, one whispered: 'His eyes – did you see his eyes?' And in the window above Dr Bradley stared and muttered to himself: 'Dear God – what sort of a boy is that?'

Randolph Haldane never fought again at the college, for there were none who wanted to risk a challenge, or even his displeasure. And the story of his final battle was told long after he had left – a tale eclipsed for the next generation of boys only by the manner of his leaving.

As Adams the gym sergeant had confided in Voss the porter, Randolph was no stranger to the inns of the town. And it was when he was leaving the Red Lion one September evening just before his seventeenth birthday that he first saw Marion Tempest.

She was the daughter of an assistant master who lived in a small house overlooking the wide High Street near the Town Hall. She was sixteen, with long shining brown hair, an elfin face and wide-set blue eyes, and a virgin figure that sent the blood rushing through the young man's veins.

He was not unfamiliar with the girls of Roxton, or a few of those around the college. Now and then there had been some rough and tumble in a barn or field, a little groping around bodices and skirts and breeches waistbands; but nothing more. In the dormitories at night there were giggling debates on the female anatomy, close questioning of boys who claimed to have had 'it' with sisters or cousins or servant girls; and among the more extrovert, competitions to decide whose erection was the most impressive. But Randolph was not particularly interested in that sort of bawdy humour; for the most part he just ignored it, as if he were waiting for something more impressive than mere talk.

From the moment he set eyes on Marion Tempest he knew he had found it. He had little difficulty in striking up an acquaintanceship, even though friendships between college boys and any local girls – let alone the daughter of a master – were strictly forbidden. Marion, whose education had already been broadened by two older, sexually adventurous brothers, was fascinated by the attentions of a boy whose reputation was already familiar to her, and it was not long before they were meeting secretly and regularly, first in the town and after a time in a deserted barn which was part of a run-down farm close to the college.

In the circumstances some sort of physical experiment was inevitable.

One Sunday evening early in November they went to the barn and snuggled down in Randolph's rug – that famous Marlburian necessity which boys usually wore over their sports attire, fastened at the neck by a leather strap and buckle. The rug, plus the remnants of a hay crop, provided reasonable warmth and comfort, and the isolation and intimacy of the circumstances were invitations neither could resist.

Eventually she felt it necessary to warn him: 'I'm not going to, Randy. I never have, yet. It's too dangerous. We could get – caught.'

'I never have either,' he said truthfully. 'But I want to. Do you?'

She wriggled against him as he undid the last button of her bodice and gently pushed the garment away from her shoulder.

'Yes. I want to. But don't try to persuade me. There are – other ways. You know that – for both of us.'

He leaned over her and kissed her breast, caressing the nipple with his tongue. Her breathing was loud in his ear.

'Go on,' she whispered suddenly. 'Go on – play with me. I can do it to you too. I know how.' She guided his hand.

'How do you know?' he muttered against her.

'My brother showed me,' she giggled. 'Boys often do it. He told me. You do, don't you?'

He flushed in the darkness, taken aback.

'Yes, sometimes.' He hesitated. 'Do – do you?'

She giggled again.

'Of course I do. Especially after I've been with you. I can't help it.' She began to move against him, responding to him, feeling for him. 'I want it. Go on, Randy – please. Like this. Go on – go on – let's do it together –'

They did; concentrating, learning, abandoning the caution of silence as their breathing quickened until he gasped and groaned and she arched her back and rocked her head from side to side and cried out, and the barn door opened and a lantern shone on them and Marion's father stood there in horror and fury.

Randolph was expelled from Marlborough the next day.

VII

The drive home to Roxton was very long and very painful. For almost the first half hour no word passed between them. Then Rupert Haldane said:

'I don't know what I'm going to do with you. I wanted to see you at Oxford, then coming down to the estate to take over. Now – I don't know.' A lock of his white hair drifted across his brow as he lowered his head.

Randolph took a long, slow breath.

'I'm sorry, father. I apologized to you in Dr Bradley's study. I can't keep on saying it. I know what I've done – to myself – to you – and to my mother.'

Rupert snapped: 'You had better decide what you're going to tell your mother. I certainly cannot relate to her the disgusting story Dr Bradley told me.'

'I'll tell her the truth.' The boy stared straight ahead, seeing nothing. 'I'll tell her myself –'

'You'll do nothing of the sort.' Rupert was suddenly shouting. 'It's not fit for her ears. You'll tell her you broke bounds to see a girl, and that's against the rules, and leave it at that.' He shook with anger.

Minutes later Randolph said: 'I'll find some employment. I'll take myself off your hands. Just let me gather things together. A day or two – that's all.'

He turned away when he saw Rupert's tortured face.

The rest of the journey was an ordeal for them both. They said little as the carriage jolted them homeward, except for occasional forlorn and embarrassing attempts to restore some sort of normality to their relationship.

Late that evening, after the agony of his reunion with his mother, he sat in his bedroom, staring at his books in lonely misery. He had refused a meal because he could not bear company. Now he was desperately hungry. He wrestled with the great void that seemed to stretch in front of him, totally obscuring his future. He had declared his intention to leave the Grange, but he did not know where to go.

The latch on the door clicked. He looked up to see Caroline. There was a tray in her hands and her still-fair hair caught the yellow lamplight.

'I thought you would like something,' she said gently.

And then, for the first time since that awful moment in the barn alongside the college, it was all too much, and he stood straight-backed, facing her, silent tears running down his cheeks.

She looked away, came into the room, and concentrated on setting the tray down carefully on the little table beside the bed. Then she walked back to the door before she said: 'Shall I stay a little while?'

He fought for control in silence; nodded. She closed the door quietly, and waited.

Presently his blurred voice said 'Thank you', and he sat down wearily on the bed.

'I think I'll sit down as well,' she said. Her voice was calm and her face composed. She crossed to a chair and sat carefully, arranging her skirts. And suddenly she was not his mother but a beautiful, slender, wise friend, and the age difference between them dissolved, and he saw that there were two cups on the tray alongside the teapot and sandwiches.

He gulped air and mumbled: 'That's the kindest thing you've ever done.' And the words were not those of a boy but of a man.

She shook her head.

'No. I just understand that there are times when we all need to talk. I hope you want to talk with me.'

He nodded, wordless, still confused. She leaned forward and carefully poured the tea, giving him time. Her hand was steady when she held out the cup to him.

'What happened? Tell me.'

He drank. The tea was hot and calmed him.

'I told you. I broke bounds to see a girl. It was against the rules.'

She looked at him steadily.

'I don't know much about Marlborough College. But that doesn't sound like a terribly serious offence.'

He drank again, set the cup down, straightened.

'It wasn't.' He met her level gaze, and she saw Mark Helford in his eyes. He said: 'The girl is the daughter of a master. We were in a barn – making love – and he caught us – just as . . .' His voice died.

Her face did not flicker, and her eyes did not shift from his. She was not shocked, as he had expected her to be. She simply absorbed it, considered it, understood it.

Presently she said quietly: 'I see. That is rather a different matter. Did you know she was a college master's daughter?'

He nodded, relieved, relaxing; forgetting the enormous question mark over his future, seeing his mother as he had never seen her, feeling closer to her than he had ever felt to anyone; strengthened by her calm.

'Yes. I knew. We had been friends for some time – since this – this half began.'

'Then you took an extraordinary risk, Randolph.' She was matter-of-fact about it. 'You were courting disaster. But then sometimes we all take risks we had not contemplated. Sometimes we are moved by things we cannot control. Now we must try to make the best of it. Do eat. You'll feel better.'

And now he was no longer weary. He sat straight on the bed, reached for the food, encouraged.

'There's not much to be made of it. Father made it quite clear that he did not welcome me here.'

'Your – father is upset. Understandably. He will think better of it. He needs you here. It's time you started to study the business. That's not your biggest hurdle, Randolph. You still have to face your friends – Frank – the servants – the labourers. People in the village. It will soon get around that you've left the college unexpectedly. Even if they're not told, they'll soon guess. A few of the young men may even admire you for it; most people will condemn you without ever knowing what happened, let alone understanding the things that can sometimes drive us all beyond the limits of common sense.'

He had stopped eating. Suddenly he thought part of her mind had left the little low-roofed room, as if a memory had intruded, and he could not understand. She was still looking at him, but seemed to see something beyond him.

She was talking again. 'The curious thing is that out of terrible worry and apparent disaster there can sometimes come good. There will come a time when you will look back on this and realize that it was not really such a dreadful thing.' She had shut out the ghost that had drifted, unseen but felt, between them. 'But first you will have to deal with the present. Make up your mind what you will say to your friends. Ignore the others. They will soon find something else to talk about. And –' she reached out quickly for his arm '– I would like you to stay here, if you feel you can. Trust me, Randolph.' She stood up suddenly. 'And try to sleep. No good ever came of regrets – they change nothing.'

Then she was gone, and he was left staring at the closed door, knowing that he was no longer a schoolboy; that he had met a woman he had never seen before – a woman who had treated him as if he were a man, and that through her he had grown older, and was the better for it.

Whether it was fatigue, or the feeling that Caroline had left some strange presence and strength in the room, he did not know; but he fell asleep quickly and did not dream.

Three days later Randolph stood in one of the yards of the home farm, talking to Frank Garton.

'He doesn't want me here,' he said. His voice was flat, resigned. 'He's making that clear all the time, without actually putting it into words.'

'I'd have thought he'd be glad of you,' Frank retorted. 'He's an old man now, and one day his rheumatism is going to cripple him. Who's going to run this place when he can't – except you? Mr Conway is only steward of this farm. What about the rest of the estate? You're the only one who can take over – the only one who should take over.'

Randolph kicked at a loose cobblestone.

'I don't think he accepts any of that. Or if he does he won't let himself consider it. He's just obsessed with the fact that I was sacked.'

'Oh hell, Randy – what's the matter with him?' Frank's voice rose in exasperation. 'It's not all that dreadful, even if it's shaken him. And it doesn't change what's here – and what this place needs.'

'That's not the point,' Randolph said gloomily. 'He can't get over that I was caught with a girl. We weren't actually having it. But not far off. And he knows that. Bradley made it pretty clear. He's so damned narrow. He's obsessed, I tell you. He looks at me as if he thinks I'm – sort of obscene. I've got to leave, in spite of what my mother says.'

Frank grinned at him quickly and gave him a mock punch on the arm.

'All right. If you go, I'll go with you. We'll find something together. Don't know what – but we will. C'mon – let's work it out –'

'No.' Randolph was firm. 'That's stupid. You've a good job here. I can tell you – Conway thinks a lot of you. I heard him telling father. He wants you to start doing some work in the estate office before long. He knows you can read and write and that your arithmetic is good. He says you've a future here – not labouring, but more important things. You stay, Frank. I can look after myself. I brought this on my own head. Don't get mixed up in any of it.'

Frank eyed him suspiciously.

'Are you just telling me that – about the estate office?'

'No. It's God's truth. I swear. You can't help me by leaving here. You'll just hurt yourself –'

A horse clattered along the drive near the house, hidden from them by a barn. They raised their heads, listening, then walked across the yard to a corner which afforded a view of the side of the house in time to see Mark Helford dismount.

Randolph said: 'Oh hell. I don't want to see him. He

doesn't know yet. I don't want to be there when they tell him. Come on – I'll give you a hand with something.'

As they recrossed the yard Frank said curiously: 'He's a close friend of your father's, isn't he? I've seen him here often. He's tough. There are lots of tales about him.'

'I know. He *is* tough. My mother told me once about how he got that scar on his face – and other things he's done. And his business – he built it up from nothing – and look at him now.'

Frank grunted as they went into a barn.

'He gives me the creeps. The way he looks at you. As if he's seeing right through you.'

Randolph nodded. He picked up a long-bladed knife and moved towards a pile of turnips.

'I know. But I like him. We get on well. I'd trust him. He's done a lot of deals with father, for a long time – always pays on the nail – sticks to his word. And he's a hell of a good horseman. Wish I could handle a fresh stallion like he can.'

They perched side by side on a bench and fell to chopping turnips – a rough, finger-aching job; and a somewhat danger-ous one, for the knives had to be sharp and used with considerable force. For half an hour they worked, until they heard Ted Oxley, the head cowman, bellowing for Frank as he prepared for the afternoon's milking. Again Randolph involved himself, washing the milk cans and the udder rags, then tipping chopped roots into the small-wheeled truck for feeding. The cattle in the next building knew the routine and raised their voices hungrily.

Then, gradually he became aware that he was being watch-ed, and turned to see Mark Helford in the doorway.

'Hullo, Randolph. Have you time to talk to me?' Crisp and deep; but quiet, not hostile.

Randolph straightened, wiping his hands on his cord breeches. Reluctantly he moved towards the door, feeling his face flush.

'Yes, sir, of course.' He hesitated, wanting to sound as if nothing untoward had occurred since their last meeting two or three months before. 'It – it's good to see you again, sir. How are you?'

Helford seemed not to hear the question. He walked out into the pale winter sunlight. Randolph followed, watching him cautiously. Helford was bearded now; had been so for a year or more. Randolph did not know that the growth was a precaution suggested by Caroline who had become increasingly alarmed by the obvious likeness between her son and his father. At 52 years of age he still had his thick black hair, and while there were streaks of grey in his beard he had the appearance and bearing of a man ten years his junior.

He waited for Randolph to come alongside him.

'Let's walk – around the garden, perhaps. I'm sorry you're in trouble.'

Randolph looked straight ahead, expressionless.

'That's kind of you, sir. You've probably gathered that it was – my own fault.'

'Things usually are, for all of us,' Helford said evenly. 'Yes – I know all about it. I've seen your father. Then I had a long talk with your mother – after your father had to return to the estate office.' He looked sideways at the young man. His meaning was clear; Caroline had told him more than Rupert was prepared to discuss.

'My father is very upset, sir.' Randolph's voice was scarcely above a whisper.

Helford nodded, said curtly: 'So is your mother.'

'She – yes, I know. But she has been – very understanding. She has helped me. I'm terribly grateful to her.'

Helford walked on in silence. They reached the walled garden alongside the house and stopped by the low wooden gate.

'What are you going to do with yourself?'

Randolph was silent for seconds. Then he half shrugged.

'I don't know, sir. Except that I feel I can't stay here. I've made up my mind about that.'

Helford turned, looking hard at him.

'Don't you want to stay here? Don't you want to learn to manage this place? It's a sizeable business, you know.'

Randolph met the uncompromising eyes without flinching. Instinctively he knew he was on trial.

'Yes. I want to stay.' His voice was flat, clear, low. 'More than anything, I want to stay. Even if there were nothing else, I want to repay my mother for her kindness – somehow. But I feel my father is against my staying. I don't know what he wants of me – but it's not here. I have to go.'

Helford opened the gate. He walked very slowly into the garden. Randolph went with him. His young shoulders were as square and straight as Helford's own. Behind a curtain in a room overlooking the garden Caroline saw them and thought, 'Oh dear God – they're so alike. Please God, don't let anybody see it.' She watched, apprehensively, as the two figures moved slowly along a path between lawns and empty flowerbeds.

Helford was saying: 'Your father has had a shock. And he is not very well. After a time I expect he will think differently. But in the interim you have to work, to gain business experience, so that when the time comes you can take full responsibilities.' He checked his stride, turned and looked at Randolph's guarded, taut face. 'I have need of a young man in my office. It's a progressive position that would benefit you. I believe you would become capable of the work, even though you are still very young. Are you interested?'

Randolph stared at him, scarcely believing what he had heard.

'Sir – I didn't expect – oh yes. Thank you. Yes – I would like to come – I'll work hard –'

'Yes. I'm sure you will. You'll see a lot of me, which will guarantee that you work hard.' There was quick humour in the dark, penetrating eyes that denied the severity of the voice. 'Shall we say you will start on Monday next?'

Randolph was still not fully in control of himself.

'Monday? Oh yes – of course – whenever you say, sir. I don't know where your offices are, but I'll –'

Helford smiled for the first time.

'That's unimportant. What matters is where you are to live. I think it would be wise if you did not try to live here, and your mother agrees. I have discussed all this with her already. In any case, it's too far from Exeter. I have a large house with unoccupied rooms, and I can accommodate you for a few days. I'll help you to find permanent lodgings. I know of several houses run by good women who will make you comfortable. You can come here at weekends, if you wish – when there is no work to do for me, that is. You will have to judge when it is sensible for you to start coming here regularly. I'll pay you enough to enable you to live reasonably.' His eyes were humorous, but the stare was piercingly direct. 'Is that a bargain between us, young man?'

From the window, Caroline watched their handshake; saw Helford put a hand on Randolph's shoulder; saw the new confidence in her son's face. A voice whispered in her mind: 'Mark – oh Mark – you said you would never let me down. I always knew you'd be there if I needed you . . .' She turned away, the tears blurring her vision.

VIII

By the time Randolph had worked in Helford's shipping office for three years the disastrous episode at Marlborough was virtually forgotten. Rupert had not forgiven but he had come to terms with the inevitable and made peace with Randolph who now spent every possible weekend at Roxton Grange. Rupert himself was now 70 and clearly an old man in body and spirit. Caroline, in contrast, seemed ageless; at 52 she was as lithe and spirited as when she had first captivated Mark Helford. Perhaps there was a little grey in her fair hair, but it was unnoticeable; perhaps there were a few more lines at the corners of her eyes, but few saw them. She still loved to ride, especially when she had an excuse to take Mark across the estate; he, for his part, remained single, increasingly successful in business and social life, a regular caller at the Grange where, as Rupert slowed, he managed to spend more time alone with Caroline. And he supervised Randolph's development subtly, closely – and effectively.

By his twentieth birthday Randolph was an authority in the Helford Shipping offices to an extent far beyond his years. He had clearly inherited his father's business acumen and commercial aggression, and his physical development kept pace. The tough and ruthless streak which had carried him so successfully through school was quickly recognized and welcomed by Helford who set about improving on it. Treating him curtly, sometimes even distantly, he nevertheless encouraged him to develop his natural skills as a bare-knuckle fighter, sent him as a pupil to one of Devonshire's most famous wrestlers, personally taught him to fence with foil and épée, and began to teach him to shoot until he realized that his son had an instinct for handling a gun and a keen eye which set him apart from anyone he had ever seen.

But as a horseman it was Helford who was the master, and he imparted as much of that mastery as he could to Randolph who practised whenever he could during his weekends at home when he also worked on the farm, studied in the estate office often with Frank Garton at his side, wrestled with him in the fields, handled and drove the cattle and the sheep flock.

In three years Randolph Haldane became a formidable young man, with a confidence in himself worthy of someone five or even ten years older.

He also became more and more like the Mark Helford of twenty years before. The same cold fury lurked inside him when he was angered; the same danger signals flashed deep in the same dark eyes; the same half-mocking humour sped across his face and touched his voice as he calculated and aimed for whatever he sought.

Mark saw it, and was secretly proud. Caroline saw it, and nursed private disquiet, even apprehension; and wondered why.

On a March evening in 1871, with a cold wind blowing high clouds across the last of the day, Frank mounted up and cantered to Exeter and Randoph's lodgings. They had a light meal, called at the livery stables where Randolph kept his dark bay hack, and rode towards the Dawlish road, hoping to meet some of the young men they knew at one or other of the inns at the edge of the city.

A few hours earlier the skipper of a fishing boat had dropped anchor in the Exe, having turned back only two hours after starting what should have been a three-day trip. As the chain took the strain and the little boat steadied against the tide, the skipper stood on the deck, a loaded pistol in his hand, and ordered the mate and his three seamen over the side into a rowing boat. All four were drunk and abusive; but none wanted to be the first to tackle the skipper and his pistol, so they went over, scrambling about the rowing boat and pushed off towards the shore, swearing foully at the man who stood up on the deck watching them go.

When they reached the shore they stumbled up to the nearest road and began the long walk towards Exeter.

They reached the outskirts of the city just as the last of the daylight faded; called at an inn for food, and then, somewhat sobered, wandered on to reach the Brandy Cask, a tavern popular with the younger men on that side of the city, around nine o'clock. They pushed through the door, blinking in the smoke and lamplight.

Randolph and Frank were sitting in an inglenook corner beside the big log fire.

At about the same time, in a small house close to the inn, Jane Dolby opened the door to Peter Pardoe, who was her lover and who had come to take advantage of her husband's absence driving the daily coach from Exeter to Plymouth. They ate supper, then climbed the creaking stairs and went to bed in a room overlooking a narrow side street which led off the main thoroughfare.

In the Brandy Cask the mate from the fishing boat, whose name was John Robbins, bought ale for his companions. As he did so he turned away from the bar, collided with Frank Garton, and spilled some of his ale down his heavy coat.

'Why don't you be more bloody careful?' he rasped, dabbing a hand down the coarse cloth.

Frank, surprised by his aggression, said: 'Sorry. I think you turned into me, really. But I'll buy you another glass of ale.'

'I can buy me own bloody ale,' growled Robbins, pushing past.

Frank shrugged, completed his order, and went back to his companion.

'What was that about?' Randolph asked.

'Nothing. He walked into me and spilled his drink. He's had too much, I think.'

They returned to their conversation. But both were aware that the fisherman was watching them across the room, his heavy features sullen and resentful. Now and then they saw his companions looking at them, in response to something the mate said.

Presently Frank leaned forward.

'I think there's trouble brewing over there, Randy.'

Randolph raised an eyebrow.

'Is there? Hope not.' He lifted his glass in a mock toast and winked.

But Frank was uneasy.

'I reckon we'd better get out, quietly,' he muttered. 'There are four of them, and they've had a lot to drink. I can see them better than you can. They're up to something. C'mon – let's go.'

Randolph clasped a hand round his glass.

'I haven't finished,' he said. 'We'll go when we're ready.'

Frank looked at his friend sharply. He knew the signs.

'We'll go now,' he persisted. 'We don't want trouble – whether we can handle it or not. That sort usually carries a knife. It's not worth it.'

Randolph looked down at his glass, then drained it quickly and grinned.

'All right. If that's how you feel. Let's go.'

They stood up and moved unobtrusively across the crowded room towards the door. Through the smoke-filled atmosphere the four seamen watched them.

Outside they took long breaths of clean air, walked along the front of the tavern and round the corner to the rails where their horses were tethered along with several others. They passed directly beneath the window of the room where Jane Dolby and Peter Pardoe were recovering from their exertions. They freed their horses, turned them in the narrow street – and saw the dark outlines of several men between them and the thoroughfare.

Randolph muttered: 'Frank – look out – I think it's the four from the inn.' He raised a foot, feeling for the stirrup. Then the men were on them.

One snarled: 'Stand still, ye fine fellers. Let's see what ye've got in yer wallets –'

In the room above, the couple in the bed heard a horse whinny, the sound of scraping boots, shouts. They both scrambled to the floor. The man pulled a coat over his naked shoulders, turned up the wick of a lamp, rushed to the window and opened it, peering out. The lamp cast a yellow glow across the little street.

Two men were on the ground, one motionless, the other trying to crawl away, moaning. Four other men fought. Then one pair broke apart, and one of the men fled down the alley into blackness. The other pair strained, swaying and grunting, locked together. Then Peter Pardoe saw one man strike upwards, vertically; heard the blow; saw the other man's head snap back, too far back, his exposed throat catching the lamplight.

Randolph, who had struck the blow with the heel of his hand to the underside of his opponent's jaw, and with terrible force, jumped back. The man dropped without a sound. Frank ran across. They bent over the crumpled figure.

'Christ,' Randolph hissed. 'Oh dear Christ. I've – I've broken his neck – he's dead –'

They straightened, looked up into the startled face of the man who held a lamp out of the window seven feet above them; heard his hoarse, panicking voice: 'Bloody hell – there's a feller killed someone – drunken bastards – in a fight – hey, you – you bastard –' His eyes riveted on Randolph's upturned face.

A woman's voice then, and the man and the lamp disappeared. Upstairs Jane Dolby dragged the man back into the bedroom, spinning him round, crying in his ear: 'Shut up, you fool – keep away – you're not supposed to be here. Keep out of it. We'll be found out if the police come asking questions.' She struggled for the lamp, turned it off. 'Get dressed, quick. Go home. We'll be found out – quick –'

In the alley Randolph and Frank stood, fear rising inside them, looking first at the darkened window, then at the shape on the ground and the head twisted sideways, the face pressed against the wall.

Suddenly they ran. Their horses were stamping uneasily down the alleyway. Within seconds they were in the saddles, spurring to full gallop in the darkness.

Behind them the alley was quiet; except for a man who groaned against a wall, blood gushing from his mouth, a few yards from two other, silent figures.

Mark Helford heard the knock on the window of his study. He sat up in his chair; heard it again. He rose, crossed the room quickly to the hall; came back with a stick, flicked the handle, and drew out a narrow sword blade. Then he turned down the lamp by which he had been reading and jerked back the curtain.

Against the starlight he saw a figure.

'Who the hell are you?' His voice barked loudly enough to be heard through the glass.

The figure came closer; the features plainer. Suddenly he thrust the sword back into its stick-sheath, grabbed the sash window and heaved it up.

'Randolph – what's this about?' Sharp, and very low now.

Randolph whispered: 'Let me in – please.'

Helford stood back, and the young man climbed over the sill and dropped into the room. His face was streaked with sweat and dust, his hair falling across his forehead. He was breathing fast and there was fear in his eyes. Helford closed the window, pulled the curtain, turned up the lamp.

'What's the matter? What are you doing here – like this?'

'Mr Helford – we're in trouble. Oh God, we're in trouble. Frank – he's out there – with the horses. I need help, sir – and advice –'

'Sit down and calm down,' Helford snapped. He crossed to a bookcase, picked up a whisky bottle and poured two drinks. He handed one to Randolph.

'Now tell me – what's wrong with coming through the front door? And what's Frank doing outside?'

Randolph held the glass in two hands. He was shaking visibly.

'He's – hiding. In the bushes. We – we didn't come to the door in case anyone saw us.'

Helford watched him with narrowed eyes, guessing, calculating.

'Then he'd better come in. Go out there and get him – through the window if you want to. Put the horses in the stable. There's room on the left. And if the trouble is as bad as you look – do it fast.'

Randolph nodded, turned to the window. Helford strode across the room, down the darkened hall and stood at the front door, listening. Slowly he opened it a few inches, listened again; heard nothing except the night wind and the distant click of a horse walking. He stood like that for almost a minute. Then, satisfied, he closed the door and softly returned to the study. The curtain stirred in the wind. He lowered the lamp light; waited. Within two minutes he heard footsteps and Randolph appeared at the window, scrambled through. Frank Garton followed. They closed the window; drew the curtain.

Helford inspected them.

'You look a sorry sight. Both of you. What's the matter?'

Randolph whispered: 'I've killed a man. We were attacked. I killed one of them. We don't know about another – Frank hit him and his head banged against a wall. We – we panicked.'

For long seconds Helford stared at them in silence.

'You mean you ran away? Is that what you're telling me? You ran away?'

They nodded, speechless.

'Where was this?'

They told him. First one, then the other; stumbling over words, their story jumbled at first then, under his prompting and questioning, slowly making sense.

'Who saw you, apart from the man in the window?' Helford demanded.

'No one – as far as we know. We didn't see anyone else. But he had a good look at us.'

'Why-did-you-run?' Helford spoke each word distinctly, like a separate sentence. His eyes mirrored anger.

Randolph said: 'We lost our heads. It was the man in the window. He called out to someone in the room with him – "There's a feller killed someone". Then he called us drunken bastards. If I'd stayed he'd have told the police it was my fault – I could tell he would. He'd made up his mind. It would only have been our word that they'd tried to rob us. Drunken bastards, the man said. He meant us. The police would have thought it was a brawl – that I'd done it in a brawl. We didn't

108

stop to see what was wrong with the man Frank put down. But he hit his head an awful crack. If he's not dead too, he's in a bad way. And one of the men ran away. He could recognize us. Mr Helford – please – please understand. We couldn't stop to think.'

Helford said: 'Be quiet. Let me think.'

They watched him. He stood, rock-still in the centre of the room, seeing nothing, showing nothing on his face. A clock ticked on the mantelpiece. Frank combed fingers through his fair hair. The knuckles of his hand were covered with dried blood. Randolph closed his eyes, trying to steady his breathing.

Helford said distantly: 'I don't know whether you did the right thing or not. The man at the window sounds like a hostile witness. The man who ran away is certainly hostile. All four of them might have a reputation for violence. We don't know. But you've been in three fights in the village in the last two years that I know about, Frank Garton. If the police accuse you they'll bring that out. And if I know anything about them they'll bring out your expulsion from Marlborough, Randolph – to try to show that you're a wild and violent pair. They could certainly make it sound like a brawl. You had been in the tavern for a long time. Then you ran away. If you'd stayed we don't know what might have happened. But you ran. That makes it ten times worse. If we tell the police now, I think you'll be in very serious trouble. A jury could easily decide it was manslaughter. No –' he held up a hand '– don't argue with me. I need to think further about it.'

They waited for a long time. Presently they sat down, weary, and Helford began to pace around the room. Then, still without speaking, he disappeared; came back minutes later with tea and bread and butter. They dared not speak, even to thank him. They ate and drank in a miserable agony of fear, their minds tumbling over the events of the night, searching desperately for a salvation.

Then Helford said: 'Go and wash. Clean yourselves up.'

Silently they left the room.

Helford sat down at the mahogany roll-top desk in a corner

109

of the room, placing the lamp carefully on top of it. He drew out paper, pen and ink, and began to write. He wrote slowly, thinking about every sentence. When Randolph and Frank returned he did not look up, and they sat down, careful not to disturb him, watching him apprehensively.

Presently he reached for envelopes, folded two letters and tucked them inside. He took a long cigar from a case on the desk, trimmed it, inspected it; struck a match and lit it carefully. Gradually he seemed to see them again.

'Randolph,' he said, 'I want to speak with you alone. Will you wait in the drawing room please, Frank – it's the next room along the corridor.'

'Yes. Yes, sir.' Frank, tight-faced, stood up. He hesitated. Randolph nodded to him, and he went out. The door of the next room opened; closed again.

Helford said: 'Can you trust him?'

Randolph nodded emphatically. 'Yes.'

'Totally?'

'Yes, Mr Helford. I'd trust him with anything.'

Helford said flatly: 'I don't think you're actually trusting him with your life; but you're certainly trusting him with your liberty. And, in view of what I'm going to do, you may be trusting him with mine as well.'

Randolph stared at him, not understanding.

'Frank is my closest friend,' he said. 'We've always been friends. We'd do anything for each other. Yes – I trust him.'

'Right.' Helford was satisfied. 'There is no way I can separate you now. You are both in this – how badly we don't know; but we must assume the worst. We cannot afford to assume anything else. By the morning the constabulary will be searching, asking questions. It will take them some time to assemble the answers. Before then you must both be away from here. There is no point in running to London, or some other part of the country. If they have a good description of you both, you could easily be found, after a time. The police are surprisingly resourceful. You'll have to get out of the country altogether.'

Randolph winced, but remained silent; watching the man

110

who had become better than a friend to him in the past three years – the man who inspired respect and, occasionally, not a little fear in him – the man who seemed to have taken control of so much of his life, who seemed to have so much influence with his parents, and to whom he had turned that night instinctively, with never a thought that he might be rejected.

Helford's deep voice again: 'I'm taking a risk helping you in the way I intend to. If the police find you, you must not tell them anything about the circumstances of your call here, or what you have told me – or indeed what I'm telling you. And you must make that clear to young Garton. Your story is this – listen very carefully – then we'll go through it again with your friend: I'm sending you to America. You are my employee, and I'm in an expanding shipping business. I'm looking for trade in Boston and New York. You are representing me. Frank Garton is your assistant – sent to gain experience. I put this requirement to you this afternoon. Is that much clear?'

Randolph could say nothing except: 'Yes, sir. That's clear.' Then he added: 'Don't worry, Mr Helford. Neither of us will ever admit that we've been here tonight – that you've helped us. I swear.'

Helford nodded briefly. He held out the two envelopes.

'There are two letters here. One is addressed to the master of the British and North American steamship *Columbia*. She is currently loading in Avonmouth and will sail for Halifax and Boston in three days. The master is a friend of mine. Deliver this letter to him twenty-four hours before sailing and he will find accommodation for you on board. You will travel as crew and he will overcome customs and passport problems for you. You will do whatever he says without question. D'you understand?'

'Yes.' Randolph was hardly breathing. 'I understand you.'

'Good. When you reach Boston deliver the second letter to the address on the envelope. Again it is to a friend. He will assist you and advise you as my representatives. He is a wise man and you can rely on him. Finally –' he crossed the room to an oil painting on the wall, lifted the picture down and revealed a small wall safe. He inserted a key, opened the safe, and drew out a metal box. From it he took a sealed packet, inspected it; held it out. '– finally, you will need money. I have three hundred and fifty pounds here. If you are careful it will last you both some time. How you divide it and what you do when it's spent is for you to decide between you. But you'll be all right until it's wise for you to return. My friend will advise you well and will be a contact point between us. And America is a country of opportunity. I have every confidence in you.'

Randolph was on his feet, staring at the envelope.

'Mr Helford – I can't do that. I can't take money. That's a fortune. I'll find a way. Frank and I can work. I'm terribly grateful – you're taking such a risk. But I can't accept money.'

'You can and you will,' said Helford curtly. His eyes held Randolph's; unblinking, penetrating, compulsive. The young man looked back, held on, focused. They stood as if physically locked, and a strange stillness crept through Randolph's mind; an awareness, suspended in disbelief; for he knew he was seeing himself. The dark, direct stare was his own. The spirit that stirred behind the gaze was his. Helford saw the dawning, the recognition, and waved the envelope quickly.

'Take it, Randolph. It's a gift. If you come back a rich man, then I might accept its return. We'll let the future decide that.'

The younger man was frozen, not knowing what he had seen, only that it had struck hard and clean inside him, and had marked him. He dragged his gaze away, to the envelope, and said: 'You wouldn't offer it if you didn't want me to take it. I will. But I'll repay you. One day I'll repay you – with interest. I give you my word.'

A smile touched Helford's mouth, briefly.

'I'll look forward to it. But – before we have Garton back in here – there's one thing we haven't talked about.'

Randolph's eyes widened.

'My parents. And Frank's.'

Helford nodded.

'You'll have to leave that with me. I'll see them tomorrow. I'll tell them as much as I think it is wise for them to know. You're not out of trouble yet. I think if you leave here

112

tomorrow morning, and travel as far as Taunton separately, you'll be all right. But we can't be sure. Keep your wits. And for God's sake don't raise your hand to any man. You don't know your own strength, boy. Now put that money in your pocket and let's talk to Frank Garton.'

RANDOLPH

Old English Randwulf – 'shield + wolf'

I

―――――――

'We can't stay here much longer. And I don't know where we ought to go.'

Frank Garton stared gloomily out of the window at the Boston street. He and Randolph where sharing a bad attack of homesickness.

Outside, under a hot sun, Boston bustled – the growlers, the horses, the people. It should have been like Exeter or, perhaps, Plymouth. But it was not; nor was it like Bristol or Southampton, or any other city they had seen. The buildings were longer and lower, built much more of wood than of brick, and hardly ever of stone; the streets were wider, the suburbs wandered away into the surrounding woodlands; the hoardings and painted signs were cruder, more aggressive – and so, they had already concluded, were the people.

They were temporary guests in the house of Tom Hogarth, to whom Mark Helford's letter of introduction had been addressed. He was a big-chested, red-faced fifty-year-old shipper and merchant, a second generation Devon emigrant whose father had crossed the Atlantic without a penny. Now the son was worth all but half a million dollars and cared nothing for who knew it.

He had welcomed the two visitors with enthusiastic and open hospitality. In accordance with Helford's instructions they had told him they were in America for experience and on the way to seek contracts for Helford's business. They wanted to stay for several months, they said, and to work while they were there in order to keep themselves; and apart from acting as free agents for Mark Helford did not care what sort of work they did as long as it paid fair wages. Hogarth had introduced them to merchants around the port, and Randolph had made preliminary arrangements for shipping several loads of grain to Helford's new storage facilities in Exeter – a trade which Helford anticipated would make him a great deal of money in coming years.

There was commission to be earned there, and Helford had also written to a Boston bank to facilitate its payment. But Randolph knew he and Frank could not make a living by that means for long, since the volume of trade on which he could call, as a lone agent, was small. So other work had to be found.

Hogarth was not encouraging about that. Boston was in danger of overcrowding and any sort of progressive job was difficult to find. He had offered them a month's free accommodation as guests in his big Colonial-style house on Beacon Hill where many of the city's best families lived and which was within ten minutes sharp ride of Washington Street, the port and the crowded offices. But now three weeks had gone and while they had spent little of the money Helford had given to them they knew it would not last long once they had to pay for a roof and their food and for travel.

Something had to be done – and done quickly. The only thing they knew was that until they were told by Helford that it was safe for them to return, they had to stay in America.

The challenge had appealed to them both – to Randolph because it was matched by his temperament; to Frank because it was a sudden and exciting transportation from everything he had known or even dreamed about, and yet he was sufficiently confident not to be awed by it. And both had come to terms with exile, and the cause of it, which now they rarely discussed.

But challenge is stimulating only when it can be met. And at that moment neither knew how to meet it.

That evening they sat in the parlour with Tom Hogarth and his buxom quick-smiling wife Louise and aired their problem. From his reaction it was obvious that Hogarth had already considered it.

'The only thing you're trained for,' he said to Randolph, 'is the management of an English small-time shipping operation. You've started some trade for your boss and I guess it could

118

grow – there's plenty of talk about a future corn trade with England. But without a lot of money to play with you'll not make a fortune. If you could do the buying I guess that'd be different. But you're just negotiating for someone else to sell it to your boss. Commission ain't good enough. You've got to be getting your fists on the dough. I'd take a chance and fund you, but I'm committed right now, at least for that sort o'money – and it's big money. And you –' he turned to Frank '– you ain't trained for any o'this stuff. You're gonna be trailing your pal around and contributing nothing. But I've been thinking about it. One thing both of you understand is farming – stock, an' horses, an' land. Right?'

They nodded. But Randolph said: 'We can't start farming without cash. You know how much we've got. There are very few farms for lease around here, and our money certainly wouldn't buy enough cattle to make any sort of living.'

'Sure – not around here,' Hogarth said. 'But you don't know much about this great country, son. You ain't got the picture. There's a whole new world out there in the west.' He waved his big hand vaguely, expansively. 'How much d'you know about that?'

They looked at each other.

'Not much,' Frank admitted. 'Indians, buffalo, Longhorns – and some very wild country. That's about all I know – except that it's a long way.'

'Right – right – and right,' Hogarth grinned. 'An' you can multiply all that a hundred times. But land is cheap, son. The injuns ain't selling it – we're taking it. I ain't sure about the morals o'that, but it ain't your worry either. You can buy good grassland for twenty cents an acre, and you buy it by the square mile. Or you can lease it from the railway companies or the mineral prospectors for next to nothing. And you can buy cattle pretty cheap out there, too – if you understand 'em. It's a trade that jumps up and down like a jackrabbit – railhead price for a steer can be as low as ten dollars or high as forty. With a trade like that there's dough to be made if you buy right, sell right – and know what you're doing in between – and you're tough.'

119

Randolph said: 'If it's that good, Tom, why don't you get out there and start a business?'

Hogarth shook his head and his wife chuckled.

'He knows nothing about it,' she said. 'Any fool could sell him a steer, and it'd die tomorrow. And he wouldn't know the first thing about land and what to do with it.'

'That's right, son,' Hogarth said. 'I'd be a sucker. And I don't much care for the thought of all them injuns. Maybe a lot've been pushed into the reservations. But a lot more are still riding loose around the plains, and I don't like what I hear about 'em. I don't much care for one-horse towns, either. I'm a city man, son. Me an' Louise, we like to be good and comfortable. I ain't young enough for that sort of business. But a coupla fellers like you – that'd be different. You know about farming, and you look like you could handle yourselves – y'know what I mean? It's rough out there, son; rough fellers and rough country. But there's fortunes to be made, if you've got the guts and you know one end of a steer from another.'

Again they looked at each other; but this time with a spark of excitement.

'We don't understand your sort of farming,' Frank said. 'We don't understand big prairies and virgin grassland, or your sort of cattle.'

Hogarth raised an eyebrow.

'You understand English cattle,' he said. 'Are you telling me you can't learn our ways good an' quick, if there's dough at the end of it?'

'No. I'm not telling you that,' Frank retorted. 'I'm telling you it might not be as easy as you think. One sort of farming isn't always like another.'

'A steer's a steer. Grass is grass. You don't make money outa keeping cattle – you make money outa buying 'em and selling 'em. And you don't make money outa growing grass – you make it outa feeding it to cattle. Ain't that what you do in England? What's different?'

Randolph said quickly: 'No difference – except in the buying and selling. That we'd have to learn. Learning isn't difficult – but it could be expensive. And money is what we don't have to risk.'

'Money is always at risk if you use it to make more money,' said Hogarth. He leaned forward. 'Tell y'what I'll do, son. You get yourselves out there. Get jobs riding trail or punching cattle or fencing – anything – there's plenty of work. Learn fast. Then write me and tell me what you reckon to need to turn five thousands bucks into twenty thousand inside two years. If you reckon you can do the job, and I like the sound of it, I'll do a partnership deal with the two of you. I'll put up the dough. Is that a deal?'

It was. They were on their feet, pumping each others' hands excitedly. Where should they go? Kansas, said Hogarth. Railroad to New York, then Chicago, then Kansas City. After that they'd be on their own. Keep away from women and Indians, keep away from gambling and liquor, get Winchesters and learn to use them. He loaned them rail fares and the price of two horses.

Three days later they were gone.

They stayed in Kansas City for two weeks, watching the cattle driven through the pens at the railhead, watching the sellers and buyers, listening to the bargaining and the strange rapid-fire language of the auctioneers – so different from home sale-rings; learning what sort of cattle brought the best prices, talking to the men who handled them and to the agents, taking in the gossip about Dodge and Abilene and Wichita, about the plains to the west and the hard country between Kansas and the Texas Panhandle and the new ranches further over in Colorado. They heard about the Chisholm Trail and the great drives of a thousand, two thousand cattle. And they heard about the Kiowas and Comanches and the way the Indians fought, how they treated their white enemies and how they were treated in their turn; and about sidewinders and coyotes and mosquitoes and buffalo.

They took rooms in a small hotel, paying as little as they could, spending as little as they could on food. They kept a low profile in the saloons, watching the honest men, the fools and the thieves, the gamblers and the women, staring covertly at those men who carried guns stuck in belts beneath their long coats. They changed their eastern clothes for check shirts, rawhide boots and buckskins, and bought wide-brimmed hats to keep the sun out of their eyes. They bought a Winchester rifle each, and a belt and cartridges, and felt self-conscious carrying their new weapons.

On the fourth day they saw a gunfight.

Two men, both wearing several days' stubble on their faces and with mean eyes and dirty shirts and stained leather, played poker, squatting in the dust in a corner of one of the stockyard pens. Other men watched, Randolph and Frank among them. Neither heard the start of the argument, but quickly realized that one man had accused the other of cheating.

Suddenly both were on their feet, backing away from each other, and the spectators scattered when they saw the hate in the bloodshot eyes, and one man's hand dart for a gun under his coat and the other was quicker, a blur of hand and metal and a twist of a body as the gun roared and the first man jack-knifed backwards into a cloud of dust with a half-scream choked as he vomited blood. Then he was kicking on the ground, quivering, then still, his eyes open and blind in the sun.

Neither Englishman spoke. Sweating with fear, they watched the victor holster his gun, heard him proclaim hoarsely: 'Yuh seed him – he went fer his gun – he drawed first –' Then the crowd closed in, the body was dragged out of the pen, and Randolph and Frank walked away. Both felt sick.

'God – this is a hell of a country,' one said. 'I've heard about it, but I didn't know it really happened – like that.'

Back in their hotel they looked at each other. Randolph said: 'I think we ought to get guns – revolvers.'

Frank shook his head.

'No. If we had them we couldn't use them – did you see how fast he was? We couldn't do that in a million years. Better not to have one. And better to keep out of trouble all the time. If we don't have a gun, we won't look as if we want trouble.'

Little more than a week later they were on the train to Dodge City, bracing themselves against the hard seats as the coaches jolted at twenty miles an hour across the wide expanses of grass and scrub. At Dodge they climbed stiffly down to the dusty earth and had their first glimpse of the sun-baked dirt streets and hastily constructed clapboard buildings of the bustling, growing cow town.

They took rooms in a small hotel next door to a gambling saloon, paid in advance the shifty-eyed greasy-skinned clerk at the desk, and were conscious of his stare as they clattered up the stairs, shouldering the leather bags that contained their worldly goods, and opened doors onto cheap furniture and faded blankets.

The next day they walked the streets, watching closely the way the cattle men rode their horses – long-legged, lithe, not rising to the trot but apparently maintaining equilibrium, tirelessly, just out of the saddle whenever the horses broke from a walk; different from the style they knew. And they saw that there were many more guns than had been in evidence in Kansas City, and that a few men wore their holsters low on their thighs instead of directly against their belts, and that none troubled to conceal their weapons.

But not all men were obviously armed. The people who walked through the dust and along the raised boards fronting the buildings were a motley collection of all ages, including women in travel-soiled skirts and shawls and narrow bonnets tied beneath their chins, and men with beards and long hair, and children, too. The wooden buildings were crude, with clumsily painted signs over bars, hotels and stores. Citizens and cattlemen from the ranges mixed along the sidewalks and dodged the waggons and horses on the broken-surfaced streets.

The stockyard was less than a quarter the size of the vast spread at Kansas City, but still had sufficient penning for a thousand or more head at a time. It was quiet now, with the auctioneers' platforms deserted. Children clambered over the rails, and a dozen strong ponies wandered loose in a pen, kicking up dust.

The two men turned and sauntered back towards one of the three or four main streets. They passed a small, shabby hotel with a board nailed above the door proclaiming it to be Trail's End. Beside the door a wide sash window was open and a girl leaned out, smiling at them. Her face was heavily rouged and her lips bright red, and she called: 'Hi, fellers – wanna come in fer a drink?' Randolph muttered, 'A drink – and then what?' and they grinned at each other, winked at the girl, and walked on, along the rough street, and watched a ragged family, a man and woman and two ten or twelve-year-old children, clamber down from a covered waggon behind two horses. The man held the horses and the woman and children climbed to the board walk and went into a drapery store. The waggon was grimy and there was a tear in one corner of the canvas cover stretched over the hoops.

Across the street, under a wooden canopy, was a saloon. They peered through a window at the dim interior, then pushed through the swing doors. Inside was a long bar with several hard-eyed men leaning against it, while others sat at tables. They ordered two beers from a bald-headed bartender with a long scar across his forehead. The man eyed them curiously, took their money and said: 'Strangers in town, huh?'

They nodded and Frank said: 'It's a busy town. There are a lot of strangers here, aren't there?'

The bartender stared at them.

'Ain't heered any of 'em talk like you. Where're yuh from, friend?'

'England,' said Frank. 'You know where that is?'

The man grinned and extended a grimy hand across the bar. They shook it solemnly.

'Sure I know. Hell of a long ways – 'cross the sea. Atlantic – thet right? What in hell're yuh doin' here?'

'Looking for work,' Randolph told him. 'With cattle.'

The man's sharp eyes inspected them.

'Plenty o' thet in Dodge,' he said. 'If yuh know what

y'doin'. Don' look t'me as if you guys hev done much so far – thet right?'

'Back home – a lot,' Randolph said. He raised his glass and drank. 'What else happens here – except the cattle business?'

The man grinned wickedly.

'Most anythin' a feller wants happens here. Women, gamblin', drinkin', fightin' when the cow hands come into town. Ornery things too – lot of folk movin' into Dodge City now the railroad's here. Suits me – good fer trade. Some of 'em even tryin' to reform the town – needs it, I guess. New church jes' bin built. Elections fer the town council next month. New taxes afore long, too – pay fer a school fer the kids. Too many settlers outa town, though – all lookin' fer land. This is cattle country, friends – an' cattle men don' like ploughin' an' corn an' fences. Bin some trouble now an' then. Guess there'll be more. Them settlers jes' don' ketch on to our ways – poor folk, too – no money t'spend.'

'Who owns the land?' Frank asked.

The man refilled their glasses without being asked.

'No one owns it – least, no one used to. Jes' buffalo an' Indian country. Cattlemen ranged right on over it, staked their claims, 'n sorted out their diff'rences best they could. With a gun, often – though there's a bit less of thet nowadays. Government agents hev moved in, takin' a lot of the land an' trying' to stop trouble. Some of 'em make more'n they stop. An' the railway company too – they grabbed land – lot of it. More'n they'll ever need fer railroads. They lease it fer grazin' cattle. Pardon me, gents – I got customers.'

He walked along the bar to three men who had just come in and were noisily demanding attention. They were tough, wide-shouldered men with ragged hair beneath big, battered hats, and wore stained leather waistcoats and patched trousers. One was bearded and the other two had long down-turned moustaches and sallow skins and looked Spanish.

Randolph and Frank drank their beers, left money on the bar and went out into the bright sunlight and the dust. They walked a hundred yards to the town centre where two main streets crossed and saw a livery stable, glanced at each other, nodded, and turned towards it.

There they bought two geldings, a bay and a black, bargaining and feeling pleased when they showed they understood horses and persuaded the owner to drop his price. Two much-used saddles and harness were next, and they paid in advance to leave the horses there overnight.

'We're looking for work,' they told the man. 'Anything with cattle.'

He was thin and rangy, with straggly brown hair and a skin lined and tanned to the colour of the saddles they had just bought.

'Where'y'from?'

'Boston – out east. Before that – England.'

'Jesus. Waddya come here fer?'

'Work. We worked on a farm in England – with cattle. Know anybody who wants a couple of men?'

'Nope. T'morrer, mebbe. Where could a guy find yuh?'

'Bay Horse – till we find somewhere cheaper.'

'Ain't nuthin cheaper in town.' The man grinned at them with crooked teeth. 'An' whatever they're chargin' yuh is too much. If anyone comes askin' I'll send 'em. OK?'

'OK,' Randolph nodded. 'Thanks.'

They walked along the dusty street, feeling taller. They had horses, rifles and wide-brimmed hats. They began to feel like cattlemen.

Three days later they were cattlemen.

A tall, thin, lazy-eyed man, newly shaven and better dressed than most, walked along the boards and turned into the hotel.

'Hear you've gotten a coupla rookies staying,' he told the clerk in a slow, and easy voice.

The clerk blinked; jerked a thumb towards the stairs.

'Twelve and thirteen,' he said, and watched the thin man nod and cross the hall.

It was nine o'clock in the morning, and Frank and Randolph were still in their rooms. The stranger knocked on the

126

doors, and both men appeared on the landing at the same moment.

'Name's Hank Whitlock,' he said. He surveyed the two men facing him, noting their height, their breadth of shoulder, their muscular arms. 'You the two guys wantin' work?'

They nodded together.

'I'm told you got horses an' you ride well. Ever ridden trail?'

'No,' Randolph said. 'We're new out here. But we're used to cattle. And we can learn.'

'I got five hundred head o' young steers an' some cows, an' I need two more men fer a drive back along the Arkansas river t'my place in Colorado. Pay's thirty bucks. Take two, mebbe three weeks. Want it?'

'We want it,' Randolph said. 'When do we start?'

'Three o'clock train brings up the last of 'em. Then we move. Waddya called, friends?'

They told him, and shook hands.

Before sundown they were riding west along the river bank with Hank Whitlock, eight other men, a herd of Longhorns and a chuck waggon.

They spread out gradually, the dust clouds rising in the still air. Hank Whitlock rode out in front, following the well-used trail and keeping within sight of the river. Behind him was the chuck waggon, jolting, lurching, creaking, with six horses strung out as spare mounts in case of accidents and as replacements for the ranch stables. Then came the herd in a giant, widening, rippling vee, point riders directing the leading steers, flank riders following and, in the thickest dust clouds, the drag riders picking up the stragglers, keeping the whole massive column moving from behind.

They rode until sundown. Then Whitlock stopped the drive and they made camp beneath a scattering of trees and alongside rock outcrop a hundred yards from the river. Shorty Owen, who was at least six and a half feet tall with a long mournful face beneath a high-crowned hat that took his overall height to well over seven feet, turned the chuck waggon to line up to the north star, ensuring that if tomorrow

127

was sunless the trail's direction could still be checked. Then he dropped the wooden flap at the rear of the waggon, and Pete Peterson and Hoppy Halton gathered brushwood and lit a fire for the iron cooking pot and the kettle as well as for warmth as the night chill crept across the plain.

The other men were curious about their new trail hands, and questions about Boston and England came quickly as they sat around the fire eating beans, potatoes and a thick beef stew and drinking strong sweet coffee. Then Whitlock allocated the watch – two men constantly riding around the cattle, on the look-out for Indians, rustlers, strays or coyotes, each night rider patrolling for two hours. Frank drew the second watch of the night, Randolph the third, and they recognized the wisdom of their introduction to the job in the company of an experienced man. Then they unwrapped their newly-bought bedrolls and stretched out on the hard ground with the rest for the first part of the night, until they were called for their watches.

At dawn Whitlock roused the camp and within an hour the herd was moving again. He had watched the two newcomers closely the previous evening as they had ridden flank where any mistakes they made could be seen and quickly corrected. Now he sent them back to ride drag, and they soon realized that this unpopular task was a rooky's initiation. As the sun climbed the sky the dust swirled up from two thousand hooves and hung in the hot air, clinging to their faces and getting into their throats. They tied sweat bands across their mouths and narrowed their eyes as they criss-crossed behind the herd, nudging lagging cattle forward, cracking whips across the flanks of strays.

By nightfall their legs and backs were aching and their hands showing blisters. They joined the group around the chuck wagon, and Randolph said to a wide-shouldered rider with close-cropped hair and a long scar across his forehead: 'Cass – how long does it take a man to get used to this? I feel as if I've been trampled.'

The man, whose name was Cassidy, grunted. He was as tired as the rest and his temper was not the sweetest.

'Depends how tough y'are. Don't tell me yore thinkin' o' quittin' this early.' He raised his voice to ensure the others heard him.

Randolph shrugged.

'I'm not quitting, sooner or later. Forget it.'

Cassidy turned to Frank. 'How 'bout yore friend? You don't look as if yuh'll be ridin' with us t'morrer, pardner.'

Frank, like the others, had just come back from the river where he had ducked his head in the water and washed away the day's dust. He pushed fingers through his wet hair and grinned.

'I'll be riding. Certainly wouldn't like to walk, anyway.'

'I'll give yuh both three days,' Cassidy said unpleasantly. 'Anybody take a bet with me?'

The others shuffled forward to the cooking pot with their tin plates and mugs. 'I'll give you a coupla bucks on thet, Cass. These guys ain't quitters,' one said.

Hank Whitlock leaned against a wheel of the chuck waggon and said: 'I'll rule your bet outa order. Find sump'n else, Cass. Nobody's dropping outa this drive. Keep your dough in y'pants.'

The incident passed and was forgotten. After the meal the men squatted around the fire, yarning and boasting and playing poker. Neither Randolph nor Frank understood the game and watched, trying to pick up the rules. The first watch came in and dismounted, heaving their saddles off the horses, and two more men rode away into the darkness. More coffee was poured into the tin mugs by the lugubrious Shorty. Presently Randolph stood up and said: 'If I don't get some sleep I'll never make my watch.'

He crossed out of the flickering ring of firelight to his saddle and pulled his bedroll down, walking back to lay it near the fire. He rolled it out, sat on it and began to take off his boots. Then a voice rapped: 'Hey – Randy – look out – rattler –' and he jerked to his feet, spinning, searching the darkness. He had never seen a rattlesnake but knew their reputation. He backed slowly away from the bedroll, then heard one of the men laugh, and others join in.

He turned slowly, looking at them, forcing a grin.

'OK. So I'm green. Trouble is, the next time somebody says that to me, I mightn't take any notice. Then someone else'll have to ride drag tomorrow.' His eyes sought Cassidy, for he had recognized the voice.

The scar-faced rider said: 'One passenger more or less – what's the difference?'

Frank propped himself up on one elbow.

'I've seen enough to know there are no passengers out there at the back of that herd,' he said in his soft, soothing Devon accent. 'I'll say one thing about riding trail – a man learns fast.'

'Think yuh know it all already?' Cassidy grunted.

'No. But I'm on my way,' Frank grinned at him, trying to defuse the situation.

Randolph said: 'I'm on my way to sleep.' He sat down on his bedroll again.

Cassidy clipped a newly-rolled cigarette between his lips.

'Better be quiet, boys,' he mocked. 'There's a guy over there can't take it.'

'Aw, quit it, Cass,' one of the riders growled. 'Leave him alone. He ain't hurtin' yuh none.'

'He's lookin' like he wouldn't mind doin' jes thet,' the rider named Pete chuckled, deep in his throat.

Cassidy said: 'Ain't nuthin' on yore mind, friend, is there?' He dragged a match across his leather boots and lit his cigarette, his eyes hard on Randolph.

'Sleep,' said Randolph, very quietly. 'And the sooner the better.' But he sat on his bedroll without any further move to prepare for it.

On the other side of the fire a rider pulled a harmonica from his vest pocket and began to play it. Somebody said: 'Aw shucks, yuh noisy sonofabitch – we kin get along without thet.' Another man muttered: 'It'd be orlright if we knew what he's a'playin'.' And a third began to hum tunelessly as the harmonica player paused for breath. But they were all watching Cassidy.

The scar-faced rider stood up, stretching his legs.

'Guess I feel like sleepin' meself,' he said. 'Trouble is, I'm on next watch. Guess I'll change thet with m'tired friend there. How's about thet, pardner? Yuh reckon yuh came to learn our ways. Ain't goin' t'be easy. No point in goin' t'bed – watch'll change afore long. An' yore on it.'

Without moving Randolph said: 'I'm not. Mine's the last one before sun-up. And I don't feel like changing.'

'Stand up 'n tell me thet.' The flickering firelight threw the rider's long shadow across Randolph's bed.

Frank's voice said softly, clearly: 'Don't do it, Cass.' Shorty took the words as a threat instead of a warning and eased himself in front of Frank, muttering: 'Best keep outa the way, Frank. Leave 'em t'settle it.' Frank looked up at the tall man and shrugged.

In the darkness, beyond the reach of the firelight, Hank Whitlock sat propped against the trunk of a tree, watching his men. He knew Cassidy well; the man was a tough drover and most of the other men acknowledged him as physical boss in the bunkhouse and out on the trail. Now there were newcomers, and Cassidy had sensed some quality in the one with the dark hair and straight gaze. Instinct drove him to assert himself.

Still Randolph did not move. He said: 'You won't hear me any better if I stand up. I don't feel like changing.'

'Then I'll persuade yuh t'feel like it – an' have some respect fer folk who know a lot more'n you do,' Cassidy growled. He stepped forward as he spoke, grabbed the corner of Randolph's bedroll and heaved it up and away, throwing Randolph sideways on one elbow.

Randolph rolled away, looking up at the man with the scar. Somewhere in his mind Mark Helford's voice said don't raise your hand to any man – you don't know your own strength; and he deliberately relaxed the tired muscles across his shoulders. The bedroll lay three paces away. He put his hands flat on the grass and pushed himself to his knees, then to his feet, walked across to the roll, picked it up and shook the dust out of it. Cassidy loomed against the firelight and the shadows of the other men, tense, watching. A coyote's bark sobbed somewhere beyond the trees. Cassidy's voice said: 'Tell me yore ridin' out next watch.'

Randolph, back half-turned, laid his roll on the trampled grass.

'I'm sleeping next watch,' he said. He heard Helford's voice again, and saw a man in a narrow lane, lying against a house wall with his head twisted sideways, terribly, in yellow lantern light against the dark.

Then Cassidy was close alongside him, pushing out a big hand, turning him round, snarling: 'Yore ridin', friend – make no mistake – yore ridin',' and Randolph saw the big hand swinging back and the fingers curling, and the muscles jerked across his back and he swayed away from the punch, saw the man's other hand flash out, felt fingers dig into his shoulder positioning him for the next blow. The dim lane alongside the Brandy Cask, so far away in Devonshire, and the still, distorted figure lying in it, blurred the face of the man in front of him and he jerked his head sideways away from the bony knuckles hammering at him. The blow ran along the side of his head, jarring, and the pain went through him and the vision was gone and before the fist could be pulled back he had the wrist in both his hands, turning, twisting, stooping and heaving it across his shoulder and the arm with it and then the whole body flying across his back, legs jerking upwards. Cassidy cartwheeled and the men scrambled out of the way as he hit the ground close to the fire, the breath exploding out of him.

Randolph straightened, watchful. Frank breathed to Shorty 'I told him not to, didn't I?' Pete muttered 'Christ a'mighty!' Then Hank Whitlock detached himself from his tree and moved swiftly and easily into the ring of firelight and said: 'That's enough. I don't want any invalids this early in the drive. Cass – get up. Randy – relax. There'll be no more fighting.'

Cassidy rolled over, pushing himself upright, holding the arm that, for one brief moment, had been used to sling the weight of his body. He swayed slightly, clearly bewildered.

His eyes searched for Randolph, but the rancher was between them.

'Take it easy,' Whitlock said. His voice was flat, hard. 'Like I told you – that's enough.' He drew the two men together. 'Now – whether it's to your liking or not, two things are gonna happen. First you'll shake hands. Right now. C'mon.' His clear eyes flicked from one to the other. Randolph nodded briefly, warily. Cassidy tried to outstare his boss, swallowed hard, shrugged, stuck out his hand. Randolph matched his grip. They stood, facing each other, easing the tension slowly. Whitlock said: 'Now the second thing. You'll take the next watch, Randy, like Cass said. Not 'cos he said it – I'm saying it now. And you, Cass, will go with him. You'll do it together, and if either of you comes back with a scratch I'll fire the other an' horsewhip him outa camp. OK?'

The three men stood, close together, still. A horse whinnied somewhere in the dark beyond the fire. One of the watchers shifted tense leg muscles.

Cassidy growled: 'One condition, boss.'

'No conditions,' snapped Whitlock.

'Gimme a chance,' Cassidy retorted. 'I'll go, and there'll be no fightin', if Randy'll show me how he pulled thet wrestlin' trick.'

The men around the fire stirred, recognizing the peace offering. Randolph nodded, still wary.

'OK. It's no secret. I'll show you.'

Whitlock's hard mouth widened into a grin.

'Wait till tomorrow. Mebbe we can all learn it.'

He walked back to his tree, sat on the ground and leaned back, tipping his hat over his forehead. From beneath the wide brim he watched the men. When he looked at Randolph his eyes were still and thoughtful.

Half an hour later the watch changed. The wiry, diminutive Blondie Wilkins rode in and said: 'Them dogies is a bit restless down by th' rocks in th' river bend. Reckon there's a rattler around. An' there's a couple coyotes up on th' hill.'

Cassidy nodded, swung up into the saddle he had already secured on his horse. Randolph gave a last tug at the girth

133

strap, mounted, moved up alongside him. Neither man looked at the other as they rode slowly away from the camp.

For a few minutes they rode in silence, looking across the backs of the herd. Many of the cattle were lying down; others stood quietly, chewing, grunting and stirring occasionally in the darkness. Beyond trees to the east, a half moon was rising. A bird hooted nearby. Cassidy reined in and leaned forward in his saddle, watching the moon.

He said: 'Haven't bin put on m'back fer a long time. Then it took two guys t'do it. Thet was a smart trick yuh pulled. Where'd yuh learn it?'

'Back home – England.'

'Know more tricks like thet?'

'A few.'

Silence then; until Cassidy reached for tobacco and cigarette papers.

'Guess yore not afraid o'many folk, are yuh?'

'No.'

'Yore sure harder'n I reckoned.' He spilled tobacco into his hand and began to roll it. 'Bin in trouble with th' law, any place?'

Randolph watched a calf nuzzle its dam, looking for milk. The moon was brighter now.

'Not that I know about.'

Cassidy finished rolling the cigarette and put it to his mouth.

'None o' my business, anyway. How old are yuh?'

'Twenty.'

'Jesus. I took yuh fer twenty-five, six, older mebbe. Yuh've done a lotta livin', I guess.'

'Some. Lot more to do.'

Cassidy flicked a match with his thumbnail; lit his cigarette. The flame caught his eyes, narrowed beneath the slanted brim of his hat.

'Yuh've come t'th' right country fer it. Smoke?' He held out his tobacco roll.

Randolph looked at it.

'I've never rolled one. Show me.'

Presently they rode on again, listening to the night noises, watching the cattle, their cigarette smoke hanging and curling in the still air. After a while Randolph realized that the ache in his legs and back had almost gone.

When they rode back, dismounted, and woke Frank and Pete to take over, Hank Whitlock opened his eyes and watched them. Mostly he watched Randolph. Then he went back to sleep.

For nearly two weeks the Bozeman trail led them westwards. For most of the days the sun burned down and a hot south wind drove dust into the faces of the riders and covered the cattle with a grey, gritty blanket. As they neared the Colorado border, having left the river and with the cattle short of water, they saw half a dozen Indians watching them from a low ridge. Presently the men mounted their ponies and began to ride parallel with the herd, a quarter of a mile to the north. Whitlock, Cassidy and Blondie Wilkins detached themselves and, rifles loosened in their saddle holsters, rode out between the Indians and the herd. Pete said to Frank: 'Kiowas. Not likely t'give us any trouble. But th' boss is jest warnin' 'em.' After an hour the Indians moved away and presently were out of sight.

The border country was arid. They followed the faint trail which gave them one water-hole a day. The heat pressed in, and then clouds rolled across the horizon and just before dawn they heard thunder roll and scrambled to pack the camp before the rain drove across the prairie and lighting split the morning sky. They rode around the cattle, quietening them; but close to a rock outcrop lightning arced to the ground, hissing as the thunder exploded above. A group of fifty or more steers panicked, breaking for open country, tails extended, wild-eyed and bellowing. It took half an hour's hard riding to bring them back, leaving the men drenched and exhausted.

The Whitlock ranch house was rough-timbered, long and strong, with a big barn and stabling attached to it, a bunk house and cover for the waggons nearby, and some well-fenced corrals. There were few trees, but a good water-hole had been tapped beside the house, and the range around was watered by a river and two tributary streams. Whitlock lived there with his tall, easy-talking wife Mary, a young son and a daughter of eighteen – and having glimpsed her, both Randolph and Frank were delighted when Whitlock kept them on the payroll for the rest of the summer. They lived in the bunkhouse with six other men, sweaty blankets on the wooden beds, equally noxious saddles on the walls, and a smoky wood-fired stove at one end, and spent the next two months learning to cut out cattle from the herd, roping and throwing calves and yearlings, branding, repairing fences.

They also learned quickly that middle west ranchers were not in favour of much social contact between their daughters and their hired hands. Whitlock's daughter Liza was slender and fair-haired and elfin-faced and attractive to any man – particularly in a society where women, except for the prostitutes who haunted the saloons in the nearby small town of Rockford, were relatively few in numbers. It did not occur to Randolph or Frank to wonder why the other men showed no particular interest in her and, singly or together, they went out of their way in their first few weeks at the ranch to talk with her.

Then one evening they saw her near the well and sauntered across the bare, stony ground and leaned on a fence and talked about the day and the work and persuaded her to ask questions about themselves. She was willing enough, for only three generations before her own family had emigrated from Gloucester and the chance to learn something about England from men who had left that country only recently was too good for her to miss. For half an hour they talked, and then Randolph and Frank carried leather buckets of water back to the ranch house for her and they bade her goodnight.

As they walked away Hank Whitlock eased himself through the door behind them and called them back. He leaned casually on a hitch rail in front of the house, his shadow long in the evening sun, and said: 'Now I hope you two guys ain't gonna take this any way personal, but I have to tell you I don't take kindly t'hired men talking over-long to my daughter. I 'preciate you ain't meaning no harm, but that's th' way I feel about it.'

Frank and Randolph looked at each other, momentarily taken aback.

'We certainly did not mean any harm, Mr Whitlock,' Frank said. His face flushed slightly. 'We were only talking about ordinary things – she was interested in hearing about England, and –'

Whitlock held up a hand.

'Mebbe. Mebbe. Don't make no difference. Like I say, it's nothing personal. I'd say the same to any hired hand. So I'm gonna ask that from now on you just extend th' usual courtesies any man should to a lady, and then leave it alone. OK?'

Randolph said flatly: 'You pay the wages, Mr Whitlock. We'll respect your wishes – just as we respect your daughter.'

Whitlock's lazy, easy eyes never wavered. He said quietly: 'That's just fine then. Goodnight t'you both.'

He watched them thoughtfully as they walked away. When they were out of sight he turned and went back into the ranch house kitchen where his wife was preparing the following day's food. For a few moments he watched her.

Presently he said: 'Just spoke t'the two new hands. Them guys from England. They bin paying a bit too much attention to Liza. I told 'em I don't like hired hands doin' that, an' they took it. Won't happen again.'

She nodded, looking sideways at him as her fingers worked through a basket of vegetables.

'It's wise. But they're two well-behaved fellas. Always courteous. They won't give Liza any trouble.'

'Don' aim t'let 'em,' Whitlock said easily. 'But they wouldn't be the sorta guys I'd welcome trouble with. The fair one's tough but quiet. It's the dark one, Randy, who could be a real handful. On the trail he put Cass on his back quick's a lightnin' flash with some wrestling trick. And sure's I'm born he was really holding hisself back like he was afraid t'let go and really fight. Reckon he coulda hurt Cass real bad if I hadn't stopped it. And the way he looks at folk is strange –

137

and I ain't sure I like it. He never takes his eyes off a guy. There's something deep inside him. I just wonder why he's in these parts – if he's running from something.'

'He's a good worker,' Mary Whitlock objected. 'You said that yourself.'

'Sure. Fer a greenhorn he's pretty good. They both are. Worth paying. And they don't carry guns – 'cept Winchesters, o'course. That's another thing. When we were driving them cattle, one night the boys started throwing bits o' rocks and branches and shootin' at 'em, and betting on who was best. Randy cleaned 'em out. Never seen a guy shoot much better in m'life. But he don't boast about it. Don't talk much at all, really. He's a different sorta guy t'all the others.'

Mary dried her hands.

'He's a good worker,' she persisted. 'Stop worrying about him. He won't be around too long, anyway. Come the fall you'll be paying several men off.'

And when the fall came, with the light fading earlier each evening, Whitlock paid them two hundred and sixty dollars each and they rode to the nearest town. Within a week they had picked up another herd for a drive back into Kansas, and a month later rode into the town they had left earlier in the summer, no longer rookies but hardened and experienced cattle handlers, their legs toughened and their skin burned by the sun and wind, their hands calloused by rope and leather. They went back to the straggle-haired owner of the livery stable and bedded down in the loft above the horses for a dollar a week each.

The next night they ambled down the main street, pushed open the swing doors of the saloon, and walked straight into trouble.

With two glasses of rye whisky on their table and a thin cigar each, they watched a group clustered around a barrel-chested, stubble-chinned ox of a man with ginger-brown hair, whose harsh voice and raucous laughter echoed across the low-raftered room. A small, wiry whiskered man who might have been anywhere between fifty and seventy years old had pushed up to the bar and nudged into the back of one of the group who snarled over his shoulder: 'Watch yerself, runt. Yuh cain't be thet thirsty.'

The man shifted away from the group quickly, but the big man lurched forward.

'I didn't hear yuh 'pologise t'my pardner.' He pushed a finger at the small man who backed away.

'Thet's 'cos I didn't, Red. But no offence. It wur an accident.' The voice was low and nervous.

The big man grinned and poked his finger again.

'Accidents kin cost a guy dough – like rye fer me an' m'friends.' He leered at the bartender. 'Set 'em up, Billy-boy. Th' old timer's payin'.'

The small man bridled.

'I ain't payin' nuthin', Red. There's no call fer –'

Then he was in the air, his feet kicking clear of the ground, the group howling their laughter as the ginger-haired man held him aloft with two great hands, shook him, then hurled him away like a struggling bundle of rags, back across the floor and spreadeagled over the table where Randolph and Frank sat.

Neither carried guns, whereas the big man called Red had a Smith and Wesson strapped to his thigh. Both kept their hands well in view, stood up slowly, and helped the little man to his feet.

'Steady, friend. You hurt much?'

The big man lurched nearer, peering through the smoke.

'Hey – kid. Say somethin' agin, will yuh? What sorta talk's thet?'

Randolph stood loosely by the table. The warning lights were in his eyes. Frank hissed: 'Cool it.'

'I asked him if he was hurt much.' Randolph's voice was low and clear and suddenly the saloon was quiet.

The ginger head went back with a bellow of laughter.

'Hey fellers – listen to it. Yuh ever heared fancy talk like thet? "I arsked him if he wos hurt much."' He roared his laughter again at the attempt to imitate Randolph's English accent. 'Talk agin – c'mon – let's hear some more o'thet fancy talkin'.'

139

The little man who had crashed across their table whispered: 'Get out of here.' Randolph said to Frank: 'Come on – let's go.' They moved away from the table.

The big man roared: 'Hey – pimp with th' fancy talkin' – I'm doin' th' talkin' now.'

Frank kept walking. Randolph checked, turned, eyes burning; then moved again towards the doors. A man laughed and a girl giggled nervously. Suddenly the big man's right hand dropped, and he dragged his gun up. The giggle turned into a thin scream and the gunshot was deafening in the room and the bullet smashed into the wooden boards at Randolph's feet.

'Stay where yuh are, punk.' The hoarse voice cut through the smoke, no longer shouting but sharp and deadly.

Randolph stood still, hands well away from his sides, half-turned. Frank was already through the doors. Someone said: 'Hey, Red – he ain't got a gun – take it easy.' The big man snapped: 'I know he ain't. But he ain't walkin' out when I'm talkin'.' His gun levelled and two shots splintered the floor. Randolph jumped sideways, his hands wide from his body, palms outward. The big man bellowed: 'Go on, punk – dance. See if yuh kin dance like yuh kin talk.' Two more shots, and Randolph stood still, legs apart, the hate in his dark eyes. Another shot, and still he did not move, and the big man spun with his empty gun, snatched another from the man at his side, thumbed the hammer and fired again. The bullet grooved the side of Randolph's boot and the force twisted his foot. The man bellowed 'Dance, will yuh – dance – dance –' and the next shot hit Randolph in the lower leg. He spun, breath hissing, crumpling. The man fired again, and the bullet went wide. Randolph clutched his leg, leaping on the other foot back towards the door, falling, scrambling, heaving himself on the back of a chair, hitting the doors with his shoulder and tumbling on to the sidewalk. He staggered down the steps, fell onto the dirt street. Then the man burst through the doors behind him, bellowing drunken laughter, a bull whip in his hands, and the lash cracked across Randolph's body and he screamed once, rolling over and over, out of reach of the lash, scrabbling to his feet. The man came after him, the lash curling, cracking across Randolph's shoulders, round his chest. He spun with it, falling again, dragging himself onto hands and knees, trying to run. Twice more the lash found him, then men closed on either side of his tormentor, wresting the whip away, and Randolph scrambled and hopped away into the darkness, across the shafts of light from the windows and into darkness again, into a space between buildings, and lay on his face, quivering.

Frank, who had run blindly from the saloon back towards the stables where their Winchesters lay in the loft, saw him silhouetted against the windows and ran back, bending over him, touching him, afraid of what he might find.

Randolph twisted his head, grunted recognition.

'Help me to sit up.' He turned over, heaving himself on one elbow, agony on his face. 'The bastard hit me – in the leg. Come on – grab me – get me back to the stables.'

Frank helped him to his feet, feeling the blood running from his back through the torn shirt. He half carried him along the street, muttering through his teeth: 'I'll get the bastard. Soon as you're back there – I'll get him. I'll kill the bloody swine.'

Randolph hissed: 'No. For God's sake. If you get him with a Winchester it'll be murder. In this town you wouldn't stand a chance. They'd hang you. Get me back. We'll talk about it. Just get me back – do something – have a look at this leg.'

In the stables Randolph could not climb the ladder to the loft. Frank brought a lantern, lit it; grunted with fury when he saw the tattered shirt and the bloody weals. He dragged off the injured man's boot as gently as he could, slit the trouser leg with a knife, held up the lantern to examine the wound.

He said: 'You're OK. It creased you. I don't think the bullet's there. I'll get some water.'

He walked to the door and in the dimness found himself looking at the small wiry man with the grey moustache and side-whiskers.

'What the hell do you want?' he growled.

'Come t'see if I kin help any,' the little man said softly. 'Guess yuh might do with an extra hand.'

Frank said: 'If you know anything about bandaging, you can help.'

The man slid into the stables.

'Lived by meself fer twenty years. Guess I know 'bout bandages.'

Half an hour later, with Randolph's wounds washed and the calf of his leg bandaged with the cleanest cloths they could find, the man straightened and said: 'Guess I should introduce meself. Name o' Dan Smith. Called Tex, 'cos I came up here from Texas 'bout five years gone. Guess I'm sorry I caused yuh fellers all thet trouble. Who are yuh?'

Frank told him. Tex said: 'Yuh livin' here?'

'In the loft – till we get more work.' Frank looked down at Randolph who sat, pale and shivering slightly. 'Though it doesn't look as if that'll be as soon as we'd hoped.'

Tex said: 'Yuh know thet Red McLean – feller as shot up yer buddy?'

'No. Never seen him before.'

Tex shook his head sorrowfully.

'He's rough as they come. Mean as a coyote. I'm tellin' yuh. Real mean. If he ketches sight o'yuh after this, he'll make trouble agin. Yuh gotta git outa this town fer a time. I gotta cabin an' some cattle a day's ride north. Guess yuh orta move in – least till yore buddy's leg's fixed.'

Frank looked down at Randolph. Red McLean apart, he recognized the wisdom of the argument. The stable was no place to nurse an injured man. He said: 'What d'you think, Randy?'

Randolph said through clenched teeth: 'OK. Whatever you say.' He looked up at the little man. 'Thanks, Tex.'

Half an hour later they rode slowly out of town, Randolph between the other two men, his leg protected by a splint, Frank's hand on his elbow.

Randolph's leg healed quickly, although it remained stiff and awkward in the saddle for some time. The weals across his back and chest healed too, leaving white scars on his dark skin.

But his mind was more deeply scarred. He spent long periods sitting outside Tex Smith's cabin while Frank and the old man were working in the corral and round the buildings, staring across the plain; or leaning on the paddock fencing watching any Longhorns grazing nearby, but scarcely seeing them. Frank grew more concerned for him, for he understood him well; but Smith, with the experience of a lifetime in a violent land, counselled caution: 'Leave him be. A man needs t'come t'terms with hisself after sump'n like that – sure as hell.'

Tex Smith had scarcely done justice to his property in his initial description of it. Certainly he lived in a cabin; but it had three rooms and was well built in the shelter of trees. And around it was stabling for six, a store shed and covered accommodation for his buckboard and other equipment as well as for any sick animals. But all the buildings needed some sort of repair, and some of his fences were broken, giving the place a run-down air; yet around it were 2600 acres or more of reasonable grassland which, until a few years before, had been buffalo grazing ground, and a tributary of the Arkansas river provided water. He had bought the land with money he had made in a small Colorado gold strike in 1862 – and in what Frank began to suspect had been cattle rustling between Colorado and Texas in the following years. He was sixty-eight years old, smoked black tobacco in an old pipe that was rarely out of his mouth, and drank more than half a bottle of whisky a day – except on Sundays when, in deference to his Quaker upbringing in Missouri, he kept the whisky locked in a cupboard – 'so's the good Lord kin see I ain't fergettin' him'. He lived by himself, hiring men only for round-up, branding and drives to the railhead.

He provided food for Frank and Randolph and for their horses, and they worked for him without pay, repairing the buildings and fences when there was nothing else to do. They quickly gained the impression that as far as he was concerned the arrangement could continue indefinitely; after years of living alone he was glad of their company. And for their part they found him an engaging, wise and wily old rascal.

Four weeks after the Dodge shooting, Randolph limped out of the cabin's kitchen with the beans, ham and eggs he had cooked for their supper, set the plates on the rough table, and said:

'Need your advice, Tex. I've got to go after Red McLean. But I need a six-shooter – and someone who can teach me how to use it better than that bastard can use his.'

Frank's knife poised over his plate. He had known something like this was coming, sooner or later. Tex plied himself to the ham without lifting his head.

'Thet ain't sensible, son,' he said with his mouth full. 'Red's a killer, sure's I'm born. Folks say he's killed a dozen men. He'd fill yuh full o' lead afore yuh could get a hand t'yore gun. Ferget it. He ain't botherin' yuh none now.' He stuffed beans into his mouth, sat back and wiped his long moustache with the back of his hand.

Randolph poked at his food with a knife blade.

'I'm not arguing with you.' His voice was flat and hard. 'I'm telling you what I'm going to do. I just want your help. Tell me what sort of gun to get, and who'll teach me to handle it.'

'Ain't no sense in havin' some guy learn yuh how t'get killed,' Tex mumbled. 'Fellers like yuh an' Frank cain't shoot like Red. He's bin doin' it since he wus knee-high to a rattler. Ain't thet so?' He appealed to Frank.

Frank pushed his knife point into a slice of ham, looked at it; then glanced sideways at Randolph. He saw the mouth, the jawline, the eyes – above all, the eyes. He put the ham into his mouth; chewed silently. Then he leaned back.

'You won't change his mind, Tex. I know him better than you do – fifteen years better. He'll do what he wants to do. And I'll be helping him. If it had happened to me, I'd be talking just as he is. And don't worry. I wouldn't put a buck on McLean's chances.'

Tex said mournfully: 'I'm tellin' yuh – the guy's a killer. Plenty o'folks'll tell yuh.'

He fell silent as Randolph stood up, limped into the room he and Frank used as a bedroom; came out after a minute with a Winchester. He walked to the door, pushing cartridges into it.

'Frank – come outside. Throw a couple of cans – like we did on Hank Whitlock's place.'

Frank grinned suddenly and nodded. He came out of the kitchen with three empty cans, following Randolph outside into the fading evening light. The old man grunted, pushed back his chair and shuffled after them.

Outside Randolph worked a cartridge into the breech, held the gun loosely, one-handed, at his side; said: 'OK, Frank. Any time.'

Frank stepped forward; threw two cans, one high to the left, one low to the right. The Winchester flashed in the last of the sunlight as it came up and Randolph fired before it had reached his shoulder. The can with the low trajectory jerked and twisted away; then a second shot mingled with the echo of the first and the other can spun wildly just before it hit the ground. Randolph lowered the gun and Frank snapped, 'One more for luck,' and threw the third can hard and high, away across the setting sun. Randolph swung, the gun going with him as he slammed another cartridge into the breech and fired from the waist and the can split and rocketed skywards before falling back to earth.

Tex whistled through his few remaining teeth.

'Nice shootin', feller. Best I seed in a long time. Yuh could make yore livin' in a rodeo. Yuh never said yuh could handle a gun like thet.'

Randolph said: 'When I was a kid I once felled a young deer with a kind of throwing stick. And I could always shoot well around the estate at home. It just happens right for me. All I need is someone to teach me how to handle a Smith and Wesson or a Colt – and what sort of gun is best for me.'

Tex kicked at the ground with the toe of one dirty, dusty boot; then looked up from beneath straggling grey eyebrows.

145

'Guess if yuh've gotten an eye like thet, might jes' be able t'learn yuh sump'n meself.'

He went back into the cabin, disappeared into the room where his straw mattress lay on the floor in one corner. They heard him struggling with the mattress; then he returned carrying a gun belt. There was a gun in the holster which hung from it.

Randolph and Frank glanced at each other. Neither had seen Tex with a revolver before.

'This here's a Colt, son. Used t'be able t'shoot with it, purty good. Guess I don't see none too good now. But thet ain't no reason why I cain't learn yuh how t'use it.'

He slid the gun from its holster, flicked the cylinder and spun it. Satisfied that it was empty he held the belt out to Randolph.

'Put it on, son.'

Randolph pulled it round his waist, buckled it, letting the holster drop half way down his thigh.

The old man nodded. 'Tie it down.'

Randolph did so, dropping his hand to the holster, moving it on his leg until it felt in the right position. Tex nodded approvingly.

'Ain't much wrong with thet, son.' He held the gun out in his right hand, palm upwards, opening and closing his fingers around the butt, forefinger on the trigger, thumb on the hammer. 'Balance has t'be right. So's yuh kin keep it in y'hand, nice an' easy. If the barrel's draggin' it ain't right – yuh'll shoot low or waste time liftin' it. If it ain't heavy enough it'll jerk at the sky. My hand's 'bout the same size as yorn – mebbe it'll suit yuh.'

Randolph took the gun, turning it over in his hand, balancing it, feeling it. He slid it into the holster and out again. It came out smoothly, faster than he had expected. He looked down and realized the holster was oiled and polished, and knew that only men who needed to draw their guns very fast bothered to treat the inside of their holsters. He looked at the old man with new respect, and wondered.

'Feels pretty good to me,' he said.

146

'OK. We'll find out if it is t'morrer. Too dark now. I jes' cain't see a thing in th' dark. T'morrer we'll see what yuh kin make of it.'

The lessons started the next day, and Tex Smith took on a new dimension in their eyes. His little, wiry body crouched, twisted, smooth and fast as he demonstrated stance, turn, shooting straight ahead, shooting sideways left and right, always in balance, always moving – ' 'Cos if yuh stand still, yore a dead man'; raising the gun, not too far but far enough, levelling the barrel straight out of the holster, dropping the shoulder to bring gun and hand closer together; one-handed shooting, two-handed shooting, thumbing the hammer and fanning it with the other hand. It went on until Randolph was tired, all without a single shot being fired. Then, while Randolph rested his leg it was Frank's turn, and the old man's pride in his pupils glowed in his craggy face and his fading eyes.

At the end of the day he said: 'Th' gun ain't right. But we'll shoot with it come sunrise. Then I kin tell what yuh need.'

The next day they set small stones up on a fence, firing at them at ten paces, then fifteen, then twenty. Throughout Frank was the better shot; Randolph was consistently shooting over the targets. But when they asked the old man to use the gun he shook his head.

'Nope. I never told yuh. I kin hardly see where them pesky stones is. Kin hardly see th' fence at twenty yards. Warn't like thet once, though. Could see a sidewinder's eye – an' hit it. Hit a feller's gun hand afore he could reach his holster.' He chuckled suddenly, remembering.

Randolph said quietly: 'You were a gunfighter, I guess.'

Tex Smith looked sideways at him, his eyes narrowed against the sun.

'I bin a lot o' things – some I don' like to think about – some I do. Scoutin' in the war – enjoyed thet. Take a damn Yankee's head off afore he saw m'gun. Workin' through th' scrub at night, pickin' off th' stragglers – see th' rest runnin'.' He cackled, then the laugh faded. 'Man learned a lot o' lessons then. Had a girl – injun. Yankee bastards caught her.

When they'd finished she wus dead. Know what they done?'
He shuddered, but kept on talking. 'Dozen o' th' bastards.
Held her for each other. Then pegged her out on th' ground
an' cut off her breasts an' threw knives at her.' His eyes filled
up. 'Said it wus injun punishment. It warn't. Injuns would hev
skinned her an' left her for th' ants.'

Frank said: 'Did you catch them, Tex?'

The old man wiped a hand across his eyes.

'Caught three. Made 'em tell what they'd done.'

He stopped without saying how he had made them tell.
Another shudder passed across his body. Then he pushed the
past away.

'Guess I'll take a ride. Thet gun's right fer you, Frank. But
it's too light f'yore hands, Randy. Yuh want me t'get yuh
sump'n thet'll suit yuh?'

Randolph nodded. 'Yes – if you don't mind . . .'

Tex Smith blinked at him.

'If I minded, yuh wouldn't be here, son,' he muttered.
'Take it easy.'

They watched him ride away to the east, a small figure
under a big hat on a big horse; a shadow from a past that was
even more violent than the present.

When he returned two days later he carried one gun, a Colt,
complete with holster, belt and a large box of cartridges. He
handed the gun to Randolph who felt it, balanced it, weighed
it – and knew it was what he needed.

'Come sun-up, we'll see how good y'are,' Tex said. Then he
went back into his bedroom, reached under the mattress and
returned with his own gun and belt. He held them out to
Frank.

'Ain't gotten no use fer these, son,' he said slowly, as if the
words were an effort. 'Yore eyes kin see better'n mine. Guess
yuh'd make more use of it 'n I could, if yuh gotten into
trouble. I ain't givin' yuh nuthin' really – s'no good t'me.'

Frank took the gun carefully. He looked up to see the old
man peering at him.

Very quietly he said: 'I'll borrow it, Tex. It's just a loan.
And I'll look after it.'

148

'T'ain't fer yuh t'look after, son,' Tex growled. 'Pesky thing'll look after you – if yuh keep learnin' yerself.'

He turned and shuffled into his bedroom.

For another two months they worked on the old man's ranch until the buildings and fences were smart and the whole place took on a new, sharper look. And all the time they practised gunplay under his critical, fading eyes; facing each other with empty weapons, trying to out-draw and outflank each other; then loading up and shooting at tins, stones, sticks – anything one could throw for the other. And now it was Randolph who was the more accurate, his natural eye for a target producing results that brought cackles of approval from Tex and open admiration from Frank.

One evening, when Randolph was outside inspecting a lame calf, Tex nodded Frank into the kitchen.

'Time I told yuh, son,' he said. 'Yore pardner's th' best gun-slinger I ever seed – an' I seed a few. Better'n me – better'n I ever wus. He's fast an' he's on th' target. But Frank –' his hand went out to the younger man's arm in appeal '– try an' talk him outa goin' fer Red McLean. It's real dangerous, son. I keep watchin' him – kin see th' way he looks – like he's seein' thet ginger bastard ev'ry time he pulls his gun. But McLean's a killer, an' he's got a crowd o wild fellers always around him. Randy don' listen – I tell him but he don't listen. You tell him, son. He ain't jes' tacklin' Red – there's his boys too.'

Frank nodded.

'He won't be by himself, Tex,' he said quietly. 'Don't let it worry you.'

The old man looked at him, blinking, shaking his head.

'Yore as bad as he is,' he muttered. 'Don' rightly know what gets into a man.' Then he looked away, remembering. 'Guess I do, though. Dammit.'

Now it was late in the year, and the rains came and turned the ground around Tex Smith's buildings into a swamp. After that the wind brought snow, and the old man's winter stock of food

149

became essential, for the ride into Dodge became an uncomfortable and even hazardous journey. It was a harder winter than usual, with deep frosts and several snowfalls, and the three men made inroads into their stock of wood for the fire and their supply of kerosene, while the herd ranged across the plain, searching for grazing. Most of the steers would be ready for killing in the spring and would have to be driven to good grazing to fatten them after the winter and before they were taken to the railhead. Then yearlings would have to be bought to take their place, for there were not enough home-bred calves to replace them. And all the time, while they watched the weather and the cattle, Randolph stalked the buildings, his gun on his thigh, whirling, drawing, shooting at the shadow of Red McLean. Several times, when the weather cleared, they rode into the town for supplies; but when Randolph leaned on the rail of the livery stables and asked about McLean he was told the big man was out of town, working on a spread thirty miles or more to the south. He was also told that early in the winter McLean had killed a man who had pulled a knife on him in an argument over one of the saloon tarts, and that one of his 'boys' had shot and crippled a man who had tried to intervene – pleading successfully afterwards that he had fired to save McLean from being shot in the back.

There were plenty of witnesses, Randolph was told, to support the story – even if most of them were either McLean's friends or were too afraid of the group to speak against them.

When the spring came and the cattle were responding to the feel of the sun on their backs, they made plans for the three hundred mile drive across to Kansas City, preferring to risk the good chance of a higher price at the main railhead instead of relying on fewer buyers around Dodge. A few miles along the trail were four hundred cattle belonging to a neighbour; with Tex's similar number ready for market they formed a sizeable herd when the drive started, with ten men and the foreman from the neighbouring ranch as trail boss. Several of the riders noted the way the two men from the Smith ranch wore their guns and sensed the steel beneath their easy confidence, and made sure they did not risk too strong an argument around the evening trail fires.

In Kansas there was a good trade and three buyers took the whole herd for seven cents a pound on the hoof – a better figure than either owner had dared to hope for. Frank and Randolph could hardly believe their luck – Tex Smith would have more money than he had ever expected; they were as pleased as if they had made it for themselves, and laughed and joked as they anticipated his excitement when they arrived back to tell him that his Longhorns had sold for almost $30,000.

But now there were yearlings to buy, and they spent four days in Kansas City watching the young stock come in, buying pens of steers until, once again, they had mustered around 800 head for the return drive – 400 for each ranch. Randolph and Frank left $13,000 in Tex Smith's account at the City Bank, taking a few hundred dollars with them to supply the old man's cash needs. How much they would get out of the deal for themselves, after eight months living and working for Tex, they did not know and scarcely considered. As Frank said, they still had nearly $800 of their own money between them, and the old man had housed and fed them through the winter.

They rode back through the cold bright spring, the westbound trail taking them close to Dodge City, a point which they reached early one evening. After a chilly night wrapped in their coats and bedrolls Frank and Randolph left the other men, and rode the mile into town leading a packhorse to carry fresh supplies for Tex.

As they dismounted and tethered their horses outside the general store, Randolph looked across the neck of his gelding and saw Red McLean and three men riding slowly up the centre of the main street.

They stood in silence by the horses. The four men passed them, reined in outside the barber shop, hitched their horses, and filed inside.

Randolph said softly: 'This is what I've been waiting for.

151

When they come out I want them in the open, with their feet on the ground.'

Frank muttered: 'OK. Forget the bodyguard.' He loosened his Winchester in the saddle holster.

'For Christ's sake don't kill anyone with that thing.'

'Don't aim to. Sight of it'll be enough.'

They waited on the sidewalk, schooling their nerves. Riders passed, men walking, a few women, but the town was quiet. It was still before ten o'clock and the breeze was thin on their faces in spite of the sun. Half an hour went. It felt like half a day. Buckboards and covered waggons rattled down the street, drivers whistling at the horses, or cursing them. Dust whirled in flurries of wind.

The shop door opened. Two men came out, then McLean.

Frank hissed: 'One still in the chair.'

Randolph nodded. He stepped down onto the street, crossing it with long easy strides. The three men stood by their horses, laughing. Frank moved up the street on the opposite side, the Winchester vertical and unobtrusive against his leg. McLean started to unhitch his horse. Randolph walked past the two men, past McLean, then whirled.

'McLean. Remember me?'

The ginger-haired man twisted, eyes narrowing. The other two backed away from the obstruction of the horses.

'Nope.' McLean barked the word, turning square to Randolph, shoulders hunching.

'Name of Haldane. You probably never knew that. Last summer in the saloon. There was an old-timer. You threw him across my table. You put a slug through my leg, then bull-whipped me. I didn't have a gun. Now I have one.' His voice cracked like ice over water.

McLean's eyes raked his face.

'Yeah. Sure – I remember. Fancy speakin' bastard.' His right hand hovered. 'Yuh come back for more?'

Randolph said: 'Tell your buddies to look across the street.'

McLean's eyes flickered sideways. The other two hesitated, glanced quickly; saw Frank twenty paces away, Winchester

152

across his body. The stance was enough; they stood still, hands well away from their sides.

'Drop your belt.' The ice cracked again.

McLean's mouth widened. Without moving his lips he said: 'Yuh bloody fool.' His hands went slowly to the buckle of his gun belt.

Watch his eyes, Tex had said. Always watch a man's eyes. Randolph heard the old man's voice – 'When a feller goes fer his gun he's thinkin' o' th' biggest target. Thet's yore body – it's bigger'n y'head. An' he'll look at his target, more'n likely. Even if he doesn't, yuh'll see sump'n in his eyes. A man cain't help it – just fer a mite of a second –'

Two riders trotting along the street reined in suddenly, seeing McLean, and the fair-haired man with the Winchester, sensing trouble. Two other men appeared at a sidewalk door. Then McLean's narrowed stare shifted fractionally and he dropped a shoulder, his hand streaking down. His fingers curled on the butt of his gun and he looked at the black muzzle of Randolph's Colt and froze, unbelieving.

More men on the sidewalks. Still men. Two or three sidled away, out of the firing line. A murmur rippled along the street.

Randolph said: 'Drop your belt.' His dark eyes burned deep.

The fingers uncurled. The hand moved up, slowly. One of the two escorts shifted on his feet and Frank's Winchester levelled in the instant; then moved again as the barber-shop door opened and a wide-eyed man, lather on his chin, stood, hand over his gun but seeing the Winchester and not moving.

Randolph's Colt inclined slightly. McLean unbuckled his belt, hesitated, let it fall. Randolph backed; said: 'C'mon. Step clear.' McLean shuffled forward, half crouching. His tongue flicked, his hands opened and closed at his sides. When they were six paces from the sidewalk Randolph said clearly: 'You bull-whipped me – right here in this street. I didn't have a gun, but you put a slug into me, then whipped me down the street when I couldn't stand straight.'

The spectators muttered, moving further back from the great-chested man they all feared and the tall man with black hair and terrible eyes who was to be feared more. Frank stepped closer, his Winchester covering the three who clustered, motionless, by the uneasy horses. Randolph moved, an arm's length from McLean now. Then his gun flashed metal and the barrel raked across the hating face in front of him, forehead to chin. The big man staggered, hands rising, a choking sound bubbling in his mouth. Randolph's gun slid back into its holster, his foot hooked behind McLean's ankle and he slammed a fist into the blood-streaked face. McLean strained against the leg trap and crashed backwards, his head jarring into the ground. He rolled, groaning, pushing himself to his feet, his right arm windmilling in a wild punch. Randolph grabbed the wrist, then the elbow, twisting, turning, as he had learned long ago from Mark Helford's Devon wrestling champion. But he did not release when, by the rules, he should, and halfway down the dusty street men heard McLean scream as the elbow dislocated and a bone snapped. The big man spun away, face contorted, blood running down his nose and chin. Randolph went with him, whipped him round, holding him by his shirt, burning eyes searing into him, hissing: 'The arm so's you won't use a whip for a long time – and a leg to remind you of mine –' and his right hand flashed up and McLean reared backwards, falling. Randolph followed, wrenching him over so that he landed face down, then stepped back, jabbed a foot behind one knee joint and levered the lower leg up, back, round, and McLean screeched and the crowd's murmur rose. One of the escorts went for his gun and the Winchester cracked and the man spun, yelping, clutching a shattered wrist, gun clattering across the sidewalk.

Then it was over, and Randolph picked up McLean's gun, slid a shotgun from a holster in one of the saddles, walked behind the motionless, grey-faced escorts and lifted their pistols from their sides, added the fourth pistol from the sidewalk to his collection; said: 'I'll drop these at the end of the street when we quit town.' He did not even glance at the moaning, jerking figure lying in the dusty street.

By the time he had stalked back to Frank the flame in his eyes was burning low.

They were an hour late returning to the herd, and muttered their apologies to the trail boss.

'We had a little trouble. Nothing to worry about now.'

The trail boss's eyes, narrowed against the sun, watched them as they turned away. He asked no questions.

With the rest of the men they drank coffee, ate sourdough biscuits, and mounted up. By midday they had the herd moving again.

Three hours later, as they approached the Smith ranch, they cut the herd into two parts and prepared to count the heads as they drove half the cattle towards the corrals. Randolph rode ahead, looking for Tex.

As he drew nearer the buildings he saw the cabin door swinging in the wind. There was no sign of the old man. He dismounted and called; pushed the door wider. The cabin was silent. He came outside, walked round the corner of the building; then stopped, aware of a strange, sickly-sweet smell.

Tex Smith lay against a wall, half on his back. His eyes were open. One arm was raised, the hand pressed against the rough timber, as if he had tried to hold himself up. The other hand was on his chest, the fingers hooked into his shirt like claws in a final convulsion of agony.

He had died as he had lived for much of his life: alone.

II

They stood awkwardly in the sheriff's office. A small, balding man in a black suit and a dangling string tie adjusted spectacles low on his nose and held up a soiled sheet of paper.

'As you know,' he said in a cracked voice, 'Daniel Smith left a will in the custody of Mr Kennedy here –' he nodded at a tall, lugubrious man who hovered in the background '– in the bank, that is. Its date –' he peered at the paper '– November 21st of last year. Daniel Smith could not write, and he dictated his will to Mr Kennedy. It was then properly witnessed by Sheriff O'Donnell here. It's a very short document.'

He peered at the paper again, holding it up to the light from the window. Sheriff Pete O'Donnell hooked thumbs in his belt, swinging a leg as he perched on the edge of his desk. He was around forty years old, with a drooping black moustache and long hair greying at the temples; a man responsible for what passed for law and order in a town which was still one of the wildest in the developing west, and who gave no sign of worrying about the responsibility.

'It reads as follows: "I, Daniel Smith, usually called Tex, now living at my ranch about forty miles from Dodge City, having no family, leave all my property, my money and all other goods to my two partners Randy Haldane and Frank Garton, to be divided equally between them or as they shall both agree."'

The bald man sniffed, looked over his spectacles at the two confused young men standing beside him, and went on:

'The will is unlikely to be challenged since, as far as anyone knows, Daniel Smith had no living relatives. Further, it was correctly witnessed by our worthy sheriff. I must therefore ask you, Mr Kennedy, to tell these fortunate young men how Mr Smith's accounts stand.'

Kennedy shuffled to his feet, cleared his throat, and consulted a notebook.

'Thank you, Mr Welbrace. There are two accounts – one here in Dodge, the other in Kansas City. The account here totals $6420; that in Kansas totals $21,700. There's also a small gold deposit valued by me at approximately $5000. As far as I'm aware there are no debts, and the property known as the Smith ranch was the late Daniel Smith's property absolutely, to the extent of around 2600 acres. That is all I have to report, except –' he cleared his throat again '– except I would like to say I will be pleased to act in the interests of the two fortunate beneficiaries if they wish to entrust their affairs to me. I have a good reputation in this town, gentlemen.'

He closed his notebook with a snap.

Frank fingered the old Colt in the shiny holster on his thigh, and stared down at the floor. Randolph glanced at him, looked away, and slowly shook his head.

'I hope the old guy's found peace,' he said quietly. 'I'd rather have him back than – any of this.'

Mark Helford's final instructions before Randolph and Frank had left Exeter had been that they should write to him at his office to indicate their health but were to give no address or other indication of their whereabouts in case the information might be dangerous to them if it were seen by others. They had done as they had been told, once from Boston, again from Kansas City.

Now, a year after their departure, Randolph said: 'I guess it's time we took the risk of telling him where we are. After all this time it can't be a risk at all – particularly sending a letter to his office. We'll give the bank address.'

So he wrote:

> Dear Mr Helford – You will see from this letter that we are now established citizens. Fortune has smiled. I will not go into details here, but we have become ranchers in partnership with each other on 2600 acres

of good grass. At the moment we have 500 Longhorns of different ages and enough capital to look for more, up to the stocking capacity of the land – which we think is greater than some other ranchers reckon. We have had some remarkable adventures, and are well. We think of you all a great deal and hope that one day we may see you all again. Please convey our warmest affections to those whom we love.

He signed the letter simply with initials, caution getting the better of him at the end.

Then he wrote a second letter, this time to Tom Hogarth in Boston.

Dear Tom – When we left you last year you indicated that you would be interested in a secure investment if we could arrange it. We are happy to tell you that an excellent proposition is now possible. By good fortune we own 2600 acres of good grass stocked with 500 steers and will shortly buy a few more. But there is a limit to the stocking capacity of this land, and if we are to expand we need to buy more land – another ranch, in fact. There are opportunities in this area, but we do not have the capital to buy more than around 1000 head ourselves at about ten dollars for good yearlings, if we are to retain safe working capital. If we are to stock that number we would have to buy at least 4000 acres at about twenty cents an acre – perhaps $800. That we can afford. But we would be happy to partner you in a bigger venture if you so wish, and would anticipate a profit on the cattle of at least $15 a head in two years. We would welcome an indication of how you now regard this enterprise. Our bank is Kansas General.

Please convey our best wishes to your good wife. We trust this finds you both well – Randolph Haldane and Frank Garton.

By the time the reply reached them they had added another hundred yearling steers to their herd, and felt they were now in danger of overstocking the land.

Hogarth wrote simply:

> Excellent news. I will put up $25,000 in anticipation of the return you indicate – as much of it as possible to be put into cattle rather than land, if you please. I have instructed my bank to write to yours immediately and a deed of partnership covering my investment will follow.

Within two months they had bought a further 3500 cows and yearlings and a 12,000-acre spread close to the Colorado border. It was 1872 – just a few months before the market collapsed and finished steers were being dumped on the Kansas City stockyards for ten dollars a head or less. They had few cattle ready to sell in 1873 and responded to the collapse by buying another 500 young cattle for as little as five dollars each. As Frank said, 'It's panic, so now's the time to buy while most folk are selling.'

It was July, and they were on a train returning to Dodge from Kansas City where they watched cattle passing through the stockyards and talked with their bank manager and enjoyed three days in the relative luxury of a hotel. The city had boomed since they had first seen it only four years before; in spite of the stock market panic that had knocked millions of dollars off share values overnight there was every sign of affluence and confidence in the new buildings, the dress of the men and women, the content of the stores and shops.

Now, sitting on the wooden seats of the jolting carriage, they were leaning forward to glimpse the vast cereal acreage which had startled them when they had journeyed in the opposite direction. When they had first moved west they had stared in amazement at the rolling corn lands of Illinois and Missouri. Now the tide had moved further across the new lands, stretching into Kansas which, as harvest approached, seemed from the train windows to be an unbroken sea of waving wheat and barley interspersed with later-maturing sweetcorn. In eastern Kansas the buffalo grass of the plains was giving way to the plough as far as the eye could see, and while the revolution petered out within fifty miles of Kansas City, and with still 250 miles to go before they reached Dodge, there was no mistaking the change that was rolling across the developing lands of the middle west.

Randolph said: 'The way this is going, America will soon have more wheat than she can possibly use herself. We know there's already a trickle going across the Atlantic. How long will it be before it's a flood – and what's going to happen to British agriculture? It's thirty-five years since the Corn Laws were repealed, and there's no chance of anything like them being introduced again.'

Frank braced himself as the carriage lurched on the uneven track.

'It'll hurt the folks back home,' he said. 'Now that steamships are moving so fast, and getting bigger all the time, merchants will be able to ship as much grain as they like. It'll be costly, I suppose. But when you're growing on a scale as big as this you can afford a lower price than we can –' he grinned and corrected himself '– than they can, back in England.'

'All it needs,' said Randolph, 'is a reaper that will bind as well. McCormick and others are working on it, so the papers say – and may be selling something before too long. That will really speed things up. And threshing machines will get better, too, especially with the new high-pressure boilers. That will make them lighter and more portable. The horse sweep will go. It'll all be steam – and that will help to move the grain out of here fast – on its way east. And there's so much virgin land out here, Frank – more than we can imagine. The expansion's only just begun.'

A poker game started between four men on the other side of the car, and they watched idly. Both had respected Tom Hogarth's advice to avoid gambling – and women, too – and had stuck rigidly to their resolve, although they played cards frequently with each other in the long winters. Now they watched the dollar bills piling up, and sensed the tension rising.

But Randolph's mind was only half on the poker game, for another dimension of the vast American grain expansion had come to him. Mark Helford was in the shipping business; and while his small fleet was entirely under sail, and the Atlantic was becoming increasingly dominated by steam, the potential was so great that there would be room for any sort of transport before long; and, in any case, Helford was a merchant as well as a shipper, and used other companies' ships to fulfil his contracts.

Maybe before long he would be able to tell Helford about it: maybe even make some contracts for him before he returned to Devon. *If* he returned to Devon. He was becoming part of this exciting new country. The narrow lanes and hedges and small fields of the west of England were far away, and seemed even further in his mind. It was a lonely life; he and Frank had made few friends, mainly because of their determination not to gamble; and they had spoken to few respectable women in the whole of the time they had been here. But Randolph rarely felt the need for friends, beyond Frank. He was at home on the wide plains with their big skies. He enjoyed nights under the stars, and days under hot sun, and he could cope with the bad winters. The slump would pass soon, he was certain; and then there would be a great deal of money to be made. Maybe he would get into corn production as well as ranching. He could lease land from the railway companies or Government agencies.

Away against the horizon he could see a cluster of low wooden shacks. Homesteaders – small farmers. They were scattered all over the West, trekking out in wagon trains, looking for new land, new hope. Many were immigrants; others refugees from the eastern cities. America proclaimed itself the land of enterprise, where everyone had an equal chance; but there was only scope for enterprise that could stand up to other enterprise, and that was a situation that always favoured the biggest and the most ruthless for they had

161

the money and the powerful friends and knew the politicians and, as a last resort in this pioneer country, had the most guns. Not much different from home, really, he thought – except for the guns. There were no pioneers in Britain; but there were plenty of struggling smallholders and farm labourers, and the big landowners were really the equivalent of the ranchers out here. He was a rancher – and the son of a British landowner. At least he was consistent. He could see Frank at the edge of his vision, still watching the card game. Now *there* was a contradiction: son of a poor labourer yet now a partner in a twin-ranch business with more than 15,000 acres – not large by American standards maybe, but colossal when set against Britain. How did Frank square his conscience? He had stumbled into this great adventure and had been swept along with it. Randolph knew that left to his own devices in the first place, Frank would probably not have come out to the west; more than likely he would have tried to start farming in Massachusetts or one of the other semi-developed eastern states – and if he had, he might later have been among the settlers seeking better things in the new lands of the west.

The train trundled around a long bend in the track and sun slanted through the swaying windows. Randolph tipped his wide-brimmed hat over his eyes and stretched his long legs. Don't fool yourself, he thought – Frank isn't the only one who has come a long way in a short time. Who in Roxton would recognize Randolph Haldane now, with his part-share in 4500 cattle and his rolling acres, his leather-patched pants and high boots and black cigars, and his Colt and his Winchester?

The winter was a quiet one. They divided their time between the Smith ranch and the new Colorado property, High Range, and saw little of towns or other people except for occasional excursions to buy supplies and on one occasion to seek a fresh horse after one of their mares had broken a foreleg over rocky ground close to the Colorado ranch house and Frank had shot her. It was a lonely existence and one that tested their patience and their friendship.

In the spring they recruited a dozen cattlemen, divided their forces and set out from the two ranches to round up the herds and check them for injuries and losses. The market was still low and they considered themselves fortunate that they had few cattle fit to sell and little need of money, so they could sit out the slump and wait for the recovery.

On a summer evening they returned to the Smith ranch after a slow ride along the nearby river. There had been little rain for three months, the water level was low and they had been checking the possibility that cattle had wandered across onto the neighbouring ranch. The river was the dividing line between them and they were glad of its normally substantial presence for the land beyond was owned by Henry Hanson, a rough, tough and ruthless Canadian, who had moved south several years before and who had an unsavoury local reputation as an Indian hunter and a womanizer.

They found no sign that cattle had forded the river and saw nothing of their neighbour – until they reached the ranch buildings and saw two horses tethered against the corral and two figures leaning against the fencing. As they drew nearer they recognized Hanson, with his wide shoulders, long arms, grey-bearded face and shoulder-length hair. The other man, shorter and stouter and older than Hanson's forty years, was a stranger to them.

They dismounted and walked towards the visitors.

'Howdy,' Hanson said. 'Hope you don't mind a call – little business t'discuss. This hiya's Don Morgan – his spread's way over th' other side o'mine.'

The four men shook hands briefly. Frank said: 'Come inside. You want coffee?'

'Mighty kind,' Hanson said. 'Sorry we don't see much of each other – bein' neighbours. How're you two guys weatherin' these hard times?'

'OK, I suppose,' said Randolph. He followed them into the cabin which had now become a comfortable ranch house with a wide verandah, and eyed them speculatively. 'What sort of business can I do with you, Mr Hanson?'

Hanson perched on the edge of the table, Morgan sat on a

hard chair and spread his legs wide to balance himself, while Frank stirred the fire embers and pushed the iron kettle over the half-consumed logs. Randolph stood in the doorway, watching them, noting that both men wore guns.

'I jes' wondered if you guys hed heard anythin' o'the trouble over in River Bend,' Hanson said. 'Where them pesky homesteaders is farmin'.'

Randolph shook his head.

'Haven't heard of any particular trouble. About a dozen families, aren't there?'

'All of that,' Morgan growled. 'An' every one with as many kids. Came out here with Washington money, grabbed a slice o'good land up agin the river, an' started ploughin' an' fencin' an' breakin' up the range. I used t'hev cattle crossin' the river there – it's a good shaller place – an' afore I knowed it there was fencin' an' croppin' an' the like. An' they're sich miserable bastards – all religious – allus callin' on the Lord for sump'n.'

'So?' Frank stood with his back to the flickering logs. 'What's the trouble there?'

'There's more of 'em comin',' snapped Hanson. 'They sent word back into Missouri t'all their friends t'come an' praise the Lord in River Bend an' build a church an' all thet sorta stuff. They're aimin' t'set up a town, right in range country, an' start farmin' all around it. Yuh know what thet means? I'll tell yuh – less land fer cattle, an' less water if they spread along the river. We need t'keep all the cattle there is right now, beef bein' such a poor trade. Cain't afford t'see good grass bein' ploughed up by miserable Missouri homesteaders – an' we don't want no fences. So I'm hiya to make sure all the cattlemen stand together.'

Frank reached for tin mugs and a jar of ground coffee.

'And what do we do when we're standing together?' he asked.

Hanson slid away from his perch on the table and thumped his fist into the palm of his other hand.

'We go out there an' see 'em,' he said grittily. 'Mebbe thirty of us. An' we take guns, so's they kin see we mean business.

No shootin', y'understand – jes' so's they kin see we mean it. An' we warn 'em off – remind 'em this hiya's plains country an' cattle country, an' we don' want no ploughin' an' fencin', an' folks's think like thet'd better go back t'Missouri or some other place.'

Randolph said: 'As I understand it they came here with Government grants and were allocated the land by Government agents. We've no power to move them.'

'Them agents don' understand this hiya country,' Hanson retorted. He took the mug of coffee offered by Frank. 'It's a political matter, an' we gotta look after the politics, soon as we can. But thet takes time. Them guys is hiya now – an' more of 'em's comin'. If we wait fer the pesky politicians we'll be over-run, an' neither you nor me nor Don nor any other cattleman'll hev any real range left. With prices bein' like they are, we gotta move now, t'protect our interests.'

Randolph nodded.

'OK. I see your problem. But it's not mine. River Bend isn't near my land. It's six or seven miles from here and my range runs in the opposite direction. So I've no personal grounds to object to what's happening there. Don't know what Frank thinks, but I'll keep out of it.'

'I guess that's right,' Frank said slowly. His face was expressionless, but Randolph knew he was troubled. 'This is a political problem, and since I'm not directly affected by it I'd prefer to keep out of it too. Good luck to you, Mr Hanson – but don't reckon we'll be there.'

Within five minutes the visitors had gone, scowling and sharp-tongued but holding their tempers in check, for the two men at the Smith ranch were big and hard-muscled and had cold eyes; and after they had cantered away past the corrals and along the dusty trail against the setting sun, Frank said: 'Guess you didn't like that any more than I did.'

Randolph drank coffee and grimaced.

'It stinks of mob violence,' he said. 'I never did go for that sort of thing – ever since that night back at the Dog and Partridge in Roxton all those years ago – remember? There'll be trouble at River Bend if Hanson and the rest ride in there.

Some of those homesteaders may be very religious, but from what I've heard of 'em there are others who'll lift a shotgun quick enough – especially the Swedes and Germans, and there are a lot of those moving west out of Illinois and the Missouri River country.'

'I'm on their side,' Frank said quietly. 'Hell, Randy – we've seen a few of 'em. Poor as church mice. Not much better than the labourers back home – my sort of people. I can't forget that – it's where I come from, even though things have changed for me. My mother and father are still there, in that cottage, with hardly enough to live on; these settlers in their shacks are the same, even though they're working for themselves. I know that if too many of them come they'll break up the ranges. But until the bottom fell out of the markets last year ranching was a licence to print dollars – look at the money we made in a year or so – and the money poor old Tex made, sitting on his backside and just watching it. God didn't give this country to cattlemen.'

Randolph felt for a cigar, bit off the end and spat it into the fire.

'He gave it to Indians,' he said wryly. 'But that's no argument – after the stories we've heard of the way the Apaches and Comanches and Pawnees and the rest savage each other as well as the white man, they don't arouse any sympathy in me. No – this is about politics. It's about money fighting government – rich men fighting poor men, if you like. I want no part in it.'

Frank moved to the door and stared moodily across the plain and away to the distant higher land on the western horizon, turning red and purple now as the day ended.

'Rich men fighting poor men.' His voice was as far away as the trail receding across the flat land. 'Somehow I thought we'd left that behind. We grew up with that, the two of us. When I was a little kid I hated you because you were a rich boy. I wanted to beat hell out of you because that would have been beating hell out of everybody who was rich. It changed soon enough, I suppose. But it was the way all my sort of kids felt. And most of 'em still do, now they're grown up – and their kids'll feel the same, because nothing changes much. Why're you different, Randy? With your background you shouldn't have wanted to know people like me – except as damn' near slave labour.'

Randolph scraped a match and put the flame to his cigar.

'Because I was brought up to think about people. My father always did. Men like Callan and Griffiths didn't love him for it. But he wasn't alone. D'you know something – that even Mark Helford's like that? He's as hard a man as I ever met; but he's generous, too – and he doesn't take account of whether men are rich or poor, or live in a cottage or big houses. He treats them all alike. He used to lecture me about that. I'm not so different. There are plenty more.' He drew smoke from the cigar. 'I wonder if anything will happen at River Bend.'

'We'll hear about it,' said Frank.

Two days later they saw it – a smudge of smoke on the horizon, growing quickly to a low grey-white cloud that spread out slowly as it rose. They watched it for a long time in silence, until it began to subside, and Randolph said: 'I think I'd like to go and take a look.' He pushed a Winchester into his saddle holster and strapped a gunbelt around his waist before he swung into his saddle and Frank, without a word, did likewise.

They rode at a steady canter along the western trail, then left it to follow the river. The buffalo grass was burned by the sun and had been grazed hard by cattle through the summer, and their horses kicked up dust as they went. The cattle they saw – their own, then neighbouring BJ ranch Longhorns, and finally Hanson's cattle – looked fit, though some were lean and would remain so until the autumn rains brought the late flush of grass. The river, a tributary of the wide Arkansas, was shallow and brown, and the mud where cattle had wandered down to drink was baked hard under the scattered cotton-woods that pointed towards the smoke, now little more than a smudge low against the sky. They talked little as they rode.

Before they reached River Bend they knew what had happened. The community of wooden shacks was close against a loop in the river, as the name suggested, with cropped land radiating from it towards the south. The corn should have been high now, but it was gone, blackened and shrivelled under drifting smoke; several hundred acres of forlorn and tangled stalks stretching across the land, with patches of potato tops between, brown instead of green after being swept by the flames; and men and women wandering amongst the wreckage, staring, helpless.

Randolph and Frank dismounted and led their horses forward. A woman stood by a cabin on the edge of the little cluster of ramshackle buildings, face smudged and hair bedraggled, dirt on her long coarse grey skirt. She looked around sixty, although Frank thought that an hour previously she might have looked fifteen years younger.

He touched the brim of his hat and said: 'We saw the smoke, ma'am. What happened here? Is anybody hurt?'

She looked at him. Tears had coursed channels down the soot patches on her face. They were still in her eyes.

'Twenty of 'em. An' more. Came an' tol' us t'get off the land – said this is cattle country.' Her voice was cracked and broken and despairing. 'They didn' come fer that, though – they came t'do what they did – rags soaked in kerosene – fired 'em an' trailed 'em through the crops. We don' hev no other crops, mister.'

A man approached, then another; tattered, thin, blackened men, with suspicious eyes and shoulder-length hair. One said: 'Where're yuh from, strangers?' The words were weary.

'Down the river – six miles. We saw smoke. Who the hell did this?'

'Cattlemen.' Hate in the voice and in the eyes. 'Lookin' t'drive us off. You cattlemen, strangers?'

Randolph looked at them. They were not wearing guns. He said easily: 'Yes. Smith ranch. Name's Haldane.' He nodded to Frank. 'My partner Frank Garton.'

'Cattlemen ain' welcome here,' the man said. 'Yuh better git ridin', strangers – less yuh kin tell us how t'live. They even killed four of the milch cows, yuh know thet? Shot 'em as they rode off. Git goin', strangers.'

'We came to help,' Frank said. 'Though by the look of it there's nothing that can help. Do you know who did it – any names?'

'Don' do no good to know names. They'd prove they was some other place. There ain' no justice in this country. Now git ridin'.'

Frank put a foot into a stirrup and swung up into the saddle. He looked down at the drawn, hostile faces.

'OK. But just to prove all cattlemen aren't alike, we'll bring a few cows over in a day or two. I guess we've some too many.'

He turned his horse and Randolph mounted, drawing in beside him. They rode away together, leaving the silent group watching them, aware that others were watching too. The acrid air stung their throats and their eyes.

Presently Frank said: 'Hope you agree – about giving them a few cows. I thought it might defuse the situation a little – and help them. God knows they need help. What the hell will they live on?'

'They look as if they're used to hard times,' said Randolph. He added without enthusiasm: 'Yes – you did the right thing.'

Frank stared moodily ahead at the river.

'This country's no better than home,' he said, half to himself. 'No justice – unless you have money. I suppose they're better off back in Devon – at least they don't shoot each other. Or they hadn't started up to when we left. Wonder what's happening back there, Randy.'

Randolph lowered his head beneath the branch of a cotton-wood.

'I wonder sometimes. One day we'll find out – if we're lucky.'

They were silent then as they rode; depressed, with slack shoulders and eyes down.

A few days later they cut four cows out of the herd, each with a heifer calf, and drove them over to River Bend. Three teams of oxen were out, dragging ploughs through the blackened earth and the stubble. Two of the ploughmen came to meet them, and then another man who had been sat outside a shack. From the same shack came the woman they had seen

169

on their first visit. The air was cleaner and fresher now under the bright sun, but the eyes were still hostile.

Randolph addressed the woman. He tipped his hat and said: 'We came the day your crops were fired – remember? We promised some cows to replace those the raiders shot. They're here. You can have the calves too – they'll make useful cows one day.'

No one spoke. The eyes took in the cattle and returned to the two horsemen.

Frank said abruptly: 'Do you want 'em?'

One of the men stirred.

'Guess we need 'em, stranger. Real bad. We cain't pay yuh.'

'We didn't come for payment,' Frank said. He caught Randolph's eye and raised his hand in a half salute. 'So long.'

The group stood, wordless, as they rode away, leaving the cows wandering aimlessly towards the shacks and the calves trotting behind.

They exchanged few words during the ride back. Yet each knew what was in the other's mind: a sick disenchantment with the new world that had once been so golden and exciting that its crudities could be excused. Power, violence, oppression; the strong growing stronger and the weak weaker. No man doffed his hat to another, as in the land they had left behind; instead men backed away, frightened of violence, even death, and had no recourse or protection.

A week later Randolph rode out on the northern loop of the Santa Fe trail, picking up a stage coach and two four-horse waggon teams for company, and headed west towards the Colorado ranch where he had left a foreman and two hands. He wanted to look over the condition of the cattle before the autumn. They would sell nothing that year, they had decided already; and the market slump was so widespread that they felt it was unlikely to recede until Washington's own financial crisis was beaten. The newspapers reported thousands of men out of work in the cities to the east, and heavy investment losses.

But in the following year the beef trade steadied and began

to recover, and there were better reports from the stock markets. They sold two hundred steers that were ready for slaughter, losing a little money, but held on to the rest of their herds, knowing that things were going to improve and that if the next winter was not too hard and they did not lose more than an average number of cattle in the snows and rains, they stood a good chance of big profits in the spring.

And so in March 1876 they rode into Dodge, studied the encouraging market reports and picked up a letter from Mark Helford which told them that there were no obstacles to their return home – all enquiries over what he referred to as 'the problem' had ceased and, he assured them, would not be revived. He also told them that their parents were well with the exception of Rupert whose health was failing although he was still in full control of the estate.

But their excitement over Helford's news was overtaken by that conveyed by the clicking telegraph from the Kansas stockyards where trade was already brisk and expected to improve with up to thirty-five dollars a head for quality steers, while from Colorado came even better reports, for Government agents there were looking for cattle after a severe winter which had hit the Indian reservations hard.

A drive for their entire herd, starting at the Colorado border ranch and picking up steers from the Smith ranch on the way, was a massive undertaking, and there was a danger of flooding the still-nervous market; so they decided to trail the Colorado cattle west on the long ride to Denver and also south into New Mexico where there was a strong trade to be had with Government agents at Fort Sumner. Then the rest would go east to Kansas City.

Comanches and Kiowas were still a danger in the New Mexico territory, and other Indians were reported in Colorado. So thirty well-armed men were recruited, and the army notified, before the cattle destined for Denver were moved off, with Frank as trail boss. A few days later, with a group nearly as large, Randolph set out to cross the plains country to Fort Sumner.

It was early summer before they met again, very much the

richer, and decided to rest for several weeks before starting the drive to Kansas City. In the evenings they sat on the verandah and watched the sun setting across the range, smoking their black cigars.

Two weeks after their return Frank asked the question that had become more and more insistent in his mind.

'Randy – d'you think much about home?'

'M-m. Sometimes.' Randolph frowned at the smoke from his cigar.

'So do I. Particularly about my parents. We're fairly wealthy men, Randy. I haven't worked out how much we've got – how much we could be worth. But back home my mother and father are living in that little cottage – hungry, sometimes – cold in the winter. I could change their lives if I sent money to them – or if I went home.'

Randolph rocked his chair back on its legs.

'My folks don't need it like yours do.'

They watched the low sun, and the faintly purple light as evening came across the wide horizon. The wind was warm.

Frank said: 'The trouble is, if I send them enough money to be useful – to make a real difference to them – I'd cut back on our investment potential. It would have to come out of the business, in some way.'

Randolph blew cigar smoke; watched it eddy above them. The phrase registered – investment potential; what a hell of a change, he thought, since the days back at Roxton – from the village boy to this hard-headed rancher able to talk the language of business without effort or affectation. Frank might not have been the leader – Randolph was under no illusions about that – but he had matured dramatically in the five years of their exile. Cattleman, landowner, stock dealer, with a Devon accent now hardly noticeable under the American Midwest overtones; shrewd eyes and a sharp calculating mind – and yet sympathetic eyes and a concerned mind, for his roots were never far below the surface. Now that sympathy and concern were in conflict with the shrewdness and the calculation. Home and distant memories were suddenly bright and beckoning; in contrast, cracks had appeared in the glittering façade of the great new world. Randolph had seen the signs for days in uncharacteristic irritability and withdrawal. He studied the grey ash on his cigar. The dream was fading; Frank was waking from it, disturbed by the transition, torn between loyalties: the ranch house and the cottage, the vastness of the range and the smallness of the fields, the paddock fencing and the high hedge banks; the present generation and the last.

He kept his eyes on the cigar, seeing the ash crumble and the flakes drift in the warm evening wind. Soon there would be only the ash; then that would disintegrate and disperse.

Frank watched him at the edge of his vision. The silence was a barrier between them. Trust – there had always been trust; unspoken, undefined, unquestioned. Yet they were so different. Frank had always been aware of the difference, even though he kept the awareness to himself. The boy of rich parents, the public school boy, the protégé of the successful businessman, the land and farming at his back. And the physical ruthlessness that was manifest in the lean frame and the secret, dangerous depths glimpsed in moments of total commitment through the mirror of his dark eyes – that, too, was different. He was defensive, offensive, with secret corners in his mind; a single-minded guardian of his own self. And the business of ranching had become his own self totally.

Frank stared gloomily across the purple range. For the first time since their childish battles for the sake of battle, he was in conflict with this magnetic, ruthless, generous, selfish man who had been part of his core for seventeen years from childhood through crisis to success. Nothing had been voiced; no word of disagreement. But it floated in the air between them, unseen but oppressive. The bond was strong. But it was not unbreakable.

Randolph stood up; walked to the rail and leaned on it; long legs crossed, sun and wind-tanned face and arms darker in the evening light. Frank watched his back, felt the silence as a physical burden, and remembered the dreadful stillness in Mark Helford's study when their futures were weighed in scales that were beyond their touch; remembered watching

173

the black-haired Helford apprehensively, not daring to speak. Strange that he should see Helford now, in that dark, booted, leather-clad figure at the ranch house rail.

Randolph's voice drifted against the dusk.

'We could split. I could borrow to cover it – no trouble, I guess.'

Frank's breath was long, slow.

'I suppose so. I haven't worked it out. And I don't know what to do anyway – I just feel I have to do something. I know I have to.'

Randolph's cigar glowed. Then he flicked it; watched the red spark arc away and drop onto the bare earth. He turned, thumbs hooked into his belt, and leaned against a post.

'I'll tell you. We quit. We don't belong here. This is a great country – but it's a hell of a corrupt country, too. There are too many things we don't like. We came together – we'll go back together. I owe Mark Helford three hundred and fifty pounds. It's time I paid him.'

Frank came slowly off his chair.

'You don't have to do that.'

'No. I don't. You don't either. But you've good reasons to want to. The best reasons. You think about people more than I do, Frank. You remind me, now and then, of the important things. What's all this –' he waved a hand '– compared with people? I remember your parents. They could do with real help. Let's give it to 'em. I wouldn't mind seeing home again, to tell the truth. Tom Hogarth's investment has matured anyway – half the cattle we've sold already were his. We pay him out, sell the rest of the herd in Kansas City, sell the two places we have, pocket the money, and get the hell out. OK?'

Frank moved across the verandah.

'I didn't think I'd ever hear you say that.'

Randolph shrugged.

'Neither did I. But it isn't the first time I've thought about it. On that long trail, riding without talking, days and days of it, a feller gets to thinking. You know that. I thought about it plenty. Is it a deal?'

Their leather and rope-toughened fists met, and suddenly

174

they were grinning at each other. The barriers that had stirred between them had gone.

In the half dark the last of the abandoned cigar glowed as the night wind stirred, and the ash blew away.

III

They sold their property and young stock to a Texan looking for expansion and left the deal in the hands of their bank. They wrote letters home and sold the last of their cattle in the Kansas stockyards, hitting the market at a high point and averaging thirty-six dollars a head. Then they sold their Winchesters and their Colts and bought two small Derringers – 'just in case of trouble on the way back'. After that there was just the long railroad ride to Boston, a couple of nights' stay with a satisfied Tom Hogarth, another train to New York and, with few formalities, embarkation on a transatlantic steamship.

In Southampton they bought a change of clothing – 'so we don't scare the natives,' Frank said. There was now a good rail service from Southampton to Exeter and Plymouth, and they reached Exeter one afternoon in late September. They hired a carriage and driver and came to Roxton at six in the evening, with the day's rain clearing and a pale sun lighting the fields and the hedgerows and the shabby cottage where Frank's parents lived. As he climbed down from the carriage and collected his baggage Frank's face was serious.

'I'm scared of this, somehow,' he muttered. 'It's been a long time.'

Randolph nodded.

'I guess we both feel the same.' Then he grinned. 'We'll have a party at home for your folks and mine – tomorrow night. I'll walk over as soon as I can.' He stuck out his hand, still grinning. 'So long, pardner. And – thanks.'

Their handshake was brief and hard. It was the end of the adventure.

Wordless, Frank stepped clear, Randolph signalled to the driver and the carriage clattered away. Frank took a deep breath and turned to the cottage door as his father, attracted by the noise, opened it.

In the drive of the Grange the carriage swept round to the front of the house. Randolph stepped down and looked around. The slanting sunlight caught the red bricks and the ivy and the grey chimneys, and the low range of farm buildings beyond the poplar windbreak. He turned to the house and saw movement at a window. He hesitated, aware of tension in his chest. He paid the driver; said, 'Unload the baggage, please.'

Then the door opened, and Caroline was there, still tall and slender against the lamplight glowing yellow in the hall. She did not move, but held out both her hands, and when he went to her she wept against his shoulder. It was the first time he had ever seen her cry.

He put a finger beneath her chin and raised her face, his eyes searching, remembering.

'Hey, lady – we're supposed to be happy about this.' His voice, deep and gentle, with its slight American slant, was almost new to her.

'I am. Oh yes – I am.' She brushed the tears away; then pushed him to arm's length. 'You look – so different – older; so much – a man.'

'I am older – remember?' His mouth widened. 'But you're not. You're the same. Still a beautiful lady.' His hand reached out and his fingers touched her hair. 'No more grey – just the same.' He kissed her forehead and she clung to him for a moment, as to a close, special friend rather than a son. Then they stood apart.

'Well – aren't you going to invite me in?' He was teasing her.

She stepped back, and then he saw a shadow in her eyes.

'Yes – I'm sorry – how dreadful to keep you on the doorstep.'

She took his hand and led him inside, to the warmth of the big hall and the logs burning in the fireplace; and Mark Helford.

For an instant Randolph hesitated. But Caroline's fingers

were tight around his and she brought him forward. His eyes flickered over the hall, but no one else was there. Then he concealed his surprise and extended his hand.

'You look well. It's good to see you again.'

Mark Helford, bearded, dark frock-coat over grey waistcoat and trousers, bow tie against high-collared shirt, came to him and returned the handshake. And Randolph knew he was tense. There was a hint of reservation in his smile.

'Good to see you too. My word – America has done great things for you. You look – enormously fit.'

There's something wrong, Randolph thought. They're holding back. Where's father?

He turned to Caroline, his eyes questioning now, and she saw it.

Very quietly she said: 'Randolph – I'm sorry – this is not the happy homecoming we had all hoped for.'

Then he knew. Mark Helford's guarded face, his mother's troubled eyes.

'My father. You don't have to tell me. My father is dead.' His voice was flat, controlled. The tension he had felt outside the house settled cold and heavy in his mind and body.

Caroline said: 'He died four months ago. He was 76, and he'd been failing for a year or more. We – I wrote to you. Then your letter came, saying you were selling everything and coming home. I realized you would almost certainly leave before my letter could reach you. There was no other way to tell you, until now.'

Four months. Where was he, four months ago? Riding trail across the plains country into New Mexico, with fifteen hundred cattle and a bunch of hard, weather-toughened gunslingers who would fight Indian or white man if they were paid for it. He felt the sun on his back and the plains wind on his face and it was cold in the house. Outside, wheels crunched the gravel and a horse snorted. The driver who had brought him to Roxton shook the reins and turned his carriage away towards the gates. The hall was quiet except for the crackle of the logs in the grate. He thought: I ought to be more shocked. This was my father. But we could be talking about a friend – just a friend; a long-standing friend, but not a close one. Images careered across his mind – incidents from childhood, culminating in the great rift after his expulsion from Marlborough. Rupert Haldane was a distant, indistinct shadow in it all, and he could not communicate with the shadow. He suddenly realized that he had been drawn home by the memory of his mother, the farm, the estate – and Mark Helford. No one else.

He heard his voice, as if from outside his body.

'I am terribly sorry – for us all. I hope he didn't suffer.'

'Very little. At least – very little pain.' It was Helford's turn. 'His heart gave out. Your mother took great care of him. It was a long and trying time.'

He nodded. Automatically his hands searched his pockets, produced one of the long black cigars he had come to enjoy. Without thought he bit off the end; then remembered where he was and checked the instinct to spit it away. He took it from his teeth and threw it into the fire, watching it burn as he found matches, flicked a thumb nail across one and lighted the cigar.

'I'm sure it was. I'm sorry I didn't get your letter. It would have made this moment easier for us both.' He was addressing Caroline, stiffly, distantly; still wrestling with his private confusion; wanting to be deeply grieved instead of only shocked. His cigar glowed. Then he took it from his mouth, looked at it and said: 'I'm sorry – I shouldn't have lighted this without asking your permission. It's a habit. In a – an all-male society you never think about such things. It will take me some time to become – civilized.'

Caroline's smile was quick, reassuring, and the room was warm again.

'I don't mind. I enjoy the smell. It – suits you, somehow.'

He moved closer to her and put an arm around her shoulders.

'My poor lady. I'm so very sorry I wasn't here to help you.'

She looked up at him, eyes searching his face, trying to read him.

'You couldn't be. We managed. Everyone here was

wonderful – very kind. And Mark became our prop. He has been our guide and strength – truly.'

Randolph looked at the silent figure by the fireplace and said: 'Thank you. If I'd known about it, I'd have expected no less. That places us all in your debt – I was the first.'

He saw their eyes meet, momentarily. Helford's deep voice said: 'There's no debt between friends, Randolph. Your mother and I are close friends – and so are you, to me.'

Randolph thought: She called him Mark. And they are very close friends. There's a private communication between them. They don't need words. He felt no sense of surprise.

'There's one debt I have to repay,' he said. 'A strictly practical one. You funded me, and Frank, when we left and when we desperately needed help. As I hope my last letter indicated, we'll have no difficulty repaying you – with interest. And I promised I would repay. But tell me first – how the estate has gone since father's death. How have you managed?'

Caroline said: 'Well enough, thanks to Mark – and to Sam Veryan. He's steward now – Stanley Conway has retired and lives in one of the old cottages we rebuilt for him and his wife. But we'll talk about that later. You haven't even taken off your coat or brought in your luggage. There's so much to tell – and so much to ask.' The shades of Rupert Haldane had gone from her eyes. 'Let's try to make it the sort of reunion we've all wanted.'

He grinned at her then, and the weight eased from his mind.

'Sure. I reckon that's the right thing to do.'

He went to the door to collect his baggage. When he returned he saw his mother and Mark Helford standing before the fire, side by side, close together. Again, he felt no surprise.

Over dinner, after the delight and excitement of Nora and a meeting with Sam Veryan, they began to piece together the jigsaw of the past six years.

The 'problem', as Helford still called it, had been forgotten by the police. Two men had died that night; then a year later, the other two had drowned at sea. The only witness, Peter Pardoe, had been discredited in a public brawl after being discovered in Jane Dolby's bed by her husband. But Helford knew that a disturbingly accurate description of Randolph and Frank had been circulated by the police and was convinced that had they remained in the area they might have become involved in enquiries.

Mark Helford's business had expanded further, not least as the result of Randolph's small introduction of American grain which had given Helford Shipping a toe-hold in a trade which was now growing rapidly as the big steamships began to transport loads regularly across the Atlantic. Helford's own ships were all still under sail, but as a merchant he was contracting with other shipping companies and had storage facilities close to the Exeter canal. His slice of the total trade was small, but it was a significant boost to his turnover.

But in parallel the Roxton estate farms, like all the farms in Britain which grew cereals, were beginning to feel the effects of competition on a scale which had never been previously envisaged. Domestic prices had begun to fall in 1874 and the decline had continued in the following year and was forecast to worsen now as the 1876 harvest approached. All the Roxton farms relied as much on livestock as on cereals, so there was some benefit in the shape of a small drop in the cost of feed; but that did not offset the reduction in profits on wheat, and Sam Veryan was concerned. He was well aware that Caroline's understanding of farming and estate management fell a long way short of Rupert's, and his anxieties had grown with her indecision, for it would not be long before ploughing and future cropping decisions would have to be made. Mark Helford had been her constant consultant, but admitted that he understood the books much better than the livestock and the land.

Randolph detected his mother's eagerness to discuss the estate's future, but Helford wanted to hear about the expansion of the American wheat crop, and how it was harvested on such large acreages, and what he had seen of storage silos in Boston and New York; and both wanted an account of his adventures. He tried to condense the story, but made no mention of the Red McLean episode until Caroline asked if men really carried revolvers and shot at each other, as the newspapers reported; and if they did, had he been able to avoid such violence? His smiling 'Yes – most of the time' only served to prompt more questions until he said:

'OK – there was a time in Dodge when I got myself into a spot of trouble, and picked up some lead through a leg. I didn't catch up with the man who did it for nearly a year – but he regretted it then, I guess. No – I didn't kill him – although it was a temptation, I have to admit. I was lucky – dear old Tex Smith turned out to be a retired gunslinger, and he taught me everything he knew and a bit more besides about handling a Colt revolver. There's always liable to be a fight in those frontier towns, and Dodge City's one of the roughest. So knowing how to use a gun – as well as those marvellous Winchesters – was useful. Apart from that there wasn't much trouble that I remember – a few Indians tried to rustle the horses away from the chuck waggon on the last trail and there was a little shooting, but nothing much and they cleared off before anyone was hurt.'

Helford was watching him closely, deep-set dark eyes narrowed a little.

'What are you going to do, Randolph? It sounds as if you've made a lot of money.'

Randolph turned his brandy glass, watching the lamplight reflected in the liquid.

'Yes. I've made quite a lot. And it's going to be strange for a time now – very quiet, in a law-abiding country, I guess. Out there you get into the habit of being aggressive and standing your ground – you have to do that. I must be careful how I speak to people.' He laughed, but without much humour, and felt in his pocket for another cigar. He studied it before lighting it, and they watched him, waiting and trying to read his quiet eyes and thoughtful face. He sliced the end of the cigar carefully with a knife, conscious of the unfamiliar action.

'What am I going to do? Stay here, if you'll have me – if I can be useful. It sounds as if there are a few problems. I might be able to help with them.' He glanced at Helford as he stuck the cigar in the corner of his mouth. 'I owe you both a great deal – everything. And this is where I belong. I want to put my money into the estate, if it can be of benefit. And help Frank find a place of his own. He wants to get his parents out of that terrible little cottage, and take a farm. I think he might have enough money to make a start.'

Caroline looked quickly at Mark Helford, who said: 'That's interesting. One of the tenancies here is coming vacant – ought to be vacant now. You remember George Charlton – old George at Lane Ends? He's past seventy and can't carry on. Your mother wants to help find a little house for him and his wife, and get him out of the farm before it starts to run down. Maybe Frank would be interested – if he fancies us as landlords.'

Us. Us as landlords. Nothing registered on Randolph's face as he flicked a match and drew smoke from his cigar.

'That could be good news. I don't know what he wants yet, except a place of his own. I'll have a look at the farm, if you like, and talk to him.'

Helford said: 'That's sensible. But you, Randolph – d'you really want to stay here? After all this time?'

He nodded, blowing smoke towards the ceiling.

'Where else? As long as there's a place for me – a proper place, so that I can contribute.' He picked up his brandy glass and shot a cautious, questioning glance at the two of them before he drank.

Caroline said softly: 'We need you, Randolph. Very much. I can't run the estate without Mark's guidance – and he has his own business, which gets more complicated every year. And neither of us can cope with the home farm – we're just leaving that to Sam, and he's not sure where his authority ends, and we're not sure how much authority he should have. This place ought to be yours now. Your father's will left it to me, because

183

he said he thought you would never come back. And I'm saying I want you to take over. You can't do it all at once. But gradually, at your own pace, you should – it's yours by right. When you've had a little time to settle down, to be sure that this is what you want, we'll turn it into a partnership, or maybe a company.'

He sipped brandy again, conscious of the sudden chill of Rupert Haldane's memory in the room.

'I told you – this is where I belong,' he said. 'And I realize you must have thought a great deal about this, since you knew I was coming home.' He addressed the implied question to both of them.

Caroline nodded.

'Of course we have. If you want to stay, nothing would please us more, I promise you. It's our dearest wish.'

The long cigar jutted from the corner of his mouth, curling blue smoke. He narrowed his eyes against it as he looked first at one, then the other. We have. Nothing would please us more. Our dearest wish. The plural again. And the total communion between them. Eyes that spoke words, and were understood.

He said: 'Do you have something else to tell me?'

The room was still, except for the lazy spiral of cigar smoke. A log crackled in the fire. Then Caroline's hand reached out across the table to Helford's arm.

'You're very perceptive. Yes – we still have the most – the most important thing of all to tell you. One day – when time has gone by – but you know. I can see you know. Do you mind?' The tears were clear in her eyes as she looked at the man who sat silently, gravely, with her. Then she looked at Randolph again, pleading with him. 'He has been so kind, for so many years. We have grown to love each other very much.'

Very slowly, Randolph took his cigar from his mouth, slanted it into an ashtray. His dark, steady eyes moved first to his mother, then to her motionless, watchful companion. Dark, steady eyes looked back at him; mirrored him. Again the chill of Rupert Haldane in his mind; a ghost of conscience drifting. What was in those eyes? There was something in

184

them; something for him. But he could not read it. He pushed
the ghost aside and remembered – Marlborough, the offer of
work in the Exeter office that had been his salvation, the help
and guidance and patience and training, the dramatic and
unfaltering hand extended to him in his worst moment of fear
and despair and all that had followed his grasping of that
hand; and his mother and the things he had scarcely noticed at
the time but recalled now with startling clarity. So kind, for so
many years. Many years. How many? What did it matter?
The present mattered – whenever the present was, whoever it
was.

He found himself on his feet, and thought he saw fear in
Caroline's face.

He said, very gently: 'You are my beautiful lady. But I
don't mind sharing you. Be happy – both of you.' He looked
at Mark Helford. 'Keep on taking care of her. I guess you've
been doing it for a long time. Thank you for that – and for
taking care of me when I needed it.' He picked up his brandy
glass, contemplated it. Faint lines of humour creased the
corners of his mouth. He raised the glass.

'A toast, I guess. To my lady. And her man.'

IV

Randolph walked into the small stone-built estate office beside the house, with Sam Veryan at his heels. It was ten in the morning and he had been back at Roxton little more than eighteen hours.

'I need to know a lot, Sam,' he said. 'We won't get through it all today or for many days to come. But we can make a start.'

He pointed to a hard chair and, as Veryan settled, perched on the edge of the old desk that had been the heart of Roxton estate business for two generations.

Veryan said cautiously: 'Are you taking over, Mr Randolph?'

'In practical terms, yes. At least for the time being. The future will take care of itself.'

Veryan took a long breath. He was eyeing the tall, sun-bronzed man who was virtually a stranger to him, and seemed to like what he saw.

'That's good news, sir. With respect to your mother, we haven't had a real boss here since your father's last illness started – a year, mebbe. I can only go so far, and sometimes I've needed a lot more'n I could decide. Your mother, bless 'er, didn't always know what t'do, and neither did Mr Helford, although he talked to me a lot and tried to help.'

'All right. Now you talk to me,' Randolph said. 'Tell me what's wrong – not the detail, just the outline. What's urgent? What do we do first?'

Veryan stirred, feeling in the pockets of his tweed jacket for his pipe and tobacco.

'Home farm's not making as much money as it should, Mr Randolph. Since your father became worse ill, I've been trying t'do the books – the trading account. Haven't been able t'do it very well, because I haven't known everything. But I've done my best. An' I know profit's dropping, mainly because of wheat. You know the price, sir? Down to forty-six shillings a quarter. We've nigh on 170 acres of wheat ready for harvesting now. I don't expect it'll average more'n forty-four shillings, by it's all sold. That's ten shillings less than three years ago. Barley's down too, though that don't matter quite as much because we feed most've what we grow.'

'Are the tenants feeling the same pressure?'

'I hear so, Mr Randolph. Not just Roxton tenants, sir – every farm around here. And everywhere else, I've no doubt.'

'How many cattle do we have?'

'Nigh ninety cows 'n heifers milking or calving. Thirty young stock. Thirty Devon and Shorthorn cross steers for beef. We could carry more.'

'Sheep – what's the flock size now?'

'Small, sir – small. Your father took agin sheep. The market wasn't too good round about the time you left us, sir, and he sold off a lot of the ewes. Say forty, plus lambs – and we lost a few lambs last spring in the bad weather.'

'What's the trade for lambs this summer?'

'Fair – quite fair. Exeter and Tiverton markets – fair.'

'Sounds a reasonable balance, even if the stocking's light. Apart from the price of wheat, what's your problem?'

Veryan stuffed the last shreds of tobacco into his pipe and scowled at it. He looked at Randolph, one long leg swinging on the desk edge, hard eyes unwavering, and took a firm hold of his courage.

'I daren't have said this to your father, Mr Randolph – and no disrespect to him. But some of the Shorthorns are the wrong sort. Don't give enough milk, sir – and eat too much compared with what they give. And two of the pastures need ploughing out. Your father'd never hear o'that – he reckoned the sward was still sweet, but it don't come round quick enough after grazing, and there's too much weed in it, and no clover. We need some draining, too.' He nodded at the map of the home farm pinned to a wall over the desk. 'The two top fields left of the wood are very wet. But that'll cost a lot of money.'

'How many men do we have?'

Veryan puffed a cloud of smoke around his head and glowered through it.

'Seventeen regular. Four or five part-timers – and more at harvest, o'course. Plus the estate workers – seven of those. And they don't all work as they should.'

'Why not? We pay more than most, as I recall.'

The steward looked at him uneasily.

'D'you know what's happened while you've been away, sir? The trade union act, and things?'

'No,' said Randolph. 'Tell me.'

'Nigh five years ago, Mr Randolph – Parliament passed the trade union act, and unions became legal. D'you remember hearing of Joseph Arch, sir – 'fore you went away?' Randolph nodded. 'He set up an agricultural labourers' union. Lot of men joined – some of ours. There's been trouble, especially in Norfolk and Suffolk and those counties; but round here a bit as well. Some farmers threw the men out – out of their cottages, too. They'd only hire men who promised not to join the union. There's been some fighting, up an' down. And worse. There's been devil's work, sir. Men meeting in the night and swearing foul oaths and talking of death and mutilation. There are stories of toads being nailed to doors as warning, and men and their families being attacked for not joining the union. Folks say there are secret societies. Only nobody talks about'm much – you just hear whispers. It's worst up north and in the east. But there's strange things hereabouts, too. It's spoiled the relations with the men, even on this farm. Oh, I know there was a lot wrong. But sometimes I think what we've got now is worse, in some ways. The men talk about not having any of the new steam tackle – say they'll refuse to work it if any comes. And sometimes I know they're slowing the job down – just deliberately working slow.'

Randolph eased off the desk, walked round and sat in

the wide wooden armchair behind it. He looked at Veryan steadily.

'Who's the ringleader, Sam? There has to be one. There always is.'

Without hesitation Veryan said: 'Tregoney, sir. You remember him? Bob Tregoney. He's a persuasive talker. Lay preacher, these days, like a lot of these union men. And the rest follow him like sheep. Never thought I'd live to see it, not on this farm. They're not all in the union, Mr Randolph – 'bout seven or eight are, though. And Tregoney's working on the rest all the time – and they all listen to him.' He puffed at his pipe resentfully. 'Sometimes I wonder who's steward. I tried to persuade your father to get rid of him, only he wouldn't. You know what he was like, sir – too kind-hearted – wouldn't believe one of his men could cause trouble.'

'Where's Tregoney live? In one of our cottages? Does he have a family?'

'No – no family – not married. Mebbe that's what's wrong with him. Not enough to think about. And he's not in one of our cottages, not being married – lives with his brother in the village. His father's still around – Billy Tregoney – you'll remember him too, I expect. Worked here, once over, afore you were born. Then for old Griffiths, downalong, and a couple more. Now he's odd-jobbing – filling in on any farm as'll take'm. Getting on a bit, o' course. But no sweeter-tempered on account of that, I can tell you.'

'What does Bob Tregoney do, Sam – what's his work?'

'Mostly ploughing in the autumn and spring. He's good with the horses and the tackle, but not much with cattle – no feel for 'em. Can turn his hand in the smithy, though – repair almost anything. Knows nearly as much about the thresher when it comes round as the men who work it. General labouring, otherwise.'

'How much is he paid?'

'Seventeen shillings, sir. A shilling more'n the ordinary labourers, on account of being able to plough. Our best men got eighteen shillings these days, and Ted Oxley gets twenty shillings for being head cowman. We still pay more'n most farms around, just like it always was – and still look after the men and their families.'

Randolph said: 'We're going to see some changes that Mr Tregoney won't like, Sam. In a few years there'll be self-binding reapers. There'll be fewer jobs around then, like it or not. And there'll be faster threshing with the latest steam engines. And steam ploughing's on its way, with engines and cables. Steam ploughing won't reduce our labour costs – it's quicker, but it needs as many men as horse ploughing. But all told, it adds up to change.' He stood up. 'I think it's time I talked to the men. Call them together outside the stables at twelve o'clock. The estate workers as well as the farm men. Don't tell them why. If they don't know I'm back, don't tell them that either.'

For an hour he studied the purchase ledger and the sales ledger, and the husbandry record inscribed in Veryan's sprawling hand. He wanted to look at the cattle but deliberately kept himself out of sight of men working around the buildings. Then he went into the house.

'Have you had trouble with Bob Tregoney?' he asked his mother.

Caroline came across the hall and went into the study, out of Nora's hearing. Randolph followed her, watching her walk and the set of her shoulders and the way her full skirts swept around her ankles. He thought she was the most attractive woman he had ever seen.

In the study she turned to face him. 'Why do you ask?'

'Because Sam tells me he's stirring up the men.'

She nodded. 'Do you know about the labourers' union?'

'Sam told me – the outline, anyway. I always thought we would have no trouble here from a union because we pay well and we look after the men and their families. It seems it doesn't work like that.'

'Don't blame the men too much,' she said. 'Tregoney's a strong character. He'd make trouble wherever he went. He's just naturally aggressive.'

He was eyeing her reflectively. Despite their long talk

through the previous evening she was still a novelty to him after the rough-spoken women of the American west.

'You haven't answered my question, mother.'

'What question?'

'Have you had trouble with him – you, personally? Or father, before he became ill?'

She looked up at him, a head taller than she was, with his strong jaw and wide mouth and the deep dark mirrors of his eyes. His black hair fell around the nape of his neck, touching his high collar. He wore the grey frock coat and black trousers which he had bought in Southampton the day before, with a white shirt and blue cravat – ridiculously formal wear, she thought, for a meeting with the farm steward. But he carried the clothes easily, and he was light on his feet, and there was a hardness in his face and around his shoulders and in his voice that she had never encountered in a man – not even, she thought with a moment's secret shock, in Mark Helford.

'Not especially,' she said, and knew that he did not believe her.

'But just a little, eh?' His mouth half smiled, but there was no humour in his eyes.

'Don't get excited about it, Randolph.' She put an anxious hand on his arm. 'He's a rude man, that's all. I gave him an instruction a little time ago, and he wouldn't accept it until Sam marched up and repeated it. And he says unpleasant things when I can hear – deliberately, I'm sure. He's putting on an act.'

'I'm not excited. I just wanted to know,' he said. He turned away, then said over his shoulder: 'You said last night you wanted me to take over. It'll be days before I can tell you what I think should be done about the management of the farm and the estate. When I have something to say about that, we'll talk. But I reckon the urgent thing is to make sure the men are working well, especially with harvest just around the corner. I'm taking that over now. Just thought you'd like to know.'

He went away across the hall, taking off his coat and then his cravat and throwing them across a chair. He walked with long strides and seemed to grow as he went, shirt-sleeved, through the door. She thought: Dear God – is this my son? What have I bred? What did you give to me, Mark?

Randolph crossed the carriage drive, went through the wide gate to the farm and across the face of the buildings; past the long barn and the coach house to the stables. The big double doors were open and twenty or more men were gathered there, most with their backs to him and facing Sam Veryan who was talking with head cowman Ted Oxley. Randolph was amongst them before they noticed him, and then he heard a voice say 'Bloody hell – it's 'im – young Randolph'; and another voice 'I said 'e were back – I told 'ee'. Then Randolph was clear of them. He put a foot on the hub of a waggon wheel and vaulted up onto the tail of the vehicle, turning to face them. His eyes moved over the figures, remembering names, seeing the two estate carpenters and their labourers among the farm men; and finding Bob Tregoney with his untidy hair and thick-set figure, noting the fringe of greying beard he had grown around his chin sometime in the last six years.

'Good morning,' he said. 'If you can't hear me, come a little closer.' His voice cut across the cobbled yards and echoed from the buildings beyond. Veryan thought they could have heard him fifty yards away; and yet he did not seem to shout.

'You may have been told that I had returned,' he said. 'I arrived yesterday. Today I've started work. I've spent time this morning looking at the books and the farm records. As the result of my father's illness some things have been neglected. That was inevitable, despite everything Mr Veryan has done. From now on he and I will be working closely together and there will be some changes. This farm is not as profitable as it was. That will be investigated. I shall introduce new machinery, and we shall all work harder. Those who don't want to work harder should leave.' His eyes flicked across faces, lingered for a moment on Tregoney's, then passed on to others. They stared up at him, taking in his stature and his skin darkened by the sun of Kansas and Colorado and its contrast with his white shirt, and the way he seemed to see each one of them, individually, as if selecting them from the crowd; and several men looked down, avoiding his gaze.

'I'm told that some of you now belong to the new union,' he said. 'That's your right. I'm also told that on some farms and estates men have lost their jobs because they have joined the union. That won't happen here. Whether you belong to the union or not, we shall continue to pay better wages than most other farms, and look after our men when they're ill or have other problems – just as we have always done. But don't misunderstand me. I need value for money if this place is to go on being able to employ the numbers of men now working here. That means we must have more production from the same number of men, or the same production from fewer men. I would prefer the former. If I only get the latter, it'll be your choice and not mine, because I shall provide the facilities for a better performance. In the next week or so I shall decide what new facilities we can afford and after I've discussed them with Mr Veryan I shall tell you about them.'

All the time he looked straight at faces, one after another, and every man felt he was being addressed personally, as if he were alone with this new, challenging, razor-voiced man who stood wide-legged above them and spoke as no one had spoken to them before.

'There's one more thing.' The words bounced back from the buildings behind them. 'In a month's time I shall reduce every man's wages by two shillings a week.' His eyes raked over them now, then settled on Tregoney whose shoulders hunched and whose jaw jutted. 'That will take our wage levels down to the average in this neighbourhood. But –' he let the word echo '– at the same time I shall introduce a system of bonuses and overtime payments. The bonuses will be paid on rate of work in every job and will be designed to enable every man to earn at least what he is earning now and, I hope, somewhat more. The overtime will not be compulsory. For the first time you will have recognized hours of work, and any work Mr Veryan has for you beyond those hours will earn extra money – if you want it. The choice will be yours. I want to see every man here earning more money than he can possibly earn on any other farm or estate. But before I can afford to pay it, I have to see an increase in our profits. That may not be easy if the price of corn goes on falling. But I hope that between us we can make it possible.'

He jumped down from the waggon and strode towards them. Several men fell back, making way for him. He beckoned to Sam Veryan, then faced Tregoney with his set mouth and narrowed eyes. He said, loudly enough for every man to hear: 'Mr Veryan – please bring Mr Tregoney to the estate office.'

They watched him go; silent and staring. When he had disappeared around the corner of the long barn there was an audible sigh. Then Veryan nudged Tregoney and said: 'You heard 'im – come on.'

For seconds Tregoney hesitated; then, slowly, he walked across the cobbles in the steward's wake.

Randolph waited in the office, leaning against the front of the desk. When the two men entered he gestured Veryan towards a chair, but left Tregoney standing, facing him.

He said coldly: 'Mr Tregoney, it is my understanding that in recent time my mother gave you an instruction which you did not obey until Mr Veryan had repeated it. I wish you to understand that my mother is the owner of this estate. Her instructions will be obeyed immediately they are given. The alternative is instant dismissal. Is that clear?'

Tregoney shifted on his feet, scowling.

'She don' know too much about farming. I didn't think it was –'

Randolph pushed himself forward from the edge of the desk, and now he stood a clear six inches above the stocky farm worker. He said: 'Mr Tregoney – you're paid to do as you're told – not to debate the decision. Remember what I've said, because I shan't say it again. And remember something else: if you say within my mother's hearing what she describes as "unpleasant things" you will be dismissed instantly for that as well. And if I have any evidence that you said those "unpleasant things" deliberately in order to embarrass or insult my mother, I shall spread you across the yard in front of the men and someone will have to carry you away.'

'You're threatenin' me – you ain' allowed to do that.' Tregoney's face had flushed and his voice rose. 'We've 'ad enough o' you damn' landlords – an' d'you think I'd just stand there an' let you . . .'

And then his tumbling words died and, slowly, he shuffled a step back; for he saw something in the eyes of the man who now seemed to tower over him that he had never seen in any man's eyes. Veryan saw it too, and rose slowly to his feet, wanting to inject a word of caution but unable to speak.

Randolph said softly: 'I'm sure you understand me, Mr Tregoney. My mother is a very special person. She will be treated as such.'

Tregoney swallowed, cleared his throat, then whispered: 'I understand that – Mr Randolph –'

'I'm glad you remembered my name,' the quiet voice said. 'I thought you had forgotten it. I'm not a "damn landlord", Mr Tregoney. I'm the representative of a family that has done more to help the farm labourers of this village over the years than any other landowner. And the process isn't finished.' Abruptly Randolph turned, walked round his desk and sat down. Tregoney watched him, still tense, but now slowly feeling his release from the hold of those terrible near-black eyes. 'And because it isn't finished yet you, as an active member of your union, will find no quarrel with me. But if there is any such matter you wish to discuss, speak to Mr Veryan and he will relay it to me. After that, you and I may talk about it. If there are no matters you wish to discuss I would be pleased if you would cease to create discontent among the men. I'm sure you understand.'

This time Tregoney did not reply, but stared across the desk, struggling to muster his reserves; to find some way of regaining the ground he knew he had lost. Then, to his astonishment, he saw Randolph's mouth widen.

'Let's talk about more agreeable matters, Mr Tregoney. About the changes we're going to see here. As you know we have so far used a contractor's services for threshing, since steam tackle is expensive even though it's so much more efficient than horses. I think that will change. We have more work for a portable steam engine than just threshing. We shall buy our own equipment. In that event I shall need an engineman. It is a very responsible position, requiring a lot of study before it can be properly filled. It is only right, therefore, that the man who does the job should be well paid. The wage will be nineteen shillings a week and there will be opportunities for both bonus and overtime. I think you are capable of doing that job. Do you wish me to consider you for it?'

For long seconds Tregoney gazed at him, finding difficulty in believing that he had heard correctly. The transition from total confrontation to this offer of a promotion and a big wage increase had been too fast for him. But he was quick-witted and he recovered well.

'I'd like to be considered for it,' he said steadily. 'But what about the rest o' the men? Some o' the new tackle as is around costs men jobs. We've seen it before in farming. But if it means men getting sacked an' families starving, none of 'em will have it. I'm not threatening you, Mr Randolph – I'm telling you how the men feel.'

'Let me tell you how I feel,' said Randolph. 'It's my job to make the home farm and the estate profitable. If it isn't profitable there'll be no jobs for anybody – I'll have to sell it, and then anything could happen. I'd be a fool if I told you we would go on employing the same number of men for ever. And you don't think I'm a fool, do you, Mr Tregoney?'

Tregoney's gaze was fixed on Randolph's shirt collar, for he would not risk meeting his eyes.

'I don' think you're a fool. An' the men ain't fools neither –'

'Then they won't expect me to make promises I can't be sure of keeping. You may get back to work now, Mr Tregoney. I'll let you know when I've decided what sort of steam engine to buy. Then we can discuss whether you're going to be the engineman.'

Randolph nodded towards the door in a clear gesture of

dismissal. Tregoney squared his shoulders and stood his ground for silent seconds, then turned abruptly and shuffled away without looking back. Veryan breathed out loudly as the door closed.

'Nasty bit o' work, sir. Are you really going to make him engineman?'

'If he's handy in the smithy, as you say, and good with a thresher, he'll probably be capable of doing the job. But we'll have to see how he behaves in the next few weeks. Is there anybody else who could fill the position better?'

'Doubt it,' Veryan said, scowling at the thought. 'Though whether he'll work well I'm not sure.'

'He'll either work well or not at all,' Randolph said. 'Keep your eye on him.'

The black retriever which Rupert Haldane had bought two years before his final illness and which now accompanied Randolph wherever he went, stood patiently, ears cocked, listening to the barn door creaking in the wind. Above, several tiles were missing from the roof and Frank said doubtfully: 'I wonder if the timbers are sound.'

'We'll look carefully at all the buildings,' said Randolph. 'I'm afraid there's some money to be spent around the estate – not just on this place.'

They were on Lane Ends Farm, with Frank considering Randolph's offer of a tenancy; and neither was particularly impressed.

'It's needing a lot of work, Randy,' Frank said. 'I'm still not sure whether I'd do better buying a place of my own.'

'Your decision,' Randolph shrugged. 'But you haven't enough money to buy and stock a hundred or more acres – somewhere the size of this place – so you'd have to borrow. I was brought up, by my father and Mark Helford, never to borrow unless I was two hundred per cent certain of being able to pay off the debt quickly and then make a lot of extra money as the result of borrowing. I don't think farming can offer you that sort of prospect at this moment. I don't know about you, old son, but I sense trouble – and not just because of this damned weather.'

Instinctively they looked up at the rain-filled clouds and the swaying tops of the elms beyond the farm buildings, and smelled the dampness in the air. The cereal harvest should have started by now, but some of the wheat was still under-ripe after the poor summer and the barley that was ready was not dry enough for the reaper.

'C'mon – let's walk the place,' said Frank, and they tramped across the yard, pushed open a five-barred gate and went out onto the land. They walked heads down, studying the turf and the relative density of grass and clover and weed. Occasionally Frank bent and pulled a handful of grass, inspecting the roots. Part of the farm's Devon herd watched them approach, stirring uneasily in the presence of strangers and the dog at their heels. Frank eyed them, wondering if they would be worth a bid at the forthcoming sale. There were several Hereford crosses among them, with the white faces characteristic of the breed, and Randolph nodded towards them and said: 'I reckon we ought to use more Herefords, Frank. Father used a Hereford bull now and then on the Shorthorns and the calves always did well. They don't fatten quickly, but they're good sorts when they're ready, and they sell well.'

'Why didn't he rear more of them, then?' Frank asked, and Randolph laughed.

'You know what he was like. Believed the sun shone out of his Shorthorns – nothing could improve them. I think he was wrong. So does Sam Veryan. The best are good dual-purpose cows, but there are too many of the other sort – and I have more of those than I like.'

Frank grunted. He pushed open a gate and they went into a ten-acre field of oats. As he looped the securing rope around the gatepost again Frank said: 'There's drainage needed here – back in that pasture there's a wet channel, and this looks like a patchy crop. It'll be the same problem, by the look of it.' He looked cautiously at Randolph. 'It'll cost a lot, Randy – two fields here, and there may be more.'

'Tell you something,' Randolph said. 'There's drainage needed on the home farm, too. And for all I know that may be true elsewhere on the estate. I'm going to spend some of the money I brought back from America on steam tackle. When you've a lot of acres, that's the way to handle drainage – do it yourself instead of paying a contractor – and then use the engine for cable ploughing as well as threshing. And I'm going to offer every tenant the use of the equipment, on a cost basis. It'll be a lot cheaper than contracting.'

Frank stared at him.

'D'you think you can make a thing like that work? Nobody's ever tried it before – a sort of estate co-operative with machinery. You'll have to cost it very carefully.'

'I know. But you're wrong – it has been done before. The Duke of Northumberland has done it, up at Alnwick. I was reading about it a couple of days ago. The report said it was working well. What's good enough for the Duke should be all right for us.'

Frank grinned, but without much humour.

'As long as it's been good enough for his tenants, too, Randy.'

Randolph raised an eyebrow.

'That's what I meant – it's been working well for everyone.'

'Good,' Frank said. He watched a kestrel hovering over the thorn hedge that ran the length of the barley field. 'You know this farm can't be worth a lot of money, Randy?'

Randolph nodded. He, too, was watching the hawk.

'I guess you're right. The rent will have to reflect the things that need doing here – and that it will take us a while to do these things. I'm prepared to let it initially for less than old George is paying.'

The kestrel dipped suddenly, dropping several feet and then steadying against the wind.

'There are some things you can't do anything about,' Frank said. 'And the main one is the shape of the farm – all long and narrow, with the house and buildings right at one end. It may be only a hundred acres, but it'll still be more expensive to work than a place that's nearer a square with the buildings in the middle. And it's right up close to the village, which I don't think I like very much – too easy for poachers and trespassers. There's not a very good natural water supply, either – there are some fields that just can't be grazed – and there's a heavy clay seam across it.'

The hovering kestrel dipped again, checked once, then folded its wings and dropped vertically, extending its claws as it disappeared beyond the hedge. Randolph watched it go, and when it did not rise again he turned and looked hard at Frank.

'Don't you want the farm? Is that what you're telling me?'

Frank met his gaze.

'Yes. I want it. I'm just telling you the rent will have to be right.'

'Of course it will – you should know that.'

'You're a hard man, Randy. I know you too well. And you're a businessman. That's a tough combination. You'll let this farm for as much as you reckon the market will stand, and then a bit more for luck. I don't want favours. But I'm going to make sure I pay an economic figure – or not at all.'

'What else would I expect?' Randolph's mouth widened. 'C'mon. Let's finish the walk. Then we'll go back and look at the books and see if we can settle a figure – with a triennial review which will give time for improvements to start showing results.'

Frank nodded briefly and turned away, moving briskly. Randolph followed, eyeing his friend's back speculatively, the hint of a frown across his forehead as he snapped fingers to call his dog to him.

The harvest was under way. A brisk wind from the north west had changed suddenly to a warm southerly breeze coming off the Channel a few miles away and two days of sunshine had given the reapers a good start. All along the southern quarter of England the wheat and barley and oats were going down beneath the sails, and the sheaves were being bound and stacked ready for carting. Further north, farmers watched anxiously, for their harvest was normally a week or two behind that of the south, and they hoped the weather would now hold after the poor summer.

Late in the evening Sam Veryan picked straw out of his shirt, stretched his tired muscles, and said to Randolph: 'It's gone well today, sir – better'n I thought. I reckon we'll get seven sacks an acre off this lot.'

'Good,' said Randolph. They were leaning on the white gate that separated the house from the farm. 'But we still have to sell it. The Times reported today that the first shipments of new American wheat are already here.'

'They have the advantage,' Veryan said. 'Their harvest is so much earlier than ours. And the railways take it to the ports so quick, now.' He grinned suddenly. 'Why'm I telling you, Mr Randolph? You told me that only a week back.'

Randolph chuckled. He pulled two slender cigars from his pocket and offered one to the steward. They lit them in silence, watching the reddening western sky and the dark silhouette of the distant wood. From the stable yard voices called between buildings, and hooves cracked and clanked on cobbles as the horses were wiped down ready for the night.

Sam Veryan said: 'Thought any more about the farm, Mr Randolph – what you're going to do?'

Randolph nodded. He watched cigar smoke curling away above them.

'Yes. More sheep, Sam. We can't do much about it this autumn, because we couldn't feed a bigger flock through the winter. But as soon as we start ploughing we'll make sure that next year it'll be a different story. We should be able to stock nearly two hundred ewes if we can get our summer grazing right – then fold them onto the barley stubbles and feed turnips before they go onto winter pasture with a bit of hay. Work it out, Sam. We'll cut the wheat acreage by whatever's necessary – if the wheat price is going to go on falling, and I'm sure it is, there'll be more money to be made out of sheep on a farm that's suited to livestock like this one. But don't cut down the land we need for the cattle. We'll agree on a ploughing pattern. I want better grass, and I'm going to sell some of the cows we have and replace them with better sorts. Talk to Ted Oxley about it for me, will you?'

Veryan drew appreciatively on his cigar.

'I'll be pleased to do that, Mr Randolph. Some of them cows may be well bred, but they don't milk like they should. And I don't think Ted's all that happy about either of the stock bulls.'

Randolph said: 'I'll look at them.' He had long ago concluded that for many people – and Rupert had been among them – cattle breeding had as much to do with the social status of herd owners as the milking ability of the cows; and since he had little patience with the former he could afford to pay more attention to the latter. There were cattle in the Roxton herd that had been kept because they were bred to blood lines which Rupert had considered aristocratic rather than because they milked and bred particularly well. Now there would be changes.

He eased himself away from the gate.

'There's another thing, Sam. I'll be away for a few days. I'm going to look at steam engines and cable ploughing systems and drainage equipment. We'll thresh this year's harvest with our own engine, Sam – to hell with contractors. And we'll plough out this autumn with steam – our own steam. So you can tell the men it's going to happen – and so is their new pay system. I'll start them both at the same time. No man will be worse off, unless he's idle; the best men who work the hardest and quickest will be a lot better off – and the farm will be better off too. How's Bob Tregoney behaving?'

Veryan, still digesting the significance of Randolph's steam plans, took several seconds to bring his mind to bear on the troublesome Tregoney.

'About the same, sir. He's been doing a lot of talking to the men – and they stop and walk away when they see me coming. But I've overheard 'em talking among themselves. I reckon 'e's telling 'em that steam is coming and it'll cost some of 'em their jobs.' Veryan studied his cigar, then added reluctantly: 'And I hear he don't like you very much, Mr Randolph. So you can bet he'll be trying to persuade the men to think the same.'

'We'll have to wait to find out if he's succeeding,' said Randolph, as if nothing had surprised him. 'Now call it a day. And let's hope the weather holds.'

He strolled off across the drive towards the house, calling 'Goodnight' over his shoulder, his quiet dog shadowing him. Sam Veryan watched and slowly shook his head. He welcomed the new leadership, but he could not pretend that he was not uneasy about the future.

Two days later Randolph went to Exeter, lunched with Mark Helford, walked through the quayside offices in which he had worked under such stimulating direction for three years that now seemed a lifetime ago, and climbed aboard a train for Bristol. From there he crossed the country to London, went north by stages to Bedfordshire, Lincolnshire and Yorkshire where John Fowler's pioneer company was based at Hunslett and the West Riding Steam Ploughing, Cultivating and Thrashing Company had gathered more experience than any other concern of its type in the country; and then to Newcastle-upon-Tyne where he gained an appointment with the agent of the Duke of Northumberland on the massive Alnwick estate. After that he went back to London and spent three days reading Royal Agricultural Society journals and reports before returning to Exeter almost three weeks after he had set out – with a bag full of literature and notes from conversations with four steam engine manufacturers and five landowners and farmers who had used their equipment.

A week later he called a meeting of his tenants, including Frank who was making final plans to move into Lane Ends Farm. They came, one by one on a late summer evening; eight men of whom Frank was the youngest and sixty-year-old Jonas Taylor the oldest. With the exception of Frank, all had been Roxton tenants for more than seven years and Peter Patchett who farmed the 260-acre Middle Farm, the largest of the tenanted holdings, had been on the estate for twenty-one years. They sat around the big hall and Randolph poured whisky and ale, except for Patchett who was a teetotaller, a committed Baptist and a dedicated observer of the Lord's Day every week no matter what the pressures of work and season.

Randolph perched on the edge of the heavy oak table that had stood in the hall of Roxton Grange throughout most of its 230 years, and said: 'There are two reasons for this gathering. The first is so that we can get to know each other. You are aware that this estate is now owned by my mother, and you may have gathered that I am taking day-to-day control of it for her. And we are making a number of changes which provide the second reason for our meeting, because I have a proposition for you. In brief it is this: I am planning to buy some modern steam-driven equipment for ploughing, harrowing and draining as well as threshing. It will be mostly Fowler equipment which, you may know, is among the best and most reliable that is available. I am willing to make the equipment accessible to all of you on a cost basis, taking into account loss of interest on capital, depreciation, repairs, oil, and the wages of an engineman and his assistant. I have here –' he tapped a small pile of papers at his side '– a scale of charges which will pay those costs. They vary according to the job to be done. You will find that they represent a considerable saving on a contractor's charges. I'd like you to take them away – there's a copy for everyone – and study them. Then we'll meet again in a week's time to discuss your views and, I hope, reach an agreement.'

He handed the sheets of paper to Jonas Taylor who was sat nearest to him and, as they were passed around, felt in his pocket for a cigar. He sliced off the end and felt for matches, watching the shrewd, weather-worn faces around him. He was aware of tension; a slight tightening of the muscles around his shoulders and neck. This meeting was important. The equipment he wanted would cost nearly £1800 and could not be justified for use on the home farm alone. And yet he knew it was the way they had to go. Steam power was taking over; and if the labourers were to become more militant he had to find ways of employing fewer of them and of paying higher wages to those who were left. He was certain that his scheme – based as it was upon one that had been proven already elsewhere – would help his tenants to cut their costs. But he knew enough of them to appreciate their fundamental spirit of independence. That they regarded the estate with some affection he had no doubt, for that had been a Roxton characteristic for two generations or more. But like most farmers they were still sturdily individualistic, and the idea of entering into long-term agreements with the squire – as several still called the occupant of the Grange – might encounter instinctive resistance.

He flicked a match into life and put the flame to his cigar as Peter Patchett cleared his throat.

'You'll be wanting us to ask questions, Mr Haldane?' When Randolph nodded he went on: 'Like everybody, I'll want to think about this. But I can see a difficulty already. There's nine of us. Sure as the good Lord's above, there'll be times when more'n one of us'll be wanting your equipment at the same time. I don't have to tell anybody that a delay of even a couple of days can make a lot of difference to some jobs – specially if the weather's as catchy as it's been this summer. How're you going to solve that one?'

Somebody else murmured agreement as Randolph blew smoke into the air and said: 'A scheme like this has been working well on the Duke of Northumberland's estate for three years. It depends on planning. So far you've been used to making up your minds at twenty-four hours' notice when you'll plough a certain field, or harrow it. But for threshing you've had to book the contractor weeks ahead – maybe months, even. You can do the same with most other jobs, if you try. Don't forget that you're still on your own for harvesting and haymaking. Those are the jobs where time is vital. Everything else can be planned – if you're willing to take that bit of extra trouble. I hope the savings the scheme offers will make that trouble worth while.'

William Baydon, who farmed 130 acres and whose family had lived in the Roxton area for more than a century, pulled his side-whiskers reflectively and raised a hand to attract attention.

'My brother's a contractor, Mr Haldane. He's been doing all my work as long as I've been 'ere. And he does work for two more of us – Bill, there, an' John.' He nodded at two watchful faces across the room. 'I wouldn't like to do anything to harm his business. I'm sure Bill 'n' John wouldn't, either. And I don't think it would go down too well in the village, sir. Business ain't that brisk for anybody in these parts.'

Randolph said evenly: 'That's a personal problem you'll have to face – and make your own decision. And we must all realize that for every man who decides not to take part, the charges for the rest will have to rise a little.'

Jonas Taylor pulled a pipe from the waistcoat stretched across his ample stomach and felt in the pockets of his rough tweed jacket for tobacco.

'There's a benefit you haven't mentioned, Mr Haldane. If this scheme works, one or two of us might be able to get by with fewer men. I think I could make a saving – and I'd welcome it. Farm o' the size o' mine has a big bill for labour – yours'll cost even more, I reckon, Peter?'

He nodded across at Patchett, who nodded in return as Taylor's thick fingers prodded tobacco into a big briar pipe. But it was William Baydon who interjected: 'That's something else as'd not be welcome in the village, though. My family's all there, so I got some feeling for'm. It's allus been said as steam'd be the end of the farm labourer, one day. We can't blame'm for being agin it.'

'It'll be the end of the labourer if we all go outa business,' growled Edward Robey, who had nearly 200 acres under his care and was a big, scowling man of fifty who worked hard to support a wife and five children who, to his declared disgust, were all girls. 'I reckon the last coupla years has bin a warning. You mark m'words, friends – there's worse coming. Anything as'll reduce my costs is good for me and for those men I can afford to keep paying. We'll never manage without the labourers. But mebbe we'll have to manage with fewer of'm. Steam can only help us. This plan is like having our own without paying for it. I'm prepared to thank Mr Haldane. I'm in favour.' He reached for his whisky glass and drained it, as if the matter had been settled.

They talked for an hour, sometimes soberly, sometimes aggressively, occasionally with laughter and coarse humour, until Patchett heaved himself to his feet and said: 'I think we should go, squire. It's an interesting proposition you got, and I'll be considering it. You want us to come back a week tonight?'

'Yes. With a decision, please,' Randolph said. 'We have to move quickly to make sure the equipment is working in time for threshing and autumn ploughing.'

They filed out, calling their farewells, boots clattering on the polished wooden floor and on the stone steps outside. Frank was the last to go; and as he went he looked back at Randolph who was not surprised to see him reappear a couple of minutes later.

'I didn't want the others to see me coming back,' he said, as he came into the hall. 'They all know we've been together for the last five or six years and they'll likely imagine I've worked some special deal with you if they see us talking too much.'

Randolph grinned and poured more whisky.

'I suppose so – though I'm not over-anxious about what people think.' He handed Frank a glass. 'What's on your mind?'

Frank slumped into a chair and stretched his legs.

'I was wondering, while all that talk was going on,' he said slowly, 'whether you ever wish you'd never come home.'

Randolph's eyes were suddenly quiet. He crossed the room to the window looking out across part of the carriage drive and the lawns to the trees silhouetted now against the late evening sky.

Eventually he said: 'Yes. I'm glad I came home. But I know what you're talking about. In spite of the violence there's space and opportunity and simple relationships there – and rewards. Big rewards if you work at it. Whereas here we're just running into trouble – falling prices, social problems, and the rest. Right?'

'Right. I would have done better if I'd just found a way to send money back to the folks, and stayed where I was. We'd have been very rich men inside five years, Randy. I'm sure that's not going to happen here, for me. You're different, of course. You're rich anyway.' He looked sideways, quickly, at the tall figure by the window.

Randolph caught the glance as he said: 'I guess I won't be so rich in another few years. Farming's booming over there. It's running down hill here. We have conflicts that don't exist in America. And they're going to grow. There are fundamental changes taking place in this country that won't trouble Americans because they're starting with a different society than we've ever had. Yes, in selfish terms, I guess we would both have done better to stay over there. I suppose I came back partly to see my mother – and father, too, though I was too late for that. But now she doesn't need me. Perhaps if I'd known that, it might have been different.'

Frank stared at him through the gathering gloom of the hall.

'She doesn't need you? I would have thought she needed you a great deal.'

Randolph turned away from the window and walked to one of the oil lamps.

'To run this place? Yes, I suppose so. But she would do pretty well if it was all sold. You see, one day she'll marry Mark Helford. That's confidential. I couldn't tell anyone else. I'm glad, of course, because she's happy.'

He struck a match and lit the lamp carefully, adjusting the wick until the flame was to his satisfaction, hearing Frank's intake of breath.

'Of course. He's here a lot, isn't he? I've seen him many times since we came back.'

'He's helped her a great deal,' Randolph said. 'He's been trying to run the estate for her, since father went. And don't forget that you and I owe him everything. He's a good friend to all of us. But nothing will be announced for a while – until the spring, I guess. Then they'll marry in the summer. Once the obligatory year of mourning has passed –' he checked himself, for the words had been mocking in his ears and he had not intended that.

'Thanks for telling me,' Frank said. He drank the rest of his whisky quickly, then stared at the empty glass. 'It's good to have the – the sort of relationship we have. I just hope the future won't destroy it.'

Randolph, in the act of lighting another lamp, turned, staring.

'Destroy it? What the hell are you talking about?'

'Something else that makes me think I'd rather have stayed in America.' Frank was still looking at his glass. 'There we were equals – partners. I was the labourer who'd become as good as you. Here I'm just one of your tenants. You're the squire – the master. All right – I know it makes sense for me to start this way and get a really good place of my own in a few years. But we aren't equal any more. My interests are not the same as yours, and they'll be opposed to yours in the future, sometimes. We used to fight a lot as kids. But we never quarrelled much. Now it'll be different. If we fight now it won't be with fists. It'll be with something much more damaging – our minds.'

He pushed himself out of his chair, set his glass carefully on a table, and walked to the door. As he went he said: 'That's really what I came back to say, Randy. Goodnight.'

Within two weeks Randolph had the agreement he needed with all his tenants except William Baydon, and he wrote letters ordering two Fowler engines, a four-furrow plough, a mole plough and pipe layer for drainage, a cultivator and a harrow, and the necessary steel rope and rope porters. He completed the equipment with a thresher and a water cart and pump bought second-hand from a bankrupt local contractor, and warned Sam Veryan that he would probably have to sell four of the farm's twenty draught horses by the end of the year, and that two or even three men might have to go.

Then he sent for Bob Tregoney and said: 'The new equipment will be here in a few weeks. I've discussed with Mr

Veryan the job of engineman. He recommends you for it. The wage is nineteen shillings plus the new work bonus and as much overtime as Mr Veryan considers necessary. Do you want it?'

Tregoney knew that few of the farm men anywhere in the neighbourhood were earning as much as that. He squared his shoulders.

'I'd like it, Mr Randolph,' he said. 'But not if it's going to cost men their jobs –'

'You don't lay down the conditions,' said Randolph tersely. 'If you try, you won't get the job. So if you've nothing else to say you'll find your new wage will start as soon as the engines arrive. Study them carefully, Mr Tregoney. The agent will instruct you in their use.'

Tregoney's jaw jutted and his lips clamped. Then he turned abruptly and left the office. Randolph watched him from the window and said aloud to himself: 'It might work out well – or it might be a big mistake.'

The news got around the village quickly and one day soon afterwards Mark Helford tethered his black gelding alongside the estate office, walked in and said: 'Do you know there's gossip about this place, Randolph?'

Randolph, in the act of drawing a new map of the estate for printing in Exeter, showed his surprise.

'No. Tell me.'

'It's being said that you're going to ruin the village – that you're a tough Americanized businessman without any feelings for the traditions that have kept communities like this together, and that you're ruthless and unfeeling in your dealings with men. Your new steam equipment scheme with the tenants is undercutting local contractors and it won't be long before other landowners are copying you. You've told your men that soon there may not be work for all of them. Robey and Patchett have already sacked one man apiece and more are expected to go.'

Randolph looked up at him.

'So that's what they say. Some of it's true, some of it isn't. Either way I can't stop it.'

Helford perched on the edge of a chair, his eyes questioning the younger man.

'It might be as well to understand them, though. There are sixty or seventy men in regular employment on the estate and many more who look to it for casual work. They've forgotten Randolph Haldane as a boy. They only know Randolph Haldane as a man who has appeared suddenly out of the wild American middle west, who even has a touch of American in his speech, and who has hit this easy-going, benevolent and slightly run-down place like a hurricane – not least with new equipment that will probably mean fewer jobs, and with a new pay system on the home farm that no one yet believes will mean other than less money for the majority.'

'I've told them it will mean more for every man who does a proper day's work,' Randolph said flatly. 'And their picture of Randolph Haldane doesn't interest me. I know what I am – and what I'm doing.'

'I still think you should be aware that a lot of people are worried, and for the most fundamental reasons.'

Randolph put his pencil on the desk top and stood up.

'They're worried? I'm worried, too – about the future of the home farm and every tenant and every worker on the estate. What would you do?'

They faced each other; dark hair, dark eyes, skin tanned a little deeper than the sun could justify, tall and wide-shouldered. Only Helford's beard and greying temples and the age gap separated them.

'I'd do the same,' Helford said. 'But there's a difference between us. People say I'm a hard businessman. But they also say I'm fair and that I'll help a man who is down as long as he's square with me. And I've gone out of my way to foster that image, because it's good for business relationships. It's all calculated, Randolph. You haven't had enough time yet – but I give you the recommendation for what it's worth.'

'You're devious,' Randolph said. Then he grinned. 'I haven't time or inclination to be devious. This place needs shaking up, and I'm shaking it. People will feel better when their teeth stop rattling. We can't stand still. Things are

211

changing around us and we have to adapt. Incidentally, I'm going to do something with the woodlands. There are hardwoods and softwoods which need thinning, and there's need for new plantings – some quick-maturing trees and some which will benefit my children and grandchildren.' He laughed quickly. 'If I ever have any.'

Helford chuckled.

'You'll never have time,' he said. And Randolph laughed again, retorting: 'I will, if the lady can run fast enough.' Then his mind darted to another subject. 'How's your American grain trade? Are you importing much?'

Mark Helford looked at him curiously.

'Too much, I imagine you will think – in view of what it's doing to home prices. I'll be handling around 4,000 tons this season. But for the sake of Helford Shipping I could do with more.'

Randolph shrugged.

'Neither you nor I will stop it. If you don't import it someone else will. It's big international business now.'

'And it's becoming very well protected on this side of the water,' Helford said. 'Contracts are tying it all up before it lands here.'

'So if you want more, you have to go out there and get it at source?'

'That's what it looks like.'

'Do you agree with me that there's a great deal more to come – that we've only seen the first trickle before the flood?'

'I do. But you know more about it than any of us – you've seen the start of the expansion across the prairies.'

'That's what I was thinking about,' Randolph said. 'There is absolutely nothing to stop the revolution that's going to hurt British farming a lot. We have to learn to adapt to it. But meanwhile there's no reason why you shouldn't derive some benefit. Before long I'll be able to afford to take some time away from here. I wouldn't mind another look at America. Would you like me to go back and see if I can get you some new contracts, right there at the American ports? If I go in April I'll be nicely ahead of the harvest – just when the

212

merchants and shippers are looking for new business.' He grinned. 'I might even do it without commission – if you pay the expenses.'

And that was how he met Laura Falkland.

V

Max Falkland was fifty, five feet six inches tall and weighed more than two hundred pounds. His frock coat was well tailored, his waistcoat carried a heavy gold watch chain across his considerable stomach, there was a diamond pin in his silk cravat, and his round face would have been self-satisfied had it not been for his quick and eager eyes.

He was a grain merchant – one of the new breed of gamblers in a volatile, complex and growing market which had driven some men into bankruptcy but was making fortunes for others. He had a keen buyer in Chicago and another in Kansas City and he had storage in Boston right up alongside the port. For ten years he had made money steadily; now, with the explosion of exports to Europe getting bigger every year, he was half a millionaire, which was more than sufficient to satisfy the ambitious Southern belle whom he had married nearly thirty years before and who had come close to returning to her family's home in Virginia when the civil war had devastated the central southern states. Max Falkland had saved his marriage, but at the cost of allowing politics into his home, for Mary Falkland had become a significant figure in the growing movement for the enfranchisement and liberation of women.

Wyoming, to the astonishment and dismay of almost every male in America and the majority in the pioneer state itself, had given women the vote in 1870, and this success had fired the female legions. Mary saw herself walking in step with Belle Starr, Laura Fair, Esther Morris and Calamity Jane, and desperately wanted her two daughters to do the same. Elizabeth, the elder, was more than willing to comply; but Laura, two years younger, was far more interested in men than women, and by the time she was twenty-four was in her second engagement – this time to Melvyn Ashley, son of a Boston fishing fleet owner. He had supplanted a young writer and journalist in her affections because both his financial prospects and his physique were better, even though Max Falkland was slightly concerned that both might be threatened ultimately by the whisky for which Ashley seemed to have a considerable capacity.

Randolph glimpsed Laura first at the start of a three-day Democratic convention in Boston at which Mary Falkland's cause was a minor but nonetheless stimulating topic. They were in a cocktail lounge at the hotel which was the scene of the gathering – he as the guest of Tom Hogarth after a week of meeting grain merchants around the port, she in the company of her parents. Their glances met across the hubbub of conversation – and locked for several seconds.

She was tall, with long dark hair, a small nose and wide sensual mouth, and an hour-glass figure encased in blue silk; and all her mother's fiery independence and disregard for convention were in the flash of her eyes.

Randolph, who felt he had been too long out of the company of young women, said to Hogarth: 'Who's the gorgeous creature in blue – by the pillar?'

Hogarth, who seemed to know half the population of Massachusetts, glanced across the room.

'Laura Falkland – daughter of Max Falkland who's in the grain trade. You ought to meet him. Family live out towards Worcester somewhere. Town house, too. And you're too late – she's set to marry a guy called Mel Ashley.'

Without shifting his gaze Randolph asked: 'Is he here?'

Hogarth looked around.

'Don't see him. Hear he's not much interested in politics – which doesn't please Mama Falkland any. But they say Laura has a mind of her own.'

'Do they, indeed?' Randolph murmured, as much to himself as to Hogarth.

For several minutes he watched; and she was aware of him, for he was a commanding figure in that pale-faced, over-weight company.

Presently he said: 'Introduce me, Tom – or find someone who will.'

Hogarth looked sideways at him and grinned.

'I'll find someone. But I told you – you're too late.'

Randolph said softly: 'Being late means you just have to go faster to catch up.'

Five minutes later he was presented to Laura Falkland and her parents, and felt the interest in her eyes as he acknowledged her casually and immediately gained Max Falkland's attention with his talk of grain export opportunities. When Falkland learned of his circumstances in England and the reasons for his current presence in America his eyes sharpened – Randolph swore later to Helford that he had seen dollar signs dancing in them – and he found Randolph more than ready to agree with the suggestion that 'This is no place to talk sensible business – how's about you coming to lunch with me tomorrow?'

Then Randolph turned to Mary Falkland, who was as thin as Max was fat and who had an astonishingly strident voice and aggressive manner for a lady who was only a little above five feet tall.

'And what is your interest here, ma'am?' he enquired cordially, to which she retorted in tones which cut through the hubbub of conversation around them: 'Women, Mr Haldane – women. The underprivileged of American society. And from what I hear, of British society too. The enfranchisement of women is the most important single issue now before the American people. We're marching, sir – and our army is growing every day. And the issue is not only one of the vote. Women have been enslaved since the dawn of time, with little opportunity to express their potential. Equality is the cornerstone of this great country, Mr Haldane – but so far it has been equality for men only. Now times are changing. I'm proud to be among the pioneers – to be flying the flag for American womanhood –'

It continued for minutes and Randolph became fascinated as he waited to see how long it would be before she paused for breath. Then, gradually, it became apparent that the diminutive orator was embracing into her audience any who as much as glanced at her – and many did, for her voice dominated the confusion of words around them. He watched her in grudging admiration, and caught Laura's scarcely concealed amusement. She edged close to him in the crowd and whispered: 'You didn't realize what you were starting, I guess.'

His mouth widened and his eyes held hers.

'It's an impressive performance,' he murmured, then stepped back willingly to make way for a bald, loud-waistcoated man who barked: 'You may have some right on your side, Mrs Falkland, but not enough to impress the voters.' Mary Falkland whirled on him and Randolph backed further away, keeping Laura beside him with a hand on her elbow. He said: 'He's a courageous man – I wouldn't fancy arguing with her. Are you among her supporters?'

She laughed at him.

'I? Certainly not. I have neither the time nor the inclination. I'm all in favour of votes for women, but I'm happy to let others fight the battle. But it seems you have a business interest which appeals to my father, Mr Haldane. Perhaps we shall see more of you in less frenetic circumstances.'

'You will,' he promised easily. 'But if you're not interested in politics, what are you doing here?'

'Family duty,' she said, and not for an instant did her eyes leave his. 'And it's a convivial occasion – although I confess that by the time the next couple of days are over I'll be thoroughly bored with it. How long do you intend to stay in America?'

He almost said: 'I'm leaving in three days.' But her face and her provocative eyes and her exquisite figure persuaded him to say instead: 'I don't know. It depends on – business. I had intended to leave soon, but I may change my mind. People here are so – interesting.'

She read him clearly, as he had intended, and said: 'I'd like another drink. Do you think you could find one for me?'

He did, and they stood together in the crowd, forgotten by Mary Falkland and by Max who by this time had found another business acquaintance and the possibility of another

217

deal; unnoticed by anyone except the observant Tom Hogarth who glimpsed them and their easy amusement with each other and thought: Hell – he's going fast enough to catch up with a dozen Mel Ashleys.

When they parted, much later, he took her fingers and raised them to his lips and murmured: 'I'll say goodnight rather than goodbye – I'm sure I shall see you again.' And she inclined her head, allowing her hand to be held just a little longer than was necessary, and said: 'I hope so, Mr Haldane. I'll look forward to it.'

She watched him move away through the crowd, Tom Hogarth at his side, and felt a pulse beating in her throat. She thought: He's a magic man. Are all Englishmen like that? But she knew they were not – and told herself that there was no one, in Britain or America or anywhere in the world, like the man whose eyes were still vividly in her mind, whose voice was still echoing in her ears, whose fingers were still brushing against hers and leaving them tingling, whose presence had eclipsed a hundred people in a noisy room and had left her feeling utterly alone now that he had gone.

He lunched with Max Falkland the following day, and it took more than two hours for them to debate the grain trade, the opening up of the American west, the expansion of the railroads across Kansas, Nebraska, Colorado and Wyoming in the years which had followed the historic link between Union Pacific and Central Pacific in Utah, and the avalanche of wheat now coming back east through Missouri and Illinois to the great industrial cities and the eastern seaboard ports. Then, with his arm around Randolph's shoulder, Max said: 'I reckon I'll be pleased to do business with you, son. I'll also be pleased to have you dine with me and my family at our home this evening.'

When he arrived at the Falkland house he greeted Laura with easy but proper courtesy and a secret familiarity as their eyes met. He endured Mary Falkland's intense conversation, Max Falkland's jovial but unending discourse on investment and interest rates, and the shrewd Elizabeth Falkland's scarcely-concealed suspicion of him; and it was all worth while when, shortly before he left, Laura contrived two minutes alone with him and he said: 'What I need now more than anything is the promise that you'll see me again. I'll be lunching tomorrow at the Atlantic Hotel. Will you join me?'

She laughed at him.

'I may have to be chaperoned,' she said. 'But I'll endeavour to avoid it. Either way, I'll be there.'

She was, having made the excuse to her family of the need for a morning's shopping, and she arrived alone. They talked and laughed, their conversation ranging over economics and politics – although not about the enslavement of women – and Washington and London scandals, the price of land and the cost of food and the discomfort of the railroads and of steamships, and it was not until they were drinking coffee that she said suddenly: 'Do you realize, Randy, that I'm risking my reputation being here with you? I'm engaged to be married. Someone who recognizes me could easily see us and report back to my family – or worse, to Mel's.'

He said: 'You must have thought of that before you came. Where is he, anyway?'

'In New York,' she said. 'He's in his father's business, and they're developing it there. He's often away.'

'Do you trust him?' he asked abruptly.

'No. I don't think I do. I suppose that's why I persuaded myself that I was justified coming here to see you. Of course, I think he'll settle down when we're married.'

He thought she said it without conviction and observed: 'Some do – and others don't. I wonder if I shall ever meet him.'

She looked straight at him across the table.

'I don't think you should, Randy,' she said.

'Why not?'

'Because I might be there too, and then I'd have to choose between you.' She said it quite calmly, as if it were the most ordinary comment of the day.

His fingers searched a pocket for his cigar case. He opened it carefully, chose a cigar and contemplated it.

'That might be difficult,' he said. 'Because I haven't asked you to marry me.'

She said: 'One day you would – if it were not for Mel.'

He held up the cigar, and a passing waiter hurried across, sliced it, and struck a match for him. He drew smoke, watching her all the time, remembering the steamship berth that would be waiting for him the next day.

'How do you know?'

'It's in your eyes. It's been there since I arrived. Have I shocked you?'

Without hesitation he nodded.

'Yes. And that's not an easy thing to do. I think you're entering an unhappy marriage, Laura – whether I'm around or not.'

She shook her head.

'Not unhappy. It will be very civilized – plenty of money, agreeable friends, interesting places to visit, children. Very civilized.'

'Is that what marriage is about?'

'What do you think it's about?'

'Two people,' he said. 'Two people who don't need money or friends or places to visit or even children. Two people who long to go to bed together every night and long to get up in the morning so that they can be with each other every day. If there's money and friends and children, they're a bonus.'

She whispered: 'Last week I'd have said that was idealism – perfection which people only dream about – that in reality we all have to settle for less.'

'Last week?'

'Before I met you. Before I saw you across the heads of people all jabbering and drinking at the party. Before I saw you looking at me and wanting me.'

'Was I so transparent?'

'Yes. And I'm glad. Otherwise we wouldn't have been talking like this.'

'And what now? I haven't told you – I'm booked on a ship tomorrow.'

Her eyes widened and she covered her mouth.

'Oh, God. Tomorrow?'

'Yes. If I come back in eight weeks will you marry me?'

Her hand came away from her mouth, slowly.

'You're crazy. We don't know each other.'

'I've known you for a million years. Will you?'

'I haven't known you for a million years.'

'Stay with me for the rest of the day. That'll be long enough. Will you?'

'You said I shocked you. Now you've shocked me.'

'We'll both get over it. Will you?'

She slid a hand across the tablecloth towards him. It was her left hand, and he saw a diamond and sapphire ring gleam on her finger. He reached out and, gently but firmly and deftly, he twisted the ring and slid it from her finger.

'Now will you marry me?'

She made no attempt to reclaim the ring, but found his hands instead, twining her fingers around his. Her eyes were very big and very serious.

'Randy – I'm volatile, and unpredictable, and I speak before I think. I started this without thinking. But I felt something – something I've never felt before. No one has ever gotten into me the way you have. No one has ever made me feel the way you've made me feel. Yes.'

'Yes what?'

'Yes please, I'll marry you. If you come back in eight weeks or eight years, I'll marry you.' And then, without warning, her eyes were bright with tears and her fingers hurt his and she whispered: 'Please don't let me down.'

He leaned forward, picked up her purse, opened it, and dropped Mel Ashley's ring inside. Then both his hands covered hers.

'I'll never let you down,' he said softly. 'Not for one day in all our lives.' Then he thought for a moment and added: 'Are you strong enough to go through with this? There's bound to be a row.'

She nodded, blinking back the tears.

'Yes. Of course. I don't care. I only care about us. I'll show them I only care about us. The convention dinner is tonight. I'm supposed to go. But I won't. I'll tell Mama that I'm dining with you and that I'm not going to be chaperoned. Where shall we go?'

'Here,' he said. 'We'll celebrate right here. At this same table.'

It was when they had left the hotel and had climbed into a cab that he looked at her, startled, and said: 'Laura – do you realize? I haven't told you I love you. Not once.'

She leaned her head back against the high leather seat, watching him in the dimness of the cab.

'Tell me now. Please.'

'I love you. I didn't know there was such a feeling. I love you.'

She closed her eyes for a moment.

'I'm glad. Because I love you with everything there is in me.'

He leaned across, taking her chin gently and turning her head towards him and he thought his heart would stop as he kissed her and felt her warmth and her eagerness and her surrender in the jolting cab and the noisy street.

She climbed out of the cab when they reached the Falkland house and ran across the sidewalk and up the steps, paused briefly to wave to him, and was gone. And when he called for her again, five confused and excited hours later, she was waiting beside the curtains in the room next to the hall and darted out in the half-light of dusk before he could leave the cab to greet her, radiant in a dark blue coat and slanting bonnet and a silver dress which swept around her feet as she hurried to him.

She shrugged off his questions about how her parents had reacted to her news, and about how she would tell Mel Ashley, and spent half the evening asking him about England and his house and the farms and Roxton village and his mother, and he told her everything he could think of and yet knew it was not enough. Then it was his turn to question her, and she told him of her childhood and her schooling and the big house in Worcester, of Boston society and her mother's politics and her father's tolerance. She even told him about Mel Ashley, and he thought she was sad – not for herself but for this man he did not know but who had come so close to the happiness which now surged through him. But when he hinted at that she shook her head and said: 'No – not Mel. He'll regret it. But he'll soon start thinking of himself again. He's very self-reliant. A bottle or two of whisky and he'll forget me.' And she changed the subject quickly to hide her own flickering conscience, then forgot it when they talked of when he would return and where they would marry and what they would do after that, and where they would live.

Much later, when they were almost ready to leave, she whispered to him: 'I'd almost forgotten. Tonight I've a room booked at the convention hotel. Mama and Papa and Liz are staying there too – it's all part of the event. Take me there, Randy – and come up to kiss me goodnight.' She shivered at the thought, but in excitement.

The convention dinner was still in progress, and they went quietly and unnoticed to her room and she held the door open for him without a word. When he had closed it they came together, and it was their first full, private embrace and it lasted for minutes. The room was still in darkness, but not totally for the lights of the city were beyond the windows and the curtains were drawn back, so there was just enough to be seen to add to their excitement as they laughed and whispered and thrilled through the tedious but essential process of undressing each other.

In bed they lay close for a long time, not moving, their lips touching, listening to each other, and wondering, until his fingers caressed her neck and her shoulders and traced the curves down to her nipples hard against him and she moved in ecstasy and her muffled voice said: 'Randy – please – love me a little, but not too much. Be careful with me. I want you, and I'm afraid.'

His hands were still and he held his breath momentarily. Then he closed his eyes and schooled himself down and down until he could open them again and look at her paleness against her hair on the pillow.

Very gently he said: 'Laura – my dear, dear love – is this your first time? Is that what you're telling me?'

'Yes.' Her voice blurred and he thought she was crying. 'I'm sorry. Should I tell you I'm sorry? I want it to be right for you . . .'

His fingers found her lips and pressed against them. He was fighting all the way, secretly, inside, and he was winning.

'Then it won't be tonight,' he whispered. 'I'm glad you told me. I'm glad it's your first time. We'll save it.'

He felt the tears running along his fingers.

'I wanted to prove to you – before you went away – how much I'm yours – in case you wondered –'

Then he felt the tears in his own eyes, and his mouth smothered hers, and they lay still until she was calm and he had won his own battle deep down. After that they talked softly and for a long time, until he slid away from her and dressed and came back to kiss her and to make his promises all over again, and went quietly out of the room and out of the hotel and into the night as if in a dream.

He stretched his long legs and leaned back in his chair. His fingers smoothed the ears of the retriever which lay beside him, watching for his movements as he said: 'I can't tell you why I did it. I don't know. It wasn't something you stop to ask yourself about. It was right, that's all – though I accept that you're bound to think it's madness.'

'I think it's dangerous,' Caroline said candidly. 'Though if you're going to marry an American you can hardly have time to get to know her well. But Randolph – three days – you're taking a terrible risk.'

'It doesn't feel like a risk. And it's not because she's beautiful – though when you see her I'm sure you'll have to admit she's that and more. That was only what made me notice her at first. After that it was – so much more. Something inside that happened between us. I don't know if such things happen to other people so quickly. I guess they do, sometimes. And when they happen you don't stop to think because there isn't any point.'

Across the room Mark watched and, just for a moment, his eyes met Caroline's and a smile ghosted across his mouth and a tiny movement of her head answered him, for they both knew what it meant when things happened between two people so quickly that they didn't stop to think because there wasn't any point.

He said to Caroline: 'Stop worrying.' And to Randolph: 'I'm delighted, and I wish I could tell the lady so. There'll be two weddings this year, then. I'm sorry we shan't be with you. But if you go back to Boston when you plan to, and marry fairly soon, you should return in time to be with us. So we'll make that a double celebration. In the meantime we should have seen the wheat from the contracts you brought back. By next week I think I'll have found buyers for most of it.'

'Max Falkland is more than anxious for a deal,' Randolph told him. 'So if you can get rid of more, I think I can buy it reasonably for you – six pounds six, eight or ten shillings a ton port price, according to quality – though God knows what it's all going to do to farming here. Still' – he shrugged – 'as I've said before, if you don't import it someone else will because there's no shortage of buyers.'

Ten minutes later he walked into the estate office with Sam Veryan, looked at the steward's face and asked: 'What's troubling you?'

Veryan said: 'Tregoney, Mr Randolph. He's working all right. But he's not getting any more men into the union and I'm hearing whispers in the village that men are being threatened, not by Tregoney but by fellers he's putting up to it. And he's preaching fire in the chapel on a Sunday, folk tell me. All about slavery on the farms and men losing their jobs because of the new machinery and low prices because of American wheat and the greed of the merchants in Bristol and Southampton – and Exeter, too. It's –'

'What does he say about Exeter merchants, Sam?'

Veryan looked at him keenly.

'Haven't heard of him naming names, sir. Nothing about Mr Helford, if that's what you mean.'

'Let me know if you hear anything like that,' Randolph said, and looked through the window to see Frank tethering a gelding on the other side of the drive.

For half an hour they talked, and Randolph told him about Laura and enjoyed Frank's wide-eyed astonishment, then about Tom Hogarth, and finally about Max Falkland and the grain trade, and Frank's enthusiasm faded.

'Is that really why you went? To bring even more American wheat here? Are you serious?'

'Mark Helford might as well have his share of what's available,' said Randolph. 'Oh, I know as well as you do what's depressing British farming. But buying another 5000 tons for Mark isn't going to make the slightest difference – first because it's a drop in the ocean compared with the rest of the imports, and second because it would come here anyway – Boston and Chicago and New York are full of buyers haggling over prices and quality and delivery dates. The Americans can sell as much as they want to put on the market.'

Frank shook his head.

'It's the principle, Randy. You're helping your family – and he's damn' near your family – to make money out of the very thing that's crucifying agriculture. And agriculture is your own life. It's crazy. If Mark Helford wants more grain he should be told to get it himself – and not to boast about it to you afterwards.'

Just for a second, Randolph's eyes narrowed.

'He's quite capable of getting what he wants. But the fact that I got it for him is no ground for criticizing either of us. I've told you – the grain would come here anyway – I haven't increased the quantity by an ounce –'

'I know. I heard you,' Frank said shortly. 'Let's forget it. I came for something else. I need a new byre at the farm, Randy. Without it I can't increase the size of the dairy herd, and if I don't do that I doubt if I'll be able to pay the rent in a couple of years time.'

Randolph shook his head.

'It'll have to wait,' he said. 'Certainly until this financial year is out. I'm not putting up new buildings for anyone until we've a better idea how farming's going to fare through next winter and beyond. In the present climate if I build you a new byre I'm going to need a rent adjustment, and I doubt if you'll take kindly to that.'

Frank sat upright in his chair.

'I've got to get more milk. Corn isn't worth growing unless I feed it to my own stock, and the present byre won't house more than twenty-five, as you know well enough. And if I can't increase the dairy herd, and I can't make money out of growing cereals for sale, what do I do with the land? Put it down to more grass and put beef on it? You know damn' fine what finished cattle are fetching – next to nothing – certainly not enough to leave a profit. And sheep are –'

'I can't do it this year,' Randolph said sharply, 'much as I'd like to. Let's look at it in January. Things might have improved –'

'You know they won't improve.' Frank snapped at him. 'They'll get worse. We're in to the worst depression farming has had since the 1820s – and it'll go on just as long. The men know it, too – that's why there's trouble looming there. You know about that? Do you know that there are some men who are afraid to go out at night now because they won't join the union? There's that much bitterness. There are all sorts of stories about black mass. Probably three quarters of them are lies, but strange things are happening. One of Peter Patchett's men has a sow – she farrowed three weeks ago and somebody took one of the piglets and nailed it to his door. Now he carries a bayonet when he goes to work. We've got to stop the rot, Randy. And landlords have got to contribute as well as tenants. We've got to make farming more profitable so that we can stop sacking men, even if we can't pay them more money. That's why I need that new building.'

'And others will want new buildings, probably for reasons just as important to them,' said Randolph. 'The estate has to balance its books, Frank. I've cut everybody's costs with the new machinery-sharing scheme – but it took a lot of capital to do it. I've drained over a hundred acres so far, with more to come – and that's costing a lot of money. I've repaired the big barn on your farm, and four buildings on others – at a fair cost. When I came back here the whole place was in a mess. It took me three months' work on the books to find out that we were actually losing money and had been for two years. I injected every penny I had into it – and you know how much that was – and now I'm trying to turn the whole lot into profit. But with cereal prices as they are, and beef sliding, and pigs not making enough to pay the wages of the man who looks after them, the home farm isn't going to make much profit this year – and unless I raise rents the estate won't show a profit either. Yet if I do raise rents, you and the other tenants will be struggling even harder. So let's be realistic. I'll build you a new byre as soon as I can justify it.'

Frank stared across the office at him, shaking his head slowly.

'Dear God – what a mess,' he said. 'Just think what it was like when we left Kansas – just starting a boom –'

'But only after a slump – remember? A lot of people went out of business in those two years across Oklahoma and Kansas and Colorado and the rest of the beef country. We were lucky. It caught us just right. But that's farming, Frank – good for two or three years, then bad for a spell. And I reckon this spell is going to last for a long time, because it's not only American cereals that we have to fight. There's talk of the new refrigerated ships bringing carcases from South America and even Australia before long. I think we're in for a ten-year depression with our markets flooded and the politicians not caring a damn. All we can do is spend as little as possible and hope that our management is good enough to enable us to survive.'

Frank stood up.

'Thanks,' he said. 'That's the sort of view I needed – just to make the day brighter.' And he left without his usual farewell grin, and did not look back as he crossed the drive to his horse.

A month later Sam Veryan knocked on the door of the Grange and said to Randolph: 'Bob Tregoney is asking to talk to you, sir. The men know by now that we won't be growing wheat after this season, and he reckons he's been asked to find out if any of 'em are going to lose their jobs.'

'I don't recognize Tregoney as spokesman for anyone but himself,' Randolph said. 'Tell him, and be sure to tell the other men too, that if anyone wants to see me I'll be in the big barn at ten in the morning to talk to them.'

And so they gathered: Tregoney and four others at first; then, as some of the rest gained courage they came forward as well, until a dozen men were waiting when Randolph crossed the wide yard between the buildings, opened the barn doors and perched on the edge of a flat cart. His dog sat, alert, at his feet, as if ready to protect him.

'Mr Veryan tells me there are questions you'd like to ask,' he said. 'Now's your chance. I'll tel you as much as I can, about anything that concerns you.'

Inevitably Tregoney was the first to speak.

'We understand there'll be no more wheat grown after this harvest. How many men'll lose their jobs?' His voice was harsh and clear and Randolph pictured him standing, as he did on many a Sunday, in the little chapel at the far end of Roxton's main street, lecturing the congregation on the cruelties of the world and God's promises to favour the poor and destroy the rich and those who indulged the sins of the flesh.

'I can't answer that because I don't know,' Randolph said. He looked around at them and saw sullen, anxious faces as they crowded together in their rough breeches and heavy boots. The day was warm and their woollen shirts were mostly open to the waist. Tregoney's fringe of beard was grey now, but the hair on his chest was as dark as the thick growth around his broad head. 'But I can tell you that I hope no one will lose his job. We're going to keep a few more dairy cows, and even though beef is a poor market there'll be some more steers. We'll keep on some of this season's lambs for breeding, too, so we'll need more grass and more roots. And there'll be another fifteen acres of barley for feeding. So there'll be plenty of work.'

'But less than there would have been,' Tregoney retorted. 'Three years ago we grew a hundred and more acres of wheat. Now it's down to fifty. Next season there'll be none – and only fifteen more acres of barley. So there'll be less work in the spring sowing, an' less at harvest. More grass means less ploughing. And keeping beef don't make work for any man.'

'What would you have me do, Mr Tregoney? Grow wheat for less than forty shillings a quarter and lose money on it? If the farm doesn't make money I can't pay you or anyone else. There have to be changes.'

'There are changes all right, Mr Randolph,' Tregoney growled. 'I remember twenty-five men on this farm. Now there are eighteen. And why? 'Cos of all that bloody corn coming from America. It's the same on the other farms. Seventy men once worked on this estate, taking all the farms into reckoning. Now there's no more'n fifty, and there'll be fewer by Christmas. You've been in America – you've just been back there. I'm told there ain't many men working on them big farms there, acre for acre, and those who do work gets paid next to nothing. I reckon it'll be the same here afore long. Is that what you're heading for?'

Randolph said shortly: 'We're not here to talk about America. We're here to talk about Roxton. Let's keep this discussion to the things that matter.'

'It does matter,' a voice muttered. 'There weren't no changes 'ere till you'd been there.'

Randolph's eyes darted over the faces.

'There are changes going on all over Britain,' he said steadily. 'Are you suggesting I'm responsible for those, too? We're in a national recession. And it's a lot worse in the eastern counties than it is here. If you didn't work on a livestock farm, half of you would be out of a job now. Be thankful for what we have here – and what, if everyone works hard, we have a fair chance of keeping.'

'It's not worth much keeping on eighteen or nineteen bob a

week – including the bonus,' Tregoney rumbled. 'And some men don't earn that much –'

'Then try some of the other farms,' Randolph said quietly and clearly. 'And see how much you earn there.' He eased away from the waggon side. 'I'm sorry, gentlemen – I thought you wanted to talk about how we farm here, and why. Since you don't seem to have anything else to ask about that, I suggest we all get back to work.'

He strode across the cobbles towards them, the retriever padding silently at his heel, and they shuffled apart to let him pass. As he walked away he heard a voice grate: 'Bloody Yankee-lover – buyin' corn for that feller from Exeter who's allus 'ere –'

For an instant his stride checked. Then he walked on, hard-faced, past the buildings and towards the white gate. He thought: How the hell do they know that? But men talked. Probably a clerk in Mark Helford's office on the Exeter quayside who might have a relative in Roxton village. Yankee-lover. His mouth twisted into a wry grin. They'd soon have more to talk about.

The next morning he found that somebody had drawn a crude version of the American Union flag in chalk on the front door of the Grange.

The church of Christ the King was crowded to the doors, for Max Falkland had many friends and his wife Mary had made sure that her own cohorts were well represented among the congregation. Randolph sat quietly at the front, Tom Hogarth beside him. He had returned to Boston nine weeks after his proposal to Laura to find her at the dockside, her hands held out to him and her eyes shining when she saw him. For two weeks they had spent every moment of every day together, shopping for the wedding, rehearsing the ceremony, enduring a round of celebratory parties with the Falkland family's friends and acquaintances, laughing and holding hands and drawing closer together with every hour. Then, the night before, he had dined quietly with Tom and

Louise Hogarth whose elegant house was not a quarter of a mile from Max Falkland's; and now he waited for her with a strange calm steadying his nerves until he heard the organ's herald and Hogarth elbowed him and whispered: 'Now for it, son!'

He turned and saw her, tall and white and exquisite in his eyes beside the portly and dignified Falkland, and his gaze held her and embraced her until she was beside him and he reached for her hand and, slowly and carefully as if it might break, without taking his eyes from hers, he raised it to his lips, and the faintest murmur crept across the watching people.

After that it was solemn and slow, with clear voices and hazy memory, chanted words and robust singing, quiet prayers and secret glances that joined them to each other long before their hands were held together and the ring was on her finger and the organ's triumph escorted them down through the church and out into the summer sun.

Later, the speeches done and the excited crowd left on the railroad station, they relaxed on the jolting train in a compartment which Max Falkland had reserved for their private use and travelled to the secret hotel which Laura had chosen for them. They dined in their room and strolled beside the river which ran close to the hotel, and when their day ended they lay close between the cool sheets in the wide bed and she put her arms around his neck and whispered to him: 'Do you remember when I asked you to be careful with me – to love me just a little?'

His lips brushed her forehead.

'I remember. And I remember how hard it was to leave you then – how I had to fight myself.'

'You told me more about yourself in that moment than I could have learned in a year,' she said softly. Then she moved her body against him and murmured: 'Now you don't have to fight, or to be careful with me, because I'm not afraid and I want you. Love me, Randy – love me –'

VI

'Have you seen the Western Daily Telegraph today?' asked Mark Helford.

Randolph was at the window in the office on the Exeter quayside, looking down at the canal below and the two basins that divided from it. Small vessels crowded against the wide quays. Several horse-drawn waggons waited, and a steam-driven crane hoisted crates from a lighter up onto one of the waggons. Alongside, the warehouses were grey against the sky and a narrow-gauge engine pulled three trucks towards wide doors, puffing and fussing under the watchful eyes of labourers waiting to unload them.

'No.' Randolph turned and crossed to the great battered desk. 'What's in it?'

'There's going to be a new railway bill in the next Parliamentary session.' Mark picked up the newspaper and pointed to a headline. 'It proposes an extension of the Great Western line out of Exeter, up through Roxton and beyond, with halts to serve half a dozen communities and with the track then branching to Honiton and up to join the main line to Taunton. And Roxton will have its own station.'

Randolph reached for the paper, frowning at it.

'Have you seen what a mess a new line makes of the countryside?' he asked. 'Great banks of clay heaped up and spread out over the fields on either side – no attempt to tidy up afterwards – hordes of men trampling everything in sight and breaking down the hedges and fences and then forgetting to make them good afterwards – to say nothing of theft and fighting and sometimes rape in the villages while the navvies are around. I don't welcome it, even though it's supposed to be progress in the end.'

'It *is* progress,' Mark said quietly. 'And in spite of the short-term problems, it'll bring benefits to a lot of people.'

Randolph read part of the report, then nodded.

'Quicker transport, cheaper movement of goods – oh yes, I know. But it will ruin Roxton. We've lived in a quiet back-water, a very rural place. The village and the other little communities around it will never survive as we've known them. New people will move in – maybe even small industries. That means employment and I know we can do with that. But the character and tempo of life will change. In ten years we'll scarcely recognize it. The feeling of space and quiet living will go. I don't welcome the thought.' He glanced at the paper again, searching through the report. 'I suppose there's no chance of Parliament rejecting it?'

'No chance at all.' Mark shook his head. 'If you read further you'll see that this bill doesn't only deal with the East Devon development. There are half-a-dozen other new lines proposed elsewhere. And you know as I do that when the railways want something they usually get it, and quickly. Money talks in Parliament. I reckon it'll be law by the spring.'

Randolph brushed the paper aside and sat down.

'If we can't stop it, let's forget it,' he said. 'I came to talk about the wedding, anyway.'

It was a Monday in September. Five days later Mark and Caroline were to marry in the church of St Thomas in Roxton. Randolph was to give his mother away, and Laura was to attend her. There would be forty guests at a small reception at the Grange, but they already knew that many more people from the village would be at the church, for however mixed the feelings about Randolph, Caroline was still Roxton's favourite lady, as she had been for more than thirty years past; and there was scarcely-concealed local curiosity about Laura who had returned with Randolph only four weeks earlier.

'I saw your wife's wedding dress yesterday,' said Mark, who spent every weekend at the Grange and who had long ceased to pretend to Randolph that he passed the nights in the solitude of the room set aside for him. 'She took my breath

234

away. I must say she is quite the most beautiful woman I've ever seen.'

Randolph shook his head.

'No, Mark. One of the two most beautiful. You're marrying the other.'

Mark eyed him.

'What self-satisfied, self-congratulatory men we are,' he said, and they grinned at each other, and fell to a final check through the arrangements for the following Saturday.

Laura's impact on Roxton had been a quiet one. No one beyond Mark, Caroline and Frank, plus Nora Penryn, had known of his marriage plans, and it was only after his reappearance with the tall and elegant New England girl on his arm that the stories had been relayed from the farm to the village. Then, two weeks later, the local newspaper had received a dispatch from an enterprising Boston journalist reporting the wedding, and suddenly all East Devonshire knew that Roxton Grange had a new lady to take the place of Caroline.

Randolph had not told his wife about the scrawled Stars and Stripes on the door of the big house, and what it had meant, for he hoped it had been only an isolated indication of somebody's prejudice and would not recur. But he did not forget it, for it would have concerned him even had he remained a bachelor. Now he knew that if there was significant antagonism it was likely to be aggravated by the presence on the estate of his American wife. But he was determined that nothing should mar her introduction to her new life and put the matter to the back of his mind as he arranged dinner parties at the Grange, escorted her into Exeter on shopping expeditions and to meet Mark's business acquaintances, and took her riding across the rolling countryside surrounding Roxton – making sure when he did so that she met his tenants and was seen by the farm workers.

She accepted it all eagerly and confidently. She had not concealed from Randolph her apprehension about leaving her own country and starting afresh 3000 miles away in a strange land and among people whose customs and circumstances were so unlike anything she had experienced. But in those first few weeks she began to feel as if she belonged to Roxton, as if the people she had met had been her friends for years; and knew that with Randolph's guidance she could make this new world everything she needed for all her life.

For the rest of that week the wedding plans dominated all their thoughts and, when Saturday came, the church in the narrow village street was full, with a hundred or more people crowding to see Mrs Haldane become Mrs Helford, and her tall son giving her away and his captivating new wife walking close beside them. They saw his proud approval, and the widening of his mouth in that curious half-smile he had, when he looked at the man who was to be his mother's husband. Strange how alike they were, stepson and stepfather; but such coincidences were not unknown. The village nodded wisely; they were clearly good friends, which was the most important thing. At least the family would not be divided by this marriage.

But as they walked from the church to the carriages at the lychgate a man stood at the window of a nearby cottage and said over his shoulder: 'Must say your boss an' his family'd make anybody stop an' look twice.'

Behind him Bob Tregoney growled: 'Not me. I see enough of 'em.'

William Tregoney, five years younger and milder-tempered than his brother, turned round.

'So you've said, many a time. But they're still a 'andsome lot. Mrs Haldane allus was a good-looking lady, an' that girl Mr Randolph's brought back from America – God, imagine taking 'er to bed –'

'Shut up,' Bob Tregoney retorted. 'America – America – that's all I hear. It's America as is ruining us – and Randolph Haldane's helping it. British farming weren't good enough for 'im – 'e had to go out there and waste 'is time. D'you know 'e's been buying American wheat for that feller you've been looking at – the feller who's married his mother? Not many know that, but it's true, take it from me. Making a profit outa the death o' British farming. And now a British woman ain't

236

good enough for'm – he's brought a damn Yankee to parade around the place.' He turned suddenly to the window and pointed. 'Look at 'er in 'er fancy clothes, riding in 'er big carriage –'

Will Tregoney laughed loudly and jeered: 'Riding in her carriage? I wouldn't mind riding 'er in 'er bed – just think about that, eh –'

'You fool,' rasped his brother contemptuously. 'What good does that sorta talk do? It'll not change a thing. But there're going to be changes, I'll promise you that. Pa put 'is curse on them Haldanes once. I heard'm. And he'll be proved right one day. The land is their power – and the land's going to be taken from them. The French people did it more'n eighty years ago. It'll soon be our turn. Maybe we won't be chopping off any heads, but it'll 'appen just the same. And then Haldane can bloody well go back to America – if 'e's got enough left to pay 'is fare.'

'Now *you're* the fool,' said Will, hitching his breeches by the broad leather belt around his middle. 'Who d'you think's going to do that for you? No Government will. We're a long way from a French revolution 'ere, an' you know it. Just because you got a union doesn't mean you'll get what you want. You 'aven't enough members to make anybody take any notice. An' the fellers as set it up are all quarrelling among themselves, half wanting to fight for men's wages an' the rest wanting to take all the land an' give it to the people, like the rubbish you're talking. It's time you grew up, brother, an' stopped dreaming an' preaching all that stuff in the chapel on Sundays. Neither God nor man'll do much for you.'

Bob Tregoney looked across the dim room of the cottage and hunched his shoulders.

'Then I'll 'ave to do it for meself,' he said. 'There'll be changes, you see. They won't be bosses for ever – Randolph Haldane in his big house with them fancy women. One day it'll be different.'

Half a mile away, when the carriages turned in between the big gate posts in front of the house, there were men and women leaning on the fence and the white gate that led to the farm, and they applauded and grinned and several called out 'Good luck, Mrs Haldane'. Caroline waved to them happily, knowing that they were looking forward to the tea that was to be served later to all comers in the big barn. But Randolph looked instinctively for Bob Tregoney, although he was scarcely surprised when he did not see him.

As Mark had forecast, the new railway bill passed through Parliament with maximum speed and with such little debate that it received scant notice in the newspapers. It was, after all, little different from many that had gone before; only the localities had changed. But by the spring Randolph knew that not only would life in the village never be the same again, but that he and the Roxton estate were about to be thrust into the forefront of a major dispute.

It began when Frank Garton was tramping the fields of Lane Ends Farm on a fine morning. He had a gun under his arm and a Springer at his heel and he was looking for rabbits. But in the southernmost field of his farm he saw three men. He watched them with interest and then with growing suspicion as he walked towards them. They carried long poles and laid tape across the edge of a new barley crop. Behind them he saw another man with an instrument on a tripod which was planted well into the crop.

When they saw him approaching they stood with their heads together for a moment, and then one man came forward. He wore dark narrow trousers which were badly creased around the knees and thighs, a long coat which flapped open and was marked up one side with a streak of mud, a bow tie at his neck and an old-fashioned tall black hat. His side-whiskers came down to the angle of his jaw and then forward almost to the corners of his mouth. As he reached Frank he tilted at the waist in a half-bow, touched the brim of his hat and said: 'Mornin' to ye, sir. It's a pleasant day.' He was eyeing the gun across Frank's arm, and the breadth of his shoulders.

'This is my land. Who are you?' Frank did not trouble to conceal his hostility.

'Oh, I do apologize if you consider us trespassing, sir.' The man repeated his little tilting bow, and smiled ingratiatingly. 'We are surveyors. We needed to come down into your field to check our levels. It seemed such a long way to your house – we trusted you would not object –'

'Who sent you?' asked Frank coldly. 'Who are you working for? What are you surveying for?'

'Oh yes, sir – of course. For maps, sir. It's a long time, many years, since the maps of this pleasant part of the country were checked and redrawn. It's our task –'

'Where is your authority? Show it to me.'

'Authority, sir? But of course, sir. My authority.' The man's hands patted his pockets, dipped under his flapping coat, felt along his waistcoat. 'Dear me – I don't seem to have it with me. A letter of instruction, you understand. I cannot find it –'

'Who gave you the letter? Who gave you your instructions?'

'Who, sir? Oh yes. My employers, sir. The council in Exeter, sir. The city council –'

The other two men stood silently, watching. In the distance the man with the tripod was also watching. All three wore rough tweeds and small bowler hats with curled brims, and their eyes were wary.

Frank said: 'If you are what you say you are, I shall have no objection to your crossing my land, nor measuring. But I want your letter of authority. Now please get back to the lane. If you want to continue your surveying, bring your letter to my house. Now go.'

The man glanced round to his companions, and they moved a couple of steps closer. Frank backed off, the dog at his side, and lifted the barrel of his shotgun slightly. The men stood still, looking at the gun.

Frank said: 'You heard me. Get off this land.' He dropped his left hand to the lowered barrel of the gun.

The man in the tall hat blinked several times, and the

ingratiating manner dropped away from him like a discarded cloak.

'If you're threatening us with that gun, you'll regret it. I've seen too many of you bloody farmers not to know how to deal with 'em –'

'I'll regret putting shot into you – but not half as much as you'll regret it when I do,' Frank snapped. He retreated several more steps so that they could not approach him from two sides. Now his gun was level, and there was something in his stance that told the men that his threat was not idle.

The spokesman said: 'You'll be sorry about this. We'll come back – and you won't get rid of us then, even with a gun. I'm warning you –'

'Bring your authority showing that you are map-making and you won't see a gun,' Frank told him. 'But I don't think you will, because I don't think you can. Now move.' He gestured with the gun barrel, and the men turned, hating him with their eyes, and marched together across the field. In the distance the man with the tripod gathered up his equipment and walked away also, trampling across the barley. Frank's dog snarled, but made no other sound until they had gone through the gateway; then he began to bark until Frank silenced him. The men walked along the lane to where their ponies were tethered and rode slowly away. Not once did they look back.

An hour later Frank had reported the encounter to Randolph, adding: 'It's your land. You'd better be aware that somebody's trespassing – and that there's something crooked about it.'

Randolph said: 'A high-crowned hat, a tripod, long poles and tape. They were surveyors, all right. But not map-makers. Engineers used to wear stovepipe hats – railway engineers particularly; and still wear tall headgear, for some reason. And tripods carry theodolites which are the first tools in the railway engineer's kit when he's looking at land over which he wants to lay lines. They were from the railway company, Frank. It looks as if they're planning to lay their new line across that land.'

Frank's shock was obvious.

'Across my land? But they can't do that – not unless you sell it to –'

'I know that. But the technique's well established. They carry out their surveys, decide on the best route, then approach the landowners. Some will sell because the money's usually attractive. Others won't – but then find themselves under pressure not only from the railway company but from neighbours who want to sell. Unless everybody sells, the line can't be built. So they play one man off against the next. They're ruthless, and half of them are liars. The men you met today were liars. If I go to see their employers they'll lie too, probably.'

'Those surveyors will be back – they sounded as if they were used to being ordered off land –'

'They'll be back, all right. And if they run true to form they'll bring three or four Irish navvies with them, all spoiling for a fight. That's the usual pattern. They'll spread out and risk a shot or two – then get at you while you're re-loading. So I'll tell you what to do. Lay barbed wire round the hedges and across the gate – a quick rough job will do. I've some wire in the stable if you want it. Then pick the half-dozen cows that are nearest to bulling, put them in the nearest grass field – and put the bull in there with them. That'll keep visitors out for several days, if I know that damn' stock bull of yours. The other fields we'll patrol – you, me, Sam Veryan – all with guns – plus three or four men I'll bring over from the farm here. We'll also take several dogs. With or without navvies, they won't tackle that lot. So we'll flush 'em into the open – force them to approach you, or me, and state their business or abandon what they're trying to do and go somewhere else. Meanwhile let's both go out and talk to other people – if we can find anyone else who has had trouble, we may get some idea of the route the railway company is favouring. Get two of your men over here to pick up the barbed wire and start laying it.'

Twice during the next week they saw groups of men in the lanes alongside Frank's land, watching the bull grazing with the selected cows. One man climbed through the thorn hedge, but the bull's belligerency was immediately apparent and the invasion ended within seconds. The next day several men called insults across the field but did not risk a closer approach in the face of the guns and the dogs. The accents floating in the wind were clearly Irish and the men were big and hard-muscled.

By then Randolph knew that surveyors had been busy to the south and west of Lane Ends, and when he marked the sightings on a map it was clear that the route being examined ran across the major part of Frank's land.

Then, on a chill bright morning, with the barley ripening and a wind disturbing the tall poplars, a carriage swept through the gates of the Grange, and two men stepped from it. Both wore dark overcoats and black silk hats and carried small cases. One was heavily bearded and the other scowled at the front door of the house over a large drooping grey moustache.

They announced themselves to Mrs Mountford, who had succeeded the ageing Nora Penryn as housekeeper, as representing the Great Western Railway Company and requested a conversation with Mr Randolph Haldane. Randolph deliberately kept them waiting in the hall for a quarter of an hour before he appeared. When he did so the bearded man advanced in a manner which clearly indicated his authority over his companion.

'Good morning, sir. My name is Faversham. David Faversham. Here is my card.' He flicked a white strip between his fingers. Randolph glanced at it without touching it. 'You will see that I am senior regional manager for the Great Western. Mr Robert Drake –' he gestured to his mournful companion '– is a solicitor representing our interests in certain matters. May we discuss those matters with you, sir?'

Randolph pointed to the heavy leather armchairs in the big hall.

'It depends what they are. You may certainly start by telling me that.'

He watched the two men settle in the chairs, placing their

242

cases carefully on the floor at their sides. They looked up at him, waiting for him to take a chair also, but he remained standing, his cold eyes on the bearded Faversham who cleared his throat loudly.

'You may be familiar with the proposal to build a new railway line from Exeter to Roxton and further north-east, Mr Haldane,' he began. His voice was loud and echoed in the hall. 'The matter was incorporated in a Parliamentary Bill which received the Royal Assent recently. Are you aware of this?'

'I am.'

'Ah. That facilitates our discussion,' Faversham announced. 'Well, sir, I am here to tell you that the route chosen for the new line incorporates land close to the village of Roxton which is, I am given to understand, owned by the estate of which you are the principal. I also understand that the land is currently rented out to a farmer, Mr Frank Garton. My company is anxious to buy such land as may be necessary for the construction and maintenance of the new line and I am happy to say has authorized me to make a most generous offer in order to progress our negotiations to a speedy conclusion.'

Randolph said: 'Show me the route.'

Faversham nodded to the silent Drake who opened his case and extracted papers, balancing the case precariously on his knees as he sorted through them and selected a folded map. Faversham took it from him, looked up at Randolph, then rose to his feet, holding out the map.

'Here, sir, is the route. You will see the line clearly marked.'

Randolph accepted the map, glanced at it, then looked back at Faversham. He was almost a head taller than the older man.

'Kindly be seated, Mr Faversham,' he said, and his voice was as chill as the unseasonable wind around the house. He stared at his visitor until the man had backed to his chair and sat down. Then he studied the map.

The inked line on it bisected Lane Ends Farm from south

243

to north, cutting its already-narrow shape into two even narrower strips. Randolph knew immediately that the route would make what was left of the farm unworkable on any sort of economic base.

He placed the map carefully on the table, moving so that as he looked down at Faversham the man was forced to tilt his head awkwardly backwards in order to see his face.

'How much land are you asking me to sell to you, Mr Faversham?'

Faversham eased backwards in the chair, trying to reduce the strain on his neck.

'We calculate that approximately thirty-five acres of your land are involved in the route proposed,' he said stiffly. His voice was now not quite so loud. 'We would be prepared to negotiate over forty acres in order to secure your own best interests – my company is always anxious to do business on a generous basis if at all possible. Now as to price –'

'And what would your company propose I should do with the remainder of the farm, Mr Faversham?'

The grey beard was still for a moment, and the eyes over it blinked.

'Do with it, sir? I don't follow you – I would have thought –'

'No, Mr Faversham. You have not thought. If you had done so you would have realized that your proposal would leave me with two strips of land, divided from each other by a railway line, with drainage seriously disturbed and so narrow that their commercial value and practical use would be nil. So if I were prepared to sell it would be only on the basis of the whole farm – approximately one hundred acres.'

Faversham twisted in his chair, and Randolph took a half-step towards him in order to make his position still less comfortable.

'But my dear sir, we have no use for such an area of land –'

'Neither would I have use for it after you had built your railway,' Randolph said evenly. 'Now tell me what that square means on the map, at the side of the line adjacent to the farm.' He pointed.

Faversham glanced at the map, then looked up at Ran-

244

dolph again. One hand stroked his beard as he considered his reply.

'That is of – er – little significance, Mr Haldane. A number of options are open to us at this time, of course –'

'It was of some significance to whoever put it there,' Randolph interrupted.

'Oh yes – at the time – naturally –'

'Stop fencing with me, Mr Faversham. What does that mark mean?'

'Well, sir, at this moment nothing has been decided, you understand.' Faversham's fingers felt his beard anxiously. 'But there is to be a small station at Roxton, and that particular site is among those being considered.'

'And if it is favoured it will occupy part of the forty acres you say you wish to buy from me?'

'Indeed, Mr Haldane, that would obviously be so.'

'In that case my land would be worth at least twice as much to you as the figure you intended to offer to me when you came here, since the position of a station is dictated by a variety of factors other than the land itself. The position is vital in relation to the road and the village. You are, I trust, prepared to pay for that?'

Faversham, still trapped awkwardly in his chair as Randolph stood over him, shifted umcomfortably, tilting his beard as he inclined his head, and looked at Drake.

'The price we are prepared to pay takes all the factors into account. Perhaps Mr Drake may be permitted to go into –'

'No, Mr Faversham, he may not be permitted.' Randolph produced a cigar. He did not offer one to either of the visitors. 'He is here to do your bidding. I shall continue to discuss the matter with you.'

'But Mr Drake is our solicitor, sir, and has –'

'Precisely. He is employed by you. I am not calling in an employee to negotiate with you. You are the principal on your side; I am the principal on mine. We shall confine this conversation to principals. And also to principles, Mr Faversham. I regard it as an important principle that I should be

245

adequately compensated for trespass upon my property, for inconvenience and anxiety caused to my tenant, and for the insult implied to me personally by such trespass and inconvenience. I shall expect the most generous recognition of that.'

Faversham drew breath audibly. Randolph flicked a match and began to light his cigar. But not once did his eyes leave those of the man in the chair; and through the smoke they seemed to shine into him, to impale him so that he could not look away despite his overwhelming desire to do so.

Drake came to his rescue with a plaintive 'Mr Haldane – you really must explain what you mean – there has never been any question –'

'You know what I mean, Mr Faversham.' Randolph did not even glance at Drake. 'I know it is sometimes your custom to send out your surveyors to take initial measurements without asking permission to enter land, and where possible to avoid contact with landowners; otherwise to claim that they are map-making. I am surprised you still do it – the deceit is widely known and has been so for thirty or more years. In this case your men were seen by my tenant who asked them to leave when they were unable to produce satisfactory credentials. To persuade them to do so he had to go to the extremity of pointing his gun at them. They then returned together with several navvies who were obviously there to attempt to frighten my tenant. He was not frightened. Neither was I. Neither were the others who were there waiting with us. I had to take considerable precautions to keep your intruders off my land, Mr Faversham – to protect my property and my tenant's crops – at considerable cost both directly and in terms of disruption of my own business and my tenant's. We shall both expect compensation for that, before I am willing to discuss the sale of the land. Shall I tell you what compensation I expect, Mr Faversham?'

'Really, Mr Haldane, this is nonsense, and quite unacceptable.' There was a hint of panic in Faversham's voice. 'If there has been any untoward conduct by our employees we shall of course look into it. But a precondition of that kind, and in

your somewhat-ah-aggressive presentation, is quite out-
rageous –'

'Do you want to buy my land, Mr Faversham?'

'Yes, sir. Of course. That is why I am here.'

'Excellent. I want to sell it.' Randolph pointed down at the
man with his cigar. 'But before I am prepared to discuss it, I
require compensation for the factors I have already outlined.
I would be prepared to accept five thousand pounds. My
tenant, whose livelihood is at stake and who has been
grievously affronted, will require much more than that – and I
am not prepared to settle until he is satisfied. Once those
preliminaries are dealt with we can discuss the purchase of the
land.'

The silence lasted for several seconds, during which Faversham continued to endure Randolph's penetrating eyes.
Then, suddenly, he wrenched his gaze away from the tall dark
figure above him and clambered out of his chair, almost
striding across the arm in order to avoid making physical
contact with Randolph.

'Really, sir – this is ridiculous.' His voice was loud again, as
if sheer volume would strengthen his response. 'You are
talking nonsense. Five thousand pounds twice over, and more
besides – even if there were any question of compensation,
and there is not, that would be a preposterous figure –
much more than the land itself is worth, as you well know.'
Behind the beard his face was flushed with anger and he tried
to draw himself up as if to reduce Randolph's height advantage.

'Then you have decided not to buy my land,' Randolph said
equably. He drew on his cigar, savouring the smoke. 'In that
case we have nothing more to discuss. I am sorry I cannot
extend hospitality any further. Good day, gentlemen.'

He turned abruptly, strode across the hall to the door and
held it wide.

Faversham and Drake exchanged glances. Then Drake
came slowly to his feet, picked up the map from the table,
folded it carefully and put it into his case, accepted Faversham's nod of instruction and followed him to the door.

247

Neither spoke as they walked past Randolph. He watched them go, his cigar jutting from the corner of his wide mouth. As they reached their carriage the coachman climbed down and opened the door for them. Only then did they turn and glance back.

Randolph had gone and the door was closed.

The reaction was not long delayed.

It came when Randolph least expected it, on the day of Roxton's biennial agricultural show when local farmers paraded the pick of their cattle, sheep and horses, and presented the best samples of their butter and cheese, their root crops and their honey; when their wives competed with cakes and pies and flowers and embroidery; when labourers and tradesmen received awards for long and loyal service; and when manufacturers and merchants displayed tools and machines alongside stalls manned by shopkeepers from Roxton and elsewhere.

Every two years a landowner allowed the show to be held on one of his farms, and in return for his hospitality the fields involved were subsequently ploughed and harrowed and made ready for the next crop at the expense of the show organizers. This year the Roxton estate was the host and, in acknowledgement, Caroline Helford – who was still referred to as Mrs Haldane by many of the villagers – had been asked to present the premiums and the silver trophies.

She was fifty-nine years old; the gold of her hair turning gently to silver but no less attractive because of it, her skin still smooth and her face serene. She looked, and was, supremely happy in her marriage. She wore a pale blue full-skirted dress with the customary high neck and close bodice and a small dark blue hat which sported two osprey feathers; and as she walked from the luncheon marquee out across the busy sunlit field, with Mark at her side, there were many who remarked upon their distinguished appearance among the cluster of show officials escorting them.

Presently Randolph and Laura stood with the crowd

around the main showring, watching as Caroline handed over silver trophies and envelopes containing prize money to men who came forward from the lines of cattle and horses drawn up across the ring, took off their hats and accepted their awards. Times were changing, but the traditions still held, and the men were happy to take their winnings from the lady who had been the squire's wife at Roxton Grange for so many years, and she was gracious and charming as she spoke to them, and Randolph knew they loved her for it.

Then it was the turn of the servants and labourers, and one was old Simon Smith from the Roxton estate itself. He came forward to accept thirty pounds – half provided by Randolph, the rest from the funds of the show society – in recognition of fifty years' service on the estate. He was seventy-five years old, bent with rheumatism, bald and wizened, but he still worked for three days each week on odd jobs around the home farm. Now he stood before Caroline, his hat in his hand; took his award and bowed, touching his forehead with crooked fingers before shuffling back to his place in the crowd, his lined face dignified and his old eyes shining. It was one of the great days of his life.

When the ceremonies were over and chairman Magnus Anderson had shouted his concluding speech at the crowd and Caroline had accepted a bouquet and their warm applause, Randolph walked slowly with Laura, tall among the dispersing people, proud when he intercepted the sidelong glances of the men towards his wife. She wore a grey skirt and short jacket over a brilliant-red bodice, and a wide-brimmed white hat crowned dark hair which moved in the breeze around her shoulders. They had been married for a year and now the risk they had taken after their extraordinary courtship was their favourite, private joke. Laura had adapted easily to her new life, and since Caroline had moved to Exeter had stamped her volatile personality upon the Grange and those who lived and worked around the house. She had been quickly accepted and respected by Mrs Mountford and the two maids, by Sam Veryan and his wife who lived in the big cottage close to the farm buildings, and by the farm labourers and their families who tenanted the row of cottages nearby.

But among the men, and in the village, there were whispers about Roxton's young master and his links with the American wheat that was slowly destroying them all, and about his wife who was the daughter of an American grain merchant who was growing fat on the ruination of British farming, and about Caroline who had gone to live in Exeter with a man whose living came partly from buying and selling crops from which Devon farmers could not make a profit. Randolph shrugged off the gossip, most of which was relayed to him reluctantly by Sam Veryan, knowing it came mainly from a discontented and embittered few; but he was careful to keep it from Laura.

But he could not keep show chairman Magnus Anderson from her, for the big farmer came out of the crowd in front of them and stopped, planted on his thick legs, red face perspiring under the late afternoon sun, and boomed: 'Ah, Mr Haldane – I've bin looking for ye. I trust ye've time for a few words?'

He looked questioningly at Laura, whom he had met for the first time earlier in the day, as if inviting her to walk on alone, and Randolph said easily: 'If it's business, Mr Anderson, my wife knows everything that happens at Roxton; and if it's personal to me, that concerns her too. Where would you like to talk?'

Anderson wiped his balding forehead with a bright red handkerchief and chuckled so that his second chin wobbled.

'The most private place is often the most public, I always say. I want a word about this railway business. I gather ye've bin approached.'

Randolph's eyes stilled. He nodded briefly.

'I have.'

'I'm told so. Pity you couldn't reach an agreement, I suggest.'

Randolph said: 'The company was unable to meet my request for compensation in respect of certain matters. That was a prerequisite. The matter fell down at that point. In any case I have no intention of putting a good tenant out of business.'

He remembered telling Frank about the visit of the railwayman and the solicitor and how he had dismissed them. He remembered, too, Frank saying: 'It's all begging the main question, though – would you sell my farm if the price was right?'

He had replied: 'If the price was right for both of us I'd talk about it – with you first.'

'But you'd sell,' Frank had persisted. 'I don't think my position's very secure.'

'I wouldn't sell unless your position was secure,' Randolph had assured him, to which Frank had responded: 'Does that mean I'm obstructing you? If you and I had not been friends for so long, would it be different?'

Magnus Anderson was saying: 'We don't have to be over-sentimental about tenants, Mr Haldane. In any case, I understand the railway company is sometimes willing to accommodate their position.'

Randolph's eyes were cool and watchful, and he felt Laura's tension.

'Supposing you tell me your interest in the matter. Clearly you have one.'

The red face nodded, and the red handkerchief mopped at the forehead.

'I have, sir. As you know, my land is directly south of yours. The railway line will cross my land. I have had an offer which I consider generous and acceptable. I'm past sixty, Mr Haldane, and the offer'll help me to retire. I want it. But if you won't sell, the railway will have to re-route. I'll lose the best chance I'll ever have of getting a good price for my land in these difficult and depressed times. This is a very serious matter for me and I'm not prepared to sit by and leave it to chance.'

'It's a serious matter for me as well,' Randolph said. 'And I'm not prepared to throw a good tenant off a farm.' His eyes caught Laura's and she saw the anger stirring deep in them.

'He'll be looked after well, Mr Haldane. I know of your

251

friendship with Mr Garton, just as everybody does. When this matter was raised with me I told Mr Faversham that that'd be a barrier. He said he was willing to discuss unusual tenant compensation. I think it would be in Mr Garton's interests to hear what the railway has to say.'

'I would be most surprised if that were the case. In any event I have already told Mr Faversham I'm not prepared to sell him half the land. The line projected cuts the long narrow farm into two. Lengthways. What's left on either side is useless. They'd find it a very expensive proposition. You can take it there'll be no deal, Mr Anderson. I'm sorry if that disappoints you.'

The big farmer looked at him, thumbs tucked into the pockets of his waistcoat, watch chain linking them, jacket hanging back from his thick chest. His fat red cheeks seemed to squeeze up beneath his eyes.

'See 'ere, Mr Haldane,' he said. 'I'll not mince words wi'ee.' His rolling Devon accent became thicker. 'This is a private conversation, an' we both be men o' the world. I suggest to 'ee that there's good reasons why it'll be in your interests to sell. I'd just like to remind 'ee how important the milk job is to us farmers now corn an' beef's so bad. I couldn't manage without a good dairy paying me a good price an' I'm sure you couldn't – an' Mr Garton couldn't either. You an' Mr Garton both sell to the same dairy – I know that. So do most of your tenants. An' I also know that that dairy's a bit overstocked wi' milk these days, times being 'ard, ye know. They wouldn't take much persuading to stop taking supplies from a few farms. Indeed they're looking at it already. An' as you know there's no other dairy wi' business around these parts for a quantity o' wholesale milk.'

Now cold night eyes were hard on the florid face.

'Tell me what your influence is with the dairy, Mr Anderson.' The words were flat, steel-hard, yet scarcely audible above the buzz and shuffle of people around them.

Anderson met stare with stare.

'No influence, Mr Haldane. Just a coincidence – Mr Oliver Culrose, who owns the dairy as you know, is married to my

252

wife's sister. Just a coincidence. That's 'ow I know 'e's considering the future of several farms as suppliers. I'll leave 'ee to take account o' these matters.'

He turned away across the showfield, calling to a passing steward, his wide figure rolling slightly from side to side as he walked, and Randolph heard Laura's quick intake of breath.

'Randy – that's terrible.' Her fingers curled round his arm. 'He's threatening you – threatening to destroy your business, and Frank's, if you don't sell. What are you going to do?'

The meeting took place in the drawing room of the Grange. With Randolph and Laura were Frank, Mark and Caroline, and Philip Ragley who was the estate's solicitor as his father had been before him.

Randolph said: 'I've been through the home farm's books again. Almost two-thirds of our revenue comes from the sale of milk, cheese, calves from the dairy herd and cull cows; and we're getting some useful beef steers by putting the Hereford bull on those Shorthorn cows we don't want to use for pedigree breeding – without the dairy herd there'd be none of those. On the other side, without the dairy herd we would save around forty per cent of our total farm costs – labour and feed, principally. So we would be materially worse off on the basis of that simple calculation. Moreover all the barley and oats we grow goes into rations for the cattle so we would have to find other outlets for that. And seventy per cent of the grass acreage which is essentially for our crop rotation is required for the dairy cattle – and the rest is for sheep and beef. To make use of that we would have to expand the sheep flock much further and feed a lot more beef, and neither would yield the net profit we get from dairying. So if we can't sell our milk we're in real trouble. So is Frank. I'm not concerned about the other tenants – I don't believe they are threatened. Culrose wouldn't want to lose that quantity of milk.'

Frank sat forward in his chair, elbows on knees, scowling at the floor.

'It would ruin me,' he said quietly. 'Lane Ends is essentially a dairy farm, in size and soil. I can grow some beef and sheep on it, but profits wouldn't compare. There's no future in wheat, or in barley and oats that aren't fed at home. My land wouldn't suit vegetables, and in any case the local market is small. I could go in for pigs but they're a gambler's trade and prices are down at the moment. And that's about the sum of it.'

'I know Culrose.' It was Mark's voice, deep and angry. 'He has an unenviable reputation in Exeter for using any method to hand if it will serve his business. There can't be much doubt that he'll do exactly as Anderson is suggesting if he thinks his family might benefit.'

'No doubt at all,' Randolph said. 'I went to see him yesterday. It was a waste of time. He takes an average two hundred gallons a day from us, about half that from Lane Ends. I thought it was a remarkable coincidence when he told me he was handling around three hundred gallons more than his trade could justify. He said he had not taken a final decision – it would depend on what he called "other business circumstances" which he didn't wish to discuss but which would have to be resolved within two weeks. It was a plain case of negotiation under duress – yet he never put a word wrong. Everything he said could have been construed quite properly. But he was giving me an ultimatum. What's your opinion, Mr Ragley?'

Philip Ragley coughed. He prefaced every speech with a cough. He was tall, thin, younger than his balding head suggested, and his winged collar was so high that it seemed to cause him physical embarrassment as he turned his head.

'I've listened very carefully to what you have said, Mr Haldane,' he replied cautiously. 'I do not think you can legally defend yourselves against what does seem to be an attempt to bring pressure upon you. You cannot proceed against Mr Anderson or Mr Culrose in consequence of anything they have said to you. There is nothing to compel Mr Culrose to continue to trade with either of you. So in essence I am saying that I cannot assist you other than to act for you and

254

Mr Garton should you decide to sell and to obtain for you the best terms possible.'

'You have nothing to fight with, Randolph,' said Caroline. She had sat throughout the meeting, listening to the explanations, the questions and the answers, without comment. Now they all turned to her. She spoke calmly and quietly. 'Mr Ragley's advice is as I would have expected. I can see two courses open to us: we can refuse to sell and cope with the financial consequences as best we may – and that is something upon which I can offer nothing original or constructive; or we can squeeze as much money as we can for Frank and for the estate out of the railway company. The first priority there would be to get enough to ensure that Frank could buy or rent another farm and continue in business without financial loss. My opinion is that we have little choice. However unpalatable we may find it, we have to yield.'

They were silent again, considering what she had said. Then Frank muttered: 'I wouldn't rent again. I don't want to be a tenant any longer.' He did not look at Randolph. 'I want a place of my own.'

'Then you must work out how much compensation you will need to inflate your present capital to the point at which you can buy the sort of farm you want,' said Caroline. 'After that Mr Ragley can proceed for us. The estate's requirements are simpler – if we sell we lose a certain income, a certain potential, and a certain capital asset. It should not be difficult to calculate all three.'

Ragley looked at them, each in turn. When no one spoke he said: 'Do I take it that those remarks summarize my instructions? If so I will need a set of figures – your minimum requirements. Then I shall see the other parties and try to better those minima.'

Caroline looked at Frank and, almost imperceptibly, he nodded. Then she looked at Randolph. He was leaning back in his chair, staring at the ceiling. After several seconds she said quietly: 'Randolph?' And his gaze came down and settled on her, and small lights seemed to shine from the dark depths of his eyes and his mouth was hard and straight.

He said: 'We fight. We say to Faversham – "take your railway somewhere else". We say to Anderson – "find your retirement money some other way and not at our expense". We say to Culrose – "tear up your contract, we don't need you". And then we pool our milk output and retail it ourselves – right here under Culrose's nose. Three hundred gallons are more than enough to ensure continuity of supply, and we can apportion costs and profits according to our respective inputs. We've been partners before, Frank. We can do it again. And to hell with Culrose.'

He was on his feet, taking cigars from a box, throwing one each to Mark and Frank, trimming one for himself and then lighting it; and all the time watching them and waiting for their reactions, standing wide-legged against the light from the big windows, straight-shouldered, angry, spoiling for a fight.

Still no one spoke. They were all looking at Frank. He sat still, turning the cigar over and over between his fingers, his fair hair falling across his forehead, his face carefully expressionless. He struck a match and seemed to hide behind the smoke as he lighted the cigar. Then, slowly, he emerged from it, and now he looked up at Randolph.

'It's a great idea,' he said. 'It would be a struggle. It might work. But I don't want it. I'm sorry, Randy. I want to know how much they'll offer me. I hope it will be enough to give me a chance of my own farm. That's what I want.'

Randolph blew smoke in a long thin stream.

'And back off?' His voice grated. 'Back off – bow to Anderson and Culrose? Let them beat us? Is that what you're telling me you want?'

'No.' Frank shook his head. 'No. I'm telling you I want to get out. I don't want to be a tenant. I want my own place. The railway might pay me what I need. I have capital already – you know that. But I must have more. I could get it from the Great Western. I don't give a damn about Culrose and Anderson. I don't care if they do beat us – because they could just give me a chance to win my own fight. I've told you before, Randy – being landlord and tenant hasn't been the same for us as our past relationship. I don't want it to go on. I can't force you to come to terms with these people. But I can tell you that if you don't try, you'll have robbed me of the opportunity I've longed for. At least, that's what I'll always believe if we never ask them what they'll settle for.'

It was beyond argument. There was no point in trying to save Lane Ends if Frank wanted the alternative; no point in entering the retail milk battle if Frank did not want to join in. If the compensation was not enough, the story might turn out to be different. But it could be enough, and Randolph knew it. He relaxed, letting the excitement and tension flow from him, easing his shoulder muscles, struggling to see Frank's view – fighting to forget Anderson and Culrose and the prospect of surrender to their device. But that was his sticking point and he recoiled from it. So he turned to Caroline.

'Adjudicate,' he said. 'You're half the estate, and the senior partner. You decide.'

She nodded. She was composed, neat in blue satin skirts and a white laced bodice, her hair loose and brushed back away from her ears. She did not hesitate.

'The loss of Lane Ends is not serious to us,' she said. 'Indeed we would not be averse to the realization of some capital in these increasingly difficult times. But we have to consider Frank first. His livelihood is at stake. After what he's told us we must negotiate a sale if the details are satisfactory. The instinct to fight is strong, Randolph. But reason must prevail.'

Ten minutes later the meeting had ended and Randolph called his retriever to his side and wandered slowly out across the carriage drive to the white gate and leaned on the top rail, looking across at the farm buildings and the fields rising beyond. He could hear cattle and occasionally men's voices. A horse's hoof struck a cobblestone and he imagined the spark. He felt depressed and angry – a frustrated anger that was a physical ache deep in his chest.

Then he heard footsteps and turned to see Laura, her skirts rustling around her ankles, drawing a shawl about her shoulders against the fitful breeze as she came to him. She stood close and said:

'It was the right decision. You'll have to accept it. Don't let it disturb you so.'

'I'm being beaten,' he said distantly. 'I'm losing without fighting. I've never done that in my life.'

'It's a wise man who knows when a fight isn't worth the victory,' she said. 'It isn't Culrose and Anderson who are beating you – it's the circumstances. You should be glad that the man who's been your closest friend stands a good chance of benefit. I haven't been here long. But even I know that losing Lane Ends isn't going to harm the estate – especially if you get a good pay-out. Anderson is doing you no harm, and he's doing Frank a lot of good.' She put a hand on his arm. 'See the best side of it, my love. There is one, you know.'

He turned slowly to face her, and saw the warmth in her big dark eyes and the anxiety for him, and said: 'I need you. I need your common sense and your calmness and the way your voice makes me calm. You're so like my mother it's incredible; but because you're my wife you're closer to me, deeper inside me, and you know me better than I know myself. Yes – there is a good part to all this. But the best part is the way you make me understand it.'

She slipped her hand down into his and said: 'The best part is the way we understand each other.'

He felt the pressure of her fingers and the intimacy of her closeness, and the tension eased away from him and was replaced by the familiar quick surge of desire for her.

He whispered: 'I want you. Come on –'

Still holding her hand he turned towards the house, but she pulled back, startled.

'Darling – we can't – your mother and Mark are here – how can we –'

'We march in – across the hall – straight up the stairs. They may not even see us. If they do – just take no notice.'

She fell into step with him, looking up, seeing the grin widening his mouth and the change in him, and her eyes loved him.

Behind, beyond the white gate, Tregoney stood at the corner of the stables, watching them; and the dog at Randolph's side turned its head several times, looking back, its eyes wary.

Frank said: 'In three weeks we'll be gone. It'll be a strange feeling to leave this place. But I'm looking forward to it. The new farm will give me greater scope to fight this recession.'

He and Randolph were walking across the fields of Lane Ends, inspecting the line of the poles which were already in place to mark the route to be taken by the railway. It was autumn.

'I'm glad Ragley was able to get enough out of them, that's all,' Randolph said. Even now he was still smarting from his acceptance of the ultimatum presented to him. 'I think he did well for both of us. We have to agree that Laura is right – it's only my pride which has been hurt.'

But in the village there was a different view. Twelve men had lost their jobs on Anderson's farm, six on Frank's place, and fifteen on other farms further north. Of the thirty-three, twenty-four had secured promises of work on the railway gangs, although few relished the prospect after their lifetimes in agriculture – even though the wages were better.

Of the nine who were left, one was married to the sister of William and Bob Tregoney, and another was among their cousins.

Anderson and the other farmers to the north came in for little criticism, for the circumstances had been familiar in Britain for forty years and more. It was recognized that the railways offered generous terms when they needed land and that few owners were likely to resist on the grounds of money alone. But the villagers looked askance at the sale of Lane Ends, for Randolph's long-standing relationship with Frank was well-known and, in the popular mind, here was a young tenant farmer being thrown out by a landlord who had claimed to be his friend until a fat cheque was waved in front of him. Local feeling was heightened by the coincidence that,

259

of the nine men left unemployed around the village, four were among the six who had worked on Frank's farm.

Nothing was said directly to either Randolph or Frank; but, as usual, Sam Veryan passed on the whispers that came to his ears; and a week after the matter became public knowledge someone chalked a red cross on the door of the Grange and scrawled under it 'God forgive you – men will not'. The culprit might have been Tregoney; but the wide gateway to the Grange was close at hand and there was little to stop an outsider slipping through it and up to the house at night.

A fortnight later the message was repeated. Laura took it well, deriding it and showing no sign of fear; but Randolph was concerned for her whenever he was absent from the house, and Mrs Mountford and the maids were clearly frightened.

But that was now more than two months ago. Nothing had occurred in the interim to revive apprehensions and Randolph was now inclined to put the incidents down to the same person who had once drawn the Stars and Stripes on his door and who had then apparently abandoned his attempts to express antagonism. He said to Frank: 'Whoever he is, it looks as if he's gone to ground. I think we'll hear no more of him.'

But in the village men and women still whispered, and the child of Bob and William Tregoney's sister died of a fever and some said it was because she was undernourished and that was because Randolph Haldane had thrown the father out of work. Then Peter Patchett and Edward Robey, both long-standing Roxton tenants, sacked six men between them because cereals were no longer worth growing and so there would be neither spring ploughing and sowing nor harvests to contend with; and Bob Tregoney reminded men of the story that Randolph had brought wheat contracts back from America to line his new stepfather's pockets and that the local newspaper report of his wedding had said that his new wife's father was a grain merchant with a big export business. The cause of British agriculture's great crisis and the misery of workless men and the growing number of empty cottages left to decay because others had moved away to the towns seeking employment was closer to home than some had realized. Of course there were many others in it; but Randolph Haldane was the only one they could see, and he had thrown his best friend out of a farm so that he could sell for railway money, too. God alone knew what was going to happen to young Frank Garton now. He had been a farm labourer once, and his father before him, and the village was on his side.

On a day in late September Randolph travelled with Frank to Yelverton, on the outskirts of Plymouth, to look at the 180-acre farm Frank had bought and to which he and his parents would move in a fortnight's time. They stayed overnight in a nearby coaching inn.

The following morning Mrs Mountford opened the front door of Roxton Grange, saw blood on the step and looked up at the head of a sheep tied crudely to the pillar alongside the door. Her screams echoed through the house and across to the farm.

When Laura came she stood still, looking at the sightless eyes and the hanging jaw and the bloodied skin and wool. Then she put an arm around the quivering housekeeper and said quietly: 'Go inside, Mrs Mountford. I'll take care of this.'

She swept down the steps, gathering her skirts in one hand, and went briskly across the drive to the white gate and through to the farm, looking for Sam Veryan. Although she had been in England for such a short time she did not have to be told that a sheep's head nailed or tied to a door was a devil's warning of death or disaster to those within the house and that it was a device used periodically by violent elements among farm labourers ever since the riots and rick-burnings of the 1820s and 30s.

She did not find Sam Veryan, for he was a quarter of a mile away inspecting a potato crop which was almost ready for lifting. Instead she found Bob Tregoney talking to ploughman Albert Priddy and engineman's labourer Tim Carter.

Addressing all three she said briskly: 'Will you come to the house, please, and bring a sharp knife, a bucket of water and some cloths?'

Priddy with his long drooping moustache and young Carter started to move towards the barn, obeying instinctively; but Tregoney stood still and said: 'We're not allowed through the gate, Mrs Haldane. Is something wrong there, then?' His voice and manner bordered insolence.

'You're allowed through the gate if I tell you to come,' she said sharply. 'Now do it quickly, please.'

She nodded to Priddy and he muttered, 'Yes, m'm', touched his forehead and scuttled away to the barn. Tim Carter looked hesitantly at Tregoney, for whom he worked, then caught Laura's eye and followed Priddy. But Tregoney stood still, watching as Laura turned back to the house, eyeing her and the way she walked and remembering what his brother had said about her.

Priddy and Carter brought the bucket and knife to the house, with Tregoney stalking behind as if he were supervising the operation. But when they came within a dozen paces of the door all three stopped and seventeen-year-old Tim Carter muttered: 'Christ a'mighty.'

They came closer before Priddy said: 'Don' rightly like to touch it, m'm. It's bad luck, see. That's what folk say – bad luck.'

'Don't be silly,' Laura snapped. 'Here – give me the knife.'

She held out a hand and, reluctantly, Carter passed over the twelve-inch blade with its rough wooden haft. She took it, seized the sheep's head by the ears, and slashed at the cord tying it to the pillar. Then, holding it out arm's length, she turned to Tregoney.

'Take it,' she said. 'Take it to the barn and put it in a bucket. Make sure nobody moves it until my husband returns tonight. He will want to see it.'

Tregoney did not move. Nor did he look at the sheep's head. With his insolent eyes on Laura's face he said: 'I'm paid to be an engineman an' a labourer – not to clear up the devil's work. You'd better do it yourself, Mrs Haldane.'

Priddy ejaculated: 'Bloody hell, Bob –' then stepped back as Tregoney lashed at him: 'Belt up. You ain't paid to clear it up either. We work on the farm – we're not labourers round the house.'

'Take it, Mr Tregoney.' Laura's voice was low and very clear. She stood, slim and tall, her hair shining in the pale sunlight, the breeze plucking at her grey skirt, the grotesque head hanging from her fingers.

And Tregoney laughed; a bitter, humourless sound; as bitter and humourless as the curl of his lips and the light in his eyes. Then he turned and began to walk back towards the white gate.

Laura's voice cut across the drive: 'Either take it, Mr Tregoney, or save yourself the trouble of going back to the farm, because there'll be no work for you.'

Without checking, Tregoney walked on. For a full five seconds Laura watched him, then turned to Priddy.

'Unless you want to lose your job as well, Mr Priddy, take this thing and do as I have said. And you, Mr Carter –' she swung towards the terrified boy '– you get across the fields and find Mr Veryan, wherever he is, and bring him here running. Is that clear?'

They went, pale-faced and avoiding her eyes.

When Sam Veryan arrived half an hour later she said to him: 'I have been insulted by Bob Tregoney, who has refused to obey an instruction. Kindly dismiss him immediately. Get him off the premises straight away.'

Then she told him what had happened, and Veryan's face was grave.

'That's a serious matter,' he said. 'I can get rid of Tregoney, all right. Wouldn't be surprised if he didn't put the thing there – or tell somebody else to, as likely. But it's not who did it as matters so much as why they did it. I thought such things were behind us. It's not the way to fight for wages an' men's jobs. It's like – black magic – trying to frighten people.'

'They'll frighten no one here, Mr Veryan,' said Laura. 'Can you imagine Mr Haldane being frightened?'

He managed a smile.

'Not of that, or anything.' Then the smile was gone. 'But some of the men will be scared. Some of 'em are in the union an' it's good for 'em. Others are afraid of it – an' others are superstitious. It's a bad time we're going through. Trouble is, Mrs Haldane, there's a split in the union. Folks say it'll break up. That makes men like Tregoney more extreme – just at a time when so many men are falling out of work.' He shook his head. 'It's a bad time.'

When Randolph returned in the evening she was withdrawn, almost formal, as she reported the day's happenings, until he said reassuringly: 'Stop worrying about it. Tregoney's been looking for trouble. There was no alternative.'

She searched his face anxiously.

'I was afraid,' she said. 'It's the first time I've had direct contact with the men. I was afraid I was making trouble for you – interfering when I didn't understand what I was doing. But I had to do it, Randy. It was your authority I was upholding. I had to –'

He kissed her quickly to silence her.

'It may be that he wouldn't have responded like that to me,' he said gently. 'But that's not the question. He, and the others, have to take instructions from you just as they do from me or from Sam. I've always been ready to dismiss Tregoney if he caused trouble. You had no choice. I'm grateful to you – and I'm proud of you.'

She relaxed visibly and her hand sought his.

'Thank you. I needed to hear you say something like that.' Then she was anxious again. 'But Randy – what about that – that thing. What did it mean?'

He shrugged, trying to give her the impression that it was unimportant.

'It means that last night somebody went into our flock, killed a lamb and cut it up – probably shared the carcase with two or three friends – and then presented us with the head. It's an old superstition that was revived years ago when men wanted to frighten a farmer who was a bad employer or a man who refused to join the other labourers – you know all about that –'

'But Randy – you're not a bad employer.' She was indignant. 'You pay more than anyone else around here, you help men who need a doctor, you give them food if their families are ill, you charge only a nominal rent for those in your cottages, you –'

He shook his hand.

'It's more complicated than that. Sam is my listening post – and a good thing I have one. He says there's a lot of misunderstanding. Men are frightened, Laura. A lot have lost their jobs because there's no work for them; a lot more know it could soon happen to them. They're looking for someone to blame. For various reasons some people blame me, among others. The sheep's head was a warning of some sort. But it's also the sign of a sick mind. So let's forget it.'

But he did not forget it, and that night as he held his wife in one strong arm and she fell asleep against him, he lay awake for a long time.

Bob Tregoney rarely preached now in the chapel at the top of Roxton's street, for the church elders had begun to consider his politics too radical and his inability to separate them from the Christian message a failing that the Lord would be unlikely to appreciate. Indeed, there were those who said he was not a Christian at all, but used the church only because it gave him a platform. But that Sunday the Reverend Elias Jones was preaching in Exeter, one of his lay deputies was ill and the other was nursing a sick wife. So, somewhat doubtfully, Mr Jones turned to Tregoney.

The word travelled quickly around the village and Tregoney's followers dominated the thirty-strong congregation which stared up at him now in the simple little chapel; stared at him curiously for they knew he was without work; stared at him eagerly, waiting for his solution to the troubles which beset so many of them, anticipating the excitement and the breath-stopping surge of rhetoric which always climaxed his angry sermons.

Tonight, they said with hindsight afterwards, he was possessed. Tonight he was genius, reaching out to them, swaying them, beckoning them. Tonight he led and could not be denied. Tonight he was their master and their saviour, and their corrupter.

' 'Tis man's greed that's ruining us,' he told them as he gripped the pulpit rail and swept them with eyes that were fierce in the light of the candles at his side. ' 'Tis man's eternal pursuit of worldly goods that's bringing our great heritage to its knees. 'Tis American grain, an' the profits to be made from it, that's taking away our farms an' taking away our work an' our wages. Our children are starving an' we're in misery because men set money above all else. But just as Jesus threw the moneylenders from the temple, so the great Lord above us condemns the money worshippers in our midst an' will throw them from His sight. God uses His servants to His mighty purpose. God has given us eyes to see the evil, an' hands to fight it, an' the will to perform His will. We are His instruments – the instruments of His might an' His justice. The evil is in our midst. Greedy, selfish an' wealthy men are in our midst.' His hectoring voice dropped conspiratorially. 'They have been warned already. The sign of the Lord has appeared on their doors, an' the sign of the devil at their gates. The devil is within their gates an' only the Lord can save them. But they reject the Lord.' The voice rose again, hoarse, strident, climbing. 'They turn their backs on the warnings of the Lord. Yet another shipment of grain came last week – right here into our midst in this fair countryside – down in the city of Exeter it came, taken off ships. Yet another nail was driven into the coffin of our livelihoods – openly, deliberately, for profit in defiance of the Lord.' The voice rose still higher, hammering against the rafters and against the ears of the men and women clustered together, their eyes riveted on the candle-lit figure and the long shadows thrown by the raised arms. 'The Lord condemns the slow slaughter of our children by starvation because we cannot buy food. The Lord condemns the worshippers of the devil's money. We are the instruments of the Lord an' we will destroy the devil's worshippers – in the night – by the fire of the Lord's wrath –' And then, in a whisper loud and clear through the echoes of the last shout: 'An' I will lead you – I will lead those with the courage an' the will in this special, secret service of the Lord, in this salvation of our children, in this destruction of the causes of our oppression. Evil must not be seen to triumph, for evil begets evil.' The voice soared again, jagged and beating through the charged air. 'The greatest evils must be rooted out first, for they set the pattern for others. The Lord must be served now – He cannot be denied longer – His will is written for all to read, an' we have read it an' know it an' will act upon it.' The hands clawed upwards and the shadows grew and the candle flames flickered and the voice screamed – 'We will serve you, Lord.' And all around the hands rose and the voices swelled in deep pulsating echoes – 'We will serve you, Lord – we will serve you now – now – now –'

The clock in the hall, as tall as a man, was striking eleven when the black-coated retriever growled.

Randolph looked up, watching the dog. It rose slowly, tail straight, hair lifting along it shoulders, facing the window.

'I think I should look around,' he said softly, and Laura stared at him in sudden alarm as he eased out of his chair, snapping his fingers to the dog which came to him, head turned to watch the curtained window, bristling. He touched her as he passed her chair. 'Stay in here. Don't try to follow me.'

Her hand went up to cover his. Then he crossed the hall to the kitchen door, whispering to the dog: 'Quiet, Nick – quiet.' He went through the wide kitchen to the big dark wash house and the stout door which led out to the side of the house. As he wrapped his fingers around the door key and turned it gently he felt the dog quiver against his leg and heard the snarl rise in its throat, and when he opened the door he covered the dog's muzzle with a silencing hand and stepped back instead of forward into the night.

As he did so two figures loomed against bright moonlight, one on either side of the doorway, converging, checking when they saw only blackness. Then the dog broke free, hurling itself in silent fury, and Randolph took the nearest man by a scarcely-seen outstretched arm, pulled him close and hit him with terrible force above the belt, then again in the side of the neck with the blade of his hand, turning him, thrusting him upright, lashing him across the windpipe as the second man screeched when the dog's teeth tore into his thigh. Randolph kicked aside the first man as he fell, choking, and smashed an iron fist into the face which loomed above the twisting, clawing dog which dropped away as the man reared and Randolph's foot thudded into his crotch.

Then he was outside, under the moon, running along the path beside the house to the corner close to the hall window. The moon was bright enough to throw shadows and they were moving, darting across the drive and the lawn beyond – two, three, four shadows, more – and there was straw piled against a window and he smelled paraffin and heard glass smashing and saw a match flare and his voice cut through the night with the impact of a gunshot 'Fire – fire – fire –' as a stick with a blazing rag wrapped around it arched through the air and landed in the straw close to him. He grabbed at it, kicking the straw away as it fired, jumping back from the flames as they soared to the height of his head, seeing other flames against the big window beyond the front door of the house and his voice tore from his throat again in warning, mingling with the dog's barks of alarm. He waved his arm to it, shouting 'Get him, Nick – get him –' and it streaked away across the drive and the lawn, intercepting a man who ran towards the farm buildings, flying at his legs, and Randolph saw light from the house as the door opened and Laura silhouetted and the flames lighting her hair and two men running towards her. He ran too, faster than he had ever run in his life, taking one of the men down in a flying tackle on the steps, rolling over and hammering his head against the ground and seeing Will Tregoney's distorted flame-lit face as he scrambled clear and faced Bob Tregoney who swung a stick and a flaming rag at him, singeing his hair. Laura screamed once, and there was Sam Veryan's deep voice and other men coming out of the darkness from the farm buildings and the cottages beyond with pounding scraping feet and shouts and he bellowed 'Sam

268

– Sam – look after Laura –' and faced Tregoney again as the stick and the flame whirled against the black sky and the moon and the straw blazed against the windows and he heard his voice crying 'Christ – the house – my house –' Then he was under the stick and the flaming rag and had Tregoney by the throat, then the arms and shoulders, lifting him, turning in a great surge of strength and fury, round and faster and the fiery stick was gone and Tregoney went backwards screaming into the flames which lit the window and the whole world around him.

And then, all in the same movement, he followed up and grabbed the man's foot and heaved him mightily out of the searing straw onto the drive and fell on him, rolling over on him, kneeling on him, smothering the flames until another man was with him and yet another and someone drenched him with water and Tregoney too as he lay and writhed on the drive. Men were everywhere now, fighting and cursing, and there was more water and he heard the old fire pump being dragged through the gate and rumbling and Laura was holding him and Sam Veryan was shouting orders as he lurched to his feet again.

Within fifteen desperate minutes the fires were out and he looked at his house against the moon and it was scarred but safe, and he whistled for the retriever whose ears and instincts had given, by the narrowest margin, just enough warning to save it.

But the dog did not come, for a man had clubbed it with an iron bar and crushed its skull. The same man stood now, lashed crudely with rope to a post by the farm workers who had overpowered him, and it took Sam Veryan and three more men to hold Randolph and lead him away.

Several intruders had escaped but seven, all injured, were held, including the Tregoney brothers, and there were cuts and bruises among the home farm's defenders. It was six in the morning and the daylight was creeping up the sky beyond the poplars. Two blackbirds chuntered, annoyed by the disturbance, and a thrush whistled. Randolph walked slowly, wearily, between the house and the farm buildings, Veryan and a constable on either side of him. Outside the open door of the barn two more constables stood, guarding the prisoners inside.

Bob Tregoney, bandaged roughly around both hands and one leg, face blackened, hair burned, shirt and breeches torn, twisted round and looked up as Randolph entered. The other men lay back on the hay. One groaned and swore repeatedly.

Randolph stood in the doorway and said: 'Why did you do it?'

Tregoney's tongue passed across his lips.

'It was God's will.'

'It was your will, you bloody fool. Why?'

Tregoney pushed on his elbows and raised himself. His face was contorted with pain and fury.

'Because you robbed men of their work.' His voice crackled. 'And made money out of doing it. You're evil – all of you in this place. My father cursed your father afore you were born – an' I curse you.' The voice changed pitch, rising, and the eyes were wild. 'You're the last – the last Haldane to rule this place. There'll be no more – no one'll succeed you – the land will come to the people – you're cursed –' The voice collapsed into a wheeze and Tregoney coughed and spat.

Randolph caught Sam Veryan's eye and shook his head. He turned to the constable.

'I'll lodge no complaint against these men,' he said quietly. 'I want them off here, that's all. If you insist on charging them I'll give evidence. But that will be your choice. This business took place on private property. If you get them away from here that's as much as I want. There'll be no martyrs and no platform for propaganda.' Then, suddenly, he whirled, and his finger jabbed out towards one man. 'You – you killed my dog. If you ever set foot on this place again I'll kill you. If I ever see you in the village again I'll break both your arms. I'll give you a week to clear the neighbourhood.' He swung round on the constable. 'Get him away from here first. Injured or not, throw him into the road.'

270

Then he turned, to find half a dozen of the home farm's men clustered outside – the men who had fought for him and for his house the night before. They were staring, uncomprehending.

He said to them: 'If I can find a way of rewarding you, all of you, I will.'

Then he pushed past them, leaving them to wonder.

Frank said: 'I've just seen Elias Jones. That completes it.'

He was in the drawing room with Laura and Randolph, Caroline and Mark. He had just returned from the village and this was his last call at the Grange before his move to the new farm at Yelverton.

His visit to the chapel's rector had been the final act in the drama which had divided village opinion so dramatically two weeks before. In truth it was still divided, but now there was less antagonism between the two sides and more understanding by each for the other.

The Tregoney-led attack on the Grange had been the sensation of the year. No one, not even old Simon Smith, could remember an event which had so polarized the community. The majority were openly horrified; but the bitterness of the unemployed and their relatives was significant and undeniable and even those who did not condone violence had more sympathy with the invaders than with the defenders.

But within a few days rumours were dispelled as the men from Roxton home farm told their tales in the village public houses and shops, and even the sharpest critics acknowledged that it was only by great fortune that no one had been killed and the big house burned to destruction.

Most telling had been Randolph's decision to end the affair without recourse to the courts. Even the Tregoney relatives had to admit that that was not the act of the ruthless and pitiless exploiter of men which Randolph was held by them to be.

But the misunderstandings which had provoked Tregoney and his followers remained and, as men talked, the nature of the confusion percolated to Sam Veryan and thence to Randolph. The final provocation had clearly been the sale of Lane Ends, and Frank had said simply: 'I can soon put that right.'

So he went to the village and talked to old Frederick Walton at the Rising Sun, and then to Herbert Colley at the Dog and Partridge. After that he visited George Wilkinson who owned the general store opposite the church and the vicar of St Thomas's, the Reverend Malcolm Small. Finally he called on Mr Small's Presbyterian counterpart Elias Jones who was still in shock and shame that his chapel should have been so used by Tregoney. To each he said, with suitable embellishments: 'The farm was sold because I wanted it to be sold – because the compensation helped me to buy my own farm. If I had not said yes, Randolph Haldane would not have sold it. The men who lost their jobs should blame me, or the railway – not him. And every other man without a job should blame the Government for sacrificing British farming on the altar of cheap food at any price. Please make sure that message gets round the village.'

He had little doubt that he had selected the best reporters – as he now told his audience at the Grange.

'Not everyone will hear the truth,' he said. 'And not everyone who hears it will believe it. But most will. And some of the men who work on the estate farms are very angry, and their voices will be heard. It's the best we can do, and it should be enough.'

Randolph looked sideways at him and said: 'Thanks, pardner.' And they both laughed, although without much humour.

'That makes me think of something else,' Frank said. 'If I wasn't leaving I'd be asking you to join me in a spot of hunting – with a gun. That damn' fox is still around. I saw him last night up by the wood. I reckon it's the same one that took those lambs in the spring. Remember?'

'I remember.' Randolph nodded. 'It's a pity we couldn't find him then. But I might still go out and look for him, when we get a clear night and a good moon. The right sort of bait, down on the edge of Morton Wood, might do the trick. I reckon that's where they go to ground.'

'How close can you get to a fox?' It was Laura's question.

Randolph shrugged.

'Depends how lucky you are – and how still you can stay for a long time. If you guess the line right, you can put yourself downwind of him, and if you're quiet he won't know you're there. Then if he moves out into the open and there's a bit of light, you can get him. It's nice to get within forty yards, but I can do it at twice that distance if there's enough light to see that far. In daylight it's easy at a hundred yards or more – but he usually stays to ground then, except in the middle of a hard winter when he's hungry.'

'You'd better not let the hunt know you're shooting foxes,' Caroline said, only half in jest.

'To hell with the hunt,' Randolph retorted. 'I'll do what I like on our land.'

Frank said: 'I'd rather rely on a gun than a pack of hounds – especially your gun.'

Caroline looked at them curiously.

'Could you really hit a fox at a hundred yards if he was moving?'

'With luck,' Randolph laughed. 'Luck – and light.'

'He could hit a cat at twice that distance,' Frank interjected. 'You should have seen him out in Kansas. The men there would bet on each other's shooting at posts or anything else – or things thrown in the air. Nobody would bet against Randy. It's a pity we don't still have the Winchesters. And at short range – you've no idea what your son could do with a Colt – or how fast he could pull one. It's an art – and he mastered it.'

Randolph laughed again.

'Tex was the master. And there were plenty better than I was.'

'I never saw one. Plenty nearly as good. But nearly could mean getting killed if you were in the wrong company.' He grinned. 'I've never seen or imagined anything like that time you got the drop on Red McLean. And he didn't believe it either.'

Laura asked: 'And who was Red McLean?'

'The man who shot Randy up in Dodge – and who paid for it.'

Helford's glance flickered from one to the other.

'What did happen in Dodge City, Randolph? What did you do to McLean?'

Randolph shook his head.

'I told you. By Dodge standards there was nothing to it.'

'Only enough to keep the town talking for weeks,' Frank said. 'Randy frightened me to death – and I was on his side.'

'Stop it, Frank.' Randolph interrupted awkwardly. 'You're embroidering it. The feller got what he'd asked for, that's all. He'd had it coming to him for a long time. He was just lucky I didn't kill him.'

Frank leaned back.

'It's the best story you'll ever hear,' he said. 'And it's time you heard it.'

Ignoring Randolph's protest, he described the incident, filling out the facts with his own descriptions. He told the story well and, when he had finished, his audience was seeing the saloon and the dusty street and the barrel-chested McLean and Randolph's streaking gun hand – and the savagery of his revenge.

At the end of it there was silence for seconds. Randolph stared at his shoes in embarrassment – an emotion with which he was not normally familiar.

Then Caroline said: 'Randolph – what a fool you were – what a marvellous fool – to take a risk like that. But you're so like your –' Her voice faded as she bit the word off, and she rushed on '– when you were young – so like yourself then – the risks you used to take.' Her eyes sought Mark's desperately.

He came to her rescue: 'It's difficult for us to imagine such a thing happening. I don't know how you two have settled down so well after living like that.' The words were as artificial as his voice.

Frank said: 'It wasn't difficult. But I certainly thought it would be –'

Randolph heard them like distant echoes from another

place. He had seen Caroline's lips start to form the word she had checked; had seen the faint flush in her cheeks, the panic in her eyes as she had looked at Mark.

They went on talking around him. He knew Mark and Caroline were watching him covertly, and that their voices had become tight, unnatural. Laura said something to him but he did not hear her clearly. Frank talked on, apparently unaware of the tension that had crowded into the room. Randolph thought: Keep talking, Frank; keep talking, talking. So I can think. About the word. The word that was killed. And Mark covering up, and the sudden fear lurking. It had escaped, that word; just for an instant, before it was killed. And he had seen it – just enough of it.

He said suddenly: 'Excuse me – I'll be back in a moment – I've just remembered something I must do.'

He walked quickly from the room, across the hall, outside. He knew his mother and Mark had watched him go, and felt their apprehension. But he had to get out – to get away from their eyes, and the innocence of Frank and Laura. He walked on, past the end of a barn, out of sight of the house and its staring windows. So like yourself? No. So like your father. Father? Rupert Haldane? Quiet, dull, obsessed, blinkered Rupert Haldane? In a gunfight in an American cow town – like Rupert Haldane? Violent and savage in revenge – like Rupert Haldane? Lady – my lady mother – what have you told me; from out of the furthest corner of your most secret memory, what have you released?

One of his long cigars found its way to his mouth and he bit off the end and spat it away, and remembered his first night at home after those long years, and biting the end off another cigar and Caroline saying we have grown to love each other very much. How long did it take to grow? When did it start to grow? How many years? Dark eyes. Whose eyes? Like looking into a mirror. My eyes – his eyes. My hair – his hair. Dark sun-tanned skin; would it have been so dark without sun? Would his? Horseman, adventurer, businessman, violent man: he was – we are. A girl in a barn in Marlborough. A girl in a bed in Boston. Another girl, twenty-eight years ago, in another bed. My lady. You are my beautiful lady, but I don't mind sharing you. Did Rupert share you? After ten childless years, did Rupert share you? Did Mark take you, and sire me, to please himself – or to please you, lady? Did it please you – did I please you – you and Mark together? The cigar smoke eddied in the wind, curling into shapes of hate and fear and love and young faces and older ones and his dead father who was not his father and whom he had not loved.

He threw the cigar savagely, high over a fence, and turned to see Caroline twenty paces away, like a pale statue.

For a year he looked at her; for all his life, staring, frozen somewhere in his body. He knew, by a word, panic in a glance, he knew their most dreadful secret. Had Rupert Haldane known his son was not his son, that his wife was another man's lover? No: he would not have allowed himself to know even if it had been paraded before him. A pale statue. And beautiful even now, in fear and desperation. He could see her face clearly. He was walking towards her. He had not felt himself move. They had shielded Rupert. For a quarter of a century they had shielded him. What agony had there been as he had grown up? He was close to her and she reached for him, her face saying please, please, please. He looked beyond her at nothing and his legs took him past, almost brushing her. A girl in a bed twenty-eight years ago, moving, urging, demanding, crying out. Oh God please help me. Help who? Not his appeal – her voice, behind him; whispered despair. A girl in a bed in Boston, and a man in New York who loved her, but not enough. So like your father. Please God help me – a dying whisper now. Rupert had not loved enough – except himself. So like your father. God help me too. God help us both, us all. Then she was in the doorway of his bedroom, holding a tray, holding out forgiveness to a rejected boy who had sinned, and he turned and held out his own hands and she came to him and clung as if he were the last refuge in all the world.

He kissed her hair and said: 'My lady – don't be afraid. There is no cause.'

RANULPH

Derived from Randolph

I

He was not tall, but strong; hard in the shoulder and down his muscular body, hard in arms and wide hands and thick legs; and hard in eye, too, when he was displeased. His forehead was broad and his jaw square, giving him a rugged, aggressive look emphasized by his stance and the way he moved – sure and firm-footed and abrupt. He did not look like a Haldane or a Helford, except for his hair which was black and his eyes which were of a brown so dark that most people saw them as black too.

He was heir to the Roxton estate, entitled to it by birth and the fervent wish of his father – except that he did not want most of it and had no hesitation about saying so.

He was born in 1886, ending Randolph's growing concern that Tregoney's curse might, by unhappy coincidence, be realized; but not without a struggle.

On that day Laura had been, by Dr Chester's estimate, a week overdue for the birth. Throughout her pregnancy she had been excited and happy. But now, as if primitive instincts were at work, fear shadowed her eyes and her fingers were white when she gripped the arms of her chair in the morning room of the Grange and said: 'I think it's going to be soon – very soon'; and Caroline, who had moved in from her Exeter home two days previously, sent her to bed.

By mid-morning a message had been sent for Dr Chester and the midwife to come.

After two hours with her he came downstairs, walked into the drawing room and said thoughtfully to Randolph and Mark: 'I think I shall be here for some time. Might I suggest that we would all appreciate some lunch?'

Part way through the afternoon Mark said: 'I can't stand waiting around any longer. I'm going out for a ride. If you've any sense you'll join me. Neither of us can do anything here.'

Randolph shook his head.

'I'll stay. I know I can't do anything. But I don't want to leave.'

He sat in the silence of the room for a time, listening to the big wall clock measuring the seconds, watching the birds turning slowly above the garden and the trees beyond the window, remembering Kansas and Colorado and cattle across the dusty plains; Boston and the first night of his marriage; Marlborough, his mother's calm and Mark Helford's strength; a man lying in an alley with a broken neck and another sprawled in a far away sunlit street beneath clapboard buildings, and a whiplash across his shoulders, and he heard Laura scream.

Once. A thin, distant sound that brought him upright in his chair, sweat starting on his face and chest. Then again, desperate, imploring help. He found himself in the hall, checking as he reached the stairs, listening. His mother was there – she would look after her. Dr Chester was a good man. The midwife was experienced. Don't go up – they won't let you in – you can't help . . .

He stood at the foot of the stairs, hearing the sound of his wife's agony distorted by doors and corridor; once the doctor's voice raised – a single syllable; blurred noises he could not identify. Then that dreadful, despairing, choking scream again, and he put his head against the wall panelling and heard his voice saying: 'Oh God – I have never prayed to you before – forgive me, if you can hear me – but help her now. I have done this to her – don't let her die because of me . . .'

After that the sounds were jumbled and his mind tried to blot them out; once he put his fingers to his ears but he could not stop them. A door banged but nobody came. He sat on the stairs, shivering, and did not hear the doctor until his quiet voice said: 'You have a son, Mr Haldane. A fine boy. But your wife has had a very difficult experience. It will be some time before she recovers from it.'

When he walked softly into the bedroom he saw her lying between white sheets, her face like a small hurt child's, her eyes swollen and bruised. His mother stood in a corner of the room beside the cradle, and he thought he had never seen her so fatigued and so concerned.

He bent over the bed and kissed his wife gently on the forehead. It was only then that she seemed to recognize him. She raised a hand and he took it between his, and she pulled him closer and whispered: 'Never again, Randy – please promise – never again.'

He promised, gently, reassuringly, totally. And so, later, there were neither brothers nor sisters for Ranulph.

The choice of the boy's name was as much Caroline's as anyone's. She told them the baby was so like Randolph at birth that he could almost have been a twin. And since the family tradition was for boys' names to begin with the letter R they selected a name that was the closest they could find to his father's.

Almost coincident with his grandson's birth, Mark found the buyers he had been seeking for Helford Shipping; and the business which had begun with a capital of little more than five hundred pounds forty-three years before was taken over by a substantial national shipping line, enabling Mark to retire first to his city home and, within six months, to Roxton Grange with fifty thousand pounds to finance his future – a small fortune which he jocularly promised Randolph would one day ensure that Ranulph would get a more-than-adequate start in life.

Mark and Caroline's move to Roxton was an easy transition, for the Grange was big enough to allow them a four-roomed apartment of their own, and although Caroline was returning to her former home she was careful to acknowledge that Laura was now the mistress of the house. Gradually she began to relinquish her financial stake in the estate, and within another five years Randolph assumed total control.

But his task was becoming even more difficult. Agriculture's fortunes declined further, for now there was not only American grain to contend with but Australian also; and both countries began to ship beef and sheep carcases to Europe as refrigeration developed and more ships were equipped to carry large quantities of meat for the growing urban populations. Memories of the Corn Laws died hard among the people, and Government after Government ignored the plight of farming in favour of the votes which came from the towns and cities.

In the eastern counties more land fell into disuse as farmers were bankrupted and found there were no buyers for their profitless acres. In the western half of the country, where livestock predominated, the survival rate was higher, for cheap grain meant lower feeding costs for the herds and flocks; but prices for milk and meat were low, for the disaster inflicted across the cereal land of the east produced a sympathetic backlash elsewhere. Even in the west the value of land was halved in the ten years between 1880 and 1890, and the trade for cattle and sheep which normally took young stock from rearing farms in the west across to the arable counties of the east for final fattening almost disappeared.

The Roxton farms became even more heavily dependent upon milk – to Randolph's growing concern, for he knew that if the inevitable competition between commercial dairies in the towns developed into a price-slashing war, the last prop on which his economy rested would be swept away.

But as the century's final decade began the milk trade remained stable, offsetting to some degree the consequences of the disaster which by then had reduced British farming to depths which were relatively far worse than those of the 1820s.

But Ranulph knew nothing of that. He grew strongly, attending the village school – now much enlarged compared with Randolph's days there – with a public school place reserved for him later. His childhood was happy, and he spent long periods on his grandfather's knee in the study of the Grange, listening to stories of ships and cargoes and life in the French Channel ports, his dark eyes shining with the excitement of the tales.

But on a January day in 1896 his comfortable and familiar world was torn apart.

The morning began like many others that winter, with a

thin wind across the ice-skimmed fields outside the house and a hungry kestrel circling the nearby farm buildings, silent against the grey clouds as it searched for prey.

Mark breakfasted quietly with Caroline. Then at eleven in the morning he asked for his favourite mare to be saddled, put on a leather coat and a scarf over his hacking jacket and heavy riding breeches and, bare-headed as usual, set out for a ride across the fields. At eighty-one years old he was remarkably fit, upright and active, and often rode alone for Caroline had long abandoned any sort of riding in the face of what Dr Chester described as 'a little heart murmur – nothing to worry about if you take life easily – you'll still live to be ninety'.

With his grey hair blowing in the wind he cantered across Warren field – so-called because rabbits lived in the bank in one corner – rode along a fold and turned into the long pasture that ran up towards the end of Morton Wood and the valley beyond. As he crossed the field the clouds parted and pale sunlight lit the winter grass. His mouth widened with pleasure and he kneed the trotting mare into a canter. Rooks began to call from the wood, the sun brightened, and he put the mare into a long gallop, rising easily to her as she went. The low thorn hedge on his left challenged and he turned in towards it, heeling the mare and letting her run. She went over cleanly, came down on hard-frozen mud, skidded and turned, falling heavily on her side. As she went Mark kicked clear of the stirrups but one foot caught. He came away from the saddle, trying to curl his body, but was pulled and twisted. His head hit the iron ground before his shoulders, his trapped foot jerked out of the stirrup, and the mare scrambled to her feet, recovering; then stood shivering beside him, tossing her head. After a while, when he did not move, she turned away and walked slowly in a circle, broke into a trot and made towards the distant buildings.

One of the labourers found her in the stable yard and called the farm bailiff. Within minutes Randolph had been alerted and set out with three men to search the fields. He knew his father's favourite routes, but half an hour had gone before they found the still form close to the thorn hedge. Randolph swung out of the saddle, slipping on the ice as he crouched, searching for life; and knew that Mark had died as his father had died fifty years before.

The men gathered round, holding their uneasy horses, quiet, staring down, not wanting to believe. The sunlight that had brought the brief surge of excitement to Mark an hour before had faded and wind sliced between the frosted fields and the grey cloud base. Randolph raised his head, looking up at the stricken faces. For the first time since another dreadful day more than thirty years past, tears trickled down his cheeks.

A little later they returned, Randolph leading his horse with Mark's body lying face down across the saddle. The others walked behind him, heads lowered. They clattered into the stable yard in slow sad procession, and Randolph led the horse across the face of the buildings and round into the drive that fronted the house. The others followed, not knowing what else to do; then they saw Caroline on the steps and held back, watching and yet not wanting to watch.

She came slowly away from the shelter of the house; as upright as Mark had been, slender still in a dark full-skirted tight-bodiced dress with lace-trimmed sleeves, holding a black shawl close around her silver hair and small, quiet face. One of the men suddenly ran forward and took the horse's head, stroking, soothing. Randolph held out his hands and she took them, but her eyes were beyond him, on the still figure across the saddle and the hands hanging down and the grey hair hiding the dead face. Randolph tried to draw her to him but she held back, still looking, her expression as frozen as the wind. Then she freed herself, moved past him, reaching out. Her fingers touched the grey hair and smoothed it, gently, as if she were comforting someone who was hurt. Her voice whispered: 'No one who had so much life should lose it.' Then she looked at Randolph with big, wondering eyes. 'He feels so cold,' she said. 'Let's take him inside.'

They laid him on a couch in the drawing room and she knelt down and brushed his hair away from his forehead and said: 'He isn't marked. I'm glad he isn't marked.' Then she kissed the closed eyelids and her tears ran down onto his face.

Later she went to her bedroom and after a while called for Randolph. He ran up the stairs, Laura close behind him, and found his mother beside her dressing table, holding a leather-bound book. Her face was calm, very pale, and he thought her skin was curiously smooth, as if some of the lines had almost disappeared.

'I've written down the special things in my life,' she said, very quietly, very steadily. 'I started it when Mark and I were married. It goes back to when I was a child. A sort of private history. I've never shown it to anyone. Even Mark never read all of it. I've just been reading a little. Do you know what I found, Randolph?' She looked up into his face, searching it, pleading. 'It's an incredible, terrible coincidence. It was on this day forty-six years ago that you were conceived.' She opened the book and looked at a page. Her gentle voice said: 'I won't tell you what I wrote. You'll read it all soon, when I've gone, as he has gone. But it – it was very beautiful –'

They heard her breath in her throat and caught her as she fell forward, shuddering, clutching her book against her chest. There was not even time for her face to show pain.

As the winter daylight faded Randolph laid them side by side on the bed in which their love had been born. He brought their hands together, his left over her right, and walked out very quietly, closing the door and leaving them on their anniversary.

For weeks afterwards Ranulph spent long periods in his bedroom, staring out of the window. He could see the farm buildings, and he tried to picture his grandparents walking across the drive and the lawn and opening the gate leading to the farm, just as he had often seen them. He tried so hard that after a while he almost imagined they were there.

At other times he sat solemnly in the drawing room or the study, whenever he could in one of the chairs his grandfather had preferred, and thought about ships and the ports of France and the grey hair and dark eyes and deep voice; and the quiet, comforting lady who had made him tea and delicious cakes and who had given pennies to him in secret and who always made him better when he hurt himself.

But, although he was only ten years old, he never cried.

Nor did he cry in consequence of an adventure which, four years later, brought him greater pain than he had ever known.

The century had turned and there had been celebrations throughout the country. But when the boys gathered at school for the spring term of the year 1900 a small number decided that the moment had not been marked with sufficient originality.

By this time Ranulph, although still scarcely out of junior school, was a recognized leader among his contemporaries and, indeed, among some other and older boys. He was stronger than average, aggressive in combat, cutting in debate, and highly inventive in subtle, secret jokes and traps at the expense of masters as well as boys. His two greatest friends were Langley and Soames, whom he preferred as much for their relatively modest family backgrounds as for their wit and resource, for he was slowly inclining to a left-of-Liberal stance as he surveyed the social conditions of the time, and increasingly found himself at odds with the in-bred political attitudes of many of the wealthier boys. Moreover, Langley and Soames were as extrovert as Ranulph himself, and the three were known among masters as well as boys – and with distinctly varying degrees of affection – as The Trio.

It was no surprise to anyone that it was The Trio who began and stimulated the debate on ways of celebrating adequately the turn of the century. Nor was it a surprise when Langley produced a chamber pot; Soames painted on it a passable likeness of Pottenger, the school's most feared and hated master, with the figures 1900 added below; and Haldane tied a school scarf to it and volunteered to hoist it to the clock tower above the main building and secure it there for all to see.

Since the point selected was a full seventy feet above the

ground, there was none who felt like challenging him for the privilege.

The twenty or so boys involved in the plan were sworn to secrecy, and preparations began. A body belt was constructed from stout leather straps, steel D-rings were attached, and then two ropes of different lengths were spliced around snap-hooks to enable the wearer to secure himself to pipes as he scaled the building and to anything he could find as he went up the tower. Then further ropes were obtained enabling the chamber pot to be offered to the climber from a convenient window so that, until that point, it would not have to be carried. Finally, other boys were recruited, not always with their wholehearted agreement, to act as lookouts at strategic points.

A night lit by a bright moon was selected and, just before midnight, the operation began.

From a high window a rope was passed over a drainpipe stanchion and then lowered the length of the pipe to the ground, its other end being held by Langley and Soames at the window. Ranulph secured the free end to his belt and, with his short safety rope looped round the pipe, and a spare length of rope over his shoulder, was hauled up the side of the building steadying himself with hands around the pipe and feet against the wall. When he reached the level of the top window, the boys on duty there passed the chamber pot to him on the end of a broom and, when he had fastened it to his belt, began to pay out the rope, allowing him to climb the drainpipe's last few feet to the guttering. As he had feared, it proved to be of indifferent strength, and he spent two minutes searching for handholds on the roof beyond, before managing to loop his spare rope around raised ridging tiles and use it to haul himself, legs dangling over a sixty-foot drop, onto the roof itself.

The clock tower which was his objective was close by, and well provided with handholds and ledges for his rubber-soled shoes, and the moon was bright enough to enable him to see as much as he needed as he inched his way upwards for twenty feet. If he slipped he knew he would slide and fall a long way, but Langley and Soames at the other end of his safety rope at the window were solid and reliable, and he was confident that, whatever else happened to him, he would not hit the ground.

But he did not slip. He tied the pot securely above the clock face, then began the descent – which, if anything, was a more dangerous procedure than the climb for, in spite of the moonlight, he could not see below as his feet searched for ledges. Once his heart leapt as he put his weight on the guttering and it cracked loudly. But it did not break and he was still held by a rope which he had knotted around a nearby vent pipe.

A minute later the boys crouching at the window saw him outlined against the stars, clinging to the drainpipe, and began to pay out the safety rope, a foot at a time, as he continued his descent.

It was at about this moment that Darwen, a fourteen-year-old who had been a reluctant recruit to the team of lookouts, heard footsteps and realized they were too close to enable him to give the alarm. His post was the nearest to a dormitory door, however, and when none other than the dreaded Pottenger stalked into view, prompted by some instinct borne of twenty years of schoolmastering into a final inspection of the dormitory building, Darwen had gathered his courage sufficiently to walk forward and, in answer to the master's booming challenge, to explain that he was on his way to the lavatory.

'What is your name, boy?' Pottenger demanded, peering closely in the gloom of the corridor. Darwen told him, as loudly as he dared, hoping that their voices would carry to other listeners; whereupon Pottenger escorted the scared youngster to the nearby row of lavatories, waited for him, and then escorted him back to the dormitory, pushing him inside, and hissed: 'In future, boy, ensure that you attend to yourself adequately before retiring.'

By the time the incident was over Ranulph was safely on the ground, warnings had been whispered, and boys had faded into shadows; and Pottenger did not enter dormitories to check that all beds were occupied.

Three days passed before a steeplejack could be found to

remove the pot from its lofty perch and Pottenger, who was none too popular among the staff, was humiliated when the likeness painted on it was seen at close quarters. By this time the whole school had been confined to the premises for a week as punishment; and by this time also Pottenger had remembered his midnight encounter with the boy Darwen.

It took him ten minutes and two vicious strokes of the thin cane which was his favourite weapon to extract from the squealing boy the name of the principal culprit. Pottenger, as a senior master, had a study of his own, and at midday Ranulph was summoned to it and promptly denied all knowledge of the escapade.

Pottenger, his eyes glinting behind pebble spectacles, wasted no time with him. He emptied Ranulph's pockets, confiscated a penknife on the grounds that it was a mischievous weapon, then confiscated the three pounds in the boy's wallet as a contribution – he said – to the cost of the steeplejack and the repair of the gutter. Then he summoned the senior mathematics master who occupied the next study and snapped: 'Rigby – this boy was involved in that dreadful incident at the beginning of the week. I have reason to believe it was he who actually climbed the building and placed that – that object on the tower.' He picked up his cane and pointed it at Ranulph. 'Confess, boy.'

Ranulph stood, pale and tense, and said: 'No, sir.'

Pottenger said harshly: 'Bend across that chair, boy. Rigby – hold him.'

The flogging was stopped by Rigby, who was of less brutal inclination than his colleague, when he saw blood. It came from Ranulph's lower lip which he had bitten severely. But he had not made a sound, and Rigby confided to other masters later that he would not have thought it possible for any boy to endure without screaming the twelve or fifteen strokes which Pottenger had administered with the full strength of his strong arm. Seeing the blood, Rigby simply released the boy, intercepted Pottenger's next blow and took the cane from his hand, saying quietly: 'That's enough. There'll be no more of it.'

He then took the shaking boy by the shoulders, led him to his own study and said: 'Stay there, Haldane, for as long as you wish. I will explain to your form master.' He left Ranulph, grey-faced with blood running from the corners of his contorted mouth, quivering from head to foot, but still silent, and returned to the next study. There he found Pottenger polishing his glasses, perspiration beaded across his forehead and running down his whiskered cheeks, and said curtly: 'That was grossly excessive. Moreover I believe you actually enjoyed it. You have earned nothing but my contempt.' The noise as he slammed the door echoed down the corridor.

The episode had three consequences, of which the most immediate occurred three weeks later when Darwen was reported missing after evening meal. He was found five hours later in the cricket pavilion, blindfolded, gagged and tied face down to a bench, semi-conscious in agony having been severely caned. Later he told the headmaster that he had been seized in the darkness by several men or boys – he could not tell which – who had covered his head with a sack, taken him to the pavilion, and administered the punishment – all without speaking a word or giving him any chance to identify them.

The second consequence manifested itself slowly through the following years in Ranulph's emergence as a vociferous critic of established values and especially traditional authority. He became noted in the school as a debater of consequence, committed to the principles of state assistance for the under-privileged, taxation of the rich and the redistribution of wealth – especially wealth based on the possession of land. He argued his new commitments vehemently, and only Rigby was able to identify the secret spur; and, because he recognized the elements of reaction and revenge in it, was saddened.

The third consequence was delayed for four years, until the day of Ranulph's departure from the school on his acceptance by Cambridge University. He walked down the corridor which led to Pottenger's study; a man now, looking older than his eighteen years, hard-eyed and hard-faced. He opened the door without knocking, stepped inside, closed the door quietly and said: 'I have a question to ask you.'

The startled Pottenger, who had been in the process of a final sorting of papers on this last day of the school year, came slowly to his feet, jaw jutting, exclaiming: 'How dare you enter this study unbidden, boy? What –'

'Be quiet.' Ranulph's voice knifed through the schoolmaster's words. 'I am no longer under your authority. Don't address me as "boy". I have a name. Use it. And answer my question.'

The two were of similar height and build, except that middle age had thickened the man's waist and chest. They stood, a stride apart, eye to eye, as Pottenger ejaculated: 'Get out, you impertinent boy – get out of here. How dare you approach me in this manner . . .'

His voice tumbled into silence as Ranulph stepped back, reached for the cane which hung, as always, behind the door, and slashed it through the air between himself and the startled schoolmaster. And as if it were a signal, he was no longer Pottenger's size but transmitted menace of such proportion that he seemed to grow with it in an illusion of strength and stature and maturity.

'I'm sure you remember using that on me, Pottenger.' And now his voice was little more than a whisper, and the more deadly because of its softness. 'Do you also remember taking money from me? Three pounds which you said was to help to pay the steeplejack's bill? What did you do with that money, Pottenger? Did you give it to the headmaster, and tell him where it came from? Tell me, Pottenger.' The cane slashed through the air again, whistling, and the man jumped back, even though it was two feet away from him. 'Tell me quickly. And do not lie.'

And then there began the tormenting of Pottenger. It lasted for five minutes only, the quiet voice slowly over-riding the furious and then frightened responses, the cane hissing yet never once coming closer than its own length to the pebbled glasses and the sweating face, the near-black eyes hating and promising unspeakable vengeance. And yet the voice never once threatened; instead it asked questions, repeating, rephrasing, repeating again: 'What did you do with the money, Pottenger? How did you spend it? Do you think of yourself as a thief? Did you enjoy flogging me? Are you a sadist – a pervert? Do you always steal from boys when you flog them?' – every question punctuated by the hissing cane, every flash of the cane followed by Ranulph moving forward, an inch at a time, and Pottenger going backwards until his head and his back were hard against the wall and he was trying to shout but the sound was muffled and the words jumbled and the questions still came – 'Teaching is an honourable profession, Pottenger – why have you soiled it? Why do you not have the courage to attack me now, Pottenger, as you did when I was under your authority? Do you need authority before you dare to strike someone? Strike me now, Pottenger.' The cane thrust forward, handle first. 'Take it – strike me now. Or are you afraid because I'm no longer under your authority? Are you afraid of what I might do to you if you strike me now? You are, because you know I would do terrible things.' The cane hissed, backwards and forwards before the man's face, and he jerked his head, and his glasses slid down his nose and fell to the floor and his naked eyes protruded and the voice said: 'But I didn't come to do terrible things, Pottenger. I came for my money. The money you stole. The money you didn't give to the headmaster to pay for the steeplejack. The money you stole from a boy and kept for yourself. I want it now, Pottenger. Three pounds. Give it to me, thief Pottenger. Give it to me, because I will not go until you do –'

It went on, until Pottenger's nerve gave way and he snatched out his wallet and his shaking fingers spilled money onto the floor as he thrust out three pounds and babbled: 'Get out – take it and get out – take it –'

Ranulph took the money, then held the cane in both hands, horizontal beneath Pottenger's nose, and slowly bent it, further and further, until it doubled and snapped. He held up the two pieces, one in each hand, and his Helford eyes burned and transfixed the man as if they were steel. He whispered:

'The next time you flog a boy, Pottenger, remember me. Always remember me. Because I might come back.'

Then he was gone.

A minute later he was outside the headmaster's study. Again he entered without knocking. The headmaster's name was Graveston, and he was tall and very thin, with a strong grey moustache and sparse grey hair. Ranulph stood before his desk and said:

'I am sorry I have to leave by reporting a serious matter to you, Dr Graveston. Four years ago I was flogged by Pottenger. At the time he took three pounds from me, saying it was to pay for damage I had caused. He did not give the money to you, but kept it for himself. I have just reclaimed it from him. There it is.' The three pound notes dropped onto the desk, fluttering. 'I leave it with you so that you may show it to him and ask him why he stole money from a boy.'

He turned and went, closing the door quietly.

II

'It's time there were changes,' Ranulph said.

He was in the hall at the Grange, pacing around the great oak table, sitting for seconds only at the bottom of the stairs and then pacing again across to a temporary perch in one of the old leather armchairs or on the edge of the table itself. He moved constantly – arms, hands, his whole body; not nervously, but with suppressed energy and enthusiasm for his arguments. He was engaged in one of his interminable discussions with Randolph who, in contrast, was still and relaxed with watchful eyes which followed his son around the big room. Laura, as was her habit when her men were in verbal dispute, was silent; pretending to read but listening and mentally sharing the stimulation of their debate.

Ranulph was in his final year at Cambridge, reading modern history and confidently expecting a good degree. He had rowed for his college, played rugby in several trials for the university team itself without achieving the ultimate cap, shot with rifle and pistol with devastating success in representative contests not least against the best team the British Army could produce, and had twice shared a bed with his tutor's wife in adventures from which he had only narrowly escaped unscathed. But his most profound personal satisfaction lay in debate, and he had argued for his college against distinguished academics, members of Parliament and commercial intelligentsia in formal senate as well as in less significant confrontation – as a radical, a provocateur, an historian, a modern, a traditionalist, a revolutionary, according to his whim. But his discussions with Randolph were the product of conviction rather than challenge, for there was a personal involvement in their conclusion which drove him to reveal his often-concealed self.

'I don't want revolutions,' he said. 'I don't share the glorious visions of the Marxists or the anarchists' longing for blood let into the gutters. I don't believe in the arguments about the faces of the rich being stamped into the dust of the proletarian emergence and all the rest of the clichés which are supposed to show how money and land can be distributed to the people. But I do want to see people helped when they can't help themselves – and when they deserve it. If they need the attention of doctors and cannot pay, we should pay for them. If they genuinely cannot clothe their children properly, we must undertake that responsibility. We have to find ways of doing these things – and at the same time of separating the honest man from the rogue, the genuinely needy from the man whose family is deprived because he is a drunkard or a gambler or a spendthrift.'

'And supposing you find that way – how do you propose to pay for it all?' asked Randolph, who often preferred to restrict his role to that of questioner, allowing implication to state his view.

'Taxation – how else? We all pay – we insure ourselves. And the funds would be topped up by industrial taxation – levies on company profits. There are other ways – an extra halfpenny on a pint of beer or on tobacco, or a penny or two added to the price of train tickets or even some of the goods we purchase. We have to find the answers.' He sat down abruptly in a chair and thumped the arm.

'You have to be careful that the cost of bureaucracy does not exceed its benefits.'

'The cost of misery is incalculable.' Ranulph was on his feet again. 'We have to learn that everything we do is for the benefit of people – not just the lucky few, but the vast majority. When we learn that, we will see the economic benefit – and that in turn will add bonus.' He paced across the room and sat on the foot of the wide staircase. 'But nothing will be achieved while we remain an authoritarian society. Power is in too few hands.'

'Are you a communist, Ranulph?' It was one of Laura's rare interjections.

'Good God, no. Nor Labour. Half of them can't spell, let alone understand fundamental economics. If you want a label, I'm Liberal. But an outsider even there – as I've been told often enough. Say I'm a democrat. But we can't run an effective democracy by relying solely on the ballot box, because half the people who vote don't understand what they're voting for and half the people who offer themselves to the voters don't understand the implications of their policies. I'm generalizing, and that's the worst sin. But it will suffice for the moment.' He stood up, using both hands to point at his parents. 'Still generalizing, we need new ideas and above all a new collective conscience. We have to create opportunities for people who do not have them.' He wandered aimlessly across to a window. 'Look at this place. It's the same as it was when you inherited. You've struggled against depression and kept the business going when some others, less skilfully managed, have gone under. But the structure has changed little –'

'You're wrong.' Randolph abruptly abandoned his questioning role. 'The structure changed for the labourers many years ago when I introduced bonuses and voluntary overtime. The tenants have a successful equipment-sharing scheme – the estate provides the capital, they pay for the use of that capital. It's been running well for twenty-five years, in various forms which have been adapted to the needs of the moment.'

'But the structure hasn't changed.' Ranulph swung aggressively away from the window. 'The same acreage, the same functions, the same relationships. There are too few opportunities because no one believes there should be more opportunities. You charge rents according to the needs of your business and the tenants' ability to pay; they work to pay those rents – that's their primary function because if they fail to discharge it they won't be able to realize their other aim – to earn a living for themselves. They have no independence, and so they have no initiative. They are captive. You are their master, no matter how benevolent and concerned and well-regarded.'

'What do you want to do – take it from me and distribute it

around the village according to the Napoleonic code, with a bit of land for everyone? You talked a few minutes ago about politicians who can't understand fundamental economics. You're letting your enthusiasms run you into the same trap.'

Ranulph came slowly away from the window; slowly across to an armchair, and sank into it. He looked cautiously at his mother, then directly at his father, as if deciding how far he should now carry the argument. Then he said:

'I'm not. I haven't explained myself. I think I should. If, one day, I'm fortunate enough to inherit this place – and you've made it clear enough that that is what you want – I will make the most fundamental change of all. I'll retain the home farm for myself, and I'll offer all the other farms to the tenants at the lowest prices possible. I'm sorry if that shocks you. But I don't believe a man should own land unless he uses it himself. I've come back to what I was urging earlier – more individual initiative, less authoritarianism, the bonus of economic opportunity. I don't mean there should be no tenanted land. If that happened there would be no chance for newcomers – no chance for labourers to become farmers. But there has to be a happy medium, and we're a hell of a long way from it. If there were more owner-occupiers there would be better farming – and greater personal satisfaction. If I have the chance, I'll take my own small step along that road. Does that disappoint you?'

'Yes.' Randolph spoke very quietly. 'What we have here has worked for the benefit of very many people of varying economic strengths and widely contrasting intelligence for well over a century. The Haldanes aren't the only ones who have been pleased with it. I'm certain there are several tenants who would not want the responsibility of ownership. If they buy, they're on their own. As it is they have someone to lean on – and someone with greater resources than they have.'

'But it's all in our interests, ultimately.'

'Ours – and theirs. If it doesn't work for them, it doesn't work for us. There's nothing for nothing in this world. If you ever sell this estate, Ranulph, don't give the impression that you're Father Christmas with gifts – you could get some people into trouble they couldn't handle. Just remember that before Father Christmas can hand out the presents, somebody has to create them – and they cost money. There are no magic words.'

'I'm not looking for magic. I'm looking for progress,' Ranulph came back at him. 'There hasn't been much of that, for a long time.'

And so they talked, on into the night; and much later Randolph sat on the edge of the bed and said to Laura: 'Remember Tregoney? Remember I told you he cursed us – said we would be the last of our line?'

'You didn't tell me that until after Ranulph was born,' Laura reminded him gently.

Randolph shrugged, and she thought he looked tired.

'He took a long time to come,' he said. 'I'm not superstitious. But now and then, during those years, I admit I thought about Tregoney, and wondered. Then we had a son and I forgot about it. But now – well, I'm wondering again. Ranulph overstates his case, like so many students. He'll grow out of that. But in the end Tregoney's curse might still work, in a way he could never have imagined. What's the point of an inheritance if the recipient doesn't want it?'

III

'Colonel Rawley has invited us to join his private guests at the hunt ball next month,' Randolph said one morning.

His son retorted bleakly: 'Good. I hope you enjoy it.'

Randolph grinned at him.

'You're included,' he said. 'The invitation is to the three of us.'

Ranulph reached out a hand for the *Daily Telegraph*.

'Do you want to express my regrets, or shall I?'

'You may present your own apologies. But I think you would be advised to join us. It will be an enjoyable occasion – a lot of interesting people will be there, I'll guarantee.'

'Then my absence will not blight the evening,' Ranulph said with mock solemnity as he sought the day's leading article.

Randolph raised an eyebrow at him.

'Why don't you want to come? Is it the Rawleys, or the hunt – or what?'

'It's not what, and it's not the hunt,' Ranulph said from behind the paper.

'So what have the Rawleys done to you?'

'Nothing. I don't like military gentlemen, that's all.'

Randolph watched his son with growing curiosity.

'Don't tell me you've added pacifism to your catalogue of convictions.'

Slowly the paper lowered, and Ranulph's dark eyes met his father's.

'Pacifism? What's that – except a belief in fairies? Going naked through a world of wolves shouting "I'm a pacifist – I'm protected" and refusing to believe you're still alive because of the hunters' guns around you. No – you've heard my views on authoritarianism often enough, so you shouldn't be surprised that I see military rank as providing the ultimate vehicle for the ultimate mutation – autocracy. I've no interest in meeting despots.'

'Have you ever discussed that question with someone who could be called a "military gentleman"?' Randolph was casual.

'No.' Ranulph retired behind the paper, and his father knew the gesture was defensive.

'Is assumption a reasonable substitute for experience and exploration? Would you have achieved such a good degree if you had based your studies on such a premise?'

'The answer to both questions is "no" – and you know it,' said the voice behind the paper.

'Colonel Rawley is retired now, as you are aware. He is a "military gentleman" of great experience. I would have thought that now he has no primary commitment to the army he would offer interesting opportunities for discussion on the subject.'

Ranulph lowered the paper, then folded it carefully.

'I would not wish to risk being discourteous to him while I was a guest in his house, father.'

'If you approached the subject with an open mind – which you should – I would have imagined there was little risk of that. I think you would find the occasion at worst entertaining, at best stimulating.'

Ranulph looked down at the paper, then rolled it slowly into a tube, contemplated it, and brought it down sharply across his free hand. When he looked up his mouth was widening.

'Under protest, and against all my instincts – I'll go: if you allow me enough time away from my post-graduate studies.'

The subject of his studies was a source of good-natured disagreement between them in which Ranulph maintained that his father was a harder task-master than all his Cambridge tutors combined. Since his graduation the previous summer he had spent every morning working on the home farm and Randolph had overridden his reluctance with the terse comment: 'The men will respect you only if they feel you understand their jobs as well as they do. And you can't understand anyone's job unless you do it. Nor can you control a business unless you have personal experience of the way each part of it works.' But in the afternoons and at weekends he studied estate management, visited the tenanted farms with his father, called on the bank manager for long discussions on investment and tax liability, met the estate's solicitors for guidance on company and tenancy law, and once a month travelled to London for meetings of the Royal Agricultural Society and the Farmers' Club. He continued to argue his views on the future of the tenanted farms but nonetheless studied their administration closely, and it remained Randolph's hope that, in time, his son would revise his opinions and that the estate's future might be better secured in consequence.

Meanwhile the hunt ball provided a diversion, for although Randolph rarely rode with the pack he enjoyed the company of some who did. Colonel Thomas de Vere Rawley was a relative newcomer to the neighbourhood, having bought the elegant Georgian Buckfast Lodge, four miles from Roxton, only a year previously upon his retirement from the Grenadier Guards. Now he had made it available for the hunt's annual social function and the committee had welcomed the gesture, for a man of the colonel's standing would be a valuable supporter – and the Lodge a graceful venue with its great central hall and wide curved staircase with landings above supported on marble pillars.

In this year of 1908 Randolph's latest pleasure was a Lanchester, and he drove Laura and Ranulph through a frosty evening to the tall gates of the Lodge and then escorted them across the wide drive to the door and their host who received them and introduced them to Elizabeth, his wife.

Up to that point, Ranulph, with sly humour, had maintained a supercilious reluctance about the occasion. Now he was correct, if distant, in response to Rawley's greeting – an exterior which the colonel mistakenly attributed to diffidence – and courteously remote when presented to Elizabeth Rawley.

But at that point his guard was swept away and thoughts of

principles with it, for standing next to her parents was the Rawleys' eldest daughter Diane, and Ranulph hesitated visibly as she extended her hand to him.

She was a mature and accomplished twenty-year-old with smooth shining fair hair, big blue eyes and a generous, laughing mouth. She wore a wide-skirted pale green satin dress cut low at the shoulders, and stepped forward to welcome the Haldane family in unaffected confidence which caught Ranulph's breath in his throat.

Her duty was to ensure that her father's guests were comfortable in the first minutes of the reception, and she did it in a manner beyond her years, slipping easily from one group to another, drawing them together, opening conversations for them with an ease which drew silent approval from Randolph and Laura and obvious admiration from their son. She paid no special attention to him, but Laura saw her slightly heightened colour when she spoke to him and the extra brightness of her eyes, while Ranulph recovered his confidence and met her word-for-word and glance-for-glance. And later in the evening, with a small string orchestra playing on a raised staging in one corner of the hall, he offered her his arm and they waltzed between the marble pillars until they had to pause for breath, and laughed with each other, and many a guest noted them and nodded knowingly. Later still they sat on the stairs with other young couples and chinked their glasses together and whispered confidences as if they had known each other for years.

Not once during the evening did Ranulph think of Colonel Rawley as a despot. Indeed, he did not think of him at all.

Three days later he drove the Lanchester to Buckfast Lodge and asked the colonel's permission to see his eldest daughter. The couple talked for an hour and then walked for a long time in the gardens; and he had tea with her parents and met her sisters. And not for an instant did it occur to him that he should debate the subject of autocracy.

The following week he went back to the Lodge and the pattern was repeated. Then, a few days later, he returned to take Diane riding, with second sister Kate as chaperone.

The girls rode mares, a black and a grey; Ranulph was mounted on a bay gelding that was a full 17 hands. Diane wore a plumed grey hat, a black linen riding coat and a black riding skirt trimmed with a silk fringe; Kate – a pretty, emerging eighteen-year-old – had chosen a small black hat above a conventional and unadorned black riding habit.

They left the Lodge's land and entered a long fold between high hedges, Ranulph and Diane riding abreast and sister Kate a silent follower; indeed, she had scarcely spoken a word since Ranulph had arrived at the Lodge and had greeted her charmingly and – Diane had thought – slightly mockingly, as if he found the idea of a chaperone secretly amusing.

'I don't know how far you would like to go,' he said. 'I enjoy riding so much that I sometimes cover considerable distances. Please don't let me tire you.'

'I shall tell you if you do,' she said, hardly concealing her surprise. 'Though why you think you can ride further than I, I can't imagine.'

He raised an eyebrow.

'It would not be an unusual assumption,' he said. 'Men frequently have a physical advantage, for obvious reasons. And riding is a physical matter.'

'I think I can match you, Ranulph Haldane,' she said softly. 'Even though I have to suffer the disadvantage of having to ride side-saddle.'

He laughed.

'My mother and father will both tell you that even as far back as the 1870s some of the women in the pioneer states of America wore trousers and rode astride.'

Diane looked at him from beneath long eyelashes.

'What a pity the fashion is taking so long to spread to Europe,' she said. 'That sort of freedom would be most welcome.' She turned suddenly and called over her shoulder: 'Ranulph is telling me that thirty or forty years ago some American women wore trousers and rode astride. How would you like that?'

Kate Rawley heeled her mare and trotted in close behind

them. She flushed, as if the idea of women riding astride a horse was too daring to contemplate.

'I – I can't imagine what it would be like,' she said reluctantly.

'Oh, come on, Kate,' Diane retorted. 'Don't treat him like a man from another world. He's human – I promise you, I know he's human.' Her laughter was quick. 'Look – I can hold his hand, and nothing dreadful happens to me.'

She extended one gloved hand and Ranulph, laughing suddenly with her, reached out and took it, and felt her fingers squeeze and hold his, and he responded quickly. Behind them, Kate flushed a deeper pink, and then giggled. They rode hand in hand for nearly a minute, until one horse veered and they had to let go. But their eyes stayed with each other, and Ranulph gently kneed his mount so that its pace quickened, and Diane kept up with him and gradually they drew ahead of the embarrassed yet intrigued Kate.

'I spend a lot of time thinking of you,' he said softly.

She looked sideways at him, cool and collected.

'I'm glad. I'd hate to find that I was thinking of you and you were thinking of someone else.'

'You do think about me?'

'Yes. I've thought about you a great deal, ever since that first evening. Before that I'd seen you in the village. My father was more than happy to include your family among his guests at the ball – but it was because I suggested it. And I suggested it because I wanted to talk with you.'

He laughed, pleased.

'You're a conspiring lady,' he said. 'I'm glad you did, though. It was a memorable evening. Every moment has been memorable since. We seem to have done a lot of talking – though I confess I can't really remember what we've said.'

'Neither can I,' she said happily. 'But it doesn't matter, does it?'

She moved her horse a little closer to his and held out her hand. He hesitated, half glancing back at their silent escort, and she shook her head. 'It's all right,' she whispered. 'Kate may be shy, but she's on my side. Pretend she isn't there.'

He touched her fingers, then said: 'Do you mean that – really pretend she isn't there?'

She nodded. 'Of course. I told you – she's on my side.'

He reined in, swung from the saddle, held his gelding on a loose rein and took her mare's head. She looked down at him for several seconds, her hint of amusement gradually disappearing as he held her gaze. Then he leaned forward and extended his hand, and she took it and slid easily from the saddle. He was still, his eyes on hers as they stood, side by side in the silent lane; then she turned suddenly and looked back at Kate who was waiting uncertainly, watching, confused.

'Kate – I thought you were my friend – look the other way!'

The younger girl coloured, then turned her horse across the ride and stared over the hedge and the fields beyond.

Ranulph's fingers closed more tightly and, very gently, he pulled her closer to him. She looked up into his face, and he knew she wanted him to kiss her. He did, tentatively; then drew back. And she murmured: 'Ranulph – my dear. Please do that again.' So he did, but this time it was firmer, harder, and she pressed her lips against his and he parted them with the tip of his tongue. He felt a shiver run through her, but she did not draw back, and they both forgot about Kate who kept her eyes carefully away from them, and clung to each other until one of the horses stirred and he whispered: 'I don't know how long we'll have to wait. But I want you – for ever.'

She brushed aside the plume of her hat and pressed her face against his shoulder. She did not need to reply.

When they returned, with Kate now drawn into their effervescent conversation, Thomas Rawley met them at the door and knew that the shine in their eyes had little to do with the sharp, clear air outside.

That evening Ranulph looked at his parents across the dinner table and said: 'Father – at present I'm an employee on his estate. You've said that you wish me to inherit. But that was before I told you that, given the opportunity, I will break up the estate in favour of the tenants. Since then you haven't mentioned succession. Something has happened today which makes it necessary that I should know what future I have here. Will you tell me, please? And don't be tempted to spare my feelings.'

'Ranulph – don't be ridiculous,' Laura said sharply. 'What else would your father want except that you should succeed him here?'

Ranulph shook his head. His eyes were dark and deep-set and serious.

'I'm sorry, mother – with respect, I have to hear father on this. I know I have disappointed him and I am prepared for the consequences. But now I have to know what they are.'

Randolph leaned back. He thought: Dear God – this boy is worthy of my father – so direct and uncompromising and clear-minded. I should not be disappointed in him: I should be proud that he has such courage.

He said: 'Tell me what has happened that makes this so important today.'

Calmly, steadily, Ranulph said: 'I have decided that I want to marry Diane. I believe that when I ask her, she will accept me. But I cannot ask her until I know my future. Is it to remain an employee for as long as may be foreseen? Will that be the sum of my connection with this business? If so, please tell me now, for I will then have to make other plans.'

'Ranulph – she's a charming girl – I'm sure she will make a marvellous wife.' It was Laura again; quick and anxious now. 'But you've spent only a few hours in her company. Don't commit yourself too quickly. I'm delighted, of course, but . . .'

Her voice faded, for she had caught sight of Randolph's expression and the slow shake of his head as if he were mystified; and then Ranulph whirled angrily on him for he was laughing softly, and snapped: 'I wasn't aiming to amuse you. I hope the joke is well-meant.'

Randolph held up a pacifying hand.

'It's well-meant – but not at your expense. I think your dear mother has forgotten that I proposed to her forty-eight hours after meeting her for the first time.' He raised an eyebrow. 'Right, my love?'

She stared at him, then reached for his hand and laughed at herself.

'Oh dear – I am talking nonsense, aren't I. Of course you did, and I accepted you – after a little argument, as I recall. I'm sorry, Ranulph – I must be getting old.'

Her son looked at them both; and then, in spite of his obvious tension, smiled slowly.

'How strange,' he said, 'that it's difficult to imagine one's parents as young lovers. I didn't know you were so abrupt, father – or you so susceptible, mother. Be consoled that I haven't actually asked Diane yet, so I'm more cautious than you were – if only by a small margin. But I shall ask her, and before long. I can't, though, until I have more to offer than my questionable wit.'

Randolph stood up, crossed the room, and came back with cigars, tossing one to his son. He stood with his back to the log fire, and the yellow lamplight threw his long shadow across the table and Laura felt his magnetism and Ranulph his impact as he looked at them both. He held a match to his cigar, taking his time – not because he needed time to consider his reply but because he knew that this moment was one of the milestones in Ranulph's life, and in his own too, and he wanted to savour it.

He blew smoke into the air above his head and said: 'You're an employee, yes – because you still have a lot to learn. But you're learning fast. In three years you should have learned enough to be able to take your full share of decision-making. Then I hope you will want to become my partner. At some time after that I shall want to retire – I promise you I shall not soldier on into whatever old age and decrepitude may come my way – and then I shall expect you to take full control. Once the business is yours you will do with it as you see fit. My only desire is that you should have the benefit, however you may interpret that. Perhaps I shall not agree with your interpretation, but that will be incidental. Does that answer your question?'

Ranulph turned his unlighted cigar over and over between his fingers, his concentration on it a shield for his emotions.

Then he looked up, his face carefully expressionless.

'I don't know what I expected you to say. But I couldn't have wished to hear anything more welcome. Nor imagined anything more unselfish. Thank you. You make me sorry that I can't change my convictions. I hope I shall be able to meet your expectation, because I would not like to have to wait more than three years to marry Diane.' He struck a match and held the flame to his cigar.

Randolph said: 'How long you wait is your decision, because surely you have a choice. On the initial wage scale we agreed you will have sufficient income to marry well before three years are up. And the other necessary things we can discuss –'

He stopped, for Ranulph was shaking his head.

'No, father. I think you don't understand me. I can't marry until I've achieved financial independence and the status which goes with it. I mean no disrespect when I say that I cannot establish myself in my own home until I have established myself as a separate person no longer dependent upon you and subservient to you. It is not a matter of trust or affection – it is one of principle. I must be my own master, and I won't achieve that until I am your full partner in business.'

Ranulph achieved his partnership in little more than two years; and he did so through a venture which focused into one initiative his grandfather's fundamental business aggression, his father's instinct for revenge when wronged, and his own capacity for patience and ruthless exploitation.

It began on a day when Laura told him the story of Lane Ends Farm and he said in astonishment: 'But we still sell our milk to Culrose – now, a quarter of a century later we still depend upon their good will. We rely just as much upon our income from milk as we did then, and we are no less vulnerable to their whim. And Culrose is still effectively a one-man business – now it's Oliver Culrose's son Herbert who runs it. No board of directors – no one to challenge him or curb him.

The home farm, the estate farms, other farms around – all dependent upon one man. He can crack the whip whenever he likes, and we'd have to jump just as father did twenty-five years ago.'

For three months neither Randolph nor Laura heard the subject mentioned again. In the meantime Ranulph continued his regular pattern of work and his regular courtship of Diane; but he combined with it a study of population densities in the villages to the east and north of Exeter, distances, costs of transport, advertising opportunities, wholesale and retail milk margins, Culrose's market penetration and that of competitors where they existed, and much more. He said nothing at home of his studies, but Diane was his constant confidante and they spent hours together poring over figures and written proposals.

Then one day his plans were complete and he walked into the estate office and placed a large folder on the desk and said to his father: 'I have an idea. I've been working on it for a long time. I've written all the details here – there are seventy-odd pages and they will take you some time to read, so if you like I'll summarize them.'

Without waiting for an invitation he perched on a corner of the desk and went on: 'We are reliant upon farming for a living – our own and other people's. Most of the farms are mixed units, but milk is of paramount importance. Yet for its sale we are beholden to a business which is controlled by one man – Herbert Culrose. Twenty-five or more years ago you learned to your embarrassment that such dependence can be costly. Yet the situation maintains. Moreover, although agriculture's depression bottomed out at the turn of the century, it is still by no means the prosperous industry it once was, and we have a long way to go before we recoup the capital which the 1880s and 90s cost us. So if we are able to extract a greater margin from our principal product, we are serving the long-term as well as the short-term interests of our business. And we can – by retailing our milk. I propose that we form an estate co-operative. Between our home farm and our tenants we have an average production of over fifteen hundred gallons a day. I have surveyed the potential within six miles of here, excluding the outskirts of Exeter itself, and assess it as at least eight hundred and probably a thousand gallons a day. The rest could be sold into Exeter to existing dairies or sent by train to wholesalers in Plymouth or Bristol or even London. I have found two dairies in Plymouth who would each take a minimum one hundred gallons a day if we offer it at a price which I reckon is viable to us. I'm sure I can find the rest of the necessary custom if I concentrate on it for two or three weeks. But the best potential lies in those eight hundred or more gallons retailed directly. We can undercut existing dairies by a halfpenny a pint and still receive over twice the price we're getting now as wholesale sellers to the dairy which is the monopoly buyer in this area. And the costs of retailing that quantity would only account for half the difference. Finally, Roxton is expanding steadily, so the market will grow.'

Randolph, who had sat still and silent through this speech, said quietly: 'What put this idea before you?'

'You did,' Ranulph said. 'Mother told me how you reacted all that time ago when Culrose put the pressure on you – and why you had to accept defeat. You wanted to retail as a partnership with your old friend Frank Garton. I'm proposing a development of that – if the tenants want it. It would be a handsome extension of our present operations. And the capital investment would not be great. There are various approaches to that' – he tapped the file on the desk – 'and I've explored several more. All are straightforward and unremarkable methods of raising or producing money and apportioning repayment responsibilities. There would have to be enough to build a central collecting depot with stabling, accommodation for waggons and churns, and an office. It could be sited on our own land. We could start with fourteen men plus two and four-wheeled carts, horses, and a manager. Each farm would be responsible for delivering its own milk to the central dairy and providing additional labour to cover for illness and holidays. There's much more to it than that, of course. But I think I've covered most of it there.' He pointed to the file again.

'And who has the market now?' Randolph asked, although he knew the answer already.

'Culrose has seventy per cent of it. The remainder is served by two minor dairies and a number of farms retailing on a small scale. I don't suggest cutting across the farm retailers if we can avoid it. But the others are fair game. And the most exciting thing is the sales campaign that would be necessary. We could mount a full-scale operation – advertising, door-to-door canvassing, leaflet distribution, and so on.' He banged one fist into the opposite palm. 'Culrose would never know what had hit him.'

Then he stopped, staring at his father; enthusiasm suddenly replaced by curiosity.

'You're not reacting as I expected,' he said. 'Don't you approve? Don't you see this as the sort of business opportunity we should exploit?'

Randolph eyed him.

'Before I tell you what I think,' he said, 'I want to know why you've done all this. I don't think you've told me everything. Why are you interested in – to use your own word – hitting Culrose.'

The reply came back; sharp and clear and without hesitation: 'Because I don't like the principle of the biggest section of our business being controlled by one man. And because Culrose Dairy once defeated you. This is your response.'

Randolph's mouth widened slowly.

'Your response, Ranulph. Your proposition –'

'My response – your response – what's the difference? Haldane response. It's taken a long time – right through the depression and beyond. But time doesn't matter. You wait for it, until everything is in your favour. Then you settle the score. Read my report, father – and tell me if you want to settle the score now.'

Then Randolph was on his feet. He picked up the folder, opened it and flicked through the pages.

'I shall be vastly disappointed,' he said, 'if I'm unable to agree with it. And if I find problems I shall work like hell to solve them. I had forgotten I owed Culrose something. I'd forgotten too many things. I've had my back against the wall for too long. You've just taught me a lesson.'

Three months later, after long meetings between the Haldane father and son and their Roxton tenants, and further meetings with solicitors and the bank manager, advertisements appeared in shop windows, on fences, in the local weekly newspaper; leaflets were pushed beneath doors and through letter boxes in Roxton and all the surrounding villages; carefully chosen salesmen called at hundreds of houses; and Culrose Dairy received the requisite notice from nine farms terminating their milk contracts.

In the villages people rallied to the venture, for they saw prospects for increased employment and greater prosperity for farms on which many of them depended for their jobs. They knew the farms and could see the cattle grazing the fields; they knew the men who worked the land and milked and fed the cows. And those who called at the farms or the new central dairy to collect their milk knew the men who ladled it into their jugs, and others knew the men who delivered it to their homes, for they were their own husbands or sons or neighbours, and they gave them the support they needed. Within four months Culrose Dairy had lost eighty per cent of its trade in the area and then withdrew from the remainder because it was no longer economic. And the estate drew closer within its boundary fences as each farmer depended more upon his neighbour and his neighbour upon him; and all upon the big house and the two men who worked in the estate office and led them to an escalating profit on their milk and the excitement of a new venture.

Culrose Dairy remained in business – but in Exeter rather than in the surrounding countryside. Randolph did not know how much damage had been done to the company, and in time he ceased to wonder about it; but Ranulph attempted to monitor the dairy's sales and did not try to disguise his ruthless satisfaction that Roxton was out of the grip of a man he had never met, and that honour lost before he was born had finally been satisfied.

Within another six months he found himself in partnership with his father, and on the very evening of their agreement he motored to Buckfast Lodge, took Diane into the garden, and said: 'I've got what I've been working for. And you helped me. I'm my father's partner. I'm his equal – in his eyes, in my mother's eyes, and when others know of it in their eyes too. Now I can face your father. Will you marry me?'

From a window an astonished Elizabeth Rawley saw them embrace unashamedly, eagerly; and then, to her embarrassment, with increasing passion – and just as suddenly break apart and run back towards the house, hand-in-hand.

Without ceremony Ranulph confronted Colonel Rawley, still holding Diane breathless at his side, and said: 'I have been taken into partnership by my father. I can now offer to Diane the dignity and security and independence that she deserves. We want to marry as quickly as possible. Your agreement would make us extremely happy. May we have it, please?'

They got it, leaving the colonel – used as he had been to bullying sergeant-majors, brash subalterns and overbearing brigadiers – bemused and amused.

The next day Ranulph argued his way into a temporary self-contained apartment in Roxton Grange pending the building of a house nearby, took Diane into Exeter to buy an engagement ring, and went to see the vicar of St Thomas's church to arrange the first details of the wedding. The following week he manifestly enjoyed the engagement party given for them by the Rawleys, but only after he had chaired a meeting of the tenants' dairy co-operative and conferred with the estate's bank manager earlier in the day, and planned later visits to events in London and Plymouth.

Randolph watched with a mixture of amazement and admiration his energy and aggression. Tomorrow was always too late; even today was rarely soon enough. Sometimes his confidence edged a little ahead of his experience, but always he found the resource to regain step; and always Diane went

313

with him, laughing, provoking, stimulating, matching his enthusiasms yet gently cautioning and subtly guiding.

It was only in the private moments, when he was alone with Laura or by himself in the solitude of one of the farm rides or the quiet of Morton Wood, that Randolph's pleasure died in him a little and he looked across the rolling land and the red earth to distant hills and was saddened that the unity, the cohesion and the established pattern tried and tested down the years were in their final days. Through four generations and the turbulence of changing times Roxton had been held together – and those who had been part of it, he firmly believed, had benefited. He had played his own part in the story; he had fought and he had won, and Roxton was still an entity, an active combination of people and purpose bonded by common concern.

But it would not go on for much longer. Ranulph, his son whose inheritance it all was, would see to that.

IV

It was September 1914 and there was war. It was a glorious, exciting, national adventure; pals together going out to France to beat the Hun. It would be over by Christmas or spring at the latest, people said – better get there quickly so as not to miss it. Nobody thought then about machine guns and mud and mustard gas.

Ranulph said to Colonel Thomas Rawley: 'I've always reacted against the unique concept of military authority because it places so much power in individual hands. I hate authoritarianism and autocracy.'

'The alternative to discipline is anarchy, and you cannot have discipline without authority,' Rawley said. He was inspecting his son-in-law curiously, for he had not previously crossed words with him on Ranulph's favourite subject.

'But authority must be based on democracy,' Ranulph retorted. 'True democracy is an insurance against the autocrat. There can be no democracy in the army. The autocrat is fundamental to military discipline.'

Rawley, who was tall and lean with a brisk grey moustache and a skin permanently browned and wrinkled by foreign suns, was alert now.

'Military discipline is based upon consensus,' he said abruptly. 'It could never work otherwise. Consensus is obtained through training and teaching. And authority is not vested in individuals; it is vested in a chain of individuals, interlinked. It is apportioned and related. I accept that there are bullies, mostly although not exclusively among non-commissioned officers. But they are not unique to military life. And even they somehow stimulate the characteristic which emerges above all others among men in uniform: loyalty – to one's platoon, one's battalion, one's regiment; to the army as a whole, to one's companions, and to oneself. And when it is to oneself it is a euphemism for personal pride. That is something which many men would never have experienced in civilian life. The army is not just a collection of men trained to kill. It is a school, a guardian; it has a social and an economic life. It develops character among its participants and it rewards achievements with progress and security.'

'It governs men rigidly,' said Ranulph. 'It does not brook discussion except strictly between those of equal rank. It frowns upon social intercourse except between those of equal rank. Men dare not debate an order for fear of severe punishment. And always the authority rests with one man – the next one up the scale from you. He is a God-like individual whose conduct towards men subject to his authority is called into question only in extreme cases of abuse.'

Very quietly the colonel asked: 'Would you object to military service, Ranulph?'

His son-in-law flashed back: 'I would not object to defending my country, for my country means my wife and my family and my friends and my way of life. But I would object to the ultimate authority of individuals if my life and the lives of other men were at stake – or, indeed, even if they were not – unless I felt total respect for the judgement and experience of those individuals. And that is unlikely to occur very often.'

Rawley nodded slowly; satisfied.

'I don't want to sound condescending, but I have to suggest that unless you experience military life you cannot judge it, or its impact upon those who are part of it. It is a unique club. It has its dreadful times, when men are killed and maimed and there is great fear. But the loyalty to which I referred previously transcends that, and those who are left are better in consequence of the authority which breeds that loyalty.' He paused, listening to Diane talking with her sisters in the next room, and a shadow crossed his eyes as he added: 'Having said that, I hope you never have need to contemplate it beyond a simple discussion like this. I fear the present disagreeable business in France and Belgium may not be the walk-over suggested by our politicians and our newspapers.

So let's talk of other things. Diane tells me that you intend one day to sell off your farms to the tenants – against your father's wishes. Have you asked yourself what your infant daughter Ruth might think about that in years to come – and any other children you and Diane might have? Are you not contemplating taking something from them – without consulting them?'

Ranulph showed surprise.

'I didn't know you had heard about that – although there's no reason why you shouldn't. Yes, I do intend that. No, I don't think I'm taking anything from Ruth. There will remain the home farm, which is a sizeable business – and the capital resulting from the sale of the estate which can be put to other uses.'

'If you sell to sitting tenants you will find the farms are not worth a fortune – especially as I suspect, in view of your philosophy, that you will not be pressing for the highest possible prices,' Rawley said. 'And you will have lost something else – tradition, and continuity. I was talking about pride and loyalty in military life. But it has been characteristic of your family's estate, too – for generations. That will go. And so will the spirit of service to the community which, I am quite certain, has been a motivation for your parents and grandparents and others before them, however little they may consider it and however they might resist its definition. Once you are the owner of Roxton home farm only, you will lose interest in the farms which were formerly part of the estate and in the men who work them – and the new owners will lose interest in you.'

'But they will be better farmers,' Ranulph argued. 'More responsible farmers – because they will be responsible to themselves instead of being beholden to a landlord.'

Rawley stroked his moustache thoughtfully.

'Has it ever occurred to you, son, that some of them might not take kindly to that? Has it occurred to you that some of them might actually find comfort in their state? If you do give them the opportunity, I implore you not to press it upon them too strongly. Some might welcome it; but others certainly would not.'

Ranulph laughed shortly.

'You sound like my father. Perhaps you are in collusion.' He was joking, but only with some effort. 'I say to you as I have said to him – I have principles born of much thought and debate, and I believe they are reasonable.'

The lines around Rawley's eyes deepened. He said, almost gently: 'Be sure that you do not sacrifice your family's best interests upon their altar; for your first commitment is to them.'

The discussion ended abruptly as Diane came into the room carrying the six-month-old Ruth with her dark hair and dark intense eyes – and, at this instant, her vocal discontent. And, secretly, Ranulph knew he was glad of the interruption. Talk of the war, and of the future of his heritage, had left him vaguely uneasy, and he felt sudden secret anger because he did not understand it.

V

Crowds lined Southernhay in Exeter: three deep on either side of the street, men and women, children jumping with excitement, waiting for the band they could hear beyond the corners of the buildings. A poster swung from a balcony; six feet deep, flat peaked cap and bold black moustache and giant pointing finger stabbing towards everyone who looked, spurring and accusing. Cars and lorries clanked and rumbled between rows of people, skirting the slower horse-drawn carts and carriages. The sun shone brightly this summer day in 1915, catching the colour of the women's dresses and hats and then the gleaming buttons of the first of the marching soldiers as they swung into view.

Ranulph was in the midst of it. He had come to Exeter to see if he could find a suit length among the sparse offerings in the war-hit shops. 'Get one now,' Randolph had said. 'In a few months, if things go on like this, there will be hardly anything left to choose from. And while you're there have a look at the new plough Baldwins were advertising last week.' He had not found any cloth he liked and the plough was a disappointment for its price. Now the crowds slowed him and pressed around him.

The soldiers moved crisply between the people, an officer leading. He looks old, Ranulph thought. Do they really have officers as old as that? Perhaps all the young ones are at the front. But the soldiers were not old; boys they looked: much younger than his own twenty-nine years. But they marched like hard, efficient men.

He wondered what Diane's father would have thought. Colonel Rawley had died suddenly six months earlier, still upright and military in his bearing and manner to within a few days of his death from pneumonia. Ranulph wished Diane had come to the city with him. But she had stayed at home with Ruth. She would have enjoyed the parade, he thought. She was so much the daughter of a professional soldier, so interested in military matters.

There were about forty soldiers, their boots banging down on the street abreast of him now, their rifles on their shoulders. Then came the band, led by a huge baton-twirling figure in red coat and blue trousers and gold braid. Stirring music echoed from the buildings and the drums hammered their marching beat against his head. Then came a grey-painted lorry with a field gun on the back, followed by another lorry with two sergeants on the flat behind the cab. One had a megaphone.

'Come on, my merry lads,' his voice boomed. 'Join your comrades. Fight for your king and country. Enjoy the fellowship that makes the best men even better. The army's a grand life – and your country needs you. Join the men who are giving the Hun what for. When your children ask about the Great War you don't want to feel ashamed that you didn't do your bit with everyone else. March with us – march to victory with us. Come on lads – let's see what sort of men you are.'

Ranulph watched critically. He thought: you bloody hypocrite. Do you really believe that rubbish? And then he realized that it was not the sergeant's job to believe or disbelieve, but to recruit. That was what he was paid to do. So Ranulph shrugged to himself. At that moment he was given to exaggerated gestures, physical or mental, for he was ever-so-slightly drunk after a lunch-time reunion with John Langley with whom he had been to school and to Cambridge and with whom he had had a long and contorted discussion about the war. They had drunk several gins and had then shared a bottle of wine. John Langley had then gone on to Drambuie, but Ranulph had kept away from that for he did not fancy driving back to Roxton through an alcoholic haze. Eventually they had shaken hands vigorously, grinned at each other and promised another meeting in a couple of months or so; and Ranulph, attracted by the noise, had walked slowly up Southernhay to investigate.

The bass drum thumped away up the street and the crowd surged around the lorry and its smart passengers. Flags fluttered from the cab and from the windows of the buildings. Men came running, laughing, catching up and trying to fall into step with the bass drum, grabbing and pulling each other along. A boy of seventeen or eighteen at Ranulph's side shouted to his companion: 'Come on Alan – time we joined this lot – let's have a free trip to France.' He broke through the crowd, dragging the other youth by the elbow, joining the column, swinging his arms high, pretending to be a soldier already.

Ranulph stepped sideways to get another glimpse of the boy. Then there was a woman in front of him, looking at him haughtily. She was late twenties – his own age – tall in her ankle-length black skirt, tight-fitting light blue jacket and wide-brimmed flowered hat. She was holding something – a feather – thrusting it at him. A white feather. He knew what it was supposed to mean. There were a lot of women like that around recruiting parades and where crowds gathered. He turned away but the crowd pressed in around him and he could not escape. The woman pushed out the feather again. Her mouth turned down at the corners and she chanted: 'Go where the real men go – fight for your country – if you dare. I don't think you dare. Show me you dare. Show us all you dare.'

For an instant he felt himself flushing. He thought: Christ – why has she picked on me? But he was not convinced by his own surprise. He had thought a lot about the war lately. And he and John Langley had just finished a long, anxious debate about it. Everyone knew, now, that it was not going to be over quickly. Christmas had gone, and so had the spring. In a month, the 4th of August would come round again – the first anniversary of its start. And men were dying, by the thousand; everyone knew that. The newspapers were still full of patriotic clichés and vaguely-worded close-to-victory war reports that were contradicted by others a month later. But the initial enthusiasm, the heady excitement, the popular intoxication, were not quite so spontaneous as they once had been. Even so far away from the front, reality was hinting, pushing, demanding attention.

So was the woman in front of him as she thrust the feather at the lapel of his jacket. Go away, you silly bitch. Everyone knows about women like you. The only blood you've ever seen is when you've cut your finger – and you squealed then. What did old John Langley say? – soon there'll be conscription for everyone, and then we'll have no choice – they'll just push us where they want to push us? He was right, of course. Good old Johnny. He'd always been right, back at Cambridge he was always right. And he wanted to get into the army, Johnny did. Not much of a job – who could blame him? 'Fight for your country – if you dare – show me you dare –' The feather pushing at him again, and people staring and a laugh somewhere. All Johnny wanted was a push, and he'd be in. Hell, I'd better get out of this – think of Diane, and Ruth. 'Show me you dare – if you dare – show us all –' The crowd shifted and someone shouted 'Go on – show 'er' and he looked hard and clear at the woman for the first time. If it had not been for her down-turned mouth she would have been attractive. Did her mouth turn down when she was in bed? He grinned at himself, then shouldered the woman aside, and someone else shouted at him and he turned and his black eyes looked at the shouter who suddenly melted into the moving crowd.

Would there be conscription? He knew his father thought so; and his father-in-law, before his last quick illness, had predicted that soon the flow of volunteers would slow as the casualties mounted – and that was bound to mean conscription. The thought was anathema to the old professional soldier, but he acknowledged it just the same. So Johnny would be right, as always. Johnny in the army – and Ranulph Haldane in the army? What in God's name would it be like?

He heard the woman's voice again, and then realized that her feather was stuck up in his jacket. He stared down at it, and suddenly a great surge of resentment jolted through him. What the hell was all this about? A peaceful country, not perfect but at least becoming aware of its problems, disrupted

322

and distorted and deprived by war, with its men dying and mutilated in thousands – because some Austrian archduke was shot by a bloody Serbian anarchist – because a posturing autocrat in Germany believed Europe should jump because he told it to? All his old convictions, which he had long argued to a dull death, swept up in him again, and as they did so he saw John Langley.

The parade, with its soldiers, its band, its vehicles and recruiting sergeants, and its ragged followers strutting behind, had wheeled somewhere and was coming back. And now the leader was no longer the officer who looked old, but Johnny himself grinning hugely, marching with another man, waving to the crowd, six paces ahead of the officer; Johnny, six feet tall, business suit crisp and pressed, hair sleek; a trifle drunk, maybe, but smart all the same.

The white feather was still stuck in Ranulph's jacket, and somebody nudged him and said; 'C'mon, mate – you'd better do somethin' about that bloody thing – I'm goin' – show the bloody Hun what Devon men are made of – get this war finished. We'll not do it by stayin' at home.' He was small and wiry, early twenties, bright-eyed and intelligent in a cunning way. He was grinning, and Johnny was grinning as he led the parade, and the woman with her contemptuous mouth was pushing through the crowd again and wouldn't go away; and there was an autocrat in Germany who wouldn't go away either until countless more men had died, but there was no other way, and Ranulph hated autocrats, and the lunchtime wine spurred his hate. Suddenly he slapped the wiry man on the shoulder and snapped, 'All right – I'm with you', and pushed through the crowd just as Johnny came abreast of him and just as the woman came within arm's length. He grabbed her around the waist and laughed at her and said, 'Come and lead the parade with me – come on – show the men in the crowd what they ought to be doing', and swept her out into the road and her protesting bleats were lost when a section of the crowd cheered. Johnny stared at Ranulph and the woman, and the little wiry man alongside them, then waved his fist in the air and shouted 'Roxton – Roxton for ever' and weaved slightly as Ranulph fell into step behind him, then grinned foolishly at the woman who was still firmly held by Ranulph's arm around her waist and hearing Ranulph's voice in her ear – 'This is your chance – you'll get more recruits than a dozen sergeants – come on – enjoy it.'

And so they went, marching ahead of the parade, three men and a woman; then four men, a fifth and a sixth. The route of the parade was clearly indicated by the crowds and policemen keeping them on the pavements, and Ranulph and Johnny and the woman wheeled into a narrower street, the woman's voice shrill now as she shouted to the crowd, and then they were in High Street and the tall old buildings pressed behind and above the people, and the six men became eight and then a dozen, and the officer appeared, running past them, falling into step again in front of them, waving encouragement to them. They waved back and the crowd on the pavement cheered and two more men tumbled out to join them as they marched beneath the great recruiting posters and the ancient overhanging balconies of the black-and-white buildings, shouted on by men who were too old to march and women who did not know what marching meant, steered by the avenue of people; Ranulph and Johnny and the woman between them, out in front of the soldiers and the band, left right, left right, up the street, wheeling into Broadgate and then into the great square fronting the carved grey stone and the soaring towers of the cathedral, between the flags and the faces of the people, leading the parade, marching up to the recruiting tables, marching to cheers, to war.

The tables were laid out in a long line, clerks behind, sergeants in front, officers here and there, smiling, encouraging. It was then that Ranulph looked down at the woman beside him, and suddenly he hated her as much as he hated the Kaiser and the archduke and the anarchist and he whirled to John Langley and snapped 'Hey – Johnny, lift her up with me', and they chaired her on their linked arms and turned to face the crowd which was abruptly hushed and Ranulph shouted: 'Here she is – here's the lady who's recruited more men today than anyone else. Give her a cheer –' The crowd responded, and the startled woman waved and Ranulph's voice rose again: 'And now she's going to set an example – she's going to join the colours – she's going to nurse the men who are hurt – out in France with the boys – she's volunteering to be a Queen Alexandra's nurse – give her another cheer –' and the crowd roared its approval as the woman squirmed, suddenly frightened, twisting but held tight by Ranulph. He heard her voice, panic in it: 'No – no – let me go – I can't –' And his hand locked round her wrist and his black eyes looked into hers and his mouth was wide in a grin devoid of any kind of humour as he rapped: 'Yes you can. You can't do anything else now. You're going to find out what happens to the men who get your feathers.'

She wriggled, fighting her way down to the ground, whispering 'No – no –', starting to tug against Ranulph's iron hand, then checking, for the crowd was still cheering. There was a huge, shallow, open semi-circle thirty or more yards wide in front of the tables and she would have to cross it in the full sight of all the people, and they were packed shoulder-to-shoulder and she would not be able to get through. Her face was flushed in embarrassment and anguish, and Ranulph's hand led her forward to the tables and he said to the clerk: 'Here's the lady. Put her name down. She wants to be a nurse.' He whirled to face the crowd and shouted: 'She wants to be a nurse –' and the crowds cheered again, and a lieutenant marched up to him and said: 'Now then – let's get started. Give your name to –'

Ranulph said, 'The lady's first', and Johnny at his elbow echoed, 'That's right – she's got to be first – always ladies first, old boy –' The lieutenant drew himself up and snapped: 'I'll decide who's first – and call me sir.'

Ranulph faced him, and his eyes shone. He said: 'I'll call you sir when I'm in uniform. Until then you can call *me* sir, because I'm paying your wages.'

The lieutenant's jaw stiffened. He half-turned and snapped: 'Sergeant – get this thing started – quick, now.' Then he stepped back, his eyes watchful on Ranulph who grinned at him and then put his arm around the woman's shoulders and

325

said: 'Now show them what you're made of – if you dare – show us all you dare – because the crowd won't like you if you don't.'

He stood, mouth a thin line now, staring at her, and she turned to the table, her hands shaking, and the clerk asked her name and she said, 'Ann Hodges – Miss Ann Hodges', in a small frightened voice.

Around them men spread out along the tables while the band played distantly and the crowd clapped and Ranulph picked up a piece of paper from under the hand of a startled clerk, wrote his name and address on it, and said: 'There it is.' Then he turned and winked to John Langley who was patiently spelling out the necessary details to the next clerk.

Nearby the lieutenant said quietly to the sergeant: 'That man – the dark-haired man. I want to know when he's called, and where to. Make sure the clerk notes it.'

VI

———◆———

Ranulph lay in bed between clean cool sheets, listening to the silence of the big house, absorbing it, sinking into it, feeling Diane at his side and listening to her breathing. He thought she was asleep until she whispered: 'You never told us you had been wounded – never mentioned it in your letters.'

He had been home for three days and it had been only that night, as he had undressed, that she had noticed the scars on his leg and he had had to tell her.

'There wasn't any point. It wasn't bad, anyway.'

She was silent for a time; then: 'You're not wearing a wound ribbon. You're entitled to, aren't you?'

'I suppose so.'

'Why don't you?'

She felt his shoulders move slightly.

'What's the point? It's only a way of showing off – saying "look at me – I'm a wounded hero". I was lucky – lucky it wasn't worse. I shouldn't get a ribbon for being lucky.'

She said: 'A lot of men are proud to wear one. It reminds the rest of us what they've been through – how lucky we are not to have to face what you've faced.'

'Forget it,' he said quietly. 'It's not my style, I suppose.'

She turned towards him, her hand seeking his.

'Would you wear a medal ribbon, if you had one – an MC, or something?'

He was silent for seconds, then shrugged again.

'Don't know. But it's hardly likely. Never mind that. Tell me how father's managing. He looks pretty good. He's sixty-six and he doesn't look a day over fifty.'

'He's marvellous,' she said. 'He copes with everything – as if it's easy. And I know it isn't. And he never shows he worries

327

about you. Your mother shows it – so does mine. But he's like a rock. We all lean on him.'

'I've hardly talked about the business yet,' he said. 'There's plenty of time, though.' He took a long breath, relaxing. He still found it difficult to ease tension from his muscles. 'Three weeks – and then a home posting, with weekends and more leave. I still can't believe it.'

'Neither can I.' She snuggled closer to him and her hand sought his face, her fingers tracing his forehead and his cheeks. Suddenly she raised herself and kissed him. 'I'm going to live every second of it – the two of us together – and Ruth, who hardly knows you. But she's old enough now to enjoy being with you.'

He turned towards her, drawn by her warmth.

'She's beautiful. So are you. I've thought about you both, all the time. I've longed for you.' He laughed softly into her hair. 'How strange – all that time away – and then the first night at home, and I couldn't make love to you. How ridiculous that was. I could have wept.'

She held him by the shoulders, pulling him towards her.

'It didn't matter. I knew – so much had happened – terrible things. It didn't matter.' Her lips found his and she breathed: 'It was right last night, though – for both of us.' She felt his thighs against hers and shivered. 'It will go on being right now – like it used to be.'

She moved against him and he responded, and their breathing quickened until she pushed against his shoulders and rolled over with him, astride him, and he felt tears on her face and his own strength and they cried out together, softly, urgently, and then his tears mingled with hers as they joined and shared and united, desperate and overwhelmed by fear and gratitude that he was still alive.

It was June and the poplar windbreak on the west side of the house and the assorted oaks, beeches and elms in Morton Wood were in new leaf and there was the fresh promise of early summer over the red Devon soil. But the year was 1917

328

and food was scarce in the shops, clothes were shabby, and the Flanders dead were totalled in millions.

Ranulph Haldane, newly-promoted from lieutenant to captain after four months spent training young newly-commissioned officers around the camps of Salisbury Plain, was on embarkation leave for the second time. The first had been just over a year before; looking back on it, he thought it had been something that had happened to somebody else.

He had been called by the army within four weeks of the Exeter incident and, although he did not know it, his name had been passed at the same time to the lieutenant with whom he had clashed at the recruiting tables. From the lieutenant had gone a brief memorandum which was attached to Ranulph's records and which recommended that he be considered for an early commission because in the lieutenant's view he demonstrated sound leadership instincts, outstanding personal confidence and considerable natural aggression. Thus he had followed early the conventional patterns of officer-training, ultimately being selected for a commission in the Royal Artillery and thence for training in signals. Then he had gone to France and to the hell which had erupted on either side of the Albert-Bapaume road, just north of the Somme, in July 1916. He had seen men die in their countless thousands in trench actions of appalling intensity and in shattering artillery bombardments which had produced casualties even the military strategists had never envisaged.

In late August he had been hit in the left leg by shrapnel, but it was a relatively minor wound and he had come limping back to the artillery command to which he was attached after treatment in a base hospital and a week's leave in Paris. Then had come his promotion from second to first lieutenant and the further battles of the Somme which, somehow, he had survived until, with a Mention in Despatches which he neglected to report in his letters to Diane and his parents, he had been sent back to England at the end of January to pass on his experiences to the training schools.

Now he sat in the drawing room of Roxton Grange, nursing the three-year-old Ruth and watching his wife who was just at the mid-point of pregnancy – the result, they both knew, of one of the first frantic nights which had followed his return from France. She looked as if a full six months had gone, and although the doctor would not commit himself, both she and Laura were convinced that she was carrying twins.

But at that moment most of his attention was on Randolph, who was pondering whether to sell one of the estate's farms after the sudden death of the tenant. The opportunity to raise capital was tempting; equally, because the land adjoined Roxton home farm itself, it would be easy to take it in hand and extend the home farm's operations by another 150 acres.

Randolph had already decided what he wanted to do, but he still recognized his son's right to share decisions of that kind in spite of the uniform he wore and so kept his preference to himself.

Ranulph said: 'I walked the farm last week. The buildings are nothing special, although the land's in good heart. If you take it in hand you'll have to change a lot of things – you can't increase the dairy herd at the home farm because the byres aren't big enough, so you would either have to create two milking units, go for more beef and a bigger sheep flock, or grow more cereals. I think a lot of that land is too light for corn, and if you're going to do the beef job properly you would have to winter-house the cattle and that would mean spending nearly as much on the buildings as would be needed if you wanted a second dairy herd. And either way, the additional cattle will cost a good deal if you're going to stock the land fully. Sheep would graze well there, but I think the present flock is big enough.'

'So you don't want to take it in hand?' Randolph prompted.

'No. I don't think the capital outlay would be worth it currently. And if you're going to sell it, you would have to do it with a specific purpose in mind – there's no point in capital unless you're going to use it in some way. We've no pressing need for capital now – unless you have something up your sleeve I don't know about.' He grinned. 'And even if tenancies are not the best short-term investment, in the long view think it would be better to retain the farm and let a new tenant take responsibility for it.'

Randolph's face was carefully expressionless. He said: 'So we offer it for tender and see if we can get the right sort of applicant?'

'Yes – if you agree. I wouldn't like to see it go to one of the adjoining tenancies – a new man would be a good thing all round.'

Randolph glanced at his wife and daughter-in-law. Both were listening and watching, and he sensed their curiosity. He hesitated, wondering whether to pursue the subject; how far he should steer the conversation along the course which, unexpectedly, it was running.

'Ranulph –' It was Laura. She held out her hands to the little girl who scrambled down from her father's knee and as the child ran to her Randolph marvelled, as he did so often, that she should be a grandmother and yet so trim and youthful and, in his secret eyes, so desirable. 'Ranulph – tell me why you want to see the farm let to a new tenant. I've heard you say so often that you intend to sell the tenanted farms one day. Does it really make sense to accept a new tenant now – wouldn't you find it more acceptable to sell the place?'

Ranulph stretched out his legs; then abruptly, was on his feet. He crossed to the window and stared out at the garden beyond. Randolph thought he had suddenly withdrawn from them. The room was still, and he saw Laura and Diana look quickly at each other.

Then Ranulph said distantly: 'Yes. I know I've said that. And I've believed it. I still believe it, as a principle. But since I've been at home – I've given it a lot of thought.' He turned slowly and sat on the windowsill, looking at them. The summer light from the garden was strong behind him, and his face was shadowed. He said, very slowly and deliberately, as if every word mattered to him: 'Do you remember Johnny – John Langley? He joined the army when I did – remember? He had two sons – four or five years old, and a baby. He talked a lot about them. He lived in Newton Abbot. I went to his home once, when we were training – met his wife – saw the youngsters. He talked about his duty to them – it was his life's duty to provide for them, to give them everything he could – to be as successful as he could be just so that they could be better than he was, and have better opportunities.'

He was silent then, for seconds; until he turned away from them and looked out at the garden again, and Randolph knew it was because he did not want them to see his face.

'I haven't told you. I didn't want to. But Johnny can't give them anything. He was killed at Pozières. Three miles from where I was. He and I had an agreement. If one of us was killed or maimed, the other would help to look after his family. We shook hands on it. So now – now I have two families to look after, when the war's over. And Diane, and Ruth, and the baby that's coming – Johnny helped me to get you all straight in my mind. The old principles are still right, for me. But there are new ones. Father-in-law told me once to take care that I didn't sacrifice my family for my principles. There's no danger of that now. I have to make sure that Roxton will look after my children – and Johnny's children. So I have to make it the best and most profitable place in the world. We have to adapt – to circumstances.'

He was quiet then, staring out at the garden; and still, until Diane stood up and, walking very softly, crossed the room to him. And Randolph's eyes met Laura's and she gathered up the silent, wondering child on her knee and followed him, and they went out of the room together, not knowing what to say but wanting to leave Ranulph with his wife.

South of Arras was a seventeenth century farmhouse with walls three feet thick and small windows. Ranulph thought it was like a minor fortress and secured a billet there for himself in a small, bare-plastered room with a hard bed and a single rail on which to hang his uniform. The farmer, who was past seventy and looked eighty, and who had refused to leave his home despite the danger from the front-line trenches only three miles away, knew no English and understood little of Ranulph's poor French. But his wife, twenty years younger and an attractive dark-haired woman who somehow reminded Ranulph of his mother, spoke modest English, and he enjoyed breakfasts and occasional, simple, evening meals with the couple.

The narrow window of his room overlooked fields beyond which were the huts which comprised his sector headquarters, and beyond again Gouzeaucourt Wood which had escaped severe damage when the Germans had occupied the area a year or more ago. In the evenings it was possible to look from the window across the country and almost imagine there was no war and no slaughter on the other side of the fields and the trees – until the next day when Ranulph rode up the line to the forward artillery units, and beyond to the trenches and the observation posts and the field hospitals and the devastated land and the death smell.

It was towards the end of September when Ranulph, and others, realized that something big was in prospect. He was ordered to a nearby half-ruined château where a Major-General and a Brigadier spoke to an assembly of some forty officers, pointing to maps of the area, demanding an immediate improvement in communications between certain sectors, and forecasting the establishment of new liaison posts which would co-ordinate movements along an eight-mile front. New communications trenches were to be dug, new telephone landlines laid in certain patterns, and new wireless equipment installed and thoroughly tested. It was clear that an offensive was planned and it required little imagination to realize that Cambrai, three miles behind the German lines, was the principal target.

But they were told nothing about that, and later Ranulph said to Lieutenant Peter Selkirk who was newly out from England and his second-in-command over the sector which was his responsibility: 'How the hell can we get things right if we don't know what it's all about? Theory isn't good enough. It's the detail which will make the difference between a lot of men living or dying.' He remembered telling his father-in-law how he would object to the ultimate authority of individuals if his life was at stake unless he felt total respect for their

333

judgement; and he grinned wryly at the memory, for he felt little respect for the Major-General or the Brigadier because they had never been across the front line and over into no-man's-land. And yet, at the same moment, he knew that the criticism was invalid, for to have fought in fury and terror, in mud and the blood of men, did not entitle a soldier to the respect of his fellows and to their unswerving obedience. Experience had taught him a great deal; but not necessarily the things that different experiences had taught the Major-General and the Brigadier. They were doing their job; he had to do his. Different jobs, requiring different skills based on different experiences. But he still resented their power when he did not understand why it was being exercised in the pattern which had emerged on the maps and in the instructions.

The following day he went with Peter Selkirk and Sergeant John Warren, a tough Lancastrian who had been in the Somme area for nearly a year and had a Military Medal to demonstrate it, up into the third line trenches, on to the second line network and then through the muddy labyrinth of communications trenches to a dugout just behind the front line. There an infantry lieutenant said to them: 'The problem is immediately ahead of us. No-man's-land is about three hundred yards wide here, but raids are frequent – both ways. We need better communications – a delay of two minutes in reporting an incident back is vital – although I'm sure I don't need to tell you that.'

He was very young, very pale, as he held out cigarettes and indicated upturned ammunition boxes. 'Sit down – be my guests. If you want a new signals liaison post I suggest this hole in the ground would be as good as any, sir. It's central to the sector you're surveying. Communications trenches are well laid out on either side. The only trouble is it gets a bit noisy at dawn and dusk, and sometimes we get trespassers.' His mouth did not smile.

They talked on, about the new wireless equipment, about field telephones and landlines, German patrol raids and warning times, observation posts, forward posts which were

334

really excavated shell holes in no-man's-land; about the need to improve liaison with the artillery and the Royal Flying Corps. Then they pushed aside the gas curtain and walked into the front line trenches, past men who lay against muddy sand-bagged walls, faces pressed against periscopes; past others who stood or squatted on the duckboards, rifles propped beside them, and others still who played cards on broken ammunition boxes. Hardly anyone spoke as the four men shuffled along the slippery duckboards. Presently the grey clouds began to drizzle thin rain and Ranulph was glad to get back to the dugout before moving further north to the next trench network, then across behind Haverincourt Wood and on again.

The wind rose during the night and blew the low clouds away, leaving clear skies when Ranulph left the farmhouse at seven in the morning after breakfasting meagrely with the old farmer and his wife. As he mounted his horse the woman said, as she said every morning: 'You must be ver' careful today, Ranulph.' He nodded and waved to her.

Somehow he could smell Devonshire on the clean air as he rode along a sunken road, and he thought about the Grange and the home farm, and then about the rest of the estate and the men who farmed it; and wondered, as he often did, what his father had thought about his confession that day now so long ago, before his return to France. Randolph had said little about it afterwards, and Ranulph had been thankful, for he had been in no frame of mind to debate the philosophy of his change of heart. But he had debated it secretly with himself many times since, thinking of Diane and Ruth and the baby soon to be born, and then about the fatherless children in Newton Abbot and the ebullient, dead John Langley; and each time took shelter in the confused, distorted world which surrounded him. When the war was over, he thought, he would confront the problem squarely, and his conscience too.

But he knew that the decision had already been made.

He had ridden three hundred yards when he heard aircraft engines. He twisted in the saddle and saw two Fokkers coming low across the fields from the wood. They banked away from him towards the farmhouse and he heard their machine guns. He slid from his horse, slapped the animal's quarters and crouched at the edge of the shallow ditch alongside the road. The horse trotted away aimlessly. Beyond a tattered hedge the second Fokker was firing; then Ranulph saw the first turn in again. There were three red stripes painted on the fuselage near the tail. The observer was standing in the cockpit, holding his machine gun. When the aircraft was abreast of the farmhouse again he fired a long burst at it. Then, still low to the ground, the two planes turned away, back towards the wood.

Ranulph called his horse, running to meet it. He swung up and into a canter, then a gallop, back towards the house. All the time he was muttering: 'The swine – the bloody swine – why did he do that – for God's sake – why?'

The old man lay outside the house door, his coat torn apart by bullets and a gaping raw wound in his chest. Ranulph ran past him into the house. In the kitchen where he had eaten breakfast a quarter of an hour before he found the wife's body surrounded by glass splinters from the shattered window. The machine gun bullets had cut her almost in half and blood spread in a wide stream across the floor. He stood, the bile rising in his throat and heard her voice saying 'You must be ver' careful today'. Then he thought of his mother in another house alongside farm buildings and swore and swore and swore until tears distorted the horror.

He spent most of the day in tight-faced silence, speaking only when someone spoke to him. He sent orderlies to clear up the mess in the farmhouse and to dig graves in a corner of the nearest field. In the afternoon he took a prayer book and went out to supervise the burials, reading a form of service, trying to say a few words in French. He ate in the hut used as a makeshift mess and slept on a chair in the corner.

The two Fokkers came back the next morning, flying little more than fifty feet above the ground, lifting to clear trees then descending again, one following the other straight for the sector post. A sentry clanged the alarm bell and the half-dozen men on duty hurled themselves through doors to

336

get away from the buildings. The sentry grabbed the Lewis gun mounted on a ring of sandbags. Ranulph ran with the men, hearing the machine guns start up. He dived behind a lorry which had brought up the rations during the previous evening and heard bullets clang and scream against the metalwork. Thirty yards away he saw the sentry struggling with the silent Lewis gun, banging it with his hand, his face distorted with fury. A soldier ran across the front of the lorry and, without a sound, fell on his face close to one wheel, shuddering, then was still. His rifle was in his hand and Ranulph reached for it as the snarling engines passed close overhead and the aircraft dipped out of sight beyond trees. He heard the pitch rise and knew they were turning to come in again. He dragged himself up beside the truck and saw the leading aircraft two hundred yards away, banking steeply. It came closer, straightening, not heading directly for the buildings but circling, flying slowly, perhaps not more than sixty miles an hour. There were three red stripes in front of the tail and the observer was standing in the cockpit behind his machine gun.

'You bastard – you bloody murdering swine –' Ranulph heard the words as if someone else was shouting. He pushed a cartridge forward with the bolt and steadied the rifle against the side of the truck, following the aircraft, aiming ahead of the black figure with the machine gun, trying to allow for speed and distance, trying to remember everything his father had told him – everything the army had taught him.

He squeezed the trigger gently, slid the bolt back and forward, following up with a fast second shot; then realized it was only the gun he could see. The aircraft swayed and he saw the observer hanging head down beside the red stripes. Then the engine note rose and the aircraft climbed in a steep bank and the dark figure detached itself and tumbled in a confusion of arms and legs away and down, like a black rag doll, and Ranulph swung his rifle, looking for the second aircraft, but it had gone beyond the trees.

'Christ – you got him – you hit the bastard.' It was Selkirk, running towards him, shouting.

Ranulph lowered the rifle and turned away, remembering yesterday's bloody kitchen and the vision of his mother and the two sheeted bodies in the grave. He said over his shoulder to Selkirk: 'Yes – I got him.' He felt cold and remote and sick.

For the next month he worked behind the lines and occasionally in the forward trenches, priding himself that when the offensive came nothing would move in his sector without his knowledge, and that his liaison with the guns and the aircraft was at peak efficiency. Increasingly he thought about Diane and wondered if the baby had been born; but mail was slow to arrive and he did not know what had happened back in the peace of Roxton.

But one night he knew something very important was about to happen in and over the trenches that had become his home. He went back through steady rain to the command post and found it extended – and was startled to see tanks in nearby farm buildings and to meet several on the road being guided by men with shielded lights. He had never seen tanks before, although he knew they had been in action months previously with indifferent success, and found their size and noise awesome and exciting in the darkness.

Three days later a headquarters colonel called a briefing of officers at the command post. He was a slightly-built, thin-faced man, a few years older than Ranulph, with a short bristling moustache, the ribbon of the Distinguished Service Order on his tunic and a long ugly scar from his temple to the angle of his jaw.

Crisply he confirmed that Cambrai was the objective of the offensive all knew was imminent, and that it would involve the biggest tank assault of the war. Over 350 tanks were waiting within a mile of where they sat in the wooden hut, together with artillery concentrations and massive infantry reinforcements. The attack would start at six in the morning of 20 November – five days hence. This time there would be no prior artillery barrage, for the land had to be left in a fit state for the tanks; the guns would open up as the tanks led the attack with infantry close behind and would blanket targets well behind enemy lines to prevent the movement of reinforcements. Maps were shown, the pattern of the assault described and discussed, communications were surveyed. Ranulph, and another captain with similar responsibilities to the north of his sector, would move forward behind the infantry, co-ordinating the forward signals operation along half a mile of the front and in depth behind it; ensuring that the infantry knew what was happening north and south, that the guns knew what the infantry needed, that communications with ground support and observation aircraft were maintained and that those responsible for the movement of reinforcements were fully informed, hour by hour.

The briefing lasted throughout the morning, and then Ranulph left to return to his post. As he mounted his horse an orderly ran to him and handed him an envelope, grinning as he said: 'Mail for you, sir – came up the line an hour ago.'

Ranulph saw Diane's handwriting and tore the letter open. The short excited note inside told him that he was the father of twin boys.

Fighter aircraft patrolled overhead, keeping German observation aircraft away. Randolph briefed Selkirk and Warren, talked to artillery unit commanders, met three RFC officers and checked final details. At night the tanks moved forward to their ultimate pre-assault positions, concealed in woods and ruined buildings. There were men and machines everywhere; it seemed impossible that the Germans would not detect something, yet the front was quiet. Then it was time to brief the infantry, the gunners and the signallers, and the tension became physical, sickening, vast.

After dusk on 19 November there was the rumble of artillery from behind the German lines and a sharp enemy probing raid a quarter of a mile north of Ranulph's forward post. When it was signalled he said to Selkirk: 'Jerry knows there's something up. He's looking for prisoners to interrogate. Just pray he doesn't get any.'

The next morning, exactly an hour before the offensive was scheduled to start, German guns began firing again, spasmodically at first, then more generally. Troops crouched in trenches and dugouts and looked at each other questioningly, tensely. Did the Hun know? Was this going to grow into a massive barrage to disrupt the attack? Was this to be the slaughter story all over again? Were they going to be the victims this time?

Then, after half an hour and several score deaths in the British lines, the guns gradually became silent. Equipment was checked yet again. In the damp darkness men smoked; some prayed, secretly. Ranulph and Selkirk shook hands briefly, and wondered which of them would survive – if either did.

Then he heard the tanks: a low rumble like distant aircraft engines – many engines. It grew until the air vibrated. Out of the dawn half-light they came, great black shapes distorted against the dark grey sky by the huge bundles of brushwood each carried to lower into trenches and help them over, lumbering and thundering at slow walking pace to their crossing points. The barbed wire had been cut ready for them; the German wire would be flattened beneath their tracks, leaving paths for the following infantry. Ranulph watched them go in their seemingly endless procession and thought: Dear God – what's it going to be like for the poor bastards over there, seeing that lot coming at them?

Then the orders were barked and whistles blew and the infantry went over their trench walls and with a heavy, dragging weight in his chest, his pistol in his hand and grenades in his belt, Ranulph gave his own signal and followed. As he did so the artillery opened up behind him, targeted half a mile ahead. He ran forward over churned ground, positioning himself behind a dimly-seen tank a hundred yards away and the scattering column of infantry which followed it. He waited for the deadly machine guns which scythed men down in their thousands, but none fired. The black forms of men moved on, and none fell. There was gunfire ahead – the six pounders in the tanks were roaring and banging, and the Lewis guns alongside them were chattering. That meant the first tanks had reached the trenches of the

Hindenburg Line. Still no German machine guns. He stumbled into a shell hole; scrambled out again. The continuous explosions of the artillery behind and the whistling shells of the low-trajectory field guns overhead were joined now by the thunder of German guns as they started firing. Their flashes lit up the dawn all along the front. Coloured Very lights arced slowly up and over as German troops signalled for help. Then a shell exploded away to his right and he threw himself down, remembering the burning, tearing shrapnel in his leg so long ago. Two signallers were down with him. Selkirk was a hundred yards to his left, he knew. He lay for a moment, waiting to see where the next shell would land – what the pattern might be. Then he heard it, whee-ing and whining, and the great roar of its explosion – further away. He yelled 'C'mon – keep moving –' and dragged himself to his feet and began to jog forward.

Suddenly the German wire was there. The infantry ahead had already crossed, and now he picked his way over its flattened, tangled mass. One of the signallers stumbled under the weight of equipment on his shoulders and Ranulph grabbed the man's arm and helped him up. Together they went forward again and found themselves on the lip of the German front line trenches, wide and deep. The soldiers running along them, crouching, bayonets glinting, were all British. Ranulph slid down into the trench, seeing it clearly now in the misty but improving light. He moved along it. There were men ahead, coming up from a dugout. As he reached them one stuck out a hand. In the dimness Ranulph saw his teeth as he grinned.

''Ere y'are, sir – breakfast wiv Jerry's compliments.' The hand held a sausage. Ranulph took it, found it was warm, said: 'Thanks – I'll enjoy that. But watch for booby traps.' He went on, the two signallers close behind. He bit into the sausage. It was newly cooked, fresh from a hot frying pan. He passed half of it to the signaller at his elbow as they turned into a communication trench.

Within minutes they were into the second line trenches. There was no resistance. It had gone – swept away by the great tanks and the tide of British infantry, leaving only the flotsam of bodies in grey and brown uniforms, twisted and crumpled. Most were silent, death agonies over; some groaned or swore repeatedly. The thunder of the guns and the constant flashing were now part of the world and forgotten – absorbed and ignored. There was no fear; just cold, inside rather than out; nerves so taut that they pained in Ranulph's hands and legs and stomach; a voice in his mind saying I'm alive – I'm still alive – still alive – still alive –

At the entrance to a dugout he stumbled and almost fell over men who were not still alive – five or six Germans, several British, sprawled in their last anguish and their blood; and more at the next angle of the trench, pushed into a mangled heap by the men who had followed. Further on he looked at his watch, stopped, said to the nearer signaller: 'Now – first message – identity as instructed. Say "Second line trenches achieved. Casualties light. Little opposition". Ask if there are signals for me.'

The man heaved his pack off his back, opened it, plucked up his aerial, switched on his set, settled earphones on his head and began to tap out his call sign. When the message was completed, and none came back for Ranulph, they moved on. There was no sign of the other units under his command and no signals to relay.

A cautious quarter of an hour later they came out of the trench system into more open country. Evidence of fighting was all around: dead and wounded men, abandoned field guns and machine gun posts, several smoking tanks – one torn open by a shell; the air splitting under gunfire and explosions, men shouting distantly, grey light increasing over everything, trees and running men stark against cloud and mist. He paused, looking around. Away to his left a machine gun rattled and he saw tracers darting from the edge of a copse. A tank was lumbering slowly towards it, the six-pounder on one side spitting flame. A shell exploded near the tank, throwing up a column of earth. The tank still went forward. Another machine gun opened up from the copse, then a field gun flashed and banged in the trees and a shell hit the ground just ahead of the tank with a great roar that battered Ranulph's eardrums. Another tank was heading for the copse, guns firing. A platoon of infantry ran across behind the first tank. One of the machine guns hammered out of the trees and men twisted and fell.

Ranulph shouted to a signaller: 'Message – report Jerry field gun and machine guns in that copse – identify as south of Marcoing, north of Bonavis Ridge.'

There was a great explosion as one of the tanks received a direct hit from a shell. A column of flame jetted from metal that was suddenly jagged. Ranulph winced. An infantry lieutenant and a corporal materialized beside him. More men followed, fanning out, crouching. Two SE 5s appeared over Highland Ridge to the north, low, swaying, dipping, turning towards the trees. Their machine guns rattled and tracer arced up towards them.

The officer at Ranulph's shoulder bellowed: 'Two machine guns at least there. Got to put 'em out. And that bloody field gun – seen it stop three tanks.'

Ranulph nodded. There was hard, deep anger in his eyes. His mind said: You're a signals officer – that's an infantry job. But he ignored it and shouted back: 'You take some men to the right – behind the surviving tank. I'll go left and use the wreck as shelter. If your tank keeps moving you can follow him in – my lot will try a rush while Jerry's watching you.'

Then he was running, keeping low, shouting to men to follow him, not thinking except about the flames from the crippled tank and the men who had died in it and the way the machine gun had sent other men twisting and writhing in the air. He could hear that same gun now and instinct sent him sprawling. A man close to him coughed and screamed. The tank's guns were banging – flat, shattering explosions. Ranulph waved his hand and scrambled on, men he did not know following him, accepting his leadership. They reached the smoking tank. The stench of burning flesh made him choke. He crawled around the tank, found two dead men. One was sprawled across a loose Lewis gun. Ranulph heaved the body aside and lugged up the gun, cradling it. A hundred yards away the other tank roared slowly on, men scattering

343

and weaving behind. The field gun was firing and earth spouted up around the tank as it lurched forward. Both machine guns were jabbering at it and the men beyond and Ranulph roared 'Now – now – after me –'

The nearest trees were forty yards away and he ran for them, clutching the heavy Lewis gun, nerves screaming, chest waiting for tearing agony. He did not know what the machine guns were doing but heard men shouting, then a single thin shriek. He struggled on over the rutted, slippery ground and his mental voice hissed in his mind: God don't let me die – I haven't seen my sons – I must see my sons – Diane take care of them for me – Father take care of her – He reached a tree, saw grey figures beyond other trees, crouched and fired the Lewis gun. It kicked and banged deafeningly and he struggled against it. Grey figures jumped, reared, fell. Rifles exploded on either side of him. The Lewis gun stopped firing and he pushed it away, snatched a grenade from his belt, pulled the ring, barked a warning to his men, threw it, ducking behind a tree. When it exploded he drew his pistol, shouted 'Now – now – now –' and ran forward. A figure dodged into view and he fired two-handed at it. More figures – firing again – Christ what am I doing here? – Who'll run Roxton if I'm dead – I can't die – I haven't seen my sons – Diane –

The bullet which killed him was too fast for his nerves to register pain: just a single blinding flash which obliterated his mind.

RUTH

Hebrew, meaning 'companion'.

The wind sighed across the land, stirring the trees so that they sounded like waves on a distant shore. Away to the left the reddish-brown soil was smoothed and level, lying fallow before a cereal crop to be planted in the far-off spring. Ahead, Hereford beef steers grazed the sparse winter grass idly, and beyond there were sheep scattered over a twenty-acre field.

He was sixty-seven years old, that bleak day in 1917. He had not felt old until the telegram had arrived. Then he had felt too old to live. But he was tall and lithe and muscular as he had always been, even if he was slowing a little; and as the days had drifted past in agony so the false years had released him and his courage had armed him ready for the fight ahead. Until today.

The memorial service had been Laura's wish. He supposed she had been right. Many people had been there; some he hardly knew. They had had their chance to show their feelings. People wanted an opportunity to demonstrate what they could not always express. Funerals supplied the same need. But funerals came quickly after death. This service had followed four weeks of grief and had revived the worst of it. The false years had come back and lay upon him and suffocated him.

He had sat at the front of the congregation watching the round, bobbing face of the figure in the pulpit, listening to the droning voice as it floated across the church, across the heads of the pale people, between the pillars and then back from the stones and the stained glass in solemn echoes which blurred each succeeding word.

'He was the epitome of British life – of courage and resourcefulness and vigour that have distinguished our great nation through the ages . . . like so many scores of thousands before him, cut down at the peak of life – he knew the risks and he took them willingly . . . his sacrifice is our great loss, and yet our gain, for his example must be our inspiration . . .'

My son. My son who sat in these pews and walked on these tiles, and the pews and tiles are still here but my son has gone and I'll never see him here again; a little boy who grew into a man and had so little time to know what it meant to be a man. Chanted hypocrisy and cliché-mongering. Is that our only tribute to him?

The people were standing up around him. He put out an arm to assist the slight figure on his right. She swayed as she rose, holding on to him. The older woman on his left stood stiffly, head erect beneath black veil. He heard the organ and the words 'Oh God our help –' and words formed and re-formed in his mind: Oh God, if there is a god, help me to understand, if there is anything to understand. He tried to sing the words others were singing, and watched the church-man in his long surplice but saw instead the son who had gone away four months before, strong in his uniform, three stars shining on his shoulders, brown belt polished. Now he was dead, somewhere in the mud of Flanders, with nothing left except images and sounds in his mind, and the letters.

That morning, before the memorial service, he had read some of the letters again; and had wondered at their slangy, sardonic acceptance of the unimaginable. What gave a man the capacity to exist through horror and to emerge bruised yet intact in mind and spirit? Intact – until that final moment when there was no more mind and no more spirit.

He remembered the silence in the church. A meditation. Silence, except for the muffled weeping of the girl at his side. He had put an arm around her shoulders. Meditation? She dared not meditate, with a girl-child of four, twin sons of scarcely two months. No meditation would chart their futures. Son, where are you? We needed you, we all needed you; I needed you – I, who never felt the need for any man since I became a man, so strong was I. I needed you, for my life is nearly done and yours was my future, the future I would never know but could consider confidently. Not now. No future – neither yours nor mine.

Then it was over, and the villagers and the farm workers and the tenants and new friends and old friends had murmured their sadness and gripped his hand and had gone, and he had left his wife and his widowed daughter-in-law and the others, and had walked across the carriage drive to the white gate and leaned now on the top bar and looked past the stone buildings and the poplars to the fields and the distant wood and the rolling rising red land that was his because his family had bequeathed it to him and he had fought to keep it and the life and living it gave to the men and women who worked it and improved it. Grey clouds pressed upon it and a grey wind stirred the empty trees. There were people and voices across the land, and horses ploughing and men harvesting and all his life moved over it in changing sun and shadow and seasons as he watched.

His land. But soon – whose land? Did that matter? It did – to Diane, to Ruth, and to the two infant boys Richard and Robert, for it would all have been their home if Ranulph had lived. He could still will it to them, and would; but to what purpose, except its piecemeal price? Diane could not control it. When he had gone, as he would before many more years had passed, she would struggle and would lose the fight and it would all disintegrate, and there would be no more Haldanes at Roxton.

He was too old. He had been too late. He felt tears sting his eyes in the wind. He was old and he had infant grandchildren who had no father. Frustration and resentment rose in him, swelling in anger. They had such need; and he had so much still to give, but too little time to give it. Oh God, if there is a god, help me to be their father. Give me time for that.

He found himself holding a cigar in his hand. Where had that come from? He did not remember taking it from his pocket. He looked at it and, strangely, recalled other cigars, in other places. Here and far away, and long ago. It had been a good life. Bad times, yes. But most of the bad ones had produced something good. A good life. Until now. Was this

349

what it had been for? Everything, through all that time – for this? This emptiness, away and down the years into his old age, and nothing at the end?

He saw a small figure move away from the house steps. Ankle-length blue dress and dark hair with a grey ribbon around it. Solemn face and round eyes. She saw him watching her and hesitated. At four years old she did not know what was happening in her world; only that people said daddy had gone away for a very long time, and mummy cried a lot. She was standing now, tiny against the big house, afraid of his stillness. Was this what it had all been for, the good life he had had – a lost child?

He looked away, feeling he could not talk to her. For a time she waited; then, slowly but determinedly, as if she had debated with herself and reached a conclusion, she walked across the wide curving drive to him. The wind caught her hair and carried it fitfully away from her shoulders. When she reached him she put out her hand and he took it in his, still not looking at her.

She said: 'Grandad – I know why you're sad. I know why mummy and granny are sad. I know it's not true that daddy has just gone away. He has died, hasn't he? Like my rabbit died.'

And then he fought within himself the greatest and most bitter fight of his life. He fought for strength so that he could beat away his surging grief and then the pity which came up and overwhelmed the grief. He fought for the sake of the child so that she should not know his despair. After a long time his voice said, 'Yes, Ruth, he has died', and he heard it distantly, as if from another place, and marvelled that it was clear and steady.

She clung to his hand, looking up at him, and there were no tears in her eyes.

'I'll help mummy,' she said. 'Daddy wants me to help her. Before he went away he told me to help her. And then I dreamed about him, and he told me again. I'll help you, too. I'll always stay with you and help you.' She hesitated, searching his face; then, just for an instant, her lip quivered and

350

she said: 'But you'll have to help me. Because I'm afraid.'

It was then that he looked beyond her, up and away towards the house, and something stirred there and he glimpsed the memory of his mother with her incredible calm and capability and courage, and beside her his father who had given him strengths which no one else understood and who had reached out to him when he had needed help, with total reassurance and confidence.

Afraid? If this child was afraid it was because he was afraid. And Randolph Haldane had never been afraid.

Then he prayed, not to God but to those two shadows; and he whispered silently into the wind: 'Help me now, as you helped me before. Give me more of your strengths, so that it will not all have been for nothing.'

She was looking up at him with her big eyes. They were dark brown, almost black; and there was life and light in them. They looked straight into his own, questioning, searching. Helford eyes in an innocent face. And he knew that the fight was not lost. There was still a way. Somehow this child would lead him there.

And suddenly he was ageless, and he put the forgotten cigar between his teeth and an old habit returned as he found a match and flicked it into life with a thumb nail, and he looked down at the child and said: 'Never be afraid. I'll stay with you. I'll take care of you.'

He turned, back towards the house, holding her hand, and he was tall against the winter sky.

The shadows were fading. But as they went he thought he saw them smile.